Where there's
And whe
ther

Dr Alice Ma⋯
Jeremy didn't know he possessed, even
though Alice is six months pregnant—
with another man's child!

Casualty officer Keely Thompson is ready to
be a wife and mother…but is her boss Zach
willing to take a chance on her?

American surgeon Candace Fletcher fell in
love with Dr Steve Colton at first sight—
mind you, becoming pregnant *wasn't* part
of the plan…

These loving couples are about to get more
than they bargained for when they're

EMERGENCY:
EXPECTING

Carol Marinelli is a nurse who loves writing. Or is she a writer who loves nursing? The truth is Carol's having trouble deciding at the moment, but writing definitely seems to be taking precedence! She's also happily married to an eternally patient husband (an essential accessory when panic hits around chapter six) and is a mother to three fabulously boisterous children. Add a would-be tennis player, an eternal romantic and a devout daydreamer to that list and that pretty much sums Carol up. Oh, she's also terrible at housework!

Sarah Morgan trained as a nurse and has since worked in a variety of health-related jobs. Married to a gorgeous businessman, who still makes her knees knock, she spends most of her time trying to keep up with their two little boys but manages to sneak off occasionally to indulge her passion for writing romance. Sarah loves outdoor life and is an enthusiastic skier and walker. Whatever she is doing, her head is always full of new characters and she is addicted to happy endings.

Lilian Darcy currently lives in Australia's capital with her historian husband and their growing family. They also spend significant amounts of time in the United States. Lilian has written over forty novels. Lilian enjoys travel, quilting, gardening and reading, and is a volunteer with Australia's State Emergency Service. Readers can write to her at PO Box 381, Hackensack, NJ 07602, USA or e-mail tolildarcy@austarmetro.com.au

EMERGENCY: EXPECTING

Carol Marinelli

Sarah Morgan

Lilian Darcy

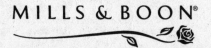

MILLS & BOON®

*First published in Great Britain 2005
Harlequin Mills & Boon Limited,
Eton House, 18-24 Paradise Road, Richmond, Surrey, TW9 1SR*

EMERGENCY: EXPECTING
© Harlequin Enterprises II B.V. 2005

*The Pregnant Intern, Emergency: Mother Wanted and The Surgeon's
Love-Child were first published in Great Britain by
Harlequin Mills & Boon Limited in separate, single volumes*

*The Pregnant Intern © Carol Marinelli 2002
Emergency: Mother Wanted © Sarah Morgan 2001
The Surgeon's Love-Child © Lilian Darcy 2002*

ISBN 0 263 84538 9

108-0505

*Printed and bound in Spain
by Litografia Rosés S.A., Barcelona*

CONTENTS

THE PREGNANT INTERN
by Carol Marinelli

EMERGENCY: MOTHER WANTED
by Sarah Morgan

THE SURGEON'S LOVE-CHILD
by Lilian Darcy

THE PREGNANT INTERN

by

Carol Marinelli

For Sam, Alex and Lucinda with love.

PROLOGUE

'YOUR blood pressure's up.'

Alice let out the breath she had inadvertently been holding. She had been trying to keep her breathing even and think only pleasant thoughts as Brett Halliday, her obstetrician, checked her blood pressure, apparently to no avail.

'By very much?'

Brett shook his head as he unwrapped the cuff. 'Not much. It's just up a touch, and still within a safe margin, but still...' He sat down at his heavy wooden desk and leant across the table as Alice, avoiding his gaze and desperately trying to avoid the ensuing conversation, concentrated rather too intently on rolling down her sleeve.

'I've been rushing around this morning, and it's terribly hot. Anyway, you know how nervous I get at these antenatal appointments.'

Brett nodded. 'All of which I've taken into consideration, but it still doesn't alter the fact that your blood pressure is a little higher than I'd like it to be.' He flicked through the pile of pathology results in front of him.

'Your blood work all looks OK, though your haemoglobin level is only scraping into the normal limits range. You're still taking your iron tablets, I assume?'

Alice nodded.

'Well, try to increase your iron intake from natural means also. Lots of green leaf vegetables and iron-rich foods—and plenty of vitamin C,' he added. 'It helps with iron absorption. You know the routine.'

'But everything is all right with the baby?' she asked anxiously.

5

Brett gave her a reassuring smile. 'The baby's doing nicely—nice size, lots of movement. It's the mum I'm more worried about.'

'Honestly, Brett, I'm fine.' Her words came out rather too harshly. Alice could hear the anxiety in her own voice and paused for a second to regain control. It was imperative to have Brett Halliday onside. With a stroke of his expensive fountain pen he could sign her off work and that was absolutely the last thing she needed at the moment. 'Really, I'm fine,' Alice said, more evenly, even managing a small smile.

But she wasn't going to escape a lecture. 'Look, Alice, you're twenty-five weeks now. Most women at this stage are starting to wind down and looking forward to their maternity leave, not about to commence a three-month surgical internship at a busy city hospital. You don't need me to tell you how busy Melbourne City is—you've spent the last nine months there for yourself. And Jeremy Foster may be a fine surgeon, but he's coming back from a long stint on sick leave. He's going to have a large backlog to catch up on and, more to the point, a lot to prove.'

'What do you mean?' Alice asked, her curiosity about her new boss for a moment overriding the issue of whether or not she worked.

'Well, it was a serious motor crash he was in. No one really expected him to live, let alone walk. And now here he is, less than a year later, returning to work, apparently none the worse for wear. There's going to be people watching him—rightly or wrongly, he's going to have to do a lot of spadework to convince them he's up to the job.'

'But he's a brilliant surgeon,' Alice argued defensively. She hadn't yet met Jeremy Foster, but you didn't have to meet Jeremy to feel as if you knew him. He had broken more hearts throughout the hospital than Alice could keep track of. But despite his somewhat scandalous reputation there had never been any question as to his surgical brilliance. 'He was the hospital's rising star—I'm lucky to have got a place on his team.'

'"Was" being the operative word. Look, Alice, Jeremy's going to be under the pump and that means more work for you.'

'I can handle it. Honestly, Brett, I'll be fine. This three-month stint will take me up to thirty-seven weeks. Lots of first babies come late, which will give me nearly a month to put my feet up and think baby thoughts. Heaps of women work practically until they go into labour these days.' She sounded so confident Alice almost convinced herself that she could handle it, but Brett wasn't about to be fobbed off.

'True,' he said, then added gently, 'But those women probably have a partner to come home to, or at least a supportive family. Someone to give them a bit of help and take away some of the strain. I know how much you need this, Alice, and I don't want to ruin your plans—but I have to be sure you know what you're doing.'

His words, however kindly meant, tore through her. The cool, confident façade melted in an instant and as she crumpled before him Brett came around the desk and handed her a handful of tissues.

'I'm sorry,' she sniffed. 'I didn't want to cry in front of you. In front of anyone,' she added.

'Cry away,' Brett said kindly. 'I see a lot of tears in here. You're not the only pregnant woman trying to make it all work. Trying to cram it all in before the baby comes along. Sometimes you need someone else to make the decision for you. To put the brakes on and tell you to slow down.'

Alice didn't answer. Accepting the tissues, she wept for a moment. She felt mortified that it had come to this: sitting in a doctor's office, begging to be allowed to work, begging for the chance to support her baby.

'If I don't finish my internship I won't be registered as a doctor and that means I can't apply to go on a GP training rotation.'

'But you can do your surgical internship once the baby comes along.'

Alice shook her head. 'I'm living in a bedsit. I can hardly afford the rent as it is. If I stop working—'

'You can claim child support,' Brett said in a practical voice. 'You won't starve.'

'I don't want my baby to start out life like that. You know how big the incentives are for country GPs. I'd have a home, a job. I could afford to have someone look after the baby while I work. I'd be able to give it a real future. If I don't do this it will put my plans back by months.'

'What about your parents? I know they're in Adelaide and you've had your differences, but maybe they're starting to get used to the idea now. Perhaps if you explained to your mum the problems that you're having, trying to make it all work…'

Her stricken look said it all. 'Then what about the baby's father?' Brett ventured gently. 'Shouldn't he be helping? After all, legally it *is* his responsibility.'

He watched as she stiffened. 'He wants nothing to do with me or the baby,' Alice said in a strained voice. 'He made that perfectly clear.'

'He might not want anything to do with you both,' Brett said, making his way back to his seat, 'but there are laws out there to protect women in exactly your position. Maybe it's time he faced up to the truth that he's about to become a father and the responsibility that entails. Even if it's only financially.'

For the first time Alice didn't have to pretend to be assured or confident; this was the one area of her life that was unequivocal. 'I'm not asking him for a single cent. He's either in or out of this baby's life—not somewhere in between. Marcus made it perfectly clear it was the latter he was choosing when I found out I was pregnant, and as far as I'm concerned it can stay that way. I want nothing more to do with him.

'Look, Brett, I really need this job,' she pleaded. 'If you think I'm stressed now, I'd be ten times worse if you told me I couldn't work. If there was any question that my baby was in danger, of course I wouldn't start, but you said yourself the baby's fine.'

Brett didn't answer for what seemed like an age. Instead, he started writing up her notes before finally looking up. 'All right, then. But I want to see you fortnightly from now on. And if your blood pressure creeps any higher, or I've even the slightest hint that either you or the baby aren't coping, I'll sign you off—and I mean it, Alice. Get yourself some support tights, eat the right food and put your feet up every chance you get.'

Alice grinned as she stood up. 'I promise.'

Brett found himself smiling back at her. He had been unsure there as to what to do. Instinct told him to sign her off, but he could understand her desperation. It was a tough call all right. Yet there was no doubt that Alice looked a lot more relaxed now she could go ahead with her plans. If he took her blood pressure now, he'd half expect it to be normal.

'Make an appointment with Madge on your way out. I do late nights on Mondays for my working mums—that'll probably suit you better.'

'Thanks.' Smiling, she made her way down the long carpeted corridor to the reception desk. 'It's OK, baby,' she whispered, gently patting her bump as she walked. 'Mummy's going to be able to take good care of you now. We're going to be just fine.'

CHAPTER ONE

WHOEVER had written in the mother-and-baby magazine Alice had read in the doctor's waiting room that there was a lot more choice in maternity wear these days either had a bottomless wallet or terrible taste in clothes, Alice thought ruefully as she dressed. Her 'bump' seemed to have grown practically overnight. Though somewhat excited by the rapid changes in her body, the down side was she could no longer get by with undoing the buttons of her skirts and wearing loose-fitting clothes. Her trip to the maternity departments hadn't been a howling success. Everything was either ludicrously expensive or trimmed with a disgusting lace Peter Pan collar or bow. Finally she had settled on a 'maternity kit' which consisted of a black Lycra skirt, swing top and trousers, and a little black dress which showed off rather a lot of her expanding bust line. Still, it was reasonably priced and, teamed with a couple of shirts, it should get her through the remainder of her pregnancy.

Settling on the black skirt and top, she pulled her dark hair back into a low ponytail and applied her make-up. The 'glow' the same magazine had promised would appear by mid-pregnancy seemed to be about as evasive as a black maternity bra. But with a touch of eyeliner and mascara on her long lashes, and a dash of lipstick on her full mouth, she didn't look too bad, Alice thought as she eyed herself in her bathroom mirror. Picking up her bag, she had a quick check in the full-length mirror and let out a groan. She looked as if she were going to a funeral. Despite the manufacturer's claims, there was obviously no such thing as 'sheer' forty denier support tights. 'You're going to be late

on your first day,' Alice warned herself as she hastily
ripped off the offending garment and grappled through her
bathroom cabinet for some tinted moisturiser. She hadn't
been near the beach in months and her pale legs needed a
bit of help. Finally—if not entirely happy with her appearance, at least feeling marginally better—Alice took a tram
the short distance to the hospital and amazingly arrived
with ten minutes to spare.

'Morning. It's Alice Masters, isn't it?'

'That's right.' She smiled at the friendly freckled face.
'You must be Josh Winters, the surgical resident.'

'The one and only. Looks as if it's only us two here.
Linda McFarlane's probably sucking a few lemons before
the ward round.'

'I'm glad it's not just me who thinks like that. I had
more than a few reservations when I first met her. She's
not very friendly, is she?' Alice said, referring to the surgical registrar who had been particularly condescending at
her interview.

'Tell me about it! Darren Barker, the other reg, is nice
to work with but unfortunately he's on annual leave for a
month now Jeremy's back. I wish it was Linda who was
on leave—she told me to get a haircut before they'd consider me.'

'And did you?' Alice asked eyeing the long shaggy locks
reaching well past his collar.

'Yes, believe it or not. Though she'll still probably take
the scissors to me herself later. We clashed a few times
when I was an intern. I must be a glutton for punishment,
coming back to do it all again. Still, Jeremy Foster on my
résumé will look pretty impressive—you can learn a lot
from him.'

Alice nodded. She had been thinking absolutely the same
thing when she'd applied for this rotation.

'I thought Linda was just giving me a hard time because I was pregnant,' Alice admitted.

'You're not, are you?' Josh asked feigning surprise. 'You poor old thing. My wife's expecting twins any day now—she gave up work ages ago. I have to say I admire you, taking this lot on.'

'Your wife's expecting twins?' Alice asked, unable to keep the surprise from her voice. Josh Winters looked like he should have had a surfboard under his arm, not a stethoscope around his neck. He certainly didn't fit the image of a young doctor, married with twins on the way.

'I know, I know.' He laughed, then added, 'Don't worry about old sour-grapes Linda. She's just peeved that the great Jeremy Foster is actually coming back. No one had written him off more completely than her. She was hoping for a nice fast ticket to consultant. And to make matters worse,' he said in undertones, 'Linda is the only woman in this hospital Jeremy hasn't even attempted to pull.'

'He surely can't be that bad.'

'You mark my words, he's insatiable. At least you're one female intern that doesn't have to worry about succumbing to his charms. That bump of yours will act like a crucifix to a vampire for our Jeremy, so at least you won't be putting Linda offside on that score. I hope she's shaved this morning.'

Alice found herself smiling, which was quite a revelation in itself. She hadn't been doing too much of that lately. It looked as if Josh was going to be nice to work with—heaven knew, she could use a few allies with the insatiable Jeremy and the bearded Linda breathing down her neck.

'There you are. I assume your letters of confirmation did explain it was *this* Monday you started.' Linda McFarlane's tone was anything but friendly. 'We're all waiting for you at the nurses' station.'

'You said to meet outside the ward,' Josh argued, apparently unruffled by her tones.

'I most certainly did not. What are you going to learn here? The medical students have been at the nurses' station, going through the patients notes and X-rays for half an hour now. At least *they're* showing some initiative.' And, turning on her heel, she walked smartly onto the ward.

'But she did say to meet outside,' Alice whispered furiously to Josh as they followed her onto the ward. Linda McFarlane, with her cold grey eyes and severe hairstyle, did nothing to endear herself to Alice.

'What Linda says and what she actually admits to are somewhat conflicting,' Josh said darkly. 'Watch your back.'

But Alice wasn't listening. The only back she was watching at the moment was the impeccably suited, wide-shouldered back of her new boss as he held an X-ray up to the light. His blond hair, expertly cut, tapered into his long neck. He looked as immaculately groomed and tastefully dressed as any film star from the glossies, and by hospital standards he was the closest thing to a legend Melbourne City was likely to produce.

'Finally, we can start,' Linda said pointedly, and Alice found herself holding her breath as Jeremy Foster turned and gave the briefest of smiles, his blue eyes flicking briefly down to her bulging stomach. Alice felt a small blush appear as she remembered Josh's 'vampire' comment.

'Pleased to meet you.' He held out his hand as the introductions were made, and Alice was painfully aware of her moist palms as she returned his handshake. No amount of gossip—and there had been plenty—had done him justice or even come close to adequately describing him: sun-bleached blond hair, blue eyes and an arrogant haughty smile. Momentarily stunned, she stared back at him, lost in her thoughts.

'We'll get started, then,' he said in a clipped voice, and Alice looked away, suddenly embarrassed.

She tried desperately to concentrate as they made their way around the ward, to ignore the flutter of butterflies Jeremy seemed to so effortlessly have started. Linda had the most to say—after all she had already met most of the patients and seemed to take every available opportunity to ram home how well she had coped. Jeremy didn't seem fazed by her attitude, listening intently. But every now and then he overrode a decision Linda had made or changed a drug regime, effectively assuring all present that he was the one in charge. It soon became apparent to everyone that Linda was having a lot of trouble accepting her boss's return. Her simmering resentment became increasingly obvious as they made their way around and at the final patient's bedside Linda let her bitterness surface.

'Mrs Marshall came in on Thursday with acute pancreatitis. She has a history of alcohol abuse. She's been nil by mouth on IV fluids with a pethidine infusion to control her pain. Currently, we're weaning her off the pethidine and she's now on five mls an hour. I was thinking of starting her this morning on clear fluids.'

'Good morning, Mrs Marshall. I'm Mr Foster, the surgical consultant. How are you feeling this morning?'

Mrs Marshall was struggling to sit up. 'A bit better, but I'd really like a drink of water.' Alice looked on. If this was Mrs Marshall looking better she'd have hated to have seen her on Thursday. Pancreatitis could either be acute or chronic. It caused severe abdominal pain and the patient rapidly became seriously ill. Although managed medically, it still came under the domain of the surgeons. In this case it had been precipitated by Mrs Marshall's ingestion of large quantities of alcohol.

Jeremy flicked through the patient's blood results as Mrs

Marshall fiddled in her locker. 'Her amylase levels are still very high.'

'But they've come down markedly,' Linda said.

'Still, it might be a bit early to be starting her on fluids,' Jeremy responded calmly.

'Just small sips—you can see yourself how agitated she is,' Linda pointed out. 'She's making a lot of work for the nursing staff, trying to get out of bed and get a drink.'

'Which is probably more related to her pain and her alcoholism. Keep her nil by mouth for now and increase her pethidine,' Jeremy said.

Linda pursed her lips. 'Surely we're just replacing one addiction with another. A few sips of water must be better than increasing her pethidine.'

Jeremy picked up the drug chart. 'Mrs Marshall is in pain, and that needs to be addressed. A PRN order of Valium might be wise also, given her withdrawal from alcohol.'

He turned from Linda's angry gaze and addressed the patient.

'Mrs Marshall, we're going to keep you nil by mouth for now. I know you want a drink but it really is safer not to at the moment. We'll increase your pain control and I've written up an order for some Valium which will help you to settle.'

Surprisingly, Mrs Marshall seemed a lot happier with his decision than Linda and leant back resignedly on her pillows.

'A psychiatric and social work referral would also be appropriate,' Jeremy said, handing her folder back to the charge nurse.

'She had all that last time she was in,' Linda said. 'That's why I didn't order the works this time around. She always swears she's going to give up this time, and then back she bounces.'

Jeremy nodded. 'Which, while mildly frustrating for us, must be absolute hell for Mrs Marshall and her family. See she gets the appropriate referrals.'

'Bravo, Jeremy,' Josh whispered, and Alice actually found she felt like cheering herself. Jeremy had certainly put the obnoxious Linda in her place.

'I'm not entirely happy with her.' Jeremy looked over at Alice. 'When we finish up here, can you do some blood gases on Mrs Marshall?'

'Sure.'

'I'll see you both later in pre-op clinic.' With a small nod he walked off, as Linda marched furiously behind him.

'I'll start writing up the notes, then, while you do the gases,' Josh suggested. 'Then we can grab a coffee.'

'I doubt it,' Alice said with a sigh. 'I've got three IVs to resite and a pile of drug charts that need writing up, and there's a couple of bloods that need doing.'

'Alice, Alice, Alice.' Josh gave her a wide smile. 'You have so much to learn. Fi,' he called to the charge nurse, who came over with a smile, 'this young intern hasn't yet learnt how to ask for favours. Do you think we should teach her?'

Fi smiled warmly at Alice. 'You're not listening to Josh, are you? He'll get you into all sorts of trouble.' Fi had delicate oriental features and a kind smile but, despite her seemingly easygoing nature, Alice knew just from this morning's ward round that Fi ran the ward with impeccable efficiency.

'That's not fair, Fi.' Josh winked at Alice. 'Fi and I worked together when I was a surgical intern,' he explained. 'Now, Fi, tell Alice the truth—didn't I always come at night when you paged me? Didn't I listen to you and call the reg when you were worried? Didn't I always bring doughnuts in?'

Fi nodded. 'And in return I had to do half your bloods and IVs.'

'Cheap at half the price. Come on, Fi, don't say you've gone all hard on me? You're the only reason I came back to this ward.'

Fi laughed. 'All right, I'll help with your bloods, *if* I get the time. But I'm on nights next week,' she warned, 'and you'd better remember your side of the deal.'

As Josh made his way to do his notes, Fi turned her attention to Alice, who was filling up a kidney dish with blood-gas syringes and alcohol swabs.

'When you've done the blood gases, I'll show you around,' she offered. 'Let you know how Jeremy likes things.'

'Thanks ever so much.'

Fi looked at her thoughtfully for a moment. 'Listen to me for a moment, Alice. I know I always look busy but I've always got time if you need to run something by me. If there's something you're not sure about, you can always come to me.'

Alice nodded. It was a kind offer that a lot of charge nurses made when new interns started and one that was much appreciated. Heaven knew, it was a busy enough job and you needed all the support you could get. But there was something about Fi's offer that sounded ominous, as if she almost expected trouble.

'I'd better get those gases done.'

'I'll get you some ice.'

Although Mrs Marshall was on oxygen, Alice removed the mask before she took the blood gases, as the blood taken while the patient was breathing only air would enable them to get a truer picture of her condition. Although obviously unwell, the increased pain control had already kicked in and she actually seemed in the mood for a chat.

'I'm just going to take a small sample of blood from

your wrist, Mrs Marshall, so just hold still while I inject some anaesthetic.'

'No one else has bothered with anaesthetic. How come?'

'Maybe you were too sick and they needed the blood urgently,' Alice suggested diplomatically.

'Maybe they were in too much of a hurry,' the patient said pointedly. 'When are you due?'

'In about three months' time,' Alice muttered reluctantly.

'Your first?'

Alice nodded. She really didn't want to discuss her private life with Mrs Marshall but, as she was increasingly finding out, her obvious condition seemed to be a licence for all and sundry to strike up a conversation about the most personal of subjects.

'Must be hard on your own.' She gestured to Alice's naked ring finger.

Alice concentrated on finding the pulsing artery. 'Hold still, please, Mrs Marshall.'

Thankfully she hit the jackpot first time and the bright red arterial blood spurted up the syringe.

'She got it first go and even gave me an anaesthetic first,' Mrs Marshall said loudly—to whom, Alice had no idea.

'Glad to hear it.'

Alice nearly jumped out of her skin as Jeremy made his way over. 'Let's pop your oxygen back on now.' He replaced the mask over the patient's face.

'I was just saying how hard it must be for the young doctor, being pregnant and on her own.'

Alice wished the ground would open up and swallow her, but she had no choice other than to stand there and press the cotton-wool swab for a full two minutes on the site where she had taken the arterial blood.

'Oh, I don't know,' Jeremy said lightly. 'Solitude has its virtues. I think you can stop pressing now,' he added to Alice.

Mortified, she followed him out of the room.

'Don't tell them so much next time,' Jeremy said, taking her to one side.

Alice, blushing furiously, looked down at her feet. Her tinted moisturiser had gone all blotchy. 'I'm sorry, I know it mustn't look very good—professionally, I mean—what with me being a single mother and all that.'

To her utter amazement Jeremy gave a small laugh. 'We're in the twenty-first century, Alice, for heaven's sake, not the nineteen-fifties. Nobody gives a damn these days about pregnant women being single.'

'Well, I do.' Alice said curtly, though the fact he wasn't bothered by her status was somehow strangely comforting.

'I know,' he said, and Alice looked up, surprised at his perception. 'I could tell Mrs Marshall's probing was making you uncomfortable. Next time tell them your fingers have got too fat to put your rings on, or tell them you don't want to talk about it. Tell them what you like. You're the doctor. It's you holding the consultation, not the other way around.'

'Thanks, I never thought of it like that.'

'You'd better get those blood gases over to ICU.'

Only then did Alice remember the kidney dish she was holding. 'I'll take them down to the lab myself. We're not allowed to use the ICU blood-gas machine for ward patients unless it's a real emergency,' she reminded him.

Jeremy screwed up his nose. 'Since when?'

'Since for ever—well, at least in the nine months I've been here.'

But Jeremy didn't look convinced. 'I've never had a problem. Maybe it's because I'm consultant,' he said pompously.

Well, you wouldn't have a problem, would you? Alice thought to herself as they entered the intensive care unit. One glimpse of those impossibly blue eyes and a flash of that ready smile and everyone melted. Even Flynn, the gay-est of porters, smoothed down his hair when Jeremy walked past. They were all so delighted to see him that Alice stood there awkwardly as they chatted away, greeting him like a long-lost friend. Finally Jeremy seemed to remember why they were there.

'I'd better get these bloods done, or we'll have to get a fresh sample.'

Far from the grumbling staff that reluctantly allowed her to do blood gases in only the most dire of emergencies, for Jeremy it seemed it was absolutely no trouble at all. They even offered to run the test for him.

'No, but thanks anyway. I just want to have a quick look at the printout and then hopefully dash off. I'll catch you all later.'

Alice could find neither rhyme nor reason for her indig-nation as she smeared a drop of blood onto the machine and punched in her request.

'Don't take it personally,' Jeremy said, glancing at her sideways as she glared at the machine. 'They probably let me use the machine because they've got a bit of a soft spot for me. I was a patient here for a while.'

Alice gave a cynical laugh as the printout appeared. The staff might well have a soft spot for Jeremy Foster, but it certainly wasn't all down to the fact he had been a patient here, or even that he was a consultant.

Ripping the result off, she handed it to him.

'Better than I thought. Good. But keep an eye on her, Alice. Given that I've upped her pethidine and prescribed her Valium, her respiration rate could go down. Tell the nurses to do strict one- to two-hourly obs and keep a close eye on her oxygen saturations.'

Alice nodded.

'I'll catch you later, then.'

As he left the tiny annexe, the baby suddenly let out a

massive kick. Alice's hands instinctively moved to her stomach and she tenderly massaged it. 'Don't worry, I haven't forgotten you're in there,' she whispered, and watched out of the window as Jeremy made his way down the unit, every nurse in the place turning her head to catch a glimpse as he left. At least she didn't have to worry about Jeremy trying his well-rehearsed lines on her. Just as well really, Alice thought to herself as she made her way back to the ward. With those blue eyes and that sultry smile she doubted whether even she would be able to offer much resistance.

Pre-op clinics always ran overtime and today was no exception, given the fact it was the intern's first day and the consultant had only just returned from sick leave.

It was Alice's job to clerk the patients, which involved taking a full medical history. From there she would order any test she thought necessary prior to the patient's admission, such as ECGs and blood tests. Then the consultant would review the patient and agree or disagree with the intern's suggestions, invariably adding or removing a test. At this point, Jeremy explained, he would like her to be present.

'There's not much point otherwise. At least we can both explain our thought processes behind the pre-op work-ups. The down side is it means we won't be out of here much before six.' He gave her a sideways look. 'Or maybe even seven. Is that a problem?'

Alice shook her head. 'Sounds fine to me.'

And so they battled away. Alice took excellent histories. Somehow she managed to get the patients to open up— maybe because she gave a bit of herself back. But under her steady, unaccusing gaze the 'occasional smoker' would admit to a twenty a day habit and even the 'social drinker' admitted to a few cans mid-week. She took Jeremy's advice, though, and somehow by remembering that it was she that was holding the consultation she managed to avoid some of the more embarrassing questions that, until now, patients had assumed it was their right to ask. Not that she wasn't personable and friendly, but Marcus's rejection and her current circumstances were something Alice was having difficulty dealing with herself without the constant, however well meaning, advice from strangers.

Jeremy, on the other hand, seemed to be taking his own advice to the extreme. He was courteous, friendly even, yet he gave nothing away about himself. Every personal comment, every attempt by a patient to make small talk was immediately and skilfully rebuffed. So skilfully, in fact, that it took Alice the full afternoon to realise he never spoke about himself other than with reference to his work.

Jeremy didn't seem remotely bothered by her apparent slowness. In fact, by the time the last patient had been seen and the clock was edging towards seven, he seemed more than happy to prolong the evening with a chat.

'That's the last, Mr Foster.'

The young nurse popped her head around the door and Alice noticed her looking pointedly at her watch.

'Thanks, Emily, you did a great job today. I'm sorry we've made you so late. And, by the way, it's Jeremy.'

Instantly the bitter expression melted.

'No problem.' Emily paused. 'Jeremy. It's nice to have you back.'

That man could get away with murder, Alice thought. Why, even the most respected consultant wouldn't be left in doubt of the nurse's wrath if he let the clinic run more than two hours over, but for some reason Jeremy could get away with it. The nurses had been just as forgiving as the patients.

'I'd just like to run a couple of things by you before you go,' Jeremy said, interrupting her thoughts.

'OK.' Putting the pile of notes she had completed into the in-tray, Alice took a seat at his desk.

'You're sure?' Jeremy checked. 'You haven't got a baby-sitter you've got to get back to or anything?'

'I don't have to worry about that for a few months yet.'

'And if Mrs Marshall's observations were correct, I can assume you don't have a husband or partner wanting his dinner on the table?'

Alice swallowed nervously. She had known it would only be a matter of time before he asked. 'Another thing I don't have to worry about.'

'Good.'

Alice looked up sharply. 'Is it?'

Jeremy gave her a brief smile. 'For me it is. Look, Alice, you've heard the gossip. I'm a has-been, I'm coming back too soon, I'm half the surgeon I used to be, and all that.'

Alice flushed. 'I've heard nothing of the sort,' she lied.

'Bull.'

His expletive hit the mark. 'Well, maybe a few remarks,' she admitted. 'But you know what this place is like. Once you've been back for a couple of weeks you'll soon put them right. Anyway,' she added somewhat more forcefully, 'what on earth has any of this to do with my marital status?'

'Everything and nothing. You know how politically correct everything is these days, Alice. Apparently, I'm not supposed to notice the obvious fact that you're pregnant. And even if it's brought to my attention I'm not supposed to let it affect my judgement of you in any way. Even by having this conversation, effectively you could run off to the anti-discrimination council and have me up to my neck in hot water.'

Alice was totally confused. 'Why would I?'

'Because, as I said, your rather large bump supposedly shouldn't affect my judgement of you in the slightest.'

'And does it?' Alice asked boldly.

Jeremy stared at her for an age. Her heavy dark hair was too much for the loose scrunchy she was wearing and was slipping from its grasp, and dark grey eyes were staring up at him as if waiting for his judgement. For a second he lost his train of thought, but only for a second. His eyes flicked downwards again, and came to rest on the soft yet firm swell of her stomach.

'Yes,' he answered simply. 'Yes, it does.'

'But why? Just because I'm pregnant, it doesn't make me any less a doctor.'

Jeremy put his hands up. Tanned, manicured, long-fingered hands, Alice noticed...surgeon's hands. 'I never meant—'

But Alice interrupted him, jumping to her feet. Suddenly she felt threatened. Maybe he was about to say he didn't want her on his team, would never have agreed to it had he been in on the interview. All she knew was that it was imperative he let her stay. 'Being pregnant makes me a better doctor. I now know what it's like to lie on an examining couch and be prodded and poked. I know how it feels to be vulnerable, to be a number in the system.'

'Whoa.' Jeremy gestured for her to sit down.

Furious with herself for reacting so violently, Alice meekly did as she was told. Not trusting herself to speak, she looked up at him.

Jeremy cleared his throat before speaking. 'Firstly, I have absolutely no doubt you're a fine doctor. Your references are exemplary, and from what I've seen today you merit every word that was written. Secondly, I'm sure you really are a better doctor for being on the receiving end of the health system. I know without a shadow of doubt that I am, or at least I hope I will be. Take Mrs Marshall today. Normally I'd have dropped her pethidine down even further, and I'm not proud of that fact. But, having been in pain myself, I now recognise it all the more.' He stopped talking and for a moment Alice thought he had forgotten she was even there.

'And thirdly,' she prompted. 'I assume there's more?'

Jeremy snapped back to attention, a wry smile touching the edge of his lips. 'I'm not an obstetrician, and with good reason.'

Alice's eyebrows shot up in a questioning look.

'Heaven knows, they make enough money.'

'Tell me about it,' Alice grumbled, thinking of the invoice from Brett Halliday sitting in her bedside drawer amongst the other pile of unpaid bills.

'What I'm trying to say,' Jeremy continued, 'albeit not very well, is that pregnant women terrify me.'

Alice started to laugh, then stifled her giggle as she realised he wasn't joking.

'You're not serious?'

Jeremy nodded. 'Deadly serious. I mean, see it from my angle. If I bawl you out, are you going to burst into tears or, worse, will I induce premature labour? If I keep you behind in a clinic or call you into Theatre at midnight, am I going to do irreparable damage to the baby?'

Alice really was laughing now. 'Jeremy, I'm not a doll. I'm not some precious Ming vase that's about to shatter, for heaven's sake. I'm pregnant, that's all. Women have been managing it throughout time, in fact.'

'I know, I know. Look, I'm probably not being fair, landing this lot on you. I know you haven't asked for special favours or anything. It's just that I'm going to be pretty full-on in the ensuing months, far more so than any of the other surgeons, and that means I'm going to be asking a lot from you. I just need to know that you're up to it and if you're not I need you to tell me.'

'I'm up to it.' Alice said with conviction, but it wasn't the answer Jeremy wanted to hear.

'You still don't understand, do you?'

Alice looked at him, nonplussed. What more did he want—an affidavit?

'If I'm piling it on too thick I need to know you'll tell me. I'm single-minded where work's concerned. What I'm trying to say is that my career is everything to me. Now, I might expect loyalty and hard work from my staff and sometimes I admit I stretch the limits, but in your case you have a baby to think of. I'm not a soft touch—anything but—and I need to know that you'll tell me if there's a problem. It might not be politically correct, or whatever you want to call it, but I can't pretend your condition doesn't exist. If I'm coming down too hard, you *must* say so.'

Alice was surprised by his words, stunned even. From what she had heard of Jeremy Foster, compassion and understanding weren't on his list of credentials, and even if his attempt at these had been somewhat bumbling and massively sexist, she was touched at his attempt. 'I will,' she said softly.

'So long as we've cleared that up, then.' Jeremy gave her a dismissive nod and Alice said goodnight. Retrieving her bag from the nurses' station, it suddenly became imperative that she thank him. Making her way back to his room, she stepped inside. Jeremy was sitting there, his head in his hands. Two soluble painkillers were fizzing away in the glass next to him. From the hunch of his wide shoulders she could tell he was tense, possibly in pain. Sensing someone's presence, he sat up smartly and turned around.

'Was there anything else?'

Alice hesitated. Suddenly she felt as if she had witnessed a side that Jeremy didn't want to be seen, as if she had somehow invaded his privacy.

'I just wanted to thank you.'

'There's really no need. You'll be calling me all sorts of names by the end of the week.'

Alice gave a small smile. She knew she should go now, but for some reason she found herself standing there. He might be her consultant, but at this moment Jeremy Foster looked nothing like the dashing, confident man she had met this morning. He looked exhausted—the day must have taken its toll—and in pain, too. 'Er, is there anything I can get you?'

Jeremy gave her a quizzical look. 'Like what?'

Alice shrugged. 'A cup of tea perhaps?'

Jeremy gave a low laugh before answering sarcastically, 'A woman's solution to everything.' When Alice flushed he added more kindly, 'At least, it's my mother's solution.' He shook his head. 'I've got a headache, that's all. I'll be fine.' And, turning his back, he started dictating his notes into a machine for his secretary.

Well, what had she expected? For Jeremy Foster to confide in her, to tell her how bad he was feeling? She let out a low moan. Imagine offering him a cup of tea! Of all the stupid things to say—in one sentence she had relegated herself to the little-woman role where Jeremy so obviously thought she belonged.

If only she had known that at that same moment Jeremy's head was back in his hands and he was thinking that maybe he should have accepted that cup of tea. Maybe a few minutes spent talking to Alice would have made things a bit easier for him if he'd told her how it was for him, that the accident hadn't left him completely unscathed. That his back was killing him and he suffered headaches that were indescribable. After all, he was going to be relying a lot on her over the next few months and he was hardly about to bare his soul to Linda. And as for Josh—well, Josh was a good bloke but he gossiped far too much. Maybe talking to Alice would have helped lighten his load. But what good could have come from it? She seemed like a nice girl, but he hardly knew her. No doubt in five minutes' flat the word would be around the hospital. Has-been, past it, came back too soon. Jeremy pulled a face as he downed the rest of the revolting medicine. He'd just have to wear it for now.

CHAPTER TWO

'COULD I have a bit more light? It's like operating in a bloody dungeon here.' Alice moved the overhead light a fraction. She was too focussed on the direness of the situation to take Jeremy's comments personally.

'Dear God, why didn't they bring him in sooner?'

Alice didn't answer. She knew Jeremy was talking more to himself than to anyone else.

'More traction,' he ordered, and Alice pulled back on the retractor holding the incision Jeremy had swiftly cut further back to allow for greater visibility. She could see the sweat pouring down his forehead. No matter how many times the nurse wiped it, only seconds later he was drenched again.

He's in pain again, Alice thought, suddenly feeling sorry for him.

She had been working with Jeremy for two weeks now, and whatever Jeremy lacked in social skills he made up for in the operating room. He was quite simply the best surgeon she had ever seen. His long fingers worked deftly, his vivid blue eyes seemed to pick up the minutest detail almost before it became apparent to anyone else. But were his skills enough to save this young life?

Lachlan Scott had been wheeled into the accident and emergency department less than two hours previously. The young medical student had been complaining of abdominal pain for a couple of days now, but hadn't thought to do anything about it. Only this morning had he turned up at his father's house, vomiting and in great pain. His father, one of the leading physicians at the hospital, had immediately rushed him in. The diagnosis of appendicitis had been

29

made even before he had hit the accident and emergency department; but it soon became clear from his rigid abdomen and shocked appearance that his appendix had already ruptured and the patient was now suffering from peritonitis. Linda and Josh had been in the middle of a hernia repair, which had left Jeremy with only the most junior of assistants.

Alice's back was killing her. Lachlan Scott had come in on the end of an already busy morning in the operating theatre, but for now her back was the least of her concerns.

'I think we're winning.' Jeremy looked up briefly and Alice could read the look of sheer relief in his vivid eyes. By the time Jeremy had stitched the last of the drains into place, which would drain any excess fluid from Lachlan's abdomen, and had covered the wound with a huge clear dressing, they had been operating for over two hours. 'Good work, everyone. Let's get him out to Recovery.'

Alice would have liked nothing more than to peel off her theatre scrubs, stand under a cool shower and follow it up with a huge mug of tea, but that luxury was going to have to wait. Lachlan had been resuscitated with fluids in the emergency department and huge doses of antibiotics had already been administered, but his post-operative IV and drug regime would have to be worked out carefully if they were to allay any of the multitude of post-operative complications he might succumb to.

'His father's just outside,' Carrie, the theatre charge nurse, prompted. Alice watched as the faintest hint of a frown appeared on Jeremy's face. 'Jeremy, he's a consultant. It will have to be you that talks to him,' Carrie said firmly.

'I know, I know,' he said irritably. 'I'll talk to him, but first I'm having a shower. I'll be back to check on Lachlan shortly.'

'Why is he so worried about talking to him?' Alice

couldn't refrain from asking when Jeremy turned on his heel and left. 'I mean, he did a brilliant job in there. You'd think he'd be the rushing off to tell Dr Scott.'

Carrie shrugged. 'Probably terrified he might have to get out his handkerchief.' She gave a small laugh and Alice heard the trace of bitterness in her voice. 'Jeremy doesn't like scenes or confrontations. If Lachlan had been a straightforward appendicitis he'd be out there now, grinning like a Cheshire cat and saying how well it had gone. You know as well as I do it's going to be pretty hard telling Lachlan's parents how sick he is. He may be out of Theatre but he certainly isn't out of the woods yet. No doubt Jeremy's hoping that by the time he's had his shower someone will have done the dirty deed for him. You'll get used to his underhand methods. I know I have.'

'I hear you've been having a bit of excitement?' Alice swung around and smiled as she saw Josh entering the recovery area. Carrie muttered something and went to check on Lachlan.

'Too much for one morning. How about you, Josh? How was your morning with Linda?'

Josh rolled his eyes. 'Bearable. At least the mask covers up her face.'

'Josh, you're terrible.' Alice giggled.

'I just say things as I see them.' He lowered his voice. 'Speaking of which, what was Carrie bitching about?'

'Nothing, she was just saying how Jeremy avoids talking to relatives when the news is bad.'

'Take everything Carrie says about Jeremy with a pinch of salt. She's just bitter because he dumped her. Or rather, he didn't dump her—he got a "friend" to do it for him.'

'Ouch,' Alice winced. 'I thought there was a bit of an undercurrent between them.'

But Josh shook his head. 'Not where Jeremy's concerned. As soon as a relationship's over, he forgets the woman ever existed and moves happily on to the next one. It's the women who are left simmering—any undercurrents come from them. Jeremy's exes probably radiate enough energy to act as the hospital's back-up generator.'

Alice's laughter was interrupted by Josh's pager. 'Now what does Linda want?' he muttered, but his face paled as he read the message.

'It's Dianne ringing,' he said, referring to his wife. Grabbing the nearest phone, he picked it up and, shaking, attempted to dial home, but kept misdialling.

'Josh, give it here.' Alice laughed. 'She probably just wants you to pick up a pizza tonight. Now, what's the number?'

But Dianne didn't want a pizza. She wanted Josh home *now* or she was going to dial for an ambulance herself.

'How far apart are the contractions?' Alice asked as Josh replaced the telephone, his face white.

'Two to three minutes apart, and from the noises she's making they're pretty full on.' He scratched his head. 'She was fine this morning, not a peep. I thought first labours went on for ever.'

'In the text books maybe, but this is real life. You'd better go now, Josh.'

'What about—?'

'*Go*,' Alice insisted. 'I'll tell Jeremy and Linda. Give me your pager. And ring me with the news,' she ordered, as he handed her his pager and notes. Josh was in such a state that he handed her his wallet. 'You don't have to pay me.' Alice laughed again.

'Wish me luck,' Josh grinned. 'Next time you see me I'll be a responsible father of two.'

Alice shook her head. 'A father, yes—responsible, no. Good luck,' she called to his rapidly departing back. And as he left Alice was suddenly filled with a hollow sadness. Josh was so excited, so ready for all that was ahead. She imagined him holding his wife's hands, working with her, guiding her through her labour. And afterwards, when their babies were born, sharing in each other's joy, united as a family. Her hand moved down to the solid swell beneath her theatre greens. Her baby was missing out on so much. And that hurt Alice, not for herself but for her unborn baby.

Maybe lots of women had babies without a partner these days, some even by choice, but it had never been her intention. She had always assumed that when—if—the time came to have children, it would be with the man she loved at her side. She knew the pain she felt now would only magnify with time. It had been hard enough at the antenatal classes, listening as the midwife had explained the role of the partner during labour. Alice had felt the weight of the pitying smiles then as she had sat alone, pretending to take notes.

What would it be like when she was actually *in* labour? When the pain got too much and there was no one she knew there to comfort her, to guide her and cheer her on? And then... Alice closed her eyes as they started to fill. How would it feel when the baby was born and there was no one to share it with, no one to gloat with and gaze in wonder at the miracle of birth?

'He's waking up.'

Alice snapped back to attention at Carrie's words, and made her way over to the gurney.

'What are his obs doing?'

'Stable. His blood pressure's good, still febrile and his temp's thirty-eight.'

'We'll just have to wait for the antibiotics to kick in. Lachlan, it's Dr Masters. I saw you briefly in the accident department. Lie still now, Lachlan, you're just coming to after an operation.' Alice kept her voice low and steady, trying to orientate and at the same time reassure the young man.

The anaesthetist had entered and was setting up a pethidine infusion for Lachlan. For the immediate post-op period a high dose of analgesic would be administered automatically, to control his pain, but as his consciousness and condition improved he would be using a patient controlled analgesia machine which would enable him to administer a safe dose of analgesic to himself as required.

'How's he doing?' Jeremy asked. Looking refreshed from his shower and, as usual, immaculately presented, he accepted the chart from Carrie. His question was directed more at the anaesthetist than Alice.

'Happy from this end. Where are you sending him?'

'There's a HDU bed on Surgical 1.'

'Josh's wife rang,' Alice informed him. 'Apparently—'

'I know already,' Jeremy answered, without looking up. 'I collided with him on my way here.'

And that was that. No small talk, no casual remarks about wishing him well, or the usual groan about twins. Jeremy obviously wasn't remotely interested.

'He said he's left his pager with you.' The blue eyes turned to her and Alice nodded.

'Well, if it gets too much, let Linda know. She'll have to pitch in.'

Which was about as helpful as suggesting she ring Josh if there were any problems. There was as much chance of Linda resiting an IV as Josh leaving his wife's side.

'How were Lachlan's family?' Carrie asked.

'Upset, relieved—the usual. I said they could pop in for two minutes before we transfer him.'

But Carrie wasn't having any of it. 'You know the rules. They'll have to wait until he's transferred to the ward, like every other family has to. Just because his father's a consultant here—'

'His father's not the only consultant here,' Jeremy reminded her. 'If you're so against staff having the occasional perk, like seeing their critically ill son in the recovery room, maybe it's just as well you work in the operating room, Carrie. Your personality wouldn't go down too well with a conscious patient.'

Alice watched as Carrie's shoulders stiffened, two spots of colour burning on her angry, taut cheeks. And though Alice knew Carrie had been out of line, the way she had addressed Jeremy, she actually felt sorry for her. Jeremy might have been a consultant, but he had by all accounts been more to her than that, and from her reaction towards him it wasn't all over where Carrie was concerned.

'Any news on Josh?'

Alice shook her head as she made her way over to Fi, who was coming out from handover. 'Not yet. I suppose he's got a million relatives and friends to ring before he gets around to letting us know.'

Fi shrugged. 'Dianne's probably still in labour. Looks like it's going to be a long hard night for womankind tonight. I suppose you're covering for Josh as well as your own work?'

'Linda's going to help out,' Alice said without much enthusiasm.

'Like I said, it's going to be a long hard night.'

Alice wasn't given to moaning about her colleagues, but Fi's inference was so spot on that Alice couldn't help but give a small smile. 'I bought some doughnuts,' she said holding out a brown paper bag, which Fi accepted with a laugh.

'Then what have I got to moan about? I'd better start doing the drugs. How about you? Do you need anything?'

Alice shook her head. 'I'm pretty much up to date. I've got a couple of bloods to do at eleven so I'll be back then. I'm going to head down to A and E—there's a couple of patients Linda wants to admit that need to be clerked before

they can be sent up to the ward, and then…' Her voice
trailed off as Jeremy and Linda walked through the ward
doors.

'Bit late for a ward round,' Fi muttered.

'How's Lachlan Scott doing?' Jeremy enquired.

'His temperature's come down and his obs are stable,'
Alice answered. 'I just left him.'

'Good. We're just going to have a quick look before I
head off.'

'Sure.'

But though Linda headed off to the HDU section, Jeremy
just stood there. 'Er, I was wondering if I could have a
word?'

'I'll get on with the drugs,' Fi said cheerfully, but Jeremy
shook his head. 'With both of you, please. Fi, do you mind
if we go into your office?' Not waiting for an answer, he
led the way. Fi and Alice followed, a worried look passing
between the two women. There must be a problem on the
ward they didn't know about. 'Sit down, please.'

Alice felt as if she were being hauled into the headmas-
ter's office for a telling-off, but when she finally looked up
at Jeremy she realised that he wasn't angry.

'I'm afraid I've got some bad news.'

Alice swallowed nervously.

'What?' Fi asked bluntly.

'It would seem that Dianne's labour wasn't very straightforward.'

Alice felt a cold shiver run down her spine.

'Apparently, the first twin, a little boy, was delivered
successfully, but there were problems getting the second
twin out.'

'Shoulder dystocia?' Fi asked, her voice shaky, referring
to a condition in labour where a baby's shoulders have
difficulty negotiating the bony pelvis.

Jeremy shook his head. 'No, Josh wasn't very clear on

the telephone but it would seem the second twin just didn't descend at all. They had to use forceps, but they couldn't get a grip. They made a number of attempts...'

Alice winced at the thought, and Jeremy shot her a look.

'Sorry, you probably don't need to hear all the details.'

But Alice shook her head fiercely 'No, tell me. I'm all right.'

'Well,' he continued tentatively, 'it would seem by the time they delivered the second twin, another little boy, he wasn't breathing and there was no output. He had to be resuscitated. Apparently it was rather lengthy, though they did get him back. Anyway, the upshot is that the baby's pretty sick. He's on PICU. He's bruised and battered from the forceps and he's got some breathing difficulties.'

'Poor Josh,' Alice whispered, almost to herself. 'And poor Dianne,' she added. Although she had never met Dianne, her heart went out to this woman and the pain she must be feeling.

'Obviously Josh will be taking some time off, which is going to mean more work for you, Alice.'

'I'll be fine,' she said, her grey eyes brimming with tears. 'It kind of puts things into perspective, doesn't it?'

Jeremy gave a brief nod. He wasn't going to be drawn into a deep discussion, but she could tell from his eyes that this news had shaken him, too.

It was a rather subdued group that made their way quietly out of the office. Linda was breaking the news rather less tactfully to the anaesthetic registrar.

'Which is just great. We've got the consultant just back from sick leave, the reg on annual leave, the resident on paternity leave and the intern about to go on maternity leave. I'm carrying the lot of them.'

'That's what I like about you, Linda,' Jeremy said dryly, as the anaesthetic reg signalled a desperate look at Linda to stop. 'Your sense of team spirit.' And without a backward glance he made his way across to Lachlan Scott, leaving Linda spluttering her excuses to his departing back.

Blinking back tears, Alice made her way down to A and E. How could it all have gone so terribly wrong? She remembered Josh's excited face just this morning. Oh, she knew things went wrong, that there were no guarantees of a perfect healthy baby, but why did it have to happen? And why to Josh and Dianne? It just wasn't fair.

A and E was busy, but wasn't it always?

'Hi, Alice.' Fay, the Unit Manager greeted her.

'Hi, Fay. I didn't expect to see you. How come you're on nights?'

'Don't ask.' Fay rolled her eyes. 'Given the fact that it's me who does the roster, I guess I've only got myself to blame. Anyway, it might be chaotic down here, but from a surgical point of view it's not too bad. There's just two for you to clerk in. Linda's seen them and ordered a few tests, but most can wait for the morning. As soon as you're done I can shift them up to the ward and free up a couple of trolleys.'

Which was an extremely nice way of saying 'get on with it'.

So she did, or at least she tried to, but no sooner had she clerked the first patient and was about to start with the second one than the sound of her pager signalled the end of her introduction to the patient.

'I'm sorry, Mr West, I'll just have to answer this. I'll be back to clerk you, hopefully soon.'

'No worries, love.'

Dialing the number as she flicked through Mr West's medical history, she was surprised when Fi answered. Normally Fi held off from paging when she knew Alice was coming back. Something must be up.

'I haven't forgotten the bloods, Fi. I've just got one more patient to clerk then I'll be up.'

But that wasn't why Fi was ringing. 'I've already done your bloods, so don't worry about that. Look, Alice, I'm a bit worried about Lachlan Scott. Would you mind coming and having a look?'

Alice didn't need to be asked twice. Ignoring the pained look from Fay, she made her way straight up to the ward.

'Thanks,' Fi said when Alice arrived. 'Hopefully I'm worrying about nothing, but he just doesn't seem right to me.'

'What are his obs doing?' Alice asked as they made the way to his bedside.

'Nothing remarkable. His temp's normal and his blood pressure's a tiny bit low, but I guess that could be put down to his analgesia.'

Lachlan Scott looked pretty much the same as when Alice had last seen him, maybe a little paler but nothing that would cause Alice too much concern. 'Lachlan, I'm just going to have a look at you,' Alice informed him, as Fi and Kate, the student nurse, helped her with the bedclothes. Lachlan gave a small nod.

'How are you feeling, Lachlan?' Alice asked.

'Tired.'

'Are you in any pain?'

Not bothering to open his eyes, Lachlan shook his head as Alice gently palpated his abdomen. Again there was no real change since the last time she'd seen him. Listening to his chest, she found the story was the same—nothing remarkable.

But Fi was worried and Alice wasn't going to ignore the fact.

Suddenly Lachlan opened his eyes. 'I should be in the library. I've got an exam in the morning.'

Alice gave Fi a worried glance.

'Lachlan, do you know where you are?' Fi asked urgently.

Closing his eyes, Lachlan nodded.

'Where, Lachlan?'

'Melbourne City.' Which, of course, was the right answer, but his moment of confusion prompted Alice into action.

'Do another set of obs and I'll ring Linda.'

Linda was particularly unhelpful. 'So let me get this straight. His obs are fine, and you can't find anything wrong on examination. Exactly why are you calling me, Alice?'

'Because the nursing staff are concerned—I'm concerned,' she said trying to sound confident. 'And, as I said, he's confused.'

'Momentarily,' Linda pointed out. 'He's had major surgery, he's on a high dose of pethidine and you've just woken him up in the middle of the night. You said yourself he's orientated now. Look, Alice, I just had A and E on the telephone complaining there's still a patient waiting to be clerked. I'm stuck on Intensive Care with a sick patient and I've still got a list of patients to see on the wards. Now you're ringing to tell me a patient I reviewed an hour ago is in the exact same condition as when I left.'

'I'd just like you to review him,' Alice said as evenly as she could. 'I'd really value your opinion,' she added tactfully.

'When I get a moment,' was all Linda could offer.

'Is she coming?' Fi asked as Alice replaced the receiver.

'When she gets time.' Alice shrugged. 'What are his obs doing now?'

'Not much change. His temp's down a bit further—it's 35.0 now.' Which was low. Not dangerously low, but low enough to set an alarm bell ringing in Alice's head.

'He could be septic.'

'But wouldn't his temperature be high then?' Kate asked.

Alice shook her head. 'Not necessarily. Sometimes when

the body's overwhelmed with infection a patient can actually become *hypo*thermic.'

Alice wasn't a brilliant doctor, she was the first to admit that. She had got into and through medical school by sheer hard work and diligence. But she was a good doctor, and she knew that, too. And part of being a good doctor involved listening. Fi, with her years of knowledge and experience, had called on her because she was worried, and now Alice was worried as well. She wrung her hands anxiously. 'I'd better ring Jeremy.' She looked at Fi for her reaction.

'Good. I'll share the flak if it's nothing.'

She had obviously woken him when she'd rung, and Jeremy listened without interruption as she relayed her findings.

'What did Linda say?'

'She's a bit busy at the moment. His temperature wasn't quite so low, though, when I spoke to her,' Alice said hesitantly. 'Maybe I should have called her back…'

'Doesn't matter now. Look, take some gases and bloods, do some cultures as well, and I'll be straight in.'

Alice, unsure whether her concern for the patient was entirely merited, was somewhat taken aback by how amenable he was being. 'I could ring Linda again,' she offered. 'Or call you back with the blood results. It could be nothing.'

'Let's hope it is,' Jeremy said darkly. 'I'm on my way.'

Linda wasn't all bad, and in fairness she did come over almost immediately. But Alice's relief at seeing her senior quickly vanished when Linda heard she had already contacted Jeremy.

'You *what*? You just went ahead and called him? How dare you, without running it by me first?'

Alice was trying to concentrate on finding a vein and didn't look up as she answered. 'I did run it by you first. I felt Lachlan needed to be seen, and urgently. I knew how busy you were.'

'So you went straight over my head?'

Alice didn't reply; she was becoming increasingly worried about Lachlan now. His veins were proving extremely difficult to find, again a rather ominous sign in a young healthy man.

'It's not your responsibility to ring the consultant. You ring me and then *I* decide. It's not your concern...'

Alice had heard enough. Rowing at a sick patient's bedside really wasn't her style. 'I'm paid to be concerned, Linda, and right now I'd appreciate your help in finding a vein. You can bawl me out later.'

'Let's concentrate on the patient, shall we?' Jeremy's rich tones filled the room, and Linda immediately snapped to attention.

'You got here quickly,' Fi said appreciatively.

'I'm sleeping at the hospital tonight.'

Alice's eyebrows shot up in surprise but she didn't say anything.

In the short space of time it had taken Jeremy and Linda to arrive, it had become obvious that Lachlan was extremely unwell. He kept pulling off his oxygen mask, confused rantings coming from his mouth.

'Linda, run over to ICU and get the gases done,' Jeremy said quickly. 'Fi, call a MET.'

Fi nodded and turned to Kate. 'You do it. Tell them the room number and bring back the resusc trolley with you.'

As the overhead chimes relayed their urgent message, Alice felt her adrenaline kick into overdrive. A medical emergency team was called when a patient was suffering a life-threatening incident. It was a relatively new innovation, and not practised at many hospitals, but it had on many occasions proved to be more than effective. Once the call was put out, the ICU anaesthetist, along with an ICU nurse and the on-call physicians, would make their way urgently to the patient's bedside to implement urgent intervention *before* the patient arrested. And though it was becoming increasingly obvious to Alice that Lachlan really was very sick, she was somewhat surprised at the dramatic measure Jeremy had taken.

From then on Alice felt she was somewhat supernumerary as a multitude of staff and equipment appeared, all far more skilled and experienced at coping with emergencies than she was. Jeremy relayed the findings to the MET team as IV fluids were pumped into Lachlan's system and his oxygen concentration was turned up. The head of the bed had been removed by Fi to allow the anaesthetist more access to Lachlan's airway, and the patient was now attached to a cardiac monitor with a probe clipped onto his earlobe to continually measure his oxygen saturation.

'Ring the lab, Alice, and ask them to step on his bloods,' Jeremy ordered, just as Linda returned breathlessly with his blood gas results.

'We'll get him over to ICU,' the anaesthetist addressed Jeremy. 'We'll need to put in a central line and do the works, but hopefully the antibiotics will kick in soon. It's lucky we got to him in time. That was a good pick-up, Jeremy. Glad to have you back on board.'

By the time Lachlan had been wheeled over to ICU it was a white, shaking Alice that stood in the empty room as Fi started to clear up the large mess that had been created. ICU wasn't Alice's domain. It was up to her to cover the rest of the wards.

'That was close,' Fi said.

'Very,' agreed Alice. 'He just seemed to go downhill so quickly.'

Fi nodded. 'Young, fit ones often do that. They hold their vital signs stable until the last minute. By the time a young guy like that drops his BP you're often too late. I'm sure there's a far more technical way of explaining it, but I'll leave that for Jeremy to explain.'

'Thanks, Fi, if it hadn't been for you…'

'Don't sell yourself short. It took a lot of guts to ring Jeremy.'

They both looked up simultaneously as Jeremy coughed, making his presence known.

'I agree.'

Alice didn't answer.

'How's Lachlan?' Fi asked. 'Will he be going back to Theatre?'

Jeremy shook his head. 'Not at this stage. He's had an ultrasound and it doesn't look as if there's a collection in his abdomen. He's septic from the infection, we think. Hopefully we can keep him going until the antibiotics kick in. His parents have arrived. I was wondering if you could come in with me, Fi?'

Fi nodded. 'I'll take them down to the day room.'

'You might as well head off to bed, Alice,' Jeremy said, without meeting her eyes.

'I've still got a patient in A and E to clerk.'

'Don't worry about that,' Jeremy said, rather too lightly. 'I've rung A and E and they're going to send him straight up—he can be clerked later. Linda's going to be up all night with me, anyway. I can tell her to head over here and do it when there's time. Is there anything else outstanding?'

'Just some two a.m. bloods.' She glanced at her watch. 'Which are just about due.'

'I'm sure Fi can help with that. If not, I'll come and do them.'

'You?' Alice said rather ungraciously. Since when did a consultant offer to do an intern's two a.m. bloods? 'Are you sure?'

'I'm sure I can handle it,' Jeremy said in his superior way, and then his tones softened. 'Let's say I owe you one.

Linda, too, for that matter,' he added darkly. A ghost of a smile touched his lips. 'Go on, get some rest. You might even cram in a couple of hours' sleep.'

It was then that Alice noticed how pale Jeremy looked. The night's events had obviously shaken him up as well.

'Thanks, then,' she said gratefully. 'But call if you need me.'

As she made her way out of the room Jeremy called her back.

'Likewise, Alice. You call if you need me as well. I'll always listen.'

Never had the thin, hard, on-call bed looked more tempting. Aching and exhausted, Alice slipped off her shoes and slowly lowered herself onto the mattress. Normally she slept on her stomach, but her ever-increasing size had meant that for the last few weeks she had been forced to sleep on her back or side, which inevitably meant most of the night was spent tossing and turning, trying to get comfortable. With a groan she placed her pager on the bedside table and flicked off the lamp, tucking a plastic-covered hospital pillow under her bump she rolled onto her side. A couple of hours sounded good from here. There was still a full day's work tomorrow to get through. Fancy Jeremy telling her to go to bed. Under normal circumstances she would have insisted she was fine, but Brett Halliday's warnings had hit home and she wasn't going to do anything to risk her health—too much depended on it. Anyway, given how the night's events had panned out, Linda probably *did* owe her one, Alice mused. Still, it had been extremely nice of Jeremy to pull rank and, in his own way, to thank her. But, then, that was how Jeremy had been all the time she had worked for him—extremely nice. Low as her expectations had been about his demeanour, he had surprised her. Drifting off into a deep sleep, her last conscious thoughts were of Jeremy, and as her subconscious kicked in, her dreams for once were not filled with Marcus and unborn babies, but a certain consultant with blond hair and a smile that set her heart racing.

CHAPTER THREE

'GOOD morning, Dr Masters, your six a.m. alarm call.'

'But I didn't book one,' Alice replied, fuddled and confused. Flicking on the light, she reached for her watch, trying to orientate herself to her surroundings. With a jolt of panic she reached for her pager. 'Has anyone been trying to get hold of me?'

'Not as far as I know,' the switchboard operator answered cheerfully. Replacing the receiver, Alice sat up slowly.

'Good morning to you, too,' she said, as the baby let out a huge kick.

Standing under the shower jets, Alice closed her eyes as the warm water slowly brought her around. Four solid hours' sleep on an on-call night was a luxury she hadn't even dared dream about. Thank goodness the switchboard operator had called, Alice thought. She was so tired she might have slept in until midday. Pulling on some fresh greens, she made her way down to the canteen, but the bleeping of her pager foiled any thought of lingering over a cooked breakfast. After purchasing a muesli bar and a coffee from the machine, she made her way over to the surgical unit.

'Morning, Fi, how has it been?'

Fi rolled her eyes. 'Let's just say I'm glad it's morning. Nothing for you to worry about, though,' Fi said quickly as Alice gave a concerned look. 'Just a couple of the old dears decided to go a-wandering. It must be a full moon. Anyway…' She grinned. 'You certainly look a lot better. Did you have a good sleep?'

'Marvellous. Luckily, switchboard gave me a wake-up call or I'd still be there now. You didn't book it by any chance?' Alice asked, but Fi shook her head.

'Maybe Linda was having an attack of the guilts. She looked positively sheepish when she came over to do some bloods. I was going to page you to resite an IV and Linda even said that she'd do it—I nearly fainted with surprise. Who knows? Lachlan Scott going off like that might be just the jolt Linda needed to bring her back down to earth.'

'Maybe,' Alice said, but she was far from convinced. Linda McFarlane might have had a bit of a jolt, but Alice was quite sure it would take more than that to soften the edges. Though not a vindictive person, Alice had a sharp memory, and Linda would need to do more than take a few bloods and book a wake-up call to earn Alice's respect. 'How's Lachlan doing—have you heard?'

'Stable. Jeremy's been in with him all night. Apparently his cultures already show a massive infection. It's lucky we got him over to ICU when we did. I wouldn't have fancied his chances otherwise.'

'Unbelievable.' Alice let out a small sigh. 'People are so sure an appendectomy is just a minor operation these days, which, of course, it would have been if Lachlan had come in earlier.'

Fi nodded and added in a subdued voice, 'Like having twins. With IVF and everything, twins are so much more common but people just don't realise the dangers of multiple births. I remember when I did my midwifery, everyone was on standby when twins were about to be delivered. It seems almost a non-event these days—until it all goes wrong, that is.'

'Have you heard anything?'

'I rang just before. Obviously they wouldn't tell me much, but apparently there's not much change. We'll just have to wait for more detail. I'm sure Josh will let us know more when he can.'

But Josh didn't ring. And by five o'clock, when the euphoria of four hours' sleep had long since worn off and Alice sat exhausted as the tram clattered along, the sight of the Women's and Children's was something she just couldn't go past. Despite the fact she had only known Josh two weeks, and had never met his wife, Josh had shown her so much kindness. She wouldn't be nosy, wouldn't ask to see the babies or anything like that. She simply wanted to let them know they were in her thoughts. If the roles had been reversed—and, please, God, they wouldn't be, Alice thought, instinctively placing a protective hand over her stomach—she just *knew* Josh would do the same. Jeremy, despite his obvious sadness as he'd broken the news, hadn't mentioned Josh all day. Babies were obviously way down on his list of priorities.

And as for Linda... Alice's lips thinned just at the thought of her. Linda might well have been more pleasant today, but the daggers coming from her icy eyes hadn't gone unnoticed by Alice. Her first impressions about Linda, Alice concluded, had been right, and she wasn't about to be fooled. One thing she prided herself on was being an excellent judge of character—except with Marcus, she reminded herself ruefully.

Not just Marcus, Alice thought in surprise as the lift doors opened to the maternity section. She had been rehearsing what to say. Her plan had been to ask at the nurses' station if she could have a word with Josh in the corridor. Jeremy had obviously had the same idea.

Both men turned as she made her way along the carpeted floor towards them.

'I hope you're here to see me and not looking for the delivery room?' Josh smiled. But despite the welcoming, half-joking words and the apparently casual hug, Alice knew he was devastated. His eyes were swollen and red-rimmed and he held onto her tightly for a second before letting her go.

'Hopefully not for a few weeks yet, Josh. How are you and Dianne doing?' She was terrified to ask after the twins in case the news had become worse.

'Holding up. Dianne's been marvellous. She's exhausted, though. Insisting on expressing milk and sitting in the intensive care unit. The nurses have just given her a couple of sleeping tablets so hopefully she'll get a few hours' rest.'

'How are the boys?' Alice asked finally.

'Declan's great,' he swallowed hard. 'I was just telling Jeremy it's not so good for Eamon.' Alice looked up at Jeremy for the first time and gave a small nod of greeting. Turning back to Josh, she was horrified to see huge tears splashing down his cheeks. 'It doesn't look too great,' Josh said, his words strangled as he tried to control his emotions.

Alice put a comforting hand on his arm. 'It's all right Josh. You don't have to go through it all for me. Jeremy can tell me. I just came to see how *you* were doing. To see if there was anything I could do to help.'

She felt so helpless standing there.

'Actually, there is something,' Josh said.

'Tell me,' Alice urged.

A hint of a blush crept over Josh's freckled face. 'Well, we left in rather a rush, as you know. Dianne didn't bring her...' He paused. 'You know... There's a chemist down in the foyer. Would you mind, Alice?'

'For heaven's sake, Josh!' It was the first time Jeremy had spoken. 'I thought you were a new age kind of guy.'

'I know, I know.' Josh replied, blushing ever deeper. 'How would you like having to buy them? That would ruin your cool image a bit, wouldn't it?'

The light-hearted jostling was a welcome relief after the previous tension.

'There's nothing to it,' Jeremy insisted. 'I'll be back in five. Get him a sandwich or something, will you, Alice? I've tried and he won't eat a thing. Maybe a woman will have more luck. He looks as if he's about to faint.'

Once Jeremy had gone Alice linked an arm through one of Josh's. 'You heard the boss. Come on, you need to eat.'

At the entrance the women's auxiliary had a small stall, selling drinks and snacks along with an assortment of hand-knitted baby goods and handmade teddy bears. Balloons with congratulatory messages for a baby boy, girl…twins adorned the stall.

Josh eyed them ruefully as Alice returned with a sandwich for Josh and two coffees.

'Not a ''get well soon'' balloon in sight,' Josh said pensively. 'You just never think it's going to go so wrong.'

Alice recalled Fi's words of that morning but didn't say anything, allowing Josh to continue.

'That's not strictly true. I imagined every possible scenario but deep down I just thought I was worrying unnecessarily, that everything would be fine.'

Alice put a hand over Josh's cold one. 'That's what we all do, Josh. You'd go crazy otherwise. But you also know deep down that, whatever happens, you'll deal with it. It's not as if we have much choice in these things.'

Josh stared into his coffee for a few minutes. 'Fancy Jeremy coming up to see me. He told me not to worry about work, to take all the time I needed. He's a good egg, Jeremy, despite what everyone says.'

'You really like him, don't you?' Alice asked, unable to keep the hint of surprise out of her voice. She was so used to hearing Jeremy derided.

'I think he's great; I always have. Why do you sound so surprised?'

Alice shrugged, not sure what to say. 'He's got such a

reputation. I mean, I know he's a great surgeon, but he's stepped on a lot of toes.'

Josh grinned. 'In his rush to get to the bedroom. Look, beneath all that smooth talk is a nice guy. Hell, if I looked like that…'

'Here you go.' Jeremy thrust a huge carrier bag into Josh's lap. 'Told you—nothing to it.'

'Jeremy.' Josh laughed. 'You've practically bought out the whole shop. 'Toothpaste, teddies, deodorant—did you hide the sanitary pads under them in the basket?'

This time it was Jeremy who blushed. 'I got them, didn't I?'

'Dr Winters.' Josh jumped as a midwife came over. 'Calm down, there's no change,' the midwife said quickly, seeing the look of utter panic on Josh's face. 'But Declan is awake and screaming at the top of his voice. Dianne will be out for a few hours yet. I thought you might like to give Declan some of Dianne's milk.'

Josh nodded eagerly. 'I'll be right there.' He gave a grateful smile. 'Thanks for coming by guys, it meant a hell of a lot.' He gave Alice a quick hug and shook Jeremy's hand before rushing off to the nursery.

Alice sat shyly after he had left.

'Hungry?' Jeremy asked.

'A bit. I might grab a sandwich myself. I can't be bothered to cook.'

'Hardly good for the baby, is it?'

Alice gave him a surprised look. 'You're an expert on maternal nutrition, are you? Actually, I was going to grab a beef and spinach foccacia. Full of iron.'

Jeremy screwed up his nose. 'Not by the time the women's auxiliary get hold of it. Come on, we'll go and grab something a bit more nutritious *and* tasty.'

His invitation was so casual it could hardly even be

called that, and Alice knew she would look stupid if she turned him down, and yet…

'Come on,' he said irritably, as she hesitated. 'Where are you parked?'

'I haven't got a car,' Alice answered. 'I came on the tram.'

'Good, that makes it easier,' Jeremy replied.

Oh, well, she thought as she picked up her bag, what choice did she have?

Sitting beside Jeremy in his slick car made Alice feel positively claustrophobic. The seats were impossibly low and Jeremy had to help her with the seat belt, which Alice rightly assumed hadn't been designed with a pregnant woman in mind. Never had she felt so huge and unattractive, and never had she been more acutely aware of the fact that Jeremy Foster was every inch a man—his expensive suit brushing her arm, the weight of him as he leant across her, the subtle scent of his cologne mingling with the heavy scent of his maleness. Alice flattened herself against the seat in a vain attempt to appear thinner, and after a couple of attempts Jeremy managed to create enough slack in the seat belt to get the beastly strap across her huge stomach. Alice thought she would die of embarrassment.

She was also painfully aware that all she had in her purse was a fifty-dollar note which she had hoped to use as a deposit for a crib. The way Jeremy had sneered at the sandwiches the women's auxiliary had on offer didn't allow Alice to hold out much hope that they would be stopping at the nearest burger bar. She was right. Sliding the car into a space directly in front of the Hyatt Hotel, Jeremy jumped out as the doorman opened the car door for Alice. Hardly stopping to retrieve his receipt, Jeremy casually strolled up the entrance steps.

'How come he's parking it for you?' Alice asked, bewildered. 'Are you a guest here?'

'Might as well be, the amount of times I eat here.'

At least the Hyatt had a massive food court. Perhaps she could steer him towards the noodles. Jeremy, of course, baulked at the idea.

'I've either been standing in Theatre or Intensive Care all day. If you think I'm going to stand in line for my dinner, you're mistaken. Come on.'

Alice bristled. He was so haughty, so arrogant and superior. How dared he just assume she wanted to sit in some five-star restaurant and dine with him?

Her acrimony didn't last long. Lowering herself into a sumptuous seat, she caught his eye and Jeremy gave her the benefit of his perfect white smile. Murder—again that was the thought that sprang to mind; this man could get away with murder. But she did have her credit card on her. OK, she had sworn it was for emergencies only, but what was this? It was hardly everyday stuff, sitting in a luxury restaurant with the most gorgeous of men, who also happened to be your boss.

Oh, well, when in Rome and all that. If she was going to use her credit card it might as well be for the benefit of the baby, Alice thought as she ordered a well-done steak with fresh garden vegetables.

Jeremy chose red snapper.

'Would sir like to see the wine list?'

Without looking up, Jeremy shook his head. 'I'll just have a mineral water, thanks. Alice?'

'The same for me, please.'

By the time their drinks had appeared, bread had been served and the wineglasses removed, Alice felt her butterflies start to disappear.

'How are you finding it?' Jeremy asked.

Alice smiled. 'Lovely. You were right. I'm sick of hospital sandwiches.'

'I meant work.'

Alice flushed. 'Oh.' The waiter appeared again and swapped Alice's knife for a steak knife. 'Work's fine, too,' she said once they were alone again.

'But not lovely?'

'I could think of other words to describe last night.'

Jeremy looked at her thoughtfully. 'I've spoken to Linda. She was always going to come, you know.'

'No, Jeremy, I didn't know,' Alice said forcefully, for the first time staring directly at him. 'I'm not interested in mind games. I accept that I'm a very junior doctor; I've got no delusions of grandeur on that count. When I rang Linda for help and she gave no indication that she was coming in time, I had to make a choice. At the end of the day it wouldn't have stood up too well in the Coroner's Court if I stated that I assumed she'd be coming and did nothing.'

Jeremy winced. 'Thank God it didn't come to that. He's a lot better this evening.'

Alice took a sip of her drink. 'Good. Look, Jeremy, to her credit, Linda did come—'

Jeremy interrupted her. 'But next time you'll think twice about ringing her?''

'Exactly. Which isn't the safest of situations.'

Jeremy stared at her thoughtfully. 'Which is why, and this is strictly between you and me, I ripped a strip off Linda last night. She *is* a good doctor, but she's got a lot to learn—mainly about how to treat her colleagues. Now, I think last night shook her up, so hopefully she'll lift her game. But don't worry, I'll be watching things closely. And if ever you are worried, I need you to promise me that you *will* ring Linda without hesitation, and if you get no joy ring me straight away. Don't jeopardise your career for the sake of ruffling a few feathers.'

'You don't have to worry about that,' Alice said seriously. 'I have no intention of jeopardising either my career or the patients' well-being. You've got no concerns there.'

'I know.'

Glad they'd at least got that out of the way, Alice started to eat the meal which had just arrived, but any thoughts of polite small talk flew out of the window when Jeremy voiced his next question. 'So, how did you get pregnant?'

Alice nearly choked on her steak. 'I beg your pardon?' she finally managed to get out when she had finished coughing. 'I would have thought that you of all people would know by now where babies come from.'

Jeremy grinned but pressed on, unfazed. 'It's a natural question to ask. Was it planned?'

'That's none of your business,' Alice retorted furiously, her eyes watering. 'You were the one who said I didn't have to reveal anything I didn't want to.'

'But that was to the patients,' Jeremy answered straightforwardly. 'I'm a friend.'

Alice looked at him, bemused. 'You're a colleague. You're my boss.'

'All right, then.' Jeremy shrugged. 'We can talk about me instead. I'm good at that.'

Again he flashed his impossible smile and Alice managed a small one back. Oh, well, what was the harm in telling him? It was hardly a state secret.

'It wasn't planned,' she admitted. 'I'd have thought that was obvious.'

'Some women choose to go it alone.' He leant over the table but didn't bother to lower his voice. 'My mother knows someone who's a ''miss'' in every sense of the word. Apparently she's found some guy who's prepared to donate—'

Alice put up her hand. 'Spare me the details.' She flushed as a smirking waiter refilled her water glass.

Jeremy laughed, and there was something about the refreshing directness of his question that made Alice tentatively start to open up. In between mouthfuls of the most delicious steak she had tasted in years, she found herself filling Jeremy in on the most painful intimate details of her life.

'Marcus and I were going out for two years. We'd never really spoken about marriage, but I just assumed it would happen one day. He was a dental student and we were both at the same uni in Adelaide. Marcus had big plans. He was going to take over his uncle's dental practice here in Melbourne—'

'And what about you?' Jeremy cut in.

'I'd do my internship here and then specialise.'

'In what?' Jeremy asked.

'I liked paeds,' Alice admitted. 'That was my first rotation, although A and E holds a certain fascination. It was paeds that got me into this mess.'

Jeremy raised his eyebrows but didn't interrupt again.

'We had a little girl in who was extremely unwell,' Alice explained. 'It turned out she had meningococcal meningitis. A few of us had been pretty hands-on with her so it was recommended that we take some antibiotics.'

'You surely knew that they interfere with the Pill, or at the very least the pharmacist should have warned you.'

'Yes to both,' Alice gave a resigned smile. 'The problem was that Marcus wasn't due to be in Melbourne for a fortnight so I assumed that the warnings didn't apply to me and promptly forgot them. When Marcus turned up for the weekend for a "surprise" visit it never even entered my head I might get pregnant.'

'What did Marcus say?'

Alice fiddled with the food on her plate before answering. 'A lot. But the long and the short of it was that he wanted me to have an abortion, and that's a polite way of putting it.'

'But you didn't—obviously?'

Alice shrugged. 'I'd love to say it never entered my head, but I'd be lying. I even made an appointment, but at the end of the day I just couldn't do it. Marcus was furious, said that I'd ruined all his plans for us, that children weren't on his agenda for years yet. I think he had a vision of us as a couple of yuppies, bringing in the big bucks and living in a penthouse.'

'And what was your vision?'

Alice thought for a moment before answering. 'I didn't really have one. Getting my registration was my next big thing, choosing an area in which to specialise. It certainly wasn't having children so soon, and definitely not on my own.'

'You'll be all right,' Jeremy said kindly, but Alice wasn't so sure.

'That's easy for you to say. The truth is, it's going to be a long, hard slog and I'll just have to make the best of it.'

'So you and Marcus are washed up? There's no chance he might reconsider when the baby comes along?'

'I doubt it. Anyway, it's entirely irrelevant how he feels. There's no way I'd go back to him after the way he's been.'

'What did your parents say?'

The flicker of pain in her eyes didn't go unnoticed by Jeremy. 'Everything Marcus did and ten times more. They really put themselves to the wall to get me through medical school—we're not really speaking at the moment.'

Jeremy gave her a sympathetic look and turned back to his meal but Alice, feeling more confident now, decided it was her turn to cross the line. 'You're still in a lot of pain from your accident, aren't you?'

Jeremy responded to her probing question in a rather

more dignified way than Alice had, but though he didn't promptly start coughing and spluttering he certainly looked suddenly uneasy.

'Has everyone noticed?'

Suddenly she felt sorry for him. He wasn't as cool as he made out. Maybe she shouldn't have mentioned it. 'No one—well, not as far as I know,' she said quickly. 'It was just that first day we started, seeing you after the clinic. I guess I realised then. And since then I've just noticed the odd couple of things, but only because I was looking. I'm sure that no one else would have.'

'I am in pain,' he said quietly. 'Not all of the time, and it certainly doesn't interfere with my work. I'd never put the patients at risk like that. But by the end of a long theatre list or the end of the day…' His voice trailed off.

'Are you taking anything for it?' she probed.

'Paracetamol—that's it. It helps a bit.'

'But not enough. Surely you could take something stronger. I mean, after all you've been through…'

'My doctor said the same, but at the end of the day I'm a surgeon. I have to have my wits about me one hundred per cent. Maybe I could take something but I have to go to my bed with my conscience. Take Lachlan Scott. It would be hard enough telling his parents if he'd died. Imagine my guilt if I'd been taking a painkiller that might have impaired my concentration.'

'But, Jeremy,' Alice reasoned, 'I'm not talking about anything mind-altering, just something a bit stronger.'

But Jeremy was resolute. 'I have to live with myself, Alice. If I need more than paracetamol to get me through then I came back too soon. I'll just have to get on with it.'

As exasperated as Alice was by his stubbornness, she also actually admired him for the stance he was taking and the personal sacrifice he was making to ensure his patients received the best of care.

'Looks like we'll both just have to lump it, doesn't it?' he said lightly.

Alice gave a small laugh. 'In my case, literally.' Raising her glass, she offered a toast. 'Here's to suffering the consequences.'

As their glasses clinked their eyes met. Again Jeremy flashed her his smile, but this time Alice didn't smile back. Her mind was suddenly in turmoil and, dumbfounded, confused, she took a hasty sip of her drink. Surely she couldn't be falling for him? Not her as well as every other female at Melbourne City?

Until that point Alice had safely assumed that your sex hormones somehow disappeared when your pregnancy test came back positive. Nothing scientifically based, of course, but for Alice it was just the way she felt. She hadn't even considered the fact she might find another man attractive. Oh, maybe somewhere a long way down the road, on the distant horizon, but it wasn't something she had dwelt on. She had enough to deal with, just concentrating on making a half-decent life for herself and the baby. But looking at Jeremy sitting across the table, immaculate, gorgeous and smiling at her, it was if she were seeing him for the first time. Suddenly he wasn't just her good-looking boss, the one with the reputation, but a man who made her laugh, who actually listened—and one with a vulnerable side, too. And for Alice it was proving to be an irresistible combination.

'What's wrong?' Jeremy asked, and Alice heard the concern in his voice.

'Nothing,' she said, flustered. 'The baby just did a huge somersault,' she lied. 'I think I'm going to give birth to a gymnast.'

'You must be exhausted. I'll get the bill.'

As he signalled the waiter Alice fished in her bag for her purse.

'Don't even think about it.' Jeremy shot her a look across the table.

'We'll go halves at least,' Alice insisted.

Jeremy seemed to find this hilarious. 'I haven't done that since I was a medical student. Anyway, that's not fair,' he joked. 'You had the steak and *two* mineral waters. Look, Alice,' Jeremy drawled. 'There have to be some compensations for spending an evening with a self-confessed male chauvinist, so at least utilise them.'

So she did. She didn't even bother to put up too much resistance when Jeremy insisted on driving her home; his leather-upholstered seats far more tempting than the tram. But as the car slid to a halt outside her block, Alice was suddenly hit by an attack of nerves.

'Er, you don't want a coffee or anything, do you?' she said, praying he would take the hint and refuse. Her poky little bedsit was hardly the Hyatt and, anyway, she couldn't remember if she'd made her bed yesterday.

But Jeremy appeared not to notice her reluctance. 'A coffee would be perfect.'

Thankfully she *had* made the bed. Jeremy instantly made himself comfortable, kicking off his shoes and flicking on the television as Alice busied herself with the coffee. Obviously strange women's apartments held no fear for him, Alice reminded herself. Luckily she had bought some filter papers at the weekend and could make a decent brew; the cheap home brand she generally survived on was definitely an acquired taste.

'I bet you hog the remote control,' Alice commented as she brought two steaming mugs through.

'Of course.'

It was a choice between the sofa or the floor, and if she sat there Alice doubted if she'd ever get up again, not in a ladylike fashion anyway, so she was left with little choice other than to sit beside him. The same feeling of awareness she had experienced in the car returned. Frantically searching for something to say, she watched as he stifled a yawn. 'You must be exhausted, too,' Alice said sympathetically. 'After all, you wouldn't have had any sleep last night with Lachlan and everything.'

Jeremy shrugged. 'Comes with the territory, though I must admit it's the first time in ages I've had to work right through.'

Alice took a sip of her coffee. 'Lucky you were on site last night and got there so quickly.' Her cheeks were burning but she couldn't stop herself. 'How come you were there?' Her grey eyes peered over the edge of her mug. Her question sounded casual enough but her heart was in her mouth as she awaited the answer.

'I was already more than a bit worried about him. I was half waiting for a call, although I admit I thought it would be from Linda. Then there's the other sickie patient we've got in Intensive Care. He's still pretty unstable. Since the accident I'm not given to speeding, as you can imagine. It seemed more sensible to stay in one of the on-call rooms when I'm on, rather than trying to make some mercy dash in the middle of the night. Safer, too.'

Even Alice was surprised at how she relieved she was that he hadn't been with a woman. OK, so who was to say that Carrie or whoever hadn't been in the on-call room with him? But at least his reasons sounded plausible.

'I don't think you fully understand how well you did last night, Alice. Cold septic shock is often terminal. We got to him just in time.'

'It's Fi you need to thank. I did nothing.'

'I've already thanked Fi. And what she said to you was right, too. It did take a lot of guts to ring me and go with your hunch. You didn't just help Lachlan last night—you made my return a whole lot easier.'

Alice gave him a bemused look. 'How?'

'As I said before, there are a lot of people watching. It would be tragic enough to lose a young fit man in any circumstances, but a fellow consultant's son…'

'No one could have blamed you, Jeremy. You did a brilliant job in Theatre, you reviewed him thoroughly postoperatively. You know better than me how subtle the signs of septic shock can be, especially in someone so young.'

Jeremy put down his empty mug. 'You're wrong, Alice. There are a lot of people waiting for me to put a foot wrong. Even if it hadn't been my fault, the consequences for me professionally would have been dire.'

'It didn't come to that,' Alice said softly.

'Thank God. Anyway, it's worked the other way, and I know that it's completely unfair on you and Fi—but I'm suddenly reaping the benefits of your wisdom. Nice as it is for now, I'm not that shallow that I don't realise it could have gone either way, and that my so-called friends slapping me on the back at the moment would have been sticking in a knife.'

'But why? Why would they want to see you brought down?'

Jeremy let out a sigh. 'Not all of them. I haven't got that many enemies. But the few I do have are pretty powerful. You know what hospitals are like, how mud sticks. I've put a few people's noses out of joint in my time, and they thought the accident was somehow my comeuppance. As you reap so shall you sow and all that.'

'Surely you can't have been that bad?'

'Of course not.' Jeremy managed a repentant grin. 'At least their daughters didn't seem to think so.'

'Ah.'

'Am I making sense now?' Those impossibly blue eyes were staring at her intently.

'Perfectly.' For a moment their eyes locked. He smiled

then, really smiled, his eyes creasing, and Alice felt her insides flip over, only this time it was definitely nothing to do with the baby.

'Can I get you another coffee?' she asked quickly, but Jeremy shook his head.

'I'd best be off.' He stood up and, smiling slightly as Alice struggled somewhat to join him from the impossibly low sofa, offered his hand, which Alice almost instinctively reached for, allowing him to take her weight as she stood up. Feeling about as seductive as a baby elephant, she managed an embarrassed laugh.

'I was fit—once. It seems like a lifetime ago.'

Jeremy grinned. 'I'm just eternally grateful it's women who have the babies.'

He made no move to go, didn't even release her hand. Instead, he stood there for a moment, his eyes searching her face. There was an unmistakable tension, but Alice assumed it was all coming from her. She was all too aware of her condition to even consider that Jeremy might reciprocate her attraction.

''Night, then, Alice.' He pulled her gently towards him and for a fleeting second his lips brushed her cheek in a casual goodnight kiss—except there was nothing casual about it for Alice. The world seemed to move in slow motion as she took in the scent of his cologne, felt his moist, warm lips graze the side of her face, her swollen stomach for a second pressing against him. It should have been no big deal, any man would have ended a pleasant evening with the same gesture, there was nothing to read into it.

But it *was* a huge deal, Alice conceded as he let her hand go. Jeremy Foster close up was every bit the exhilarating experience she had heard about. He deserved every flicker of his reputation if one tiny kiss could have that effect on a woman. No wonder they all melted, Alice reflected as he turned to leave. It would take a stronger woman than her to turn him down. 'Have a good night's sleep,' she managed to rasp.

Jeremy nodded. 'No doubt about that. I'd better book an alarm call or I doubt I'll make it.'

Alice stood there dumbfounded. 'Was it you that booked the call for me this morning?'

Jeremy gave a casual shrug. 'Sure.'

'But why?'

'I thought you needed the rest. It did Linda no harm at all to be reminded of the work an intern does. She might think she's carried the whole team for the last year, but by all accounts the only job she's been doing is mine. Everyone else had to do the rest.'

'But I told you I don't want any special treatment.' This was all too much—never had it entered her head that it might have been Jeremy who'd been so thoughtful.

Jeremy, though, seemed to think it was no big deal. 'I know you don't want any special treatment, and if it makes you feel any better I'll be sure to run you ragged tomorrow. Thirty-six hours on the go is bad enough at the best of times, Alice, let alone in your condition. You should be grabbing every opportunity to rest when you're on call.'

'Th-thanks,' she stammered.

He didn't answer. With a vague wave he opened the door and Alice stood watching as he made his way down the corridor and out through the foyer.

Walking back in, she looked at the two empty mugs side by side on the coffee-table. The scent of his cologne still hung in the air and Alice closed her eyes for a moment. Jeremy Foster was the last person she should even think of falling for. He was a flirt and a womaniser. Everything she didn't need. After Marcus, surely she had learned her lesson by now—men couldn't be trusted.

As if to prove a point, she took down a photo album from her bookshelf and opened it. Images of Marcus and herself filled the pages. This was the man whose child she was carrying, the man whom she'd thought had loved her, the man she had loved. But not now, Alice thought darkly. His abhorrent reaction to her pregnancy, his utter unwillingness to stand by her through difficult times had shown his true colours. There simply weren't any feelings of love for Marcus left in Alice, just hurt and bitterness and an overwhelming sense of sadness for her unborn baby.

Anyway, she concluded, snapping the album firmly shut, she was way out of her league where Jeremy was concerned. The gossip said he liked his woman size eight, unopinionated and uncomplicated, and Alice failed dismally on all three. Which was for the best really. The last thing she needed right now was to be yet another notch on his bedpost. Another woman in the hospital lugging around a broken heart because she'd succumbed to his charms. Maybe the safety of her bump could now provide a refuge to hide behind, because Alice knew without a doubt that if she wasn't six months pregnant it would have taken every ounce of self-control to show Jeremy the door tonight.

CHAPTER FOUR

IF, AND for Alice it was a big if, there had been some gentle flirting going on that night, Jeremy seemed to heed her warning that she didn't want any special favours and on the work front treated her not quite as one of the boys but more or less. However, on more than one occasion she caught him staring at her, and she was almost certain that the look in those devilish blue eyes showed her that he definitely saw her as a woman. And even though Alice repeatedly told herself that she didn't want a repeat of their casual date, when she visited Josh she found herself battling with a stab of disappointment when invariably she had just missed Jeremy.

Darren Barker returned from annual leave and after a month Josh came back to work, but despite the fact that the team was fully manned for the first time in ages, the workload, like Alice's girth, only seemed to get bigger.

'Hell, what's Jeremy trying to prove?' Josh remarked when he saw the theatre list for the following week. 'There's practically a full month's worth here. Thank heavens we've got Monday off or we'd be dead on our feet. We'll never find beds for them all—they're going to have to cancel some.'

Alice didn't look up from the notes she was writing when she answered, 'No such luck. Jeremy's swung it to have some of the closed-off beds opened to get the waiting times down, so I'd make the most of this weekend if I were you. We're going to be going in all guns blazing from Tuesday. Fi's having a fit—apparently she's going to have to get a load of agency staff in, what with the new patient-staff

67

ratios. Jeremy, in one week, is going to blow the whole year's ward budget.'

'The budget's not going to be the only thing that blows. Dianne will throw a wobbly if I keep coming home late. And, looking at this list, there's not going to be much chance of getting out on time.'

This time Alice did look up. Putting down her pen, she took a grateful sip of the tea Fi had thoughtfully placed in front of her. 'How's Dianne coping now? You said she seemed pretty down.'

Josh ran a hand through his long hair. 'I think she's just exhausted. Declan's a real live wire. It was hard enough dealing with just him, but now we've got Eamon home it's too much for her to deal with. He takes for ever to feed.' Josh leant back in his chair. 'Not that we're complaining. It was touch and go for a while, and to have him home so soon and doing so well is like having all your prayers answered at once. It's just…'

Alice, without getting up, moved her chair on its wheels nearer to Josh. 'That you're both exhausted.' She finished the sentence for him. 'Don't feel guilty for feeling this way. A sick baby is hard work at the best of times, let alone with a healthy demanding twin. It's only been six weeks. No doubt Dianne's still not caught up with her sleep, let alone everything else that's gone on. It must be hard for her, especially now you've been back at work a couple of weeks. She must be feeling pretty isolated. Have you thought of getting someone in to help?'

She watched as Josh rolled his eyes. 'I did suggest it. Dianne promptly burst into tears and said that I thought she couldn't cope and was a lousy mother. I can't win.'

'Maybe it's a bit more than exhaustion, Josh,' Alice suggested cautiously. 'Dianne could well have postnatal depression. A complicated labour, a sick baby, a multiple birth—they're all known risk factors. I should know; my obstetrician gave me a pile of leaflets to read this week. I think I'm heading for it and the baby's not even born yet.'

Josh managed a small smile at the joke. 'I think you're right, Alice. Maybe I should put my foot down and just get some help in.'

'And get her to see her GP as well. Maybe ring him and mention what it's like for Dianne at the moment. She doesn't need to know you've called, but if the GP's actively looking for signs of depression it could make diagnosis easier, and the sooner she gets help the better.'

'Thanks, Alice. I just never thought being a parent would be this hard.'

'Don't,' Alice said through gritted teeth. 'I'm starting to have a touch of stage fright.'

'Sorry.' Josh grinned. 'How long have you got now?'

'Seven weeks and counting, which means just four weeks left of this place. I must admit I'm more than ready to finish. It's getting harder and harder to roll myself out of bed in the morning. Three days off sounds just what the doctor ordered. I think we should make the most of it.'

Josh nodded. 'I intend to. Maybe I should give my mum a ring see if she can come for the weekend—take the load a bit.'

Alice pursed her lips. 'You know what they say about mothers-in-law. Another woman offering endless advice might be the straw that breaks the camel's back. I'd try breakfast in bed and lots of TLC all round, and if things don't get better, speak to the doctor. Sorry,' she added. 'I'm interfering. Your mother's probably wonderful.'

This time Josh really laughed. 'I'd say you're right again. Nice save, Alice.'

Her pager broke in and, laughing as she picked up the phone, Alice felt as if the walls had suddenly fallen in as she heard the switchboard operator's cheerful voice.

'There's a visitor for you in Reception, Dr Masters. A

Marcus Collins. Should I direct him up to the ward or would you like to come down?'

For a moment Alice couldn't speak and her mind suddenly went into overdrive. What could Marcus possibly want? What if he had changed his mind, wanted her back? Wanted to play a part in the baby's life? How would she react to that?

'I'll come down,' she managed to rasp.

'Is there a problem?' Josh asked, noticing how pale Alice had gone.

'I'm not sure yet.' Alice stood up. 'Look, Josh, I'm practically finished. I've just got one more prescription chart to write up—would you mind?'

'Sure,' Josh replied amicably. 'Alice, you'd tell me if there was something wrong, wouldn't you?'

'Anything I should know about?' Jeremy's clear tones clipped through the air and they both swung around in surprise.

'Nothing's wrong,' Alice insisted. 'An old...' She paused for a moment too long. 'Friend has just turned up. He's waiting down in Reception. I was just asking Josh if he'd mind finishing up my drug orders.'

Neither man pushed further, and Alice gratefully picked up her stethoscope from the workbench and made her way down the corridors to Reception, her heart practically in her mouth as she tried to fathom what lay ahead. But even if she'd had a full week to come up with an endless list of scenarios, never could she have envisaged what Marcus had in store.

His greeting was cool, decidedly uncomfortable even, and Alice noticed that Marcus not only couldn't meet her eyes, he was also studiously attempting to avoid looking at her hugely pregnant stomach.

'I need to talk to you, Alice.'

Alice swallowed and nodded. 'We can use one of the

pre-admission rooms.' She led him the short distance along a carpeted corridor and, after checking with the admission clerk, let them into a small admitting room, which the admissions staff used to register booked patients.

Alice sat down, her back straight, her hands folded neatly in her lap, but Marcus chose not to use the other chair, instead standing uncomfortably against the closed door as if he might make a run for it at any moment. 'What did you want to see me for, Marcus? I thought you'd said all you wanted to.' Her voice, to Alice's amazement, was cool and calm.

'There's no easy way to say this, Alice. I've met someone else and we're getting married shortly.'

Alice didn't need to worry about Marcus noticing her stunned expression. His eyes were looking everywhere but at her. Again she was amazed at her ability to keep her emotions in check. 'Well, what has that got to do with me? It's not as if you need my permission or anything.'

'I know that,' he answered irritably.

'Have you told her about me? About our baby, I mean.'

'Some of it.'

Alice stood up. She was sick of having to drag out information from him—after all, it had been Marcus that had instigated the meeting. 'Which part, Marcus? That we were together for two years and you dumped me as soon as you found out I was pregnant? Or the part where you begged me to have an abortion? Does she or does she not know that you're going to become a father in seven weeks' time? Because if the answer is no, I suggest you get a move on. Don't worry, I'm not going to come begging for maintenance, and heaven knows why I should care about how you handle yourself, but don't you think a bit of honesty might go down well at the start of a marriage?'

'I've told her all right,' he snapped. 'And Yvonne took it very well. But she is a bit worried that you might start asking for money once the baby's born. She knows first-hand how messy it can all get. She's a kindergarten teacher.'

'Which makes her an expert, does it?'

Marcus sighed. 'You have to see it from her point of view. It's hardly the ideal way to start a marriage.'

Alice was as stunned as she was sickened by his insensitivity. So stunned, in fact, it took a moment or two for his next damning sentence to sink in.

'Anyway, I've told Yvonne that if you suddenly start asking for support I'm going to insist on a DNA test, just to be sure.'

Alice grabbed at the chair-arms. 'To be sure of what?' she asked through white lips. Surely she must be mistaken? Marcus, the man she had loved, couldn't be saying this—not now, not ever!

'To be sure the baby's mine.'

Bile rose in her throat. The taste was as foul as the words she was hearing.

'Is that what you've let her think? That I was sleeping around on you?' Her voice was rising and she could feel her blood pressure hitting the roof. Stay calm, she begged herself inwardly, you've got the baby to think of. Suddenly it was all too much. 'Get out,' she shouted. 'Go on, get out.'

But Marcus made no attempt to leave. Sobbing, she rushed past him. Lunging at the door, she pulled it open, and practically ran out into the hallway—straight into the arms of Jeremy.

'Alice.' His concerned voice reached her. 'Alice, what on earth's happened?'

Shaking, sobbing, she leant against him. 'Please,' she begged. 'Tell him to go.' Jeremy's eyes travelled over her head, coming to rest on Marcus as he walked out of the room.

'Alice, we need to talk—we need to clear things up.'

'I don't think now is the time, do you?' Jeremy's voice was scathing, and if Alice had looked up she would of seen a look of pure hatred in his eyes as he distastefully eyed the other man. 'Perhaps you should do as Alice asks and go.'

For a moment it looked as if Marcus was about to argue, but something in Jeremy's stance made him think twice.

'OK, OK, I only came here to talk.' Without a backward glance he marched along the corridor and, Alice swore to herself, out of her life for good.

'I assume that was Marcus?' Jeremy said dryly, leading her back to the interview room and dragging the chair behind her. As he guided her to sit down he only just stopped himself adding that he hoped Marcus's personality wasn't heritable—now wasn't the time to lighten the mood. He pulled up another chair, sat down and put his arm back around Alice.

'Did he want to try to patch things up?' She was too overcome to hear the slight unease in Jeremy's questioning tone.

'Not exactly,' she said. 'He came to warn me off. He's getting married.'

'I'm sorry.'

Alice squinted up at him through her tears. 'That's not the problem,' she gulped. 'We've been finished for months. I never expected him to spend a year in black or anything.'

'Still, it must hurt a bit,' Jeremy ventured, but Alice shook her head resolutely.

'Surprisingly, no. Well, not much,' she admitted reluctantly. 'He said if I ask for any money he's going to insist on a DNA test.'

'Ah,' Jeremy said, his grip on her tightening somewhat. 'Someone's been talking to a solicitor.'

'Why do you say that?'

'Because that's just the sort of tactic they use, dragging things out, making everything terribly complicated when the whole world knows it's really quite straightforward.'

'But I was never even going to ask him for money. I want to support my baby myself,' Alice wailed.

'Marcus probably knows that deep down, but I'll bet it made it a hell of a lot easier telling his girlfriend there was some doubt as to whether the child was his or not than the plain truth—that he simply doesn't want to know.'

His words made sense—at least enough to stop Alice crying—and once she had calmed down it suddenly dawned on her whose arms she was in.

'How come you were here?' she asked, attempting to pull herself away, but Jeremy only held her tighter.

'Because I was concerned about you. I asked the receptionist where you had gone.'

'But why?'

'Because I was hoping she'd know and as it turned out I was right.'

This time she managed to wriggle from his arms enough to look up at him. She stared at him, nonplussed, for a second. 'I didn't mean that.'

A small smile tugged at the corner of his mouth. 'I know you didn't. All right, then, I was concerned about you because I care.'

Alice was caught completely off guard by his revelation, so much so that she sat there, open-mouthed, as he tentatively continued, 'I care a lot about you, Alice.' His face moved slowly but surely towards hers. She had every chance to move, to duck out of the way, but instead she held still. Allowing his lips to rest on hers, moving her mouth slowly against his, her hands gradually worked their way up until she could feel his silken blond hair between her fingers. The millennium fireworks were nothing on the eruptions exploding in her head as she responded to his touch.

Stunned, embarrassed, yet dizzy with desire, she sat there motionless when he finally broke away. 'Surely you've noticed?' he asked gently.

She gave the faintest shake of her head. 'No. Well, maybe the night we went out, but I thought you were just being nice...' Her voice trailed off. She was trying to look him in the eye but she couldn't tear her gaze away from his full, sensual lips. Lips that had only seconds before been on hers!

'Nice! And there I was, pulling out all the stops! What's a guy got to do to impress you, Alice?'

She could hear the humour in his words, and Alice looked up shyly. 'It never entered my head you could possibly be interested in me.'

'Why ever not?'

His question was so impossibly ludicrous that Alice gave an incredulous laugh as she spoke. 'Because I'm pregnant, Jeremy. Very pregnant, with another man's baby. It hardly puts me up there on the list of Australia's most desirable women.'

'Thank God for that,' Jeremy quipped. 'Most of them are as boring as anything and I should know—I've been out with a couple.'

The fact that she was pregnant honestly didn't seem to bother him a bit, and Alice found herself shaking her head in bemused wonder that they were even having this conversation.

'I'm sorry for losing it like that, it was just all a bit of a shock. Marcus was the last person I was expecting to see.' She was trying to make an excuse for her actions to offer him an out if that was what he wanted.

But Jeremy was having none of it. 'Don't apologise, you had every right to be upset. And I was only too happy to console you. I've got a thing for damsels in distress, in case you hadn't noticed.'

And every other female with a pulse, Alice thought cynically, trying to bring herself back to earth.

'What are you doing this weekend?'

'Nothing,' she answered without thinking, then quickly added, 'But that's deliberate on my part. I've got to see my obstetrician on Monday evening and he's told me if my blood pressure is up even a smidgen then it's maternity leave for me. I'm going to take it very easy.'

'Is there any chance Marcus might come round, hoping to resume talks?'

She hadn't thought of that!

'And even if he doesn't,' Jeremy continued, not waiting for an answer, 'you're going to spend the whole time on tenterhooks or at the very least churning yourself up by going over what he said.'

'Probably,' Alice admitted.

'Well, instead of playing Russian roulette with your blood pressure, why not come with me to Sorrento? I've got a holiday home there, on the beach. It's only about an hour or so from here, and it would be really relaxing for you. There's a nice pool and you could go for long walks on the beach.'

'No, Jeremy,' Alice said straight away. 'I really don't think it would be appropriate.' She hadn't meant to sound quite so prudish, and when Jeremy roared with laughter even Alice managed a small grin.

'On the contrary, given the fact we've finally admitted we like each other, I think it would be entirely appropriate to spend some time together.'

Alice shook her head. How could she tell him that nothing sounded more tempting than what he was suggesting, but that she felt as fat and un-sexy as she had ever felt in her life? And the thought of a weekend in close proximity with Jeremy Foster would be even worse for her blood pressure than ten visits from Marcus.

'Come on, Alice,' Jeremy insisted. 'It will do you good. I'm not asking you there so I can have my wicked way. I honestly think it will do you some good and I think it will be nice for us to get to know each other a bit better away from work. And let's face it,' he added with a wink, 'with my bad back and your huge belly I doubt we'll be rewriting the Kama Sutra!'

Once she had finally agreed to go, Jeremy seemed hell-bent on getting there. So much so he didn't even want to stop by Alice's apartment for her to pack.

'You only need a few bits and pieces—we can get them there.'

Again he just assumed either she could afford it or he would pay for her. She wasn't sure which was more annoying.

'We're stopping at my place,' she said firmly, as again Jeremy battled with her seat belt.

'Surely there must be a design fault. I'm not *that* big,' she muttered, mortified at the thought of having to go through this every time she got in his car.

Tact obviously wasn't one of Jeremy's strong points. 'You're huge, Alice,' he said without thinking, then, catching sight of her shocked expression, he quickly backtracked. 'But it's all baby,' he said hurriedly. 'From behind you wouldn't even know that you're pregnant.'

When they got to her bedsit, Jeremy stood over her as she attempted to pack.

'What do you need that for?' he asked for the hundredth time, as Alice folded the flex on her hair-dryer.

'In case I want to do some cooking! What on earth do you think I need it for?'

'Alice, we're going to Sorrento, for heaven's sake, not

Outer Mongolia! I'm sure I can rustle up a few mod cons for you. I think I can even stretch to a towel,' he said, retrieving the towel she was neatly folding and tossing it onto the bed. 'Just grab some bathers, a toothbrush and a change of clothes, and we'll be on our way.'

'Bathers? You're not serious.' She held up a stringy little bikini from her drawer. 'This is all I possess in that field and I'd probably be arrested for indecency if I wore it.' She looked at the thin straps and tiny triangles and let out a wistful sigh. 'I wonder if I'll ever be that thin again?' she said, more to herself, stuffing the bikini back into her top drawer. .

But Jeremy immediately retrieved it. 'That will be fine. Who knows, you might even come back with a tan on your stomach. You'll be the talk of the maternity ward, you scarlet woman you.'

He had this incredible ability to put her at ease, to make even the most embarrassing situation somehow amusing. He was also far too used to women jumping to his tune, Alice thought to herself as Jeremy tapped his well-shod foot impatiently. Well, he would just have to wait for her, she decided, pointedly refusing to rush as she sorted out her make-up bag. 'Before you ask what the hell I need make-up for,' she said without looking up, 'I might be the size of a house with the whitest stomach in living memory but no one, and I mean *no one*, is ever going to see me without mascara. Not even in labour.'

'You should get your eyelashes dyed; it's supposed to be marvellous. Sorry,' he added as Alice shot him a withering look. 'An ex-girlfriend of mine swore by it, and I've picked up a few tips in my time.

'So much for spontaneity,' Jeremy teased as he loaded her case into the boot a short time later and Alice made a quick dash to check for the second time that she had locked the front door. As she lowered herself into the seat, and the battle with the beastly seat belt recommenced, Jeremy caught her eye and gave her a tiny wink. 'Perhaps you should have brought that towel. You know I'd never forgive you if your waters broke on my leather seats.'

It was a point she didn't care to dwell on, but for now Alice was rather more concerned with the weekend ahead. She was having serious trouble keeping her breathing even as Jeremy slid the car into gear.

He took the beach road, the Melbourne skyline glittering orange in the rear-view mirror as they followed the long road along the bay. The views were stunning and Alice craned her neck, taking it all in.

'There's a lookout point on Oliver's Hill,' Jeremy said, glancing over. 'We'll stop there.'

Pulling in, he came round to the passenger side and helped her out. Taking her hand, he led her to the lookout point nearby. Alice caught her breath in wonder. Oliver's Hill stood behind them, the houses precariously set on its jagged slopes, their windows, designed to catch every glimpse of the magnificent bay view, sparkling in the sunset. The bay glittered before her, a magnificent horseshoe of sand and sea, with the city standing tall and resplendent on the tip, the low orange sun turning the buildings into a sparkling mass of liquid gold. She followed the curve of the beach slowly, taking in all the landmarks—Brighton, Rickets Point, Frankston Pier—right along to where they were now.

'Magical, isn't it?' Jeremy said in a low, husky voice. 'I never get tired of it.'

Alice was about to agree with him, but as he continued talking she swallowed her words, listening intently as he continued.

'After the accident, when I was discharged, my mum brought me straight to Sorrento from the rehab unit to recuperate. I don't really remember much about that time, but one thing I can recall is asking her to stop here. She didn't want to, said it would be better to head straight for the beach house, but I was adamant.' He paused for a moment. 'I can remember getting out of the car and standing right here on this exact spot, just staring, drinking it all in. It was like I was seeing it for the first time.' He turned and looked at Alice. 'I've never felt so grateful to be alive.'

The wind was whipping up around them and Alice could have, if she'd wanted to, blamed her watery eyes on that, but instead she stood there silently surveying the view, imagining Jeremy, battered and confused, and how it must have felt for him that day. How it must feel for him now. She felt privileged to be standing with him, sharing a small part of his life, the tapestry that was Jeremy. With a jolt she realised it was the first glimpse he had permitted her of his deeper side. The first time he had knowingly let the façade slip for an instant. And now she'd had a glimpse, Alice knew without a shadow of a doubt she wanted to see more.

The same way that Alice had envisaged her first child would be welcomed into the world by two loving parents, part of her had also had a vague blueprint of what pregnancy would be like. Oh, not a definite plan or a set of standards that had to be adhered to—more an assumption she would have time to focus on her child within, to revel in the changes in her body. And perhaps, more poignantly, to share the tiny yet monumental landmarks with someone who found the whole process as fascinating and wondrous as she. To date, her pregnancy had been sadly lacking in all of these. But if ever there was a time in her pregnancy when she truly felt happy, a time where her dreams were met and surpassed, it was during those precious hot summer days in Sorrento.

Jeremy had more than a few mod cons; the place was

absolutely dripping with luxuries. The huge lounge with vast white walls and dark blue leather couches was so superbly designed it was like an extension of the glittering ocean that filled the massive floor-to-ceiling windows that opened onto a huge decked area. He showed her round briefly, modestly, his only intention to ensure she felt at home. Alice didn't say anything. It was all too surreal, being here with him. But as he flicked on the light to the bathroom Alice let out an involuntary groan. It was all white, with the deepest of spas, the only splashes of colour from handpainted starfish and brightly coloured shells ingrained into the tiles, and hand-blown glass bottles.

'It's divine,' she breathed.

'Why don't you have a nice bath, then?' Jeremy suggested. 'I'm sure I can rustle up a towel from somewhere.'

Alice shot him a look as he opened one of the discreet doors, and the thickest, most luxurious towels beckoned her.

'Take your time. I'll sort out some dinner.'

There was something incredibly decadent about lying in a deep bath with bubbles up to your neck, listening to a man prepare food. Judging by the occasional crash and expletive, it wasn't something Jeremy did too often, but Alice refused her initial instinct to rush out and offer help, instead lying back and watching as the warm water lapped against her huge stomach. The baby was enjoying the sensation as much as she was and Alice gazed, fascinated, as her stomach contorted, bulging and dipping as her unborn child stretched and swooped safe within its dark, warm world. Finally, when her toes and fingers were as wrinkled as the starfish on the wall and a gorgeous scent wafted through from the kitchen, she pulled the plug and wrapped herself in a huge bathrobe.

'Better?' Jeremy enquired as she padded out into the kitchen.

'Much. I'll just go and get dressed.'

'Alice, relax. We're not at the Hyatt now; you look fine as you are.'

So she did relax, curling up on the sofa as Jeremy finished off dinner preparations.

'Something smells nice. What is it?'

'It's supposed to be a risotto.' Jeremy grimaced as he brought a laden tray over to where she sat. 'But we might have to think of another name for it by the time I'm finished. It was either that or toast. I'll have to go and do a shop tomorrow.'

Strange, Alice thought. The words 'shopping' and 'Jeremy' somehow didn't equate.

'It's delicious,' Alice uttered as she took her first mouthful. 'Funny, I never imagined you could cook so well.'

Jeremy eyebrows shot up in horror. 'Me! Cook? Rose, the housekeeper, would have dropped this into the fridge this morning. All I had to do was heat it up and warm through the bread.'

'So all that banging and crashing was you just heating it up? Jeremy, I thought you were shelling fish in there.'

Jeremy flashed her an embarrassed smile. 'I should have kept my mouth shut, shouldn't I? Anyway, I grated the Parmesan—I've got the Band-Aid on to prove it.' He held up a finger and Alice started to laugh.

They sat together on the sofa after dinner. Jeremy had opened the huge glass doors, and the darkened bay provided a magnificent backdrop. He was very easy to talk to, and she found herself opening up as she had never done, sharing with him her hopes and fears for herself and her baby.

'I just worry the baby's missing out on so much, not having a father.'

'He'll have you.'

Alice looked up. 'Or she,' she pointed out, then sighed. 'But am I enough?'

Jeremy placed his empty plate on the coffee-table. 'Of course you are. From what I've seen of Marcus—well, put it this way, I think a reluctant access visit once a month and the occasional present will screw a kid up far more than having one passionate parent who really cares.'

Alice blinked in surprise. 'It sounds like you've given it some thought.'

Jeremy shifted uncomfortably. 'I have.' He hesitated before continuing, his eyes staring out at the bay and then turning back to her. 'I've never told anyone this before, not *anyone*,' he emphasised, 'because it simply didn't seem relevant. My biological mother walked out on my father and I when I was three months old. I've never seen her since, not that I remember her from then obviously. Apart from a few photos dotted in albums, I have no idea what she's like.'

Alice couldn't keep the surprise from her voice. 'So the mother you talk about isn't your real mother?'

She could have bitten her tongue off as she watched his face darken. 'Yes, she is, Alice, in every way. Mavis is my real mother.' His features softened and Alice listened as he continued. 'She came as a nanny at first, but within a few months my father and she fell in love. They had a brilliant marriage.'

'Had?' Alice ventured.

'He died a few months ago, after I had my accident. They were the best parents anyone could ask for. Mavis was the one who got up to me at night when I was teething, saw me take my first steps, picked me up from school, helped me get through uni. It was Mavis sitting day and night beside my bed when I was in Intensive Care. Mavis is every bit my "real" mum.'

'But surely you must be inquisitive. I mean, don't you ever think about your real—I mean your *biological* mum?'

Jeremy shrugged. 'Not if I can help it. Sure, when I was a spotty, moody teenager, I gave Mum a bit of hard time, saying she had no right to talk to me like that, that she wasn't my real mother, but all teenagers give their parents grey hairs.'

Alice found herself smiling at the thought of Jeremy as a moody adolescent. 'So it really didn't affect you?'

'Who can tell? I'm sure I could pay a shrink a fortune to tell me that my mother's desertion is the reason I treat women so appallingly but, as I said before, that's just a load of mumbo-jumbo. The buck stops here, Alice. I had a perfectly nice childhood with two wonderful parents.'

'So why do you treat women so appallingly?' She felt the heat rise in her cheeks as she asked him, but it was something that had to be confronted. Jeremy's colourful past was something that needed to be discussed if things were ever to move further.

Slowly his eyes met hers. They were as blue and deep as the bay outside—and just as easy to drown in, Alice reminded herself. She needed a clear head for this.

'Are you sure you want to hear this?' he asked heavily, and Alice gave a small nod. 'Because I always get away with it.' He didn't say anything for a moment. 'Not a great excuse, I know, but it's the truth.'

'Have you ever been in love—I mean with any of them?'

For an age he didn't answer, but when he slowly nodded Alice felt a surge of panic. She had asked for the truth but she wasn't entirely sure she was up to hearing it. 'Just one.' He stood up and made his way over to the decking as Alice struggled up from the sofa to join him. 'And I made her life hell.'

'What was her name?' Despite her reluctance, Alice needed the details.

'Olivia,' he said softly, and Alice had to strain to hear. 'We were together five years and I mucked it all up.'

'Did you have an affair?'

Jeremy gave a low laugh but she could hear the despair in it. 'One that she knew about and one that she didn't.'

'But why, Jeremy? If you say you loved her, how could you do that?'

'Because when we were together I didn't realise that I did love her. Looking back, I actually don't think I was capable of loving anyone then. I was so into myself there wasn't room for anyone else. Anyway, when Olivia found out she promptly dumped me and made a dash for the bush. Once she'd gone I realised how much she'd meant to me. She got sick and I went after her, but it was too late. She'd met someone else by then and didn't want to know.

'Well, you'd think I'd learnt my lesson, but instead of slowing down I just went into overdrive, chatting everyone up and living life in the fast lane. "I'll show her", so to speak. Pretty immature, huh?'

'So what happened then?'

'The accident. Too tired, too fast and I nearly ended up dead. Waking up in Intensive Care and spending three months flat on your back in traction is a pretty big wake-up call. I had plenty of time to think, to realise what a jerk I'd been.'

'Did Olivia come to see you?'

Jeremy nodded. 'I thought she'd come to gloat, but she's too nice for that. She came to my father's funeral as well, and she said that all things considered, she probably knew Dad better than she knew me. She was probably right.'

Alice felt a surge of jealousy for this woman who seemed to have a claim on Jeremy's heart. 'You still loved her?' she asked, dreading the answer.

'I hardly recognised her. She looked so relaxed, so happy in herself. I then realised how much I had hurt her. I never want to feel like that again, to be the cause of so much misery.'

'If she took you back…'

'Don't go there, Alice, it's not going to happen. She's head over heels in love and probably popping out little red-headed babies now, and I'm happy for her, I really am. I may have loved her, and I still care about her, but we've both moved on. Life doesn't stay still. Sooner or later you have to get on with living, which I intend to, only this time not at the expense of other people's happiness. Hopefully I can prove to you that I've changed, if you'll give me that chance.'

Alice stood there a moment, pondering his words. She was somewhat disarmed by what he had revealed, but also touched by his honesty. It couldn't have been easy to tell it how it was, to not cover up the truth or apportion blame for his actions. She also knew they had moved on considerably, that the road they were taking in revealing so much of themselves was leading somewhere. It was a road Alice hadn't considered she would be taking for some time yet, certainly not while she was pregnant. Yet never before had she felt such an overwhelming feeling of closeness and acceptance. The fact they were attracted to each other was a given—the consequences of acting on that attraction were what terrified her.

Standing there on the decking, swamped in a bathrobe, her hair a fluffy dark cloud blowing gently in the night's breeze around her flushed face, Alice didn't look like a woman who was wrestling with the weight of indecision.

Jeremy, just inches away, was like a magnet pulling her ever nearer. His eyes seemed to be inviting her to move closer yet he never moved, leaving it for her to take that tiny but monumental leap. Slowly, hesitantly she took a step towards him. The consent in her movement was all the encouragement Jeremy needed and he held out his arms to her. Pulling Alice towards him, he held her still for a moment.

She leant against him, feeling the bulge of her baby pressing into him, his strong arms around her. Slowly his hands moved upwards and, taking her face into his hands, he kissed her slowly, deeply. Drunk on desire, she kissed him back, his thick blond hair like silk beneath her fingers, his heady scent intoxicating her senses. His kiss was all that afternoon's had been, and more. Lost in the moment, all that filled her mind was Jeremy, but it was he that pulled away, he that called a gentle halt.

'Oh, Alice.' He buried his face in her hair, breathing in deeply her soft, slightly fragrant scent. 'You don't know how good you make me feel.'

His utterances were exactly what she was thinking, and she felt the sting of tears in her eyes as she held onto him.

'What was that?' Jeremy pulled back and gave her a shocked look. 'Was that the baby kicking?'

. Talk about ruining the moment!' There was nothing Alice could do but laugh as she nodded.

'I think you're right. You really are giving birth to a gymnast.' He looked down at her stomach and his hand hovered nervously over the bulge. 'Can I?'

Taking his hand, she guided it to where the baby was moving. Pressing his hand into her she held on and watched his face as he waited. Jeremy's eyes were wide with an almost childlike fascination. Perhaps sensing an audience, the baby refused to perform.

'Must have gone to sleep,' Alice murmured as Jeremy reluctantly moved his hand away.

'And so must you.' He gave her a small, gentle kiss. 'It's been a long day for you.'

He led her to her bedroom and gave her a slow, unhurried kiss goodnight. When she'd closed the door on him Alice lay on the bed and almost wept. She wanted him so badly she could never have turned him down, yet she was infinitely grateful to him for not pushing it, for giving her the chance to think before they went any further.

Of course, with Jeremy watching her like a hawk she had forgotten to pack a nightie so, slipping out of her bathrobe, Alice slipped between the cotton sheets naked, carefully placing the robe at the end of the bed. How long she lay there, staring into the darkness and listening to the waves lapping against the shore, she couldn't be sure. She was painfully, achingly aware that Jeremy lay in the room next to hers. Her lips were still stinging from the weight of his kiss, and every nerve in her body seemed to be tingling like pins and needles, as if awoken from the longest sleep and slowly coming back to life. She tried not to think of what Jeremy would be like as a lover, and failed.

To be held in those arms with nothing between them. To feel his hot skin against hers, his tongue exploring her. Stop it, she warned, trying to will herself to sleep. But sleep, the one thing she had been longing for all week, suddenly seemed inconsequential. She also badly needed to go to the bathroom—with the baby now firmly head down and growing bigger each day, Alice had a bladder with the capacity of a thimble. She tried to ignore it but to no avail. Getting up, slipping the robe back on and tiptoeing out into the dark hall, she padded about in the unfamiliar house, finally locating the bathroom. Afterwards, making as little noise as possible, she made her way to the kitchen, opened the fridge, pulled out the jug and poured a glass of water to take back to bed.

'Is everything all right?'

Hearing Jeremy's voice, she turned and smiled, the light from the fridge illuminating her features. 'Everything's fine. I just needed a drink. I'm sorry if I woke you.'

'I couldn't sleep anyway.'

'Why?' Alice asked, then blushed as she remembered the

reason for her own insomnia. But Jeremy, it seemed, had rather more practical concerns keeping him awake.

'I keep imagining you suddenly going into labour. Do I drive you to the nearest hospital or just head straight for the Women's and Children's, or do I call an ambulance?'

Alice stared at him, bemused. 'Jeremy, I'm not due for seven weeks yet. I'm sure I'll get a bit of warning. I'm not likely just to suddenly have it!'

'I know, I know.' He gave her a sheepish grin. 'I told you I'm terrified of pregnant women.'

'We're quite normal really. Come here.' She beckoned as the baby started to move. 'You might feel something now.'

This time when she placed his hand on her stomach the baby let out a hefty series of kicks, and Jeremy grinned in amazement.

'It's so strong,' he said in wonder.

Her eyes travelled over his near naked body, covered only by a small towel draped around his waist. A vivid raised scar held her gaze, out of place amongst such perfection. It looked angry and sore, and instinctively she reached out and touched it, her fingers, cool and soothing from the icy water, tracing the jagged edges of his wound.

Looking up, Alice caught her breath as he stared back at her.

'It looks sore,' she murmured.

She could feel his breath on her cheek, his bronzed skin beneath her fingers, and she knew then what she was feeling was good and right, that her love and desire for Jeremy was an entity, that something so intrinsically right could never be wrong. Slowly, she bent her head, her cool lips gently kissing the length of his scar. She heard him exhale, one hand burrowing into her hair as the other crept to her belt and struggled with the knot. She moved to help him, the gesture an affirmation for him to continue. Standing back a touch, she swallowed nervously as he loosened the robe and it slipped off her shoulders, tumbling silently onto the floor.

The rapt expression on his face dispelled the last trace of her nerves. Never in her life had she felt as sensual, as feminine. The effect of her naked body on Jeremy was bewitching. With a low moan he buried his face in her neck, his tongue cool and probing as she had known it would be as his hands skilfully explored the contours of her body until Alice thought she would faint with desire. Without an utterance they made their way to Jeremy's room, pulling back the sheet on the vast bed as he helped her down beside him.

'I want you, Alice,' he rasped. 'Tell me you want me as I want you.'

She answered him with a kiss. Hungrily her lips reached for him, their naked bodies blending together as they explored each other slowly, languorously. For Alice each stroke of his fingers, each touch of his tongue was a revelation. She had never imagined she could feel so sexually alive, so sensual, and it was Jeremy who made her feel this way. Every inch of him expressed his desire and they went on their journey of discovery together, both touchingly unsure of how they would get there but knowing they would in the end.

'I don't want to hurt you,' he said in a thick voice, his eyes like velvet as they gazed into hers. She sensed his hesitancy and knew she had to help him.

'You won't,' she murmured, slowly lowering herself onto him. They moved together, tentative at first but becoming bolder as desire and need took over. His hands cupped her glorious swollen breasts, his long fingers massaging her nipples, as ripe and tempting as summer berries. But through it all he held her with such gentleness, all the time careful, mindful of her condition, treating her with a certain reverence that further affirmed her new-found love.

Opening her eyes, she gazed down at his body beneath her. As if drawn, his eyes opened too, and she held his gaze. Their bodies joined, their eyes locked. They were one. Feeling the swell of him within her, she gave in to the sweet release, overwhelmed by throbbing intensity that seemed to ricochet through the entire length of her glistening, flushed body. And when the journey was over, as they lay together in an exhausted embrace and Jeremy pulled her closer to him, if that was possible, Alice knew that, really, the journey had only just begun.

'So that's what it feels like.'

His deep voice broke into her slumber. 'What's "it"?' she murmured, nestling deeper into his embrace.

'Love' came the simple, heart-rending reply.

Alice lay on her side, her dark cloud of hair fanning the pillow. Tenderly he smoothed her locks and nestled his face into her shoulder, tucking his body around hers. As he snuggled in deeper one arm pulled her closer as the other held her stomach in an almost protective gesture. Despite the joy of their love-making, despite the rapture of lying here in his arms, Alice felt a tear slide down her cheek, and she realised with a jolt that the one thing she wished more than anything was that the baby inside her could have been Jeremy's.

'Alice, is anything wrong?' His voice was deep, probing, and the genuine concern she heard prohibited her from answering in case he heard the emotion in her voice. Instead she gently shook her head.

''Night, then,' he murmured into her hair, the softest of kisses sweeping her exposed shoulder. He felt her relax against him, listened as her breathing evened out, and only when he was sure she was asleep did Jeremy finally give in and let himself start to doze. Feeling the baby swooping and kicking beneath his hands, his last conscious thought as he drifted off was that he wished the child he could feel cocooned safely inside the woman he knew now he loved was his.

CHAPTER FIVE

FOR three days and nights they disappeared from the world and lived only for each other. Long hazy days, spent lying in the sun, occasionally cooling off in the huge sparkling blue pool. They only ventured out once, walking the short distance into Sorrento where they went to a fish and chip shop which Jeremy assured her was the best in the southern hemisphere. Alice found herself agreeing as they sat on the beach, squeezing lemon over their king prawns, feeding each other as lovers do. The ferry bound for Queenscliff was setting off. Alice watched as it pulled away, idly throwing the remaining chips to the rapidly gathering sea-gulls.

'Next time we'll take the ferry over there.' Jeremy broke into her daydream. 'There's some beautiful restaurants.'

Alice shook her head with a lazy smile. 'They couldn't beat this.'

But Jeremy begged to differ. Pushing her gently back onto the sand, he kissed her slowly, deeply, with salty lips. 'Want to bet?' he said, breaking away. 'I was about to say there's also some magnificent accommodation. We could be on our way upstairs now to a massive four-poster bed in the honeymoon suite.'

'Oh, well, in that case...'

So they ambled back, hand in hand and, though there wasn't a four-poster bed, nor a silver service restaurant downstairs, their love-making was every bit as romantic and tender as that of newly-weds. She knew there were issues to be faced; they both did. They didn't have the luxury of taking things slowly—the imminence of the baby and the fact that Jeremy was here, sharing in this precious time, spoke volumes. And though they both knew there was a lot to discuss, for this weekend at least they let the bigger picture rest, instead concentrating on each other. Their deep, emerging feelings for each other in no way compromised or conflicted with their emotions for the unborn baby. Instead, they were forging a foundation on which to build before the world rushed in and had its say.

It was Jeremy who broached the subject first.

'How's your blood pressure now?'

'Hmm?' Alice half opened her eyes as Jeremy, sitting on the sofa behind her, skilfully massaged her shoulders. 'It's probably so low Brett Halliday will admit me with *hypo*-tension.'

Alice was sitting on the floor so she didn't see Jeremy's eyes narrow, but she felt his fingers stiffen on her bare shoulders and she wriggled uncomfortably.

'Why don't you call it a day, Alice? We've got one helluva week coming up, and surely it can't be good for you, or the baby.'

It was Alice that stiffened now. 'You think I'd put the baby at risk?' She shrugged his hands off.

For the moment Jeremy tried to ignore her injured tones as he gently persisted. 'Of course not,' he said, replacing his hands and carrying on the massage. 'I know it's all happened really quickly, no one is more surprised than me how things have worked out, Alice, but I'm ready for this, I really am. I feel as if I've been waiting all my life for this moment, to be totally and utterly in love. Now, if that sounds slushy, I make no apology.' He felt her start to relax again under his touch and he carried on talking, trying desperately to win her around.

'Loving you means wanting to take care of you—all of you, Alice. I don't want you to have any trouble with your blood pressure. Of course I'm concerned about you working. I want you to be at home, putting your feet up, enjoying the last few weeks of your pregnancy. Not stuck in a hot theatre and up all night on call.'

She understood what he was saying, more than understood. As much as Alice loved her job, in the last couple of weeks that was all it had become—a job, no more than that. Something you had to do, not the labour of love it had once been. Oh, she knew her vocation would return, that she would always be, and *want* to be, a doctor, but for now she was a woman. A heavily pregnant woman who was tired and needed to rest and focus on the life within her. How easy it would be to lie back against him, to throw in the towel and let Jeremy make the decisions for her. But she had made a promise to her child, and she had also been let down badly before. There simply wasn't the luxury of choice here; she had to see it through. To hide the indecision she felt, her words came out harshly.

'So the great Mr Foster will provide? Women are actually capable of making it without a man, you know.' She swung around to face him.

'I have no doubt you're more than capable, Alice. I'm merely saying it's no longer necessary for you to work yourself into the ground—'

'You'll take care of us.' It wasn't a question, more a sneering statement, but Jeremy wasn't about to be perturbed.

'If you'll let me.'

Alice paused for a moment, gathering her thoughts. She knew her words had hurt him but she needed some time to think. It was all just happening too fast.

'I can't do that, Jeremy.' She saw a flash of pain in his eyes. 'I need us to be on equal terms. If we'd been together longer, if this were our baby…' She looked at him, perplexed. 'I'm not saying that I don't trust you, that I'm not grateful for your offer, but I've thought of nothing else but getting through my internship for over six months now. I've made plans, big plans, to move to the country, bring my baby up there… I'm not saying that I'm necessarily going to go through with them, but I need to—no, *have* to have that option up my sleeve. I can't just throw it all away on the strength of this weekend.'

'Fair enough.' Jeremy took a deep breath. 'Then how about on the strength of this? Marry me, Alice.' He paused, searching her face for a reaction, and when she didn't answer he added somewhat desperately, 'Please?'

For a second Alice couldn't quite believe what she was hearing. She knew she loved him and, despite her doubts and misgivings about men, did believe that Jeremy truly loved her, but never in a million years had she expected this. And also at the back of her mind, painfully intruding and desperately unwelcome, was a small nagging voice that warned her of Jeremy's past, his previous track record, his apparent inability to remain faithful. She needed a clear head for this, she needed absolute clarity, not the cloudy euphoria of rose-tinted glasses worn in the first giddy weeks of love. Her baby deserved that at least.

'You'd never be asking me if I wasn't pregnant.'

Jeremy looked at her thoughtfully. 'I hate to point this out, Alice, but it's not my baby. There's hardly a shotgun to my head, forcing me to do the honourable thing.'

'I know,' she conceded. A small smile tugged on the corner of her lips. 'But it is the truth. Jeremy…' She took his hands and moved her face close to his. 'I'm so grateful to you for asking me, I really am, but the timing's just not right. Ask me again when I'm thin and gorgeous and the clock's not ticking. There may not be a shotgun but we are up against the clock.'

'You're taking a raincheck, then?'

Her smile widened at his answer. 'What would you know about rainchecks, Jeremy? I'm sure you've always been able to have absolutely anything you want, when you want it.'

'Until now.'

She heard the pain in his voice and she longed to comfort him, but she wasn't going to give in. Instead she put her hands up to his face and kissed him tenderly. 'Let's just say it's on hold for now. I need to do this, Jeremy, and if we really are meant to be, we'll work it out.'

With that he had to be content.

Driving back, this time they were on the right side of the beach road to capture the full beauty of the bay. Her hand resting on Jeremy's solid thigh, Alice leant back in the seat marvelling at the sight, marvelling too at how the weekend had unfolded. She had found love, had had a marriage proposal and with Jeremy's skilful help had unleashed a sensual side to herself that she never would have believed existed. She squeezed Jeremy's thigh, as if pinching herself to make sure it was all real.

'What time's your appointment again?'

'Five-thirty.'

He glanced at the dashboard. 'We'll be there in plenty of time.'

Alice nodded. For once she wasn't nervous about her appointment with Brett. Never had she felt more relaxed or content. Surely her blood pressure must have come down?

As Jeremy slid the car into a parking spot a little later, Alice undid her seat belt.

'I shouldn't be too long.'

Jeremy nodded, 'Whatever. I'll just wait here, shall I?'

Alice hesitated. 'It's up to you.'

Jeremy shook his head. 'No, Alice, it's up to you.' She couldn't blame him for being cautious after her 'back off' speech, but she had never intended to shut him out. The fact that Jeremy wanted to be there for her, to share in this time, sealed her love even further.

'Come on, then,' she said softly.

* * *

'Dr Masters, I've been trying to call you.' Madge, the receptionist, replaced the receiver and gave Alice an apologetic smile. 'Brett got called away to perform an emergency Caesarean section and he's also got another woman just about to deliver, so he's had to cancel his antenatal appointments for this evening.'

It was a scenario Alice had been warned of when she had first met Brett Halliday. 'Babies come when babies come, Alice, so if I have to rush off or miss an appointment you'll have to bear with me. It will be your turn to keep a few ladies waiting one day.' Sitting there, slim, without even a trace of a bump, that day seemed a lifetime away.

'That's no problem, Madge. Should I make an appointment for next week?'

'No, Brett wants to see you weekly—he's written that quite clearly. I can squeeze you in at ten a.m. tomorrow, or there's a four o'clock appointment available on Wednesday.'

Alice pointedly didn't defer to Jeremy, and she could almost feel him bristling beside her as she said, 'Four o'clock on Wednesday will be fine. I'll see you then.'

As soon as they stepped out into the car park Jeremy turned to her. 'Why didn't you take the morning appointment?'

'Because we've got a busy day tomorrow.'

'We'd have coped. It's important to get yourself checked.'

Alice stood by the car as Jeremy unlocked it. 'And I will, but on Wednesday.'

He didn't argue the point but Alice could tell he wasn't happy. 'Look, Jeremy, if I start rushing off to antenatal appointments whenever I like, and you start treating me like a doll, people are going to start talking.'

Jeremy shrugged nonchalantly. 'Let them talk. We've

done nothing to be ashamed of.'

'I know that, but once this gets out...' She didn't know what to say. Alice could almost hear the gossip hurtling through the wards, raising questions they hadn't even answered themselves.

'You want to keep it quiet?'

Alice nodded. 'At least until my internship's finished. Surely that's for the best?'

Turning the key in the ignition, Jeremy finally nodded. 'If it makes things easier for you, that's what we'll do. But, hell, Alice, this is the one decent relationship in my life. I'm not going to act as if I'm doing something wrong.' He gave her a small smile. 'Where do you want to go?'

And though the last thing she wanted was for this magical weekend to end, Alice had a sudden urge to be at home, amongst her own familiar things.

'Do you mind if you take me home?'

Jeremy's face was crestfallen and he couldn't hide the disappointment in his voice. 'Sure.'

The journey home was tense, and suddenly Alice was filled with misgivings. What if he was regretting what had taken place? What if he was finally realising what he was letting himself in for?

Depositing her bags on the living-room floor, Alice stood uncomfortably. 'Look, I know it's not what you're used to, but I can't explain it—I just want to be at home right now. We can stay at your place another time.'

In an instant his attitude changed, his face lighting up as he broke into a wide smile. 'I thought I was dropping you off, that you wanted to be alone.'

So that explained the mood! 'Hey, you're not as cool as you make out, Mr Foster.'

'Not where you're concerned. Come here,' he said, pulling her close. 'Now that I've found you I don't ever want to spend a night apart. I'd stay in a tent if that made you happy.'

Alice leant against him. 'I don't believe a word of it. Somehow I can't imagine you without hot running water and a marble bathroom.'

'Well, maybe not a tent,' Jeremy conceded with a teasing note to his voice, 'but I hear they've come a hell of a long way in luxury caravans.'

One of the nicest aspects of falling in love, Alice mused as she listened to Jeremy singing tunelessly in the shower, was the utter joy in even the simplest of things. The pleasure of discovering the tiniest details about each other—from how they liked their coffee to the more heady details of what turned each other on. For Alice their love-making was an utter revelation. She quite simply melted at the sight of Jeremy, and had an almost insatiable desire to have him near her, touching her, unlocking secrets of her body that Alice hadn't even known existed.

Watching Jeremy walk out of the bathroom, his gorgeous masculine body ridiculous in a small pink towel, Alice let out a gurgle of laughter.

'I'm sorry. Was that the only towel you could find? I'll have to go to the laundry tonight.'

'No, you won't. You'll be far too busy tending to *my* needs to be stuck in the laundry. I'll buy some at lunchtime when I go and get a couple of shirts.'

Alice watched guiltily as he dried the collar of his Egyptian silk shirt with her hair-dryer. Only at ten last night had they realised that his suit, tie, socks and shirt were in a crumpled mess at the bottom of his suitcase.

Finally happy that his shirt was dry, Jeremy made his way over to the bed and took a grateful sip of the coffee Alice had made. Looking down, he saw her gazing at him, a dangerous glint in her eye. 'Uh-oh, no way, we'll be late,' he said as her hand reached up and grabbed the towel.

'Then you'd better be quick,' Alice said seductively, pulling him back onto the bed beside her.

It was a slightly breathless, laughing pair that eventually pulled into his reserved parking spot at the hospital. 'How am I supposed to get through the next twelve hours without touching you?' Jeremy grumbled.

'It will make tonight all the better,' Alice promised and, reaching across, gave him a long lingering kiss. 'That will have to do for now. I'll go on in—and by the way, Mr Foster, you've been a wonderful teacher. I can hardly wait for the next lesson.'

Walking across the car park, Alice could barely keep the grin off her face. Suddenly life felt good again, as if the gods were smiling on her.

'What time do you call this?' Josh gave her a friendly wink a few minutes later as Alice joined him at the sink to scrub.

'I know, I know,' Alice said, blushing. 'I missed the tram by a millisecond. Normally I'd have run for it but I'm simply not up to it.' She was saved from any further lies by the angry voice of Linda.

'About time,' she seethed. 'And, no, I don't want to hear any excuses. You know full well what sort of day we've got ahead of us. The least you could do was get here on time.'

Alice didn't answer. In truth she was only two minutes late, but ordinarily she would have been there at least half an hour ago. Seeing Jeremy walk through the door, not quite as immaculate as usual, Alice suppressed a smile. Linda's rancour was worth it.

'Morning, all.' He made no apology for being late, neither was one expected.

The team was using two theatres this morning. All the

procedures were fairly minor—hernia repairs, circumcisions and the like—but it was an extremely demanding list just by the sheer volume of patients that were being operated on.

By eight-thirty the first patient was on the table. Alice was assisting Jeremy, but once he started operating their thoughts were only for the patient.

'Mr Jacobs, thirty-two years old, with a left inguinal hernia. Today we'll be performing a keyhole repair of the bowel wall as opposed to the traditional open repair, which will hopefully mean less risk of infection and shorter recovery time. Any questions?'

Nobody answered and Jeremy began the procedure explaining his movements every step of the way. All eyes were on the screen that showed the work he was doing inside Mr Jacobs's body and Alice watched, fascinated, as the mesh that would hold the protruding bowel back in place was inserted. Jeremy made it all look so simple, operating the guides apparently effortlessly, but Alice knew that each movement took skill and patience, and though he made it look easy it certainly wasn't.

On and on they worked, the day lengthening as the list grew shorter. They stopped only for a quick coffee at mid-morning and a hasty lunchbreak.

'All right?' Jeremy asked as Alice took a bite of her egg sandwich.

'Fine,' she lied. It had been impossibly hot in the theatre and, despite sitting down, her back was absolutely killing her.

'How's things your end?' he asked as Linda marched in.

'Shipshape,' she answered briskly. 'I've sent Josh up to the ward—the workload's building up there.'

'Good idea. Alice, why don't you head up to the wards after your lunch? Linda and I will finish off the list.'

She didn't have to be asked twice.

By the time the day had ended Alice was completely exhausted. So as not to draw attention to themselves, Jeremy had left straight after the final post-operative ward round, leaving Alice and Josh to carry out his last orders. By the time she wearily climbed off the tram and let herself into the bedsit all she wanted to do was sleep. Jeremy, it seemed, had beaten her to it. Long-legged, he lay stretched out on her sofa, his feet dangling over the edge.

Alice gave him a gentle poke in the ribs. 'I thought you'd have dinner on,' she joked.

Jeremy rolled his eyes. 'I'm too exhausted to even ring out for pizza. How about we go straight to bed?'

This time when they climbed into bed it was far from Jeremy's passionate declarations of the morning. Instead they just about remembered to set the alarm before cuddling up and falling deeply asleep.

'We're like an old married couple,' Jeremy said with a laugh when they woke up. 'First time an early night's meant just that. How do you feel this morning?' he asked, after planting a soft kiss on her lips.

Alice winced as she opened her eyes. A thumping headache wasn't the best way to start a day and night on call.

As Jeremy wandered off to make the coffee she lay there for a moment. Just three weeks or so to go. It sounded such a short time but it seemed like an eternity. If Jeremy asked her now to chuck it all in she'd be hard-pressed to refuse. Shaking her head ruefully, she headed for the shower. It was simply a question of mind over matter, she insisted to herself. She wasn't about to give in now.

Jeremy might have got the waiting lists down a fraction but there was definitely a down side to his surgical vigour. The ward round was interminably long, not helped by the fact that Jeremy and Josh had already been summoned to Theatre to perform an urgent laparotomy on a road trauma victim. Which left Alice to do the round with Linda, whose venom seemed to have taken on a stronger bite this morning. Every patient, it seemed, needed an inordinate number of tests or changes to their drugs or IV regimes, which all fell on Alice.

'Well, that was pleasant.'

Fi's sarcasm didn't go unnoticed as the two women watched Linda depart through the ward doors. 'I'd love to give you a hand, Alice, but I'm snowed under myself. Half the staff are agency this morning. Luckily they all seem excellent nurses, but half my day's going to be spent showing them where things are kept.' She gave an apologetic smile.

'I'll get there, Fi,' Alice said gloomily, staring at her long list of jobs.

And she would get there, Alice decided, if her pager didn't go off every five minutes or the nurses didn't keep asking her to write up drug orders that really could have waited.

'Er, Doctor, I've just started to do Mr Linton's dressing and I think you ought to take a look.' A young nurse Alice didn't recognise hovered nervously.

With a sigh Alice made her way over to Mr Linton's bedside.

'It's looking a bit red around the edges,' the nurse commented as she peeled back the sterile drape she had placed over it.

'I already saw it in the ward round, and it hasn't changed since then,' Alice said, trying to keep her voice even. 'Miss McFarlane's instructions were to start him on IV antibiotics and to clean the wound and apply a dry dressing.'

'But there's nothing in the notes or on the drug chart.'

Alice sucked in her cheeks. 'If you'd give me a moment alone, maybe I could get around to writing up some notes and charts.' And, turning on her heel, she brushed through the curtains.

'Damn,' she cursed through gritted teeth as she sat down at the workstation. Taking her frustration out on the poor agency nurse had made her feel no better. It wasn't the nurse's fault—she was right to be concerned about the wound. If only Josh were around, maybe they could get up to date. Massaging her temples in an effort to quell the throbbing in her head, Alice picked up her pen and started writing.

'There's a new admission up from A and E,' Fi said brightly, as a trolley carrying an elderly lady whizzed past. 'Apparently Linda wants her clerked straight away so we can commence the IV antibiotics.'

'Great,' Alice muttered under her breath.

The patient was a varicose leg ulcer. Mrs Dalton was a diabetic and her poor circulation made her prone to this type of difficulty. Even the smallest wound could create a problem for patients like her, and in this instance her ulcer had shown no improvement, even though she'd had twice-daily visits from the district nurse. Now, despite the nurse's diligence, it had become infected.

'I'm sorry, Mrs Dalton, I know you've been through this already, but I'm going to need to examine you and ask a few questions.'

'No worries, love, I know how it all works. Well, I should by now,' she joked, gesturing to the huge pile of old notes Fi had thrust at Alice.

'How long have you been a diabetic?' Alice asked as she gently lifted the sterile drape with which the nurses had covered the ulcer.

'Since I was ten.'

'So no doubt you could tell me a thing or three about it?'

Mrs Dalton laughed. 'No doubt. You ask away, love, I'm

a mine of information. At least you don't think you know it all, not like that madam I saw before. What was her name?'

Alice took a leaf from Jeremy's book and simply evaded the question. 'It looks very painful.'

'It is. Sarah, the district nurse, said you might order a needle for me before I have it changed. Normally I don't like taking anything but, 'struth, if you knew what it felt like when they start prodding and poking it. I'm not one for whingeing normally…'

Alice gave a sympathetic smile. Mrs Dalton had the tough, sun-battered face of a real Aussie battler, and from the brief look she'd had of her notes Mrs Dalton definitely wasn't a 'whinger'—she had put up with a lot from her diabetes.

'I'll write you up for something strong and the nurses will give it to you before they do your dressing.'

Even though Mrs Dalton had only come in for dressings and IV antibiotics, Alice still had to examine her patient thoroughly and take a detailed history. Her head was pounding and tiny little dots seemed to be dancing before her eyes as she wrote her notes. By the time she had finished the clock was edging towards twelve and her body, tired before the day had even begun, now ached mercilessly for its bed, yet she still had the rest of the day and night to get through. It was in that instant Alice knew she simply couldn't do it any more. Enough was enough.

The dots on the page blurred as tears filled her eyes. The sound of Fi's gentle voice came as no surprise.

'How about we take five in my office?'

Gulping, Alice nodded gratefully and followed Fi like a child. Fi let her cry for a moment before she spoke.

'Not having the best day, huh?'

'How did you guess?' Alice said, half laughing at herself.

'Well, when the agency nurse said a female doctor had

snapped at her, of course I assumed it was Linda. But when the same nurse put it down to hormones I did a double take. We all know Linda hasn't got any.'

Alice gave a small laugh, then started crying again. 'I've got this terrible headache. I thought it was because I was tired, but now I'm starting to get little spots in front of my eyes.'

Fi's expression changed abruptly. 'Since when?'

'Just in the last five minutes or so.'

Fi's slim delicate hands picked up Alice's. 'Your fingers are swollen—not much, but they definitely are. Have you had your blood pressure checked recently?'

'I've got an appointment at four. It's not been too great at the best of times.'

Fi tutted. 'You silly girl,' she said, but not unkindly. 'What on earth are you doing here?'

'I'm beginning to wonder myself.'

Fi took over. She disappeared, returning with a blood-pressure machine. Now, let's see what your blood pressure's doing.' She wrapped the cuff around Alice's arm. Feeling it tighten, Alice sat there, resigned. As Fi pumped it up even higher Alice felt in that moment all her dreams evaporate.

'How high?' she asked when Fi had finished.

Fi didn't answer straight away. 'I think you ought to ring your obstetrician.'

'How high, Fi?' Alice demanded, her voice urgent.

'One hundred and sixty over a hundred.'

And suddenly work, her internship, the GP rotation all paled into insignificance. Both she and the baby were in real danger.

'I thought I might find you in here! When you can drag yourself away from your morning coffee, there are a few patients that need to be seen.'

Alice didn't bother to look up as Linda rattled on. It was

Fi who spoke, her voice clear and calm, but Alice recognised the note of urgency health professionals reverted to when there was a real problem. 'Dr Masters isn't feeling well, Miss McFarlane. I've checked her blood pressure and she needs to go to her obstetrician *now*.'

Alice heard the subtle shift in tone on the last word.

Suddenly Linda was all concern. 'Why on earth didn't you say something, Alice?' She came over. 'Who's your obstetrician?'

'Brett Halliday.'

Linda nodded. 'I know him well. Look, do you want me to arrange transport to the Women's and Children's?'

Alice shook her head vehemently 'I'll take a taxi.'

'Nonsense,' interrupted Fi. 'I'll drive you. I'm due for a lunchbreak. Rowena Sheldon's an associate charge nurse. She can manage for half an hour while I take you.'

Alice nodded gratefully.

'That settles it, then,' Linda said efficiently. 'I'll ring Brett and tell him you're on your way. I'll let Jeremy know. Don't worry about a thing.'

As Alice handed over her pagers to Linda she knew without a shadow of a doubt she wouldn't be back; she wouldn't even be going back to her flat. The next time she came home it would be, God willing, with her baby.

Alice was infinitely grateful for Brett Halliday's professional unruffled manner. He examined her thoroughly, listening to the baby's heartbeat and checking her urine and blood pressure.

'You know I'm going to admit you, don't you?' he asked as Alice lay back on his examination couch. His hand was feeling her fundus—the top of her uterus—to check the size of the baby. Without waiting for her to answer, he continued, 'Your blood pressure's still up, you've got mild fluid retention and there's protein in your urine. Any one of these can happen, but combined in pregnancy we have to tread cautiously.'

'It's my fault, isn't it?'' she said, fighting back tears, but Brett wasn't about to apportion blame.

'Pre-eclampsia is also referred to as the disease of theories. No one can pinpoint exactly why certain women develop it. Yes, you've been working hard, and with your blood pressure a bit high, which you know was a concern, but healthy stay-at-home mums also develop it. The important thing now is to bring your blood pressure down and help you get as much rest as possible. Hopefully that will halt the progress of it.'

'But what if it carries on? What will happen to the baby?'

'Let's take it a step at a time, shall we? For now we'll get you admitted. The midwives will put you on the CTG monitor at regular intervals to keep an eye on the baby, and I'll arrange an urgent ultrasound and cord studies. If there's any signs the baby's in distress or it isn't receiving adequate nourishment we'll be straight onto it.'

'But it's too soon. I'm only thirty-four weeks.'

Brett squeezed her shoulder reassuringly. 'Let's do the ultrasound, shall we?'

Settled into bed, Alice tried vainly to calm herself down, but to no avail. Everything Brett had said she understood, but she felt as guilty as hell—and not just because she'd continued to work. A little voice inside her warned that this was payback. If she hadn't swanned off for the weekend with Jeremy, hadn't spent the time making energetic love, none of this would have happened. It never entered her head that, had Jeremy not intervened when Marcus had confronted her on Friday, she could have been in exactly this situation, only five days sooner. That lying by the pool, being massaged, fed and pampered by the man she loved, could possibly have kept her blood pressure down.

. Her self-imposed guilt only deepened when Brett returned to her bedside with the ultrasound results.

'I won't beat around the bush, Alice. The baby's not in any distress but your placenta's not functioning as well as it should, and it's not going to provide adequate nutrition to carry the baby to term.'

'Which means…'

'You'll be having the baby sooner rather than later.' He gave her a gentle, reassuring smile. 'We'll see if we can get you to thirty-six weeks. But even if you have the baby now, it's still a good size, though it will mean a stay in special care. We're going to start you on steroids, which will help to develop the baby's lungs. The most important thing you can do for your baby and yourself is to try not to worry. I know I'm asking the impossible but it really is imperative that you try and rest and eat well. Hopefully we can add a few grams to the baby's birth weight. Now, I know you don't want to get in touch with the baby's father, but is there anyone else we can get in to be with you? You should have some support—what about your parents? I'm sure if they were aware of the circumstances they'd be ready to patch things up.'

Alice shook her head. 'I'm not up to one of my mother's lectures. Honestly, Brett, it really wouldn't help at the moment.'

'Some friends, then?'

Alice thought of her loyal friends back in Adelaide. Jess would come at the drop of a hat if she called her, but it was hardly fair. Like herself, Jess was at the end of her internship.

'There is someone,' she said quietly, thinking of Jeremy. 'He'll probably be here soon.'

'Good.' Brett uncharacteristically patted her arm. 'Now, I've written you up for some sedatives. Nothing too strong,' he added, noting her alarmed expression. 'And before you ask, no, it won't harm the baby—that's what we're trying to prevent. Remember, we're all batting for the same team here. They'll just help you relax and, as I said before, that's crucial at this stage.' He smiled as a young nurse entered with a plastic medicine cup. Grumbling, Alice swallowed the small pill.

'Are you going to check under my tongue?'' she asked as Brett stood there, making sure she took it.

'I'm sure it's not necessary.'

'Giving you a hard time, is she?' Alice almost started crying again as there in the doorway, paler than usual and slightly breathless, stood Jeremy.

Brett Halliday obviously recognised him and immediately walked over and shook his hand. 'G'day, there, Jeremy. I was just telling your young intern here to lie back and stop worrying. I hope you're not going to undo all my hard work. She feels bad enough as it is about stopping work.' Brett spoke in a light, jovial manner but again Alice could hear the coded undercurrent that warned all was not well.

Jeremy obviously heard it too. 'Don't worry, I'm not here to talk shop. I just wanted to see how she was doing.' Walking over to the bed, he looked down at her. 'Linda only just told me. I came as soon as I heard.'

Alice saw a flash of confusion pass over Brett's usually impassive features, but he didn't say anything and quietly left.

Once they were alone Jeremy sat gingerly on the bed, picking up her swollen hand. 'What happened?' he asked, his voice thick with concern.

She so badly wanted to be angry with him, to somehow offload her guilt and blame him for all of this, but, looking into his worried blue eyes, she knew he didn't deserve it. 'I've got pre-eclampsia. My blood pressure's through the roof. And Brett just told me the baby's likely to be born sooner rather than later.'

'It will be all right,' he said confidently, but it wasn't what she needed to hear. Angrily she pulled her hand away.

'How would you know?'

Jeremy gave a helpless shrug. 'Because it has to be,' he said simply. As her face dissolved into a mass of tears he pulled her into his arms, holding her close as she sobbed onto his chest. 'It has to be,' he said again, closing his eyes in a silent prayer.

CHAPTER SIX

ALICE did her best not to worry. She took the tiny yellow pills and read endless magazines until the words blurred in front of her and she drifted off to sleep. She ate all the meals that were placed in front of her and only got up to go to the toilet and have a brief shower in the morning. She didn't even have to feel guilty about letting them down at work as Josh and Jeremy both told her that her position had been immediately filled by a young overseas doctor named Mai Wing. But, despite the best medical care and the most compliant of patients, nothing was going to prolong this pregnancy beyond thirty-five weeks.

'You've had a few days' worth of the steroids,' Brett said gently as he broke the news late on Monday evening. 'All the indications are that the baby will do well. Now, as it won't have the last few weeks *in utero* it won't have laid down any fat reserves so you can expect it to be quite scrawny. Also, he's going to need a lot of small, frequent feeds, which will exhaust him—'

'It's a boy, then?' Alice asked, jumping on Brett's words.

'Force of habit,' he assured her, but Alice was convinced now she was having a son.

'Just wait and see, huh? Now, I know you're keen to have a natural birth and we're going to give you a small trial of labour, but any signs that you or the baby aren't coping and I'll do a Caesarean section without question. You understand that, don't you?'

Alice nodded.

'Good. Right, then, I'll see you in the morning. Enjoy

your sleep—it's the last good one you'll be getting for a while.'

Lying back on the pillow, Alice put a shaking hand down to her stomach. 'It's all right, baby, you'll be here beside me tomorrow. Try and rest now.' Closing her eyes, she tried to think positive thoughts to stay calm, sure the baby would pick up on the utter fear she was feeling. She was concentrating so hard on the baby that it took a moment of two to register that someone had come into the room. Opening her eyes, she gave a trembling smile to Jeremy. 'All systems go tomorrow.'

He heard the break in her voice and in a second he was on the bed beside her.

'I know you hate me saying it, but things really are going to be fine. You've done very well to get this far.'

Gulping, she nodded. 'Do you really think so?'

'I know so. That extra week will have made all the difference to the baby, you know that as well as I do. It's time now, Alice. At least once it's here you can feed it up. *Everything* really is going to be all right.'

Alice lay back on the pillow. He sounded so sure she almost believed him.

'Now...' He squeezed her hand. 'About tomorrow. I know it's all happened quickly, and I know you want to wait before we make a commitment, but would it help if I was there for you tomorrow?'

Alice gazed over at him, taking in the deep blue eyes, the full mouth that had touched hers. She wanted him there more than anything, didn't want to do this alone, but it was such a huge thing to ask, such a big step in the direction of commitment.

Jeremy seemed to read her mind. 'It doesn't have to mean anything's written in stone. I've been to the medical library and borrowed all the trendy labour books.' He held up a bulging carrier bag. 'It's almost old hat to have a husband there these days—I'd be called your "support person". Apparently we're supposed to draw up a list of your wishes and desires throughout labour and if you start to stray from your chosen course I'm supposed to step in.'

His superior dry teasing tones bought a smile to Alice's lips.

'Personally I'd be screaming for all the drugs available— perhaps I shouldn't have looked at the pictures.'

Alice really laughed now. 'It will be a bit more graphic than a few textbooks tomorrow,' she warned.

'I'll stay at the head end of the bed, I think, shouting instructions from the sidelines, so to speak. That is, if you want me there.' He looked over to her almost shyly, and Alice knew it would have taken a lot for him to ask. She could almost feel the tension in the air as he awaited her decision—it evaporated as she gave a nod.

'It would mean a lot to me...'

Jeremy swept her words away and planted a brief kiss on her cheek. 'Now, you, young lady, ought to get some sleep, and I'm off home to do some reading. Did you know that in some cultures they actually eat the placenta afterwards? I think we'll skip that part and settle for a bottle of Moët.'

'Jeremy...'

He turned in the doorway.

'You'll make sure I stay presentable, won't you? I mean, I'm not into baring all in front of everyone.'

'I hadn't noticed,' he quipped, then, seeing her anxiety, he stopped the jokes.

'Leave it with me.'

As he left Alice couldn't wipe the smile from her face. He always did this to her, somehow managed to cheer her up, make her load seem a little lighter. And tomorrow he was going to be there with her every step of the way.

When the night nurse came in to check Alice's prescription chart and her IV site, half expecting to find her in floods of tears, she was pleasantly surprised to find Alice in the deepest of sleeps, her hair fluffed out over the pillow, a ghost of a smile on her lips.

'What a beautiful day to have a baby.' Bridgette, the midwife, flung back the curtains as Alice sat up slowly, blinking in surprise.

'Goodness, I did sleep well.'

'Now, I'm just going to do your obs and then you can have a shower. Do you want to wear your own nightdress or one of our gowns?'

Alice took the white hospital gown Bridgette was offering.

'Good choice. Right, I'll be back in fifteen minutes or so,' she said, after checking Alice's temperature and blood pressure and listening to the foetal heart on the small Doppler machine. 'Do you want to ring your mum again?' she asked gesturing to the phone.

Alice shook her head. 'She wasn't particularly inspiring when I called her last night. I think I'll wait till it's over.'

'Second good choice of the morning,' Bridgette said enthusiastically. 'Surround yourself with positive vibes.'

'Are you going to be with me this morning?' Alice asked, trying not to sound anxious.

Bridgette came back from the door and enveloped Alice in the biggest of hugs. 'I wouldn't miss it for the world. Now, do you have any favourite oils you'd like me to burn?'

Alice shook her head dumbly.

'Good. That means I can choose. You enjoy your shower.'

Alice smiled as Bridgette left. Normally the most untactile person, Alice was surprisingly comforted by this slightly eccentric woman. Many nights she had sat on the edge of Alice's bed and told her how she'd 'surfed the menopausal internet' and had discovered massage and aromatherapy, convinced it had calmed her raging hot flushes and palpitations. As a doctor Alice was somewhat sceptical, but Bridgette was so utterly convinced and delightfully wacky, yet still completely assured and professional, that Alice felt soothed immeasurably that it was Bridgette who would be with her during this most special of times.

After she'd showered, Bridgette took her down to the delivery suite and showed her around.

'In the first stages you can wander around. Here's the television room, but don't have anything to eat or drink. Some mums have a bath but as Brett will probably rupture your membranes we'd rather you didn't have one; you can always have another shower.'

Alice took it all in, eyeing everything nervously. Her medical training seemed to have flown out of the window and she felt a complete novice.

'We'll monitor you and the baby regularly throughout, but try and be as mobile as possible in the early stages—it helps speed things along. Here's Brett now.'

Brett was as kind and efficient as ever. 'OK, then, Alice, we're going to start you on a small dose of Syntocinon. We can always increase it if needed, but we don't want to start the contractions off too violently, especially with the baby being a bit on the small side.'

Alice watched as he checked the dosage with Bridgette and the IV infusion was connected to the bung in her arm. 'Now I'm going to rupture your membranes. It won't hurt, just be a bit uncomfortable.'

As Alice lay back through the procedure she did her best to relax and try not to feel too embarrassed. Brett would have done this a thousand times before but, still, it was most undignified. Through it all Bridgette held her hand reassuringly.

'There, now, we'll just attach you to the CTG monitor for a short while to check how the baby's doing, and then you can get up and have a wander. I'll be in to check on you a bit later.'

Bridgette stayed after he had left. 'Baby's looking fine. I'm just popping out for five—here's the call bell if you need anything.'

She returned a moment later. 'Here's Jeremy.'

'Are you decent?' His haughty tones filled the room as he breezed in, carrying a bundle of newspapers.

'For now.' Alice answered. 'You seem set for a relaxing morning,' she said, eyeing the newspapers.

'I hope so. It's not every Tuesday I get the day off.'

Alice pursed her lips and tried not to show her disappointment.

Ruffling her hair, he started to laugh. 'I thought you might like to keep them for the baby as a momento.'

'Oh,' Alice gasped. 'How nice of you. Thank you,' she managed, instantly mollified.

She had read the same books as Jeremy and both, despite their medical training, were somewhat deflated to find that Alice wasn't suddenly thrown violently into overwhelming contractions. Her confidence ebbing as the minutes ticked by, she agreed to Bridgette's suggestion that they go for a wander. Ever the gentleman, Jeremy guided her IV pole, making sure it didn't overbalance with the weight of the IVAC pump that carefully regulated the medication Alice was receiving. Alice waddled alongside him, her slippered feet not making a sound on the highly polished floor. They didn't wander far as there really weren't a lot of options. Alice peered through the theatre doors, watching as the midwives—identified by their floral paper caps—bustled along.

'Don't even look—that's one corridor you're definitely not going down today.'

'I hope not,' Alice replied nervously.

They settled in the TV room. Jeremy refused a drink at first, but when Alice assured him that she didn't feel like one anyway he eventually succumbed and made himself a coffee as Alice pretended to watch *Good Morning, Australia.*

Watching Jeremy, long-limbed in designer blue jeans and a casual polo shirt, she felt she had to pinch herself. She still found it hard to believe that he was really here with her. A small sigh escaped her lips and Jeremy was instantly by her side, the coffee forgotten.

'Anything?' he asked anxiously.

'I'm not sure,' she lied. She was saved from further explanation by Bridgette breezing in.

'Only me.' After checking Alice's blood pressure, Bridgette gave her shoulder a reassuring squeeze. 'If only your blood pressure had behaved as well as it's doing today, huh?' Discreetly moving the gown, she squirted some jelly on Alice's abdomen and listened for the heartbeat with the Doppler. 'Everything's fine.'

Alice caught her breath. A tightening in her stomach seemed to be intensifying. Bridgette didn't say anything but calmly held her hand on Alice's bulge until the tightening eased off.

'Things are starting to happen,' she said brightly. 'I'll leave you two to it.'

Trying to concentrate on the cookery demonstration taking place on the screen, Alice found she was rocking in the chair as the tightening intensified, and Alice found herself suddenly irritated by the noise of the television. Jeremy, seemingly relaxed, laughed as the TV host made one of his usual jokes.

'Turn it off, would you?' she barked uncharacteristically. Jeremy knew better than to argue and immediately flicked off the screen. 'If I'm taking up too much of your time?' Alice snapped.

Suddenly it wasn't tightenings that she was having, it was definitely pain. Alice started to rock harder in the chair.

'Can I do anything?' Jeremy asked. 'Should I get some-one?'

'Just talk to me, instead of watching the damn television,' she demanded.

'I think we ought to head back to the room, Alice,' Jeremy suggested, and something in his voice told her he wasn't to be argued with.

Surprisingly obedient, she allowed him to help her stand, unaware that he had pushed the call bell.

'Everything all right?' Bridgette appeared in the door-way.

'It would seem the TV's not the thing Alice wants to see right now!' Jeremy said sweetly, but Alice was sure he was raising his eyebrows at Bridgette.

'Oh, can you all just shut up?'

Without a word Bridgette led her back to the delivery suite and helped her onto the bed. 'Now, young lady, how about I do a quick internal...'

Bridgette was still smiling hours later as she came to the head of the bed and Jeremy swiftly arranged the sheet after another internal. 'What a clever girl. You're seven centi-metres dilated.'

'Can I have some drugs now?' Alice gasped as another contraction gripped her. Jeremy held her against him and, guided by Bridgette, placed the ball of his fist into the bot-tom of Alice's back, applying firm pressure. As the pain abated Alice listened in horror as Bridgette gently ex-plained she was too far gone for pethidine.

'By the time the drug took effect it would be useless

anyway. Keep going with the gas—it won't be too long now.'

The expletive that escaped from Alice's lips didn't seem to remotely bother Bridgette but Jeremy looked at Alice, stunned. 'She doesn't mean it,' he gasped. 'She's the most gentle, dignified—'

Bridgette cut off his excuses with a friendly wink. 'They're always the worst.'

From there on it was sheer and utter hard work. Alice sucked furiously on the gas, at times throwing it across the room in frustration, only to beg to have it back. Through it all Jeremy was beside her, slightly bemused but with an endless line of chatter that served to placate and irritate with alarming irregularity. He gave up trying to replace the sheet for the hundredth time when Alice stripped off her gown and demanded to stand. And suddenly he was behind her, taking her weight as he held her arms and she leant against him in a semi-squat. The urge to push was a wonderful relief, an almost primal instinct. No longer was the pain overwhelming her with nowhere to go. Suddenly there was something she could do. Bearing down, she grunted and gasped, pushing harder and longer as Jeremy and Bridgette urged and cheered her on. The sight of Brett tying an apron was the most welcome sight she could imagine.

'How much longer?' she gasped.

Brett gave her a steadying smile. 'That's up to you, Alice. The harder you push the sooner your baby will be here.'

It was all the incentive she needed. Suddenly an end was in sight, and with Jeremy murmuring words of encouragement, a life jacket in the stormy ocean, Alice could see land.

'Come on, Alice, one big push now—come on, Alice.' She could hear Brett's voice urging her on.

'Come on, sweetheart, I'm so proud of you. Push, Alice, one more, come on,' Jeremy urged.

And when she could push no more, when it all seemed utterly too much hard work, suddenly Bridgette exclaimed, 'Your baby's got black hair—feel it.'

Feeling the silken hair, knowing her baby was nearly out, was all the incentive Alice needed. Purple in the face, Alice took a deep breath, pushing harder and longer than seemed humanly possible. Suddenly, and far more quickly than she had imagined, a slippery bundle was being thrust into her arms, and Jeremy was gently lowering them onto the huge beanbag behind her.

Stunned, rapt, utterly shell-shocked, she gazed in wonder at the tiny angry bundle in her arms, watching as the denim blue colour of her baby almost instantaneously changed to a healthy pink, like litmus paper dipped in acid, and furious squeals of indignation poured from its wide open mouth.

'As he was so wonderful, shall we let Jeremy do the honours?'

Bridgette held up the scissors and Alice nodded, watching as Jeremy's normally steady surgeon's hand trembled with the sheer emotion of the moment when he severed the umbilical cord, tears streaming down his face.

'She's so beautiful,' he murmured.

'A girl?' Alice gasped. 'I've got a daughter? Hello, darling, hello, beautiful girl,' she crooned she held the slippery pink body to her naked breasts. 'Welcome to the world, little lady.'

Once the final stage of labour was over, and the placenta safely delivered, they had some time alone, the three of them, exploring the ten tiny fingers and toes, the sweet rosebud mouth, and the dark locks plastered to the baby's head, with the creamy vernix that had protected her inside her mother. And all the time Jeremy whispered words of endearment, telling her over and over how wonderful she had been, how proud he was to have witnessed this miracle. Bridgette joined them again, her eyes welling with tears. The wonder of birth never failed to touch her, no matter how many times she was privileged to share it.

'How about we give her a bath now?'

Normally it could have waited until Alice was more ready, but the babe was rather small and needed some warm clothes and rest, so the first bath was left to Bridgette as Alice sat shakily on a chair beside the sink, with Jeremy crooning beside her. The tiny nightie Alice had brought seemed to swamp the infant, and when Bridgette produced a lemon woolly beanie and popped it on the baby's head Alice realised for the first time just how small her baby was.

A Perspex crib was wheeled beside Alice's bed and they watched as Bridgette deftly tucked her in then placed an overhead heater above the crib. 'Just to help with her temperature, but the paediatrician's very happy with her and said she can stay beside you for now—though we'll bring her into the nursery tonight to let you rest and to keep an eye on her.'

Alice couldn't take her eyes off her. 'Can I get her out a bit later?'

Bridgette nodded reassuringly. 'Of course you can. We'll let her rest for now, though. You, too, Alice—you're probably exhausted. Have you thought of a name?'

'Maisy,' Alice murmured, looking over at her sleeping baby. 'Maisy,' she repeated, her eyes darting to Jeremy. 'Do you like it?'

She watched a smile steal across his face as he gently repeated the name. 'I think it's beautiful.' Walking over to the crib, he gently stroked the tiny soft cheek. 'Hello, little Maisy,' he whispered, and Alice thought her heart would burst.

*   *   *

After what felt like the longest, most important day of her life, Alice awoke from a deep sleep. Her eyes instantly focussed on the crib beside her and her heart beat faster as she realised it was empty. Turning slightly, she saw Jeremy silhouetted at the window, a swag of blankets in his arms, whispering baby talk to her precious daughter.

'Is she awake?'

'Wide awake,' he said softly, and, making his way over, he gently placed Maisy into her mother's arms. 'She smiled, Alice, I swear. I was showing her the moon and the stars and she smiled.'

Alice gave an indulgent smile as she held her newborn close. 'I don't think they smile this early, Jeremy, it was probably just wind.'

She looked up, holding his gaze as he moved closer on the bed, his strong hands gently reaching out for both of them. 'Thank you Jeremy, for being there today.' Her voice was shaking with emotion and the words seemed a paltry offering for the gratitude she felt, but Jeremy swept her words away.

'It's me that should be thanking you, Alice, for *letting* me be there.' He glanced down at the tiny babe. 'I wouldn't have missed this for the world.'

CHAPTER SEVEN

PHYSICIAN, heal thyself. Alice had heard the old saying a hundred times but, just as most doctors did, she ignored her increasingly obvious symptoms as she struggled on in those hormonal, exhausting postnatal days. As Josh had before her, she ignored signs most doctors would have seen at a glance if only they hadn't applied to them. A difficult pregnancy, lack of support, financial problems, custody issues, a difficult baby all pointed to an increased susceptibility to postnatal depression.

It was probably unfair to call Maisy a difficult baby, when really she was the most sweet-natured little thing. But the lack of those precious last weeks *in utero* meant that for now she needed strict two-hourly feeds, and the sight of her tiny body with a little woollen beanie tore at Alice's heart. The doubts and angsts that had plagued Alice before Maisy's birth seemed to have resurfaced and multiplied at an alarming rate, and the fact she was having great trouble with her milk didn't help matters. She felt that she had failed Maisy more than once and that breastfeeding was her chance to rectify this, but it wasn't to be.

'How are my two beautiful girls?' Jeremy breezed in, immaculate as usual, and Alice lay there defeated after yet another unsuccessful attempt at feeding Maisy, all too aware of her unwashed hair and shiny puffy face. 'I stopped by your flat and picked up your post as you asked. Here.' He placed a pile of letters on her bed. 'And I even cleaned out the fridge. Just as well I carry some latex gloves in the car—there were a few science experiments going on.'

'You didn't have to do that.' Alice gritted her teeth. 'I'll be home tomorrow. I could have sorted it out then.'

'It was no trouble,' Jeremy said airily, deliberately ignoring the tense note in her voice. 'Have you had any visitors?'

Alice shrugged as she flicked through her post then wearily placed it in her locker. She didn't have to open them to know they were all bills. 'Josh dropped by, and Fi, and a couple of other colleagues.'

'Your mum didn't come, then?' he asked gently.

'Well, it's hardly a five-minute car journey; it's over an hour's flight from Adelaide,' she said defensively. 'And it's not as if the flat's the most luxurious of accommodation. She'll probably come over once I'm home.'

'Of course she will,' Jeremy said, trying to sound more positive than he felt. Mrs Masters had barely shown any interest even when the pregnancy had gone so horribly wrong. She had also made it perfectly clear she didn't want to know until Alice had her life sorted. Privately Jeremy would have liked to have indulged in a few choice words with her but he knew it wasn't his place—yet. He hesitated for a moment, not wanting to tell Alice while she was in this mood that he really could only stay for five minutes. 'Alice, I have to get back to work, I'm on call tonight and there's an urgent lap choly scheduled this evening...'

'I'll be fine,' she said, trying to force a smile.

'What time are you being discharged?'

Alice forced her mind to concentrate 'Eleven a.m. Look, we can get a taxi. I know you'll be busy...'

But Jeremy was having none of it. 'I'll be here by eleven.' He leant over to give her a soft kiss goodnight but at the last moment she turned her face so his lips only grazed her cheek. 'I love you Alice,' he said almost pleadingly.

But Alice couldn't answer, and as he reluctantly left she

gave way to the tears that had been threatening all day. How could he love her like this? How could anyone love her when her own mother didn't even want to know? Glancing over at the crib, she watched Maisy sleeping on, oblivious to her mother's tears. She couldn't provide her own child with a father, couldn't finish her internship. Alice looked over at the bottle of formula in the jug on her locker. She couldn't even provide her own baby with breast milk.

'Only me.'

'Linda!' Alice blew her nose noisily on a handkerchief.

'I know it's after hours but the sister said you were still awake.'

'You just missed Jeremy,' Alice said quickly, searching for something to say to her surprise visitor. 'He had to rush back to do an urgent lap choly.'

Linda's forehead furrowed. 'Really? First I've heard about it.' Seeing the look of confusion flicker over Alice's face, she gave her a quick smile. 'But then what would I know?'

'But you're on call, aren't you?'

Linda shook her head. 'Not tonight—at least I certainly hope not,' she tried to joke, then, catching site of the crib, she swept over. 'Oh, Alice, she's beautiful. Josh said she was divine. Maisy, isn't it? Don't you just love those old-fashioned names?'

Alice couldn't help but be taken back by Linda's maternal tones but she forced a smile. After all, Linda was making an effort.

'So you're not on call?' Alice asked again, wondering if she'd misheard Jeremy.

'No, it's Mr Taylor's team tonight.' Linda gave her a questioning look. 'Why? Isn't work the last thing you should be worrying about with this little baby to look after?'

Alice gave a wry laugh without bothering to answer.

With Maisy to look after, work was one thing she definitely had to worry about. Almost on cue Maisy stirred in her crib and Linda wasted no time in asking if she might hold her.

'Sure,' Alice replied, trying desperately to ignore the knot of tension in her stomach. But Linda, it would appear, had eyes only for the baby. Swooping little Maisy up, she rocked her gently and Alice started to relax.

'She's beautiful, Alice, absolutely gorgeous. You must be so proud. I must admit, I do so admire you going it alone.' She glanced almost shyly over to where Alice lay. 'A dear friend of mine had a little boy a couple of years ago. I have no end of admiration for how she's coped. Mind you, she's had it tough.'

'In what way?' Alice asked, more to make conversation than out of interest. She had problems enough of her own without hearing about one of Linda's friends.

'Oh, you know, her boyfriend didn't want to know. Then suddenly when the baby was eighteen months old he found himself a nice wife, and after a year of trying with no babies coming he decided to file for custody.'

Seeing Alice's alarmed face, Linda seemed to realise the distress she had caused and begged to reassure her. 'But it's nothing like that for you. I'm sorry, Alice, I shouldn't have brought it up. Marianne—my friend—as much as I love her and everything, well, suffice it to say it wasn't straightforward like you. She'd had other boyfriends before, during and after the pregnancy, hardly the stuff to make you sound favourable in front of the family law court when you're up against the picture of domesticity—her ex-boyfriend and his charming stay-at-home wife. Still, it's not as if anything like that could happen to you—we all know how upset you were when it ended with your boyfriend. If push came to shove I'm sure the courts would come down in your favour. After all, you're the child's mother and a doctor, too. A good job must surely count for something.'

Alice somehow managed a polite murmur, but as Linda turned her attentions back to Maisy Alice felt the cold claws of panic clutching at her heart. Surely Marcus couldn't change his mind—surely not! But what if he did? What chance would an unemployed mother, living in a bed-sit, have against an affluent dentist and his kindergarten teacher wife? And as for Jeremy, if anyone wanted to fight dirty there was plenty room for mud-slinging there! Goodness, she hadn't even waited until the baby was born before jumping into bed with the biggest rake in hospital history.

Her first instinct was to grab Maisy back from Linda, to clutch her babe to her bosom and hold her, but Alice restrained herself, desperately trying to focus on the conversation. She was overreacting. Maisy was hers—surely there was no argument there?

'What happened in the end?'

'Sorry?' Linda gave her a bemused look.

'To your friend with the baby—what happened in the end?'

'Oh, it's still going on. The poor child spends half its time with each parent. Can't do it much good. Marianne is just about at her wits' end. I try to be as supportive as I can, but there's really not much I can do except listen, I guess, and try not to say "I told you so". Honestly, Alice, I'm only saying this because there's no chance of you meeting her, but I really have to bite my tongue sometimes. Marianne just carried on as if she was young, free and single. I know she's my friend and I know I don't speak from experience, but surely when you make the decision to have a baby sometimes you have to take the tough road. And if that means saying no to a hot date and staying home, well, surely that's what you have to do. The baby *has* to come first. But, then, I'm preaching to the converted. I know you'd think the same.' She gazed down at the now sleeping baby, her hard face softening somewhat. 'Wouldn't she, sweetie?' Linda crooned. 'Your mummy only wants what's best for you.'

Alice was saved from any further details by the round, smiling face of the paediatrician peering round the door. 'Sorry I took so long to get here,' Mary Healesville needlessly apologised as she came in. 'I got waylaid upstairs. I was just hoping to check Maisy over before I sign her discharge papers. I thought it would be nice to have a chat, see if you've got any questions before you take her home.'

Linda handed Maisy back to Alice. 'I'll be off, then. It was lovely seeing you, Alice.' She smiled at the paediatrician. 'It's Mary Blake, isn't it? You were a couple of years below me at medical school.'

'That's right. I thought you looked familiar.' Mary shook Linda's hand. 'Actually, it's Healesville now, I got married last year. How about you?'

'Oh, still McFarlane,' Linda replied with a slight edge to her voice. 'Work doesn't leave me much time for anything else. I'm working for Jeremy Foster now, not that you'd know it—he's been sick most of the time I've been on his team.'

'Oh, yes, he's the one who had the big accident. It must be good to have him back.' Mary turned to Alice, obviously concluding the conversation, but Linda still lingered.

'Well, the young girls seem to think so, it doesn't matter how nicely you try to warn them. They still think they'll be the one that will change him and bring him to heel. That man leaves a trail of broken hearts everywhere. When will these girls realise that a man will say anything and I mean *anything*, to get a girl into bed, and it always ends in tears?'

'Oh, well, you live and learn,' Mary said pleasantly, rolling her eyes for Alice's benefit. 'It was nice catching up with you, Linda, but I'll have to ask you to excuse us now. I really need to get on.'

Thankfully Linda took her cue this time and left quietly. Only when the door was safely closed did Mary speak. 'Is she a friend of yours?'

'Not really,' Alice replied diplomatically. 'A colleague.'

Mary gave a knowing smile. 'That'd be right, you can choose your friends.'

'I take it she wasn't the most popular girl at medical school?'

'I'll say, and from what I've heard not much has changed. Now, on to far more pleasant matters—how's this gorgeous girl of yours doing? I see she's back over her birth weight.'

'No thanks to me.'

Mary sat down on the bed. 'The breastfeeding's still not going well, then?'

Alice's eyes brimmed and she shook her head, biting on her lip to stop the tears.

'Alice, I know she's not tiny, like some of the premmies on special care, but she was still very small. With all the publicity you'd be forgiven for thinking that just under two kilos is a normal birth weight. Well, let me tell you it's not. These little ones take for ever to feed, they get easily exhausted from sucking and just when the first feed's over it's almost time to do battle for the next. It isn't any wonder breastfeeding doesn't always go well.'

'But surely it's important, particularly with her being small, that I keep on trying. The midwives said—'

'Alice, listen to me, please.'

Alice stopped talking and stared at Maisy lying innocently in her arms.

'Enjoy her, love her. That's what's most important. Don't get too bogged down in trying to do everything perfectly. They're pretty tough, these little ones. You're her mother and your best is more than good enough. Don't let anyone tell you otherwise.'

And when it was only Maisy and Alice left, and she'd struggled through yet another lengthy feed and Maisy had fallen into a rather more exhausted than contented sleep, Alice, hating herself for her lack of trust, finally picked up the telephone.

'Melbourne City Hospital. Can I help you?'

'It's Dr Masters here. I was wondering if you could tell me which surgical team is on call tonight.'

'One moment, please, Dr Masters.' The wait was agony but finally the switchboard operator with a rustle of papers came back on the line and Alice held her breath as she awaited the information. 'Mr Taylor's the on-call surgeon tonight—can I page him for you?'

'No, that won't be necessary. Thank you.'

With a shaking hand she replaced the receiver and picked up the electric breast-pump from her bedside locker. Attaching the beastly shield to her breast, Alice flicked on the switch and lay there staring at Maisy as the rhythmic pumping of the machine tried to cajole the milk from her hopelessly unyielding breasts. If only, Alice thought rue-fully as she labelled the paltry offering and wandered down to the fridge to store it, she was as successful at expressing as she was at crying. The tears she had shed would surely have stocked the fridge for a week.

That night was the worst yet. Perhaps sensing her mother's tension, Maisy was increasingly fretful, and sitting rocking her newborn, as the other babies seemed to slumber end-lessly Alice had plenty of time to think.

She loved Jeremy, that was a given. Loved the way he made her feel, the way his haughty, superior face softened when he spoke to her. Loved the way he touched her, moved her, engulfed her senses. And she loved him for outwitting the odds and making it through. Even though he had a past she loved the man it had made him—knowledgeable, aware, even sensitive, and a wonderful lover. But sometimes love itself just wasn't enough. Now, after the months of waiting, a new person had come into her life. A little lady had exploded into Alice's universe and she needed a mother, and not any old mother. The best mother in the world.

A year ago, or even a couple of weeks ago, Alice would have been prepared to hedge her bets, to ride out the storm and see where her relationship with Jeremy was leading. But now... Now she was a mother, the only parent of a beautiful daughter. What right did she have to jeopardise Maisy's security by chasing a dream?

And Jeremy was a dream, Alice acknowledged with an involuntary sigh. How could she ever hold him? What chance did she have of holding the man dreams were made of, with a new baby, no job and strapped to a breast-pump for heaven knew how long? What competition was she against the Olivias and Carries of the world? What sort of life was she going to lead if she doubted his every move, had to ring to check where he was, if he really was on call? And when it all soured, as it surely would, who would suffer most? Maisy.

'Can I get you a warm drink?' Alice jumped slightly as the midwife spoke. 'Sorry, I didn't mean to startle you, it's these rubber soles.'

'No, I'm fine, thanks. I think she's finally gone off.' Easing herself out of the rocking chair, she gently laid Maisy into her crib then kissed the softest of cheeks. 'Goodnight, darling,' Alice whispered, pulling the bunny rug around Maisy's tiny shoulders. It was Maisy that mattered and, much as it galled her to agree with Linda, for once Alice acknowledged maybe she was right. It was time to take the tough road, to focus on her baby instead of herself. Her mind made up, Alice made her way wearily back to bed. Slipping between the sheets, she felt a spasm of fear. Tomorrow she would leave the safety of the hospital. There would be no midwives, no doctors and, worst of all, no Jeremy.

Now all she had to do was tell him.

Alice deliberated long and hard as to how she was going to tell Jeremy. Her first instinct had been to discharge herself early and maybe explain later, but she knew this was unfair, and also there was some security in telling Jeremy in the hospital. There was surely less chance of there being a scene in the middle of the maternity ward. But as the clock edged past eleven-fifteen Alice wondered if she had been worrying about Jeremy's reaction unnecessarily. Perhaps he had decided already that Alice and Maisy were simply too much to take on.

Finally he arrived. 'Sorry I'm late.' He placed a breathless kiss on her cheek. 'Oh, doesn't she look beautiful?'

Maisy did look beautiful, dressed for the first time in 'real' clothes—a cherry-red one-piece with a matching red beret swamped her tiny frame. It was one of the many outfits Jeremy had bought her.

'Are you all ready for the off?'

Alice swallowed hard. 'What's this?' she asked, prolonging the agony as she pointed to a padded velour baby car seat, which looked impossibly new and ludicrously expensive. 'I was going to hire a capsule from the hospital.'

'Well, then, I've saved you a job,' he said lightly, scooping up Maisy and carefully strapping her into the seat. 'I bought the nurses a huge cheesecake. I thought you might like to give it to them for their morning tea. Is there anything else you need to do?'

It would seem Jeremy had planned for everything—everything except the words that faltered from Alice's lips.

'You didn't have to do all that.'

'I know.' He grinned. 'I wanted to.'

'You might wish you hadn't after you hear what I've got to say.' She watched his face slip as she broke the news. 'I'm sorry if I've misled you Jeremy, but I can't go on seeing you.'

'What do you mean?'

Alice swallowed a huge lump. 'Just that. I've been doing a lot of thinking. You know—about me and Maisy and how it has to be. And it can't be with you. I have to do this alone.'

Jeremy shook his head fiercely. 'No, you don't. Alice, you *don't*. Whatever the problem is, we can sort it out. I love you, Alice, don't shut me out now.'

But Alice was adamant. 'It's not going to work. It's better this way.'

'Better? Better! Better for who?'

'For all of us,' she tried to reason. 'You could have anyone, it's just your confidence is low at the moment. Sooner or later you'll get back on your feet and realise the mistake you've made, and then you'll hurt us. Not deliberately, maybe, but the day will come.'

'No,' Jeremy denied. 'No, it won't. I know that you and Maisy are what I want.'

'For now. But she's not your baby, Jeremy. One day down the track you're going to realise what you've taken on and wonder what the hell you've done. You'll look at Maisy and see she's not yours.'

She had known it would be difficult, but seeing tears in his eyes, his beautiful strong face crumpled and destroyed, Alice felt like the biggest bitch in the world.

'How can you say that?' he demanded. 'How can you say that when every time I look in her eyes I only see you. I promised Maisy that first night, when you were sleeping and I held her, I promised her I would always be there for her, always do my best for her.'

For a second she wavered. Maybe she was wrong. Maybe

she could be the one to hold him. But as Maisy let out a tiny wail she fought back her doubts. She had to stay strong.

'It wasn't your place to be making those sorts of promises. I'm sorry, Jeremy.'

'Everything all right?' Bridgette's concerned face appeared at the door.

'Fine,' Alice said, trying to compose herself. 'I was just about to ring for a taxi.

But Jeremy stood firm. 'She's not going home from a hospital in a taxi.' He picked up the handle of the car seat. 'At least let me do this for her.'

And so Bridgette came down with them to the car park. The bright sun seemed alien to Alice after so long indoors. Her legs felt unsteady and unused to the distance. Jeremy's car didn't look quite so sophisticated with a huge bolt and baby-seat holder strapped in place.

'All fitted correctly.' Bridgette tried to lighten the mood. 'You are good. More often than not, the bolt's still in the wrapper and I'm asked to install it. I should start charging.'

Jeremy gave a thin smile. 'That was nearly me. I spent the morning fiddling in the garage, then finally had to admit defeat and rush back to the shop to beg them to help. That's why I was late,' he added.

The journey home was a nightmare. Neither tried to make small talk—the only saving grace was that Maisy slept. Any attempt at independence for Alice was further thwarted when they arrived at her flat. She carried Maisy in as Jeremy followed with her endless bags. Opening the door, she thought her heart would burst as she held back the tears. No wonder he had been late. Everywhere she looked there were pink balloons and streamers, a huge banner proclaiming WELCOME HOME, a bottle of champagne chilling in the sink, surrounded by ice. A huge basket of goodies was awaiting her inspection. She stood there quite still, surveying his work, unable to speak as she heard him come up the hallway and enter the flat.

'That's everything. I'll be off, then. I expect you want to be alone now.'

Bending down, she started to unclasp Maisy. 'You'd better take this.'

'Keep it,' he said grimly.

'What would I need a car seat for, Jeremy? I haven't even got a car.'

'You still have to get taxis. You can use it with car seat belts—it doesn't need the bolt.' And then Jeremy fired the parting shot. 'Anyway, what would I need it for, Alice? Now that I don't have you.'

CHAPTER EIGHT

SOMEHOW Alice stumbled through the next few weeks. Her tiny flat only seemed to get smaller as Maisy's ever-increasing accoutrements took over. The sink seemed to be forever flowing with mountains of used bottles waiting to be sterilised. Her laundry basket was growing like a weed in compost and was threatening to invade the couch. The already cramped bathroom was now filled with baby baths and endless creams and ointments, all proclaiming to be the one that would get rid of Maisy's infantile eczema. No matter how many times she tidied and vacuumed and ironed it was time to start again. Even a hasty morning shower and a quick drag of the comb seemed decadent when Maisy was wailing to be fed. It seemed like light years since she had last plucked her eyebrows—not that Maisy cared, Alice consoled herself.

Despite the dark gloom that seemed to have descended indelibly on her life, her one shining light through it all was Maisy, and every day Alice marvelled at the miracle she had been blessed with.

Wearily climbing the stairs to the flat one day, weighed down with Maisy and a pile of freshly laundered Babygros, her mood lifted somewhat at the sight of Josh, standing grinning at her door.

'Dianne's holding a coffee morning for her fellow post-natal depressees. Not wanting to be left out, I swiped a coffee cake and thought I'd hold my own.'

'You're not wrong there.' Josh had been marvellous since she'd come home, popping in and out, not remotely fazed by Alice's tears and self-doubt.

138

'You'd be banned in a moment if you tried to get in,' he joked as he followed her in. 'They're all insisting on the merits of breastfeeding to get one's pre-pregnancy figure back, and here's you not a gram over fifty kilos with little Maisy happily on the bottle.'

'Don't go there, Josh,' she warned with a half-smile; her abandoned breastfeeding still irking.

'So, how are things?' he asked after making the coffee and dishing up two huge slices of cake.

Alice shrugged. 'Not the best. I've just spent the most humiliating morning of my life trying to explain to a clerk at the unemployment centre how a doctor can only work as a doctor once she's completed her internship. And how, just because the baby's father is a fully qualified dentist, that doesn't stop him being the biggest—'

'Alice,' Josh chided, 'that's not the sweet, smiling girl I used to know.'

'I'm sorry.' Alice blushed. 'I'm sure you don't need to hear my tales of woe. How are things with you?'

Josh fiddled with the fork, pushing his cake around the plate. 'Like a minefield,' he admitted. 'We spend most of the time trying to reassure each other that Eamon is every bit as bright as Declan, and then Declan goes and coos and gurgles or tries to roll over while poor little Eamon lies there, staring at the ceiling, and either Dianne or I crack.'

Alice put her plate down and moved along the sofa, reaching out for her friend. 'It's early days yet, Josh. He's been through so much, it's just too soon to try and compare.'

'I know, I know, but sometimes I get so scared for him.'

Glancing over at Maisy, lying on a rug, her little legs almost chunky now cycling the air in jerky movements, Alice knew then that she was the lucky one. For all the complications, for all the risks, she had a healthy baby. It made her hellish morning at the unemployment centre look like a trip to the circus.

'I'm sorry, Josh. Here's me banging on about my problems when you've got more than enough of your own.'

Josh managed an engaging grin. 'But yours are so much more refreshing. While I've got you on a guilt trip, tell me, Dr Masters, exactly what did happen between you and the dashing Mr Foster?'

Mumbling, Alice retrieved her plate and took a hefty bite of her coffee cake. 'I guess my bump didn't quite act as the crucifix you so eloquently predicted.'

'So what went wrong?' Josh probed.

Alice stared at the cake for an age, then her eyes looked over to where Maisy lay. 'I grew up.' Her voice was almost a whisper and Josh had to strain to catch what she was saying. 'Maisy needs security, and asking for that from Jeremy would be like asking for the moon.'

But Josh wasn't convinced. 'I like Jeremy, I always have. OK, I admit he's got the worst reputation imaginable, and that this time last year I'd have cracked up laughing at the thought of him changing nappies and burping a baby, but, Alice, Jeremy has changed.'

'So he tried to tell me.'

'Then why can't you believe him?'

She couldn't answer. In truth she didn't know herself where the rot had set in, where the doubts had started. But now as she sat there, scared, terrified of the future and as lonely as hell, it was an impossible dream to imagine Jeremy Foster could ever love her again.

'Alice, what went wrong?'

The cake seemed to have turned to sand. Swallowing hard, she turned her reddened eyes to Josh and for the first time that day looked at him. 'I really don't want to talk about it.'

'Fair enough,' Josh said wisely. 'But maybe you'll want

to talk about this. You know Mai Wing filled your position practically immediately?'

Alice nodded, trying and failing to appear interested as she started to fold her washing.

'Well, as usual Linda was bitching, and for once it actually made sense. Mai Wing started her internship three weeks early, which means she's going to finish three weeks early...'

Alice clutched the tiny Babygro to her chest. 'So the team will be short.'

'Got it in one. Now, in a month's time little Maisy will have had her jabs and be able to go to the crèche, which means that you, Dr Masters, will be more than able to step in and finish your internship.

'But what about the on calls?' Alice ventured, unable to believe it could really be that that simple.

'There wouldn't be that many, and if push came to shove I'm sure Dianne could manage one more.'

'Don't be ridiculous,' Alice retorted. 'She's got enough to deal with.'

'Well, I could chuck a couple of sickies and stay home to help. It would make your night a lot longer but, hell, Alice, it's only three weeks. Surely between us we can work it out.'

Suddenly there was a light at the end of the tunnel. It could work, it really could! She could complete her internship, start her GP rotation, get out of the bedsit and give Maisy the security she deserved. The only obstacle was Jeremy. Would he agree? And, more to the point, even if he did there was the fact that she would have to see him again, to work alongside him. Looking at Maisy mindlessly pedalling the air, the figures on her mobile making her go cross-eyed as she attempted to focus, Alice felt her heart-rate quicken. For that little girl she could get through anything.

'So do you want me to talk to Jeremy?'

Her eyes sparkling, her cheeks flushed, Alice threw down the laundry and made her way over to Josh. 'Yes.' She nodded breathlessly, 'Yes, please.'

The hows and whys, the practicalities of going back to work so soon, were only starting to surface when her doorbell rang later. Checking that the noise hadn't disturbed Maisy, Alice pulled open the door, her smile rapidly disappearing as she saw Jeremy standing there.

'J-Jeremy,' she stammered.

He didn't answer for a moment, his eyes, like the first time they had met, flicking over her body, taking in the huge changes. It was then she realised it was the first time he had seen her slim. But even that did nothing to bolster her confidence as she was achingly aware she must look a fright. She had wanted to look so cool and sophisticated the next time they met.

'I have a proposition for you.' His voice was stilted, wooden even, but what did she expect? Pulling the door fully open, she gestured for him to come through. Josh must have spoken to him straight away. Safe in the knowledge that she knew what he was about to say, Alice gestured to the sofa, hesitantly sitting down herself, desperate yet totally unable to meet his eyes.

'As you know, we found a replacement for you straight away when you were taken ill.' His sharp tones ruled out the need for small talk as he headed straight to business. 'Well, the upshot is it would have left us short for three weeks at the end of the rotation.'

Alice didn't answer, not wanting to appear too keen. But her solemn face slipped into one of despair as Jeremy continued.

'Mai Wing—your replacement—has just had some bad news from overseas. Obviously she has no choice but to fly home. Now, I had initially been intending to offer you the position at the end of Mai Wing's rotation, but now that isn't an option.'

Alice felt the slimy walls of panic closing in again. Just when there had seemed some hope, a way out of the mess she was in, it had been snatched back. She hardly listened as Jeremy went on. 'However, I've told Mai Wing to take a full three weeks—that will bring us into line with the rest of the rotations when she's finished. Which leaves us short for now. I've spoken with Mr Felix and, given the circumstances and our heavy workload, he's agreed that we can offer you the chance to complete your internship. You can start on Monday—three weeks from now you could be fully qualified and off to the country. How about it?'

'Monday?' she gasped. 'I can't. I'm not making excuses, Jeremy, it just isn't possible. Maisy hasn't had her inoculations yet so no crèche will take her.' She thought of Josh's kind offer but knew she couldn't land this on him and Dianne—they had more than enough troubles of her own. Her mind flashed to her mother. 'I could try Mum...' she said doubtfully, knowing deep down it would be useless.

'There's no need to do that,' Jeremy said crisply. 'I knew before I offered you the position the obstacles you'd be up against, and I've got something to run by you. You may or may not recall I told you my mother first came to us as a nanny. Well, she's a fully qualified mothercraft nurse. She's kept her registration up and still does casual shifts at the local crèche now and then. She's always eager for any excuse to come down and stay with me and fuss. I've spoken to her and she's more than happy to look after Maisy.'

'I could never afford—'

'For God's sake, Alice, not everything comes down to money,' he snapped.

'It does when you're broke,' she retorted, flushing at re-vealing her plight.

'As if I'd offer if we were going to charge you. The only down side is that there's no way my mother would stay here.' He seemed almost to sneer as he looked around her flat. 'Which would mean you'd have to move into my place for the duration.'

'So my flat's not good enough?' Why she was being argumentative she didn't know, but Alice couldn't stop her-self.

'Frankly, no.' Hell, he could be such a snob sometimes, and yet seeing his hostile face, knowing the pain she had caused and, more importantly, all they had been through together, she understood his contempt. Coming here today would have been hard.

'Why are you doing this for me?' she asked, genuinely bewildered that he would go to all this effort for her, but Jeremy wasted no time in shattering any illusions she might have had.

'Let's get one thing straight.' His eyes bored into her, cold and distant. She could almost taste the bitterness in his words as he spat out his speech. 'I'm not doing any of this for you. I'm doing it for Maisy. You may have chosen to disregard what I said about turning over a new leaf, but let me tell you this. I made a promise to Maisy and I fully intend to keep it. She deserves better than this.' He gestured to the untidy room, the overflowing ironing basket, the small electric fan battling fruitlessly against the oppressive afternoon heat.

'And you've got a chance now to give it to her. I don't expect you to make up your mind straight away, but I shall need to know by tomorrow morning. Personnel will need to be informed and obviously my mother will need to make some arrangements.' He put down a manila envelope on the coffee-table beside the remains of the coffee cake.

'These are my mother's certificates of registration. I know you won't want to take my word.' Picking up his car keys, he seemed to freeze on the spot as Maisy let out an indignant wail.

Alice walked over to the crib. Picking up her baby, she rocked her quietly against her, smelling the fragrance of baby powder and milk.

'She's grown,' Jeremy said softly. Looking up, Alice saw all the contempt had gone from his eyes, his features mellowing as he gazed on her daughter.

Alice took a deep breath. Jeremy was right, Maisy did deserve more. 'I don't need time to think about it. I'd like to start work on Monday.' She picked up the envelope and handed it to Jeremy. 'And of course I don't need to check the details; it's a very kind offer. Thank you.'

'Fine. I'll pick you up on Saturday morning. Can you be ready by ten?'

'Saturday? But…'

His face hardened again as his eyes flicked back from Maisy to Alice. 'As my mother is going to be looking after Maisy from seven-thirty on Monday morning it might be prudent for them to have some time together. Don't make the mistake of thinking you're going to be in for an easy ride over the next three weeks, Alice. You're not pregnant now.'

That was unfair. She had never asked for favours because of her condition, but, achingly aware of the pain she had caused him, she let it go. For a moment she'd thought Jeremy was softening.

'It will do you good to get back to work,' he said more kindly as he opened the door, but her illusion was soon shattered. 'Who knows? It might even give you a reason to wash your hair.'

* * *

She felt like a refugee as Jeremy loaded her bags and cases into his boot.

'That the lot?'

'I think so. I can always come back for anything I've forgotten.'

Checking for the third time that Maisy was correctly secured, she finally made her way around to the front seat and clipped on her belt. Aware of Jeremy's eyes on her, she felt a blush starting to creep over her face. 'What?' she asked rudely.

'Nothing. I was just thinking your hair looked nice.'

Alice shrugged dismissively. 'I just had a trim.' Which was a downright lie if ever she'd told one. Jeremy's comment had hit home and she had finally thrown caution to the wind and taken her credit card up to its limit, having a few low-lights and a deep conditioning treatment, as well as her legs waxed and her eyebrows plucked. Feeling somewhat more secure of her ability to provide now her work problem was sorted, she was more than aware she had let herself go somewhat. Alice wanted to look smart for her colleagues and patients—and Jeremy, she thought reluctantly before pushing the thought firmly away. That door was most definitely closed. She had made her choice and now she had to stick with it.

Any concerns she had about leaving Maisy with a stranger were laid to rest almost as soon the door to Jeremy's apartment flew open and Mavis Foster engulfed Alice and Maisy in a huge scented hug.

'You're here at last. Welcome, welcome. Don't just stand there. Come on through.'

'I'm sure Alice would if you gave her a chance,' Jeremy said dryly, but his eyes were smiling as he spoke to his mother.

'You poor thing. You must be terrified about going back

to work, but you mustn't fret. Work will be a breeze after the last few weeks.'

'Nice to hear you take my career so seriously,' Jeremy commented as he staggered in with the baby bath filled with bags. 'That's the last of it. I'll load up my stuff and be off, then. I'll see you at work on Monday, Alice.'

'Monday? But where are you going?'

'Off to Sorrento for the weekend. I thought you might find it easier to settle in without me interfering.'

Jeremy smiled as he spoke but his eyes were cold. He was obviously making an effort to appear friendly in front of his mother. Although he was probably right, and she should have felt relief at the reprieve, Alice could only feel disappointment.

'Right, Mum, I'll see you Monday night.' Alice was touched at the way he hugged and kissed Mavis goodbye.

'Right you are, darling. I'll have your favourite dinner waiting—steak and chips, just as you like them.'

Jeremy rolled his eyes and turned to Alice. 'My mother hasn't yet heard of oven chips, she still fries them in lard, and she won't believe me when I tell her that eggs and bacon no longer qualify as a healthy start to the day.'

'Rubbish,' Mavis retorted. 'A man needs a good breakfast.' She gave him a final kiss and insisted on standing at the door, waving, till the lift door closed. 'Right, Alice, before this baby of yours wakes up, how about we have a nice cup of tea and some cake and you can tell me all about her little ways?'

That night, groaning as she climbed into bed, Alice found she was actually smiling into the darkness. Full, fit to burst from a huge roast dinner and the stodgiest treacle pudding imaginable, she'd had to plead for mercy when Mavis had appeared at ten p.m. with a tray of toasted cheese for 'supper'. Who would have thought, Alice mused, that Jeremy, the coolest of cool men, would have a mother literally dripping with maternal instinct. You could just imagine her whipping out a handkerchief to wipe away a smudge from his cheeks at his graduation ceremony. More importantly, Mavis had been an absolute marvel with Maisy. Not interfering or superior, she had listened carefully as Alice had taken her through her baby's routine—not that she really had one; it was more hit and miss at the moment.

Over the weekend Alice felt her confidence grow, not only with leaving Maisy but more amazingly her own ability as a mother. Mavis seemed to instil in her a quiet confidence that as Maisy's mother she really did know best. If only her mother could have shown half as much interest, life could have been so much easier.

In fact, by Monday, as she stepped off the tram and headed into the hospital, Alice's only concerns were for the day ahead. She knew beyond doubt that Maisy was in the best possible hands.

'Welcome back, stranger.' Josh let out a low whistle. 'My goodness, you do look the part. What happened to the girl I left on Thursday?'

'Two hours in the hairdresser's and a ton of foundation. I'm so nervous, Josh. I feel as if I've forgotten everything.'

Josh gave her a friendly pat on the arm. 'Don't worry, one look at Linda and it will all come flooding back with painful familiarity. She's really in a strop this morning—her hormone tablets must have run out.'

Josh was right. Two hours into the day Alice felt as if she'd never been away. The ward round had been mercifully quick, with mostly discharges which meant heaps of empty beds and therefore heaps of admissions, but as they weren't the team on call that day hopefully she was in a for a fairly smooth first day back.

Famous last words. 'Alice, could I borrow you a moment?'

Alice looked up from the IV charts she was writing, glad of the diversion. She was desperate to ring Mavis and check on little Maisy but she had already rung once this morning. 'Sure, Fi, what's the problem?'

'It's Mrs Dalton.'

Alice nodded. Mrs Dalton had been Alice's last patient before she had gone off sick. During that time she had been discharged, only to return last week with the same problem. However, this time her ulcer was far worse and her circulation was deteriorating markedly. She was booked for an angiogram that morning to assess the severity of the blockage, and it was looking as if bypass surgery was becoming the only option.

'Her foot seemed fine on the ward round—well, no worse anyway. But she just buzzed and is saying it's agony. It feels pretty cold. I think you'd better take a look.'

Alice made her way straight over and as Fi pulled the curtains Alice slipped the bedsock off the offending foot.

'It's very painful, is it, Mrs Dalton?'

'Yes, dear. I'm sorry to make such a fuss; I know you're all busy.'

Alice looked up from the foot to her patient. 'Let's have none of that. Now, when did the pain start?'

'Just after Mr Foster left. I tried to ignore it…'

Alice knew from her previous conversations with Mrs Dalton that for her to be this distressed meant that she was in severe pain. Mrs Dalton had put up with more than enough in her life without complaint. The foot was definitely cold, not just cool, and there was some mottling around the toes and on the dorsal surface. Gently she tried to palpate the pedal pulse but after a few moments of effort and quiet concentration she took her fingers away. 'Did you have any luck, Fi?'

'No.'

Fi handed her the Doppler, and Alice squeezed some gel

onto the cold foot. Gently placing the probe, she tried to find a pulse. The speaker made some whooshing noises as Alice slowly and patiently moved it around, but despite all her efforts there was definitely no pulse to be heard.

'Shall I page Jeremy for you?'

Alice chewed her lip. 'Better not. Can you try Linda first?'

The attempt at friendliness on Linda's part obviously only extended to out of hours. Her sour voice on the end of the phone was back to its usual condescending tones and when she marched into the ward she didn't even bother to address Alice, instead directing all her questions at Fi.

'How long has it been like this?' she barked.

'Mrs Dalton said the pain started after the ward round.'

'But that was over an hour ago. Why was it left so long before calling someone? Were you waiting for it to turn blue?'

'I only just let the staff know,' Mrs Dalton said apologetically, and Alice choked back her own rage at Linda's unprofessional attitude.

'Should I page Mr Foster?' Fi ventured.

'He's already coming,' Linda barked. 'It was obvious to *me* this was an emergency.'

Which it was, of course, but, as Alice had done, Jeremy took his time examining the foot, carefully trying to palpate a pulse, listening with the Doppler and arranging a strong injection for pain while he waited for the ultrasound machine to arrive.

'It doesn't look too good, does it, Doctor—I mean Mister?'

Jeremy looked up from the ultrasound monitor. 'There's a blood clot blocking off the blood supply,' Jeremy informed her, his voice friendly but entirely professional. 'Now, we could start a heparin infusion, that would thin the blood and disperse the clot, but the down side is that may take too long. Realistically I think we ought to take you straight to Theatre and perform what we call an embolectomy. While we're there we'll also perform the bypass surgery to hopefully improve the circulation to your foot.'

'And if it doesn't work?'

Alice found herself staring at her own feet as she awaited Jeremy's answer.

'Well, I'm going to do everything I can to make sure that it does work but, yes, there is a chance, and a fair one, that it mightn't work.' He paused, allowing his words to sink in.

'You'd have to amputate?'

'Worst-case scenario, yes.' He waited a couple of moments as Mrs Dalton sobbed quietly into her handkerchief before he continued. 'Mrs Dalton, I don't like to speculate too much, and I don't like to raise false hope, but certainly that is really a last resort. My intention is to save your foot.'

For the next fifteen minutes Mrs Dalton's bedside was a hive of activity. The anaesthetist came in to do a pre-op assessment. Thankfully, as she had been due for an investigation later that morning, Mrs Dalton was already fasting, which made emergency surgery a lot safer as her stomach was empty, thus reducing the risk of aspiration. Fi, quietly efficient, performed an ECG without waiting to be asked, and by the time Mr Dalton had arrived, red in the face and dressed in the grubby jeans and an old T-shirt, Mrs Dalton was ready to be taken to Theatre.

'Fancy coming to the hospital in your gardening clothes,' Mrs Dalton chided, groggy from the analgesia. 'What will people think?'

'Never satisfied, these women, no matter what you do,' Mr Dalton tried to joke as his eyes filled with tears.

'I quite agree,' Jeremy quipped, and Alice was positive *that* little comment was aimed at her.

But there was none of that once they got to Theatre. The

only objective here was to save Mrs Dalton the trauma of losing her foot and Jeremy worked exhaustively, first evacuating a huge clot before the painstaking task of bypass surgery. Finally, when it was over, Alice could only again marvel at his skill. Mrs Dalton's foot, right down to the tips of her toes, was now a healthy pink.

'I want strict fifteen-minute vascular obs for the first two hours, then hourly for six hours and two-hourly overnight. Actually, make it hourly overnight.'

'The ward staff won't be too pleased,' Carrie warned.

'Do I look as if I care?' snapped Jeremy, peeling off his gloves and hurling them into the metal bin beside Mrs Dalton's gurney before stalking out of the recovery room.

Carrie raised a well-plucked eyebrow. 'Someone's unhappy in love. I wish I knew who she was—I'd like to buy her a drink. It's about time that bastard got his comeuppance.'

The venom in Carrie's voice was pure poison, and as she listened Alice felt the hackles on her neck rise. 'I'd like to remind you, Sister, that Mr Foster happens to be my boss and a consultant surgeon. If you can't show any respect for that fact then at least show it for your patient. Mrs Dalton may be unconscious but there can be no excuse for that kind of talk.'

'I'm sorry,' Carrie spluttered, the colour in her cheeks mounting. 'It won't happen again.'

'It had better not,' Alice warned. 'Let's leave it there, shall we?'

Making her way to the changing rooms, Alice realised she was shaking. Useless at confrontation, she normally avoided it. But hearing Jeremy so unfairly being jeered at, she had felt anger flame within her. Sitting herself down on the small wooden bench, she put her head into her hands. Who was she trying to kid? She loved him, she always had, she had never stopped. It was just so impossible. Even if she wanted to ignore his past, everywhere in this hospital there were constant reminders. Maybe it was for the best. Maybe that would serve to keep her strong and focussed and remember why she could never be with him again. Letting him go once had been agony, to do it again would be sheer hell.

CHAPTER NINE

IF THERE was some tension at work between them, it was almost bearable. Jeremy was aloof and distant, but the demands of their busy schedules and the vast difference in their status meant there was, more often than not, a reason to rush off if things got too close for comfort. But on the home front the tension was palpable. Jeremy did his utmost not to be there and, given the fact that Alice was a mere intern, it invariably meant her days were punishingly long. But there were the inevitable times when they met in the hallway on their way to the bathroom or had to make small talk over the vast three-course meals that Mavis insisted on cooking.

The one saving grace was Maisy. Her angelic presence always lightened the mood, and some evenings, when Alice was positive she would spontaneously combust if she had to sit there staring at the television with Jeremy achingly close as Mavis knitted quietly, she would jump with relief when Maisy let out her wakening cry.

He was wonderful with Maisy—there was no argument there. Though he was careful not to appear too keen when Alice was there, several times when she came home she hid a smile as she walked in to find Jeremy singing the latest pop songs to his devoted audience, or practising his lecture technique on the finer points of vascular surgery to his most affable student.

'Finally, a female who doesn't answer back.' He would shrug, blushing as Alice walked in. 'How could I resist?'

'Give her time, Jeremy. She'll learn.'

But there was too much left unsaid, too many questions

unanswered for there not to be some sort of confrontation, and three weeks was a long time when your heart was bleeding.

One night during the second week she was there Maisy was particularly fretful. Nothing Alice tried seemed to placate her. She tried more milk, boiled water, rocking her face down, as June Wicks, the maternal and child health nurse, had showed her, but nothing, it seemed, was going to silence her. Almost at her wits' end, Alice was tempted to knock on Mavis's door and ask for some welcome advice. But just when Alice had exhausted all possibilities and was about to beg the older woman's guidance Maisy, for no apparent reason, suddenly gave Alice the most delicious smile and drifted off into a deep sleep.

Wide awake now, Alice padded out to the kitchen with a pile of half-empty bottles and nappies. The sight of Jeremy sitting hunched at the kitchen table, nursing a glass, stopped her in her tracks. Suddenly she was back where it had all started, catching him unawares, glimpsing the Jeremy behind the cool façade. She was truly horrified by how he seemed to have aged—the blond stubble on his chin and the lines etched around his eyes. He didn't look up, but as she stood there, not knowing quite what to do, he spoke, his voice thick and husky.

'Is she all right?'

'She's just gone off. I'm sorry, Jeremy, I tried to keep her quiet. Are you in pain again?' she asked, knowing it was now none of her business but concerned just the same.

'Agony,' he replied. Jeremy took a sip of his drink and with a long sigh he placed the glass down on the table. 'Have you any idea the hell it is for me, listening to her crying?'

Alice was straight on the defensive. 'I said I tried to keep her quiet. Surely you must have known it might be like this sometimes with such a young baby. If it's too much we'll be out—'

He stopped her flood as he banged the glass down on the table. 'I meant listening to her crying and not being able to do anything, sitting here not being able to help because you've erected a damned "do not enter" sign around your heart. I'm sorry,' he said wearily, looking up at her stunned face. 'You don't need this. We're on call tomorrow. I'd better get to bed.'

'Can I fetch you a painkiller or anything?' she asked, not wanting to let him go like this.

A wry smile tugged at the edge of his lips. 'A painkiller wouldn't touch it.'

It was only when he had left the kitchen that Alice realised with a start that the agony he was in wasn't from his back. With a moan she realised it was she, Alice, that was causing his pain. The cool persona, the icy contempt, it was all an act—he really did love her.

Back in the sanctuary of her bedroom, gazing at Maisy asleep, one hand held high above her head as if she were doing some strange version on the Irish jig, Alice ached to go to him, to hold and comfort him—but what then? Her old fears were sniping at her heels again—Linda's painful predictions, Carrie's wrath, Olivia's pain. How could she risk Maisy and her security by throwing it away to chase a dream, delectable as it was? It took a massive effort to climb into bed, pull the sheets up tightly and will herself to sleep—anything rather than weaken now. She had come so achingly close to achieving her goals that it would be foolhardy to wreck it now.

After a night spent trying and failing not to think of Jeremy, the last thing Alice needed was the prospect of twenty-four hours on call. But Mavis, insisting she had slept like a log and hadn't heard a peep all night, fussed about seemingly oblivious to the tension, piling mountains of bacon and toast onto Alice's plate and refilling her cup with sweet, strong coffee.

'Come on. Jeremy,' she scolded gently as he appeared unshaven at the table. Obviously Jeremy wasn't relishing the prospect of being on call either. They studiously avoided each other's eyes as Mavis rabbited on. 'So if you get home before two tomorrow, fine, but if not I'll take Maisy to the child health nurse for her weigh-in. Is there anything you want me to ask for you?'

Alice had a list as long as her arm, but instead she shook her head. 'Just mention that she seems unsettled at night. I think she might even be teething, although it seems a bit soon.'

Mavis clucked happily. 'Some are born with teeth.'

'Anyway, I should be back in plenty of time to take her myself. I usually finish around midday after being on call.' She stood up, smoothing some crumbs from her smart navy skirt. 'I'd better be off.'

'But why not wait for Jeremy?' Mavis protested. 'He won't be too much longer, will you, pet?' she asked, turning to the newspaper now blocking Jeremy's face. 'It seems silly, you taking a bus or tram when Jeremy will be driving there anyway.'

'Perhaps she needs some fresh air,' Jeremy suggested curtly, not bothering to move the paper.

Planting a lingering kiss on Maisy's cheek as the baby gurgled happily in Mavis's arms, it was a positive relief to escape the unbearable tension of the apartment and step out into the warm morning sun. It was only just over a week until her internship was completed but it seemed interminable. Admitting to herself that she had never stopped loving Jeremy only made things harder, and the fact he obviously loved or at least thought he loved her made it downright impossible.

Even as she stepped on the tram, purchased her ticket

and made her way to her seat, her muddled mind never once left Jeremy. Resting her head against the cool window, she allowed her mind to wander. Suppose, and it was a big suppose, she did relent, did reveal the depth of her feeling to him and—almost more impossible—suppose he did forgive her, what then? Mavis wasn't going to be around for ever. Jeremy was hardly going to move to the country. Jeremy—with all his ego, all his immaculate, chauvinist, carefree ways—suddenly thrust into the role of a parent as she struggled to juggle work and child-raising—it could never last, and she was a fool to even hypothesise.

The wailing of a siren broke into her daydream. The tram halted at the lights, giving way as an ambulance sped past. As they waited, unmoving, through several light changes the air was filled with ever-increasing wails. Looking out, Alice saw a couple more ambulances tearing towards the hospital. Making her way to the head of the tram, she spoke to the conductor.

'What's the delay?'

'Police told us to sit tight, love. Apparently there's been a big accident. They're trying to keep the entrance clear.'

'Could you let me off?' Alice asked urgently. 'I'm a doctor, I'd better get there.'

'No worries, Doc.'

As the doors slid opened her mobile phone trilled loudly. Answering it as she ran, her heart came into her mouth as she heard the chilling message.

'Dr Masters, there's a major incident in progress. Can you please come directly to Accident and Emergency?' The switchboard operator's voice was cool and efficient but Alice could detect the tremor in it. She would have been given a list of all personnel to work through and would know exactly what to do after the endless rehearsals, but this was no mock set up. Alice knew for sure it was real.

'I'm on my way. I'll be two minutes,' she gasped as

ambulance after ambulance sped by. Something huge was going on.

The impeccable mechanism of the accident and emergency department had swung into action by the time Alice arrived, breathless, at the doors. Fay, the unit manager, donning a red hard hat to show she was in charge, was directing the traffic. 'Dr Masters, straight through to Resusc, please. Mr Donovan will direct you.'

'What happened?'

'Two buses versus a truck' came the grim reply. The casualty list would be huge.

What went up had to come down—it was a simple law of physics. On the up side, if there was to be a major incident, seven forty-five was probably the best time for it to happen. At that time the nurses were still in hand over, meaning there was double the staff. Most doctors were already there or, like Alice, on their way, while the night cover was still on site. The down side to the scenario was that if a truck lost control and collided with two buses, seven forty-five a.m. meant they would both be packed with commuters and school children.

Alice steeled herself as she entered the department in an attempt to prepare herself for what lay ahead. But despite lectures, videos and simulations of a major incident, nothing but nothing could have prepared her for the sight that greeted her. It was truly appalling. Bodies were everywhere as Samuel Donovan, the accident and emergency consultant, directed the staff while simultaneously working on patients.

Jeremy had obviously beaten her to it. He'd clearly not even had time to remove his jacket, and his immaculate grey suit was already splattered in blood as he worked on a lifeless body on the trolley in front of him. She watched as he shook his head and looked up at the clock, calling the time that this life had ended. For a second he caught her eye, and not for the first time Alice couldn't interpret the look that flashed over his face.

'Take this one into a cubicle, Alice,' Samuel ordered as the paramedics rushed a trolley in.

The young woman that met Alice's eyes as she looked down at the ambulance stretcher had a look of absolute terror on her face and Alice's heart went out to her for what she must have been through. Her face was as pale as the sheet that covered her, and Alice was certain that under normal circumstances she would have been placed straight into Resusc—but, then, there was nothing normal about to-day.

'This is Kim Earl, twenty-two years of age, passenger in bus number one. She was up the front end of the vehicle, which took most of the impact. When we got to her she was conscious, trapped by her left leg.'

The paramedic gave Alice a wide-eyed look and glanced down at the affected limb. Alice's gaze followed his. The leg was heavily splinted and covered in drapes, but Alice could see from the hideous angle at which the foot was lying and the colour of the toes the reason for the paramedic's concerned expression.

'She's also complaining of some abdominal pain, but her leg seems to be the main source of pain. She's had gas on the way with some relief.'

'Thanks very much.' Alice said when they had carefully moved Kim onto the hospital gurney. 'Are there many more to come?'

The lead paramedic gave a grim nod. 'Yep, we'd better get back to it. Oh, one thing we didn't tell you. Kim's due to get married on Saturday, aren't you, Kim?' He gave the terrified woman a friendly wink. 'They'll look after you now, Kim. Good luck. I'll come and see how you got on later.'

Alice was always impressed by the paramedics. The

scene they had just attended and were going back to would have been horrific, yet despite it all they had found the time to make the patient feel more than a number, to treat her as a young woman with a life and problems of her own, not just a nasty leg and abdo injury. It was a lesson Alice always tried to remember.

They had already established intravenous access, and as the nurses were all tied up Alice did a swift set of observations, trying to quell the mounting panic within her as she examined her patient. An accurate assessment was especially vital, given the fact that the senior staff were involved elsewhere. Kim's leg, the most obvious injury, was for the moment safely covered and secured, so there was no point concentrating on that if she had more dire injuries. Her neurological status was sound, Alice noted, with no apparent head injury apart from a few abrasions. Moving to her chest, Alice was satisfied her air intake was adequate with no breathing difficulty, though her respiration rate was high. Her abdomen, though, was distended and tender.

Alice felt a surge of anxiety. This young woman was seriously injured. Inserting another IV cannula, Alice took some baseline bloods and an urgent group and cross-match then attached a plasma expander drip. There were supplies of O-negative blood kept in the emergency department but these would already be sorely depleted. Samuel Donovan would have to ration that valuable commodity.

Alice rechecked Kim's blood pressure, which was markedly lower with her pulse-rate increasing, a sign of large blood loss. What would Jeremy do next? That was how she'd play it.

Peritoneal lavage. It was a relatively simple procedure which involved making a small incision into the abdominal cavity and allowing in a bag of warmed saline. If when the saline flowed back there was blood in it, it meant the patient needed to go to Theatre. Although a straightforward procedure, it was not one Alice had done before but, realising the seriousness of the situation, she prepared all the equipment that would be needed before rushing out.

'Mr Donovan?'

He made his way over swiftly. 'What have you got?'

'Twenty-two-year-old female with a serious leg injury, which I haven't looked at yet. It's her abdomen I'm more concerned about, though. I think she's bleeding out. I've set up for a peritoneal lavage.'

'Good.' He came straight to the gurney and, after briefly introducing himself, performed the procedure. 'She needs Theatre. OK, I'll get Jeremy. Fay…'

In a matter of ten minutes Kim was about to be taken up to Theatre. All planned ops had been cancelled to leave room for the urgent cases, and Kim couldn't wait.

'I'll see you on the ward.' Alice squeezed the young woman's hand. 'Mr Foster is going to operate.'

'What about my leg?'

It was Samuel Donovan who answered as the orthopods examined her leg.

'Kim, it's a very serious leg wound you have. We'll have a better idea in Theatre once you're anaesthetised. We'll do the X-rays up there.'

'It has to be right for Saturday.'

'She's getting married,' Alice said to the consultant.

Despite the chaos, despite the tragedies unfolding in all directions, Samuel took the time to explain to this beautiful young woman as he took her through the consent form that, although they would do everything to save her leg, it might not be possible.

'*No!*' The scream that emerged from Kim's lips was blood-curdling. 'I won't consent to that. You can't cut it off.'

Mr Khan, the orthopaedic consultant, came to the head of the gurney. 'Now, please, my dear, believe me when I say I'm going to do my utmost to save it, but it doesn't look good. I cannot and will not let you die from your leg wound. And that could be the reality. I'm not going to amputate unless I have no other choice.'

Kim looked pleadingly at Alice. 'Is that it? I'm going to lose my leg? Can't I get a second opinion? I've got private cover…'

For some reason, perhaps because she had been the first doctor present, perhaps because she was a woman or near her age, Kim needed Alice's opinion.

'Kim, when the doctors say they'll do everything, they mean it. You really need to go Theatre. I know how hard this must be.'

'No, you don't.'

Alice knew she was right. 'I'm sorry. I can only imagine—'

'Will I die?'

Alice squeezed her hand. 'We're not in the business of letting young women die. Our job is to do everything to save you, and that means you have to go to Theatre now.'

Kim's eyelids were starting to close and she struggled to open them.

'Ted, my fiancé…'

'I'll talk to him as soon as he gets here. He'll be waiting for you when you come out.'

Watching the pale, shaking hand as Kim signed the consent form, it took a superhuman effort for Alice to stay professional. Kim should be signing a marriage certificate in a few days, not a damned consent form that might render her an amputee.

Although the situation had intensified, with a seemingly never-ending stream of casualties still arriving at an alarming rate, the department seemed a lot more controlled. More staff were now present, many of them senior and able to make swift assessments and prioritise the patients. Up on the wards all patients who had arrived for planned surgery or were well enough to be discharged were being seen by doctors and sent home to free up beds for those that needed them. The overnight stay ward in the emergency department had become a makeshift mortuary.

Stunned, Alice still couldn't take in what she was a part of. The precarious line that held everyone inside a safe normality could change in an instant. Life that day had changed for all present.

'How's your stitching, Alice?' Fay grabbed her as she walked past. 'Do you mind making a start?'

And so she played her part. OK, so she wasn't up in Theatre saving a life or in the resuscitation room on the front line. But over the next five hours Alice knew that she was doing a good job. Painstakingly she picked out the never-ending lumps of shattered glass, applied local anaesthetic and cleaned aligned edges, doing her small bit to make sure the external scars people bore to remind them of this black day were as minimal as possible. Her soft voice was gentle, reassuring patients and their relatives. And sometimes when there was no need for words, when the patients just wanted to lie still and let her get on, Alice's mind drifted to Jeremy up in Theatre, doing his best to save a young woman's life. Jeremy, who had always done his best for her and later Maisy, too.

'Alice, when you finish this one, Kim Earl's parents and fiancé have arrived. I've done my best to talk to them but I was wondering if you might have a word. Samuel's not going to get there for ages and she's still in Theatre.'

'Sure, Fay,' Alice replied, placing a dressing over the hand she had just sutured. 'I'll come now.'

'A word of warning—the fiancé isn't taking it all too well.'

'Can you blame him?' Alice said sadly. 'It must be an awful shock.'

But Fay shook her head. 'His greatest concern is the fact she might lose her leg. Look, I'll let you judge for yourself. Just tread carefully.'

Bill and Sheila Earl looked every bit as devastated as any parents would, confronting the events that had been thrust upon them. Bill sat staring at the wall ahead, his heavily tattooed arm around his wife's shoulders. Sheila was gently rocking, not making a sound as tears coursed down her cheeks. A younger man, dressed in a trendy single-breasted charcoal-grey suit, his dark wavy hair cut closely to his head and slicked back with gel, introduced by Fay as Ted Caversham, paced relentlessly up and down the tiny room.

Alice pulled a chair up and sat down opposite the parents, and as gently as possible took them through her dealings with Kim.

'The sister said her injuries were serious.' Bill cleared his throat. 'How serious? She's not going to…?'

'She was bleeding internally, I'm not sure from where. Rather than wait for further investigations which would have taken up a lot of time, particularly due to the demand on equipment this morning, it was considered far safer to take her directly to Theatre. I'm sorry I can't be more specific, but I really don't know much more than that. However, what I can tell you is that she was taken to Theatre very quickly, and the surgeons that are operating are first class. She was conscious throughout. I spoke with her and she told me all about the wedding.'

A trembling smile wobbled on Sheila's lips, then as the realisation dawned again it vanished and she gave way to hysterical tears.

'But what about her leg?' Ted turned an angry stare on Alice. 'We've been told she might lose it.'

Alice swallowed. 'It does look a real possibility. Her leg was partially severed below the knee. I personally didn't see it but the orthopaedic consultant said that it was a very serious injury, though I must reiterate that everything will be done to save it.'

'Rubbish. They'll be rushing to get the next case in. I tell you now that if everything, and I mean everything, isn't done this hospital is going to have the biggest lawsuit—'

'Mr Caversham, I understand you're distressed—'

'You bet I'm distressed. You calmly walk in here and tell us that Kim's probably going to lose her leg—'

'The important thing,' Alice interjected, 'is that she gets out of Theatre. Once we know the extent of her injuries, the doctors can give more definitive answers to your questions. At the moment it's pure speculation.'

'If Kim loses her leg, she might as well die.' Alice fought to hold her tongue as Ted Caversham continued, 'You might think I sound harsh, but you don't know her. She's a model, for heaven's sake. She simply won't cope.'

Privately Alice rather thought it was Ted that wouldn't be able to cope with the loss. Standing up, she picked up her stethoscope from the coffee-table. 'As soon as we hear anything further, we'll let you know.' She wanted to stress that at the moment Kim's leg, although a tragedy in itself, was really the least of her problems, but bringing Ted down a peg or two could only exacerbate Bill's and Sheila's pain. 'I'm sorry I can't give you any more answers.'

Fay was waiting for her as she came out. 'A charmer, isn't he?'

'He's probably just upset. People react strangely.'

Fay gave her a knowing look. 'Yes, people react strangely, but I can't help but think he's more worried about his image than poor Kim. How all this is going to affect *him*.' Taking Alice's arm, she led her to the staff room. The canteen has sent down some refreshments.' With a final glance back towards the interview room Fay shook her head. 'Tell me, Alice, where have all the good guys gone?'

'Here's where you're hiding.'

Alice smiled as Josh entered, then flushed as she realised Jeremy was directly behind him. There was the answer to Fay's question. Jeremy looked terrible, his grim face set with tension. He had been operating without a break since eight-thirty that morning, and Alice couldn't help but wonder how he was coping with his back. Alice poured the two men coffee while Fay piled a couple of plates with sandwiches.

'I needed that.' Never had a cup of coffee and a cheese and Vegemite sandwich been more welcome.

Fay grinned. 'Me, too.'

Finally a sense of normality was emerging. Though A and E was still full, no case now was particularly urgent and a welcome break was most definitely in order. Glancing at her watch, Alice gave a yelp. 'Heavens, it's three o'clock! What time are you due to finish, Fay?'

'Seven hours ago' came the rueful reply.

'You were on last night? Oh, Fay, you must be exhausted.'

'Actually, no. I'm quite sure if I went to bed now I wouldn't be able to sleep. If you knew how much time I've spent in meetings and mock-ups, preparing for this day, hoping it would never happen but trying to be sure that if it did we'd be able to cope. I think we did well.'

'I don't think we could have done any better,' Josh agreed. 'Everyone was marvellous, pitching in. What was the final casualty count?'

'Fifty. We saw twenty-eight, the rest went on to the Women's and Children's or were flown to the trauma centre.'

'How many fatalities?'

Fay let out a long breath. 'Eighteen. Unbelievable, isn't

it? People like you or I just setting off to work or school. How's it going up in Theatre?'

Josh didn't answer until he had demolished a couple of sandwiches. 'Bloody awful—literally. There's a couple down here for Theatre still, aren't there, Fay?'

'Yep. When do you think you'll be able to do them?'

Jeremy stood up, speaking for the first time. 'Now. Theatre four was just finishing up.' He turned to Josh. 'You finish off your food. I'll go and see them then meet you in Theatre, say in half an hour.'

'How did Kim Earl do?' Alice called as he made to leave. She watched as his departing back stiffened. Turning only slightly, not meeting her eyes, he replied curtly, 'Perforated bowel, lacerated liver. She had to spend an age in Recovery but she should be transferred to the ward soon. Really she needs to be in Intensive Care, but those beds were snapped up long ago.'

'What about her leg?' Alice persisted. 'How did it go?'

'It didn't.' And without any further explanation he left the room. Fay raised an eyebrow.

'How's Jeremy? He went as white as a sheet when the call came in—it must have brought all the memories of his accident back.'

Josh didn't look convinced. 'He's seen enough trauma since he's been back, but maybe you're right. There's definitely something wrong.' He shot a look in Alice's direction. 'He's not exactly been sociable the past few weeks, but today he's far worse. There's something up—not that it's stopped him performing miracles I hasten to add. That guy's a brilliant surgeon; he's like a machine down there.'

'And Linda?' Fay asked, smiling as she anticipated a smart crack from Josh.

'Loving every moment. It's the most excitement she's had in years.' He gave a lewd grin before adding, 'Of any kind. First time I've seen her wearing lipstick. She's hoping to make it onto the news. Oh, well, back to it.'

The short interlude over. They all stood up, marginally refreshed, ready to do battle again.

Fi looked as immaculately in control as ever, her soft voice relaying instructions and answering queries as the ward struggled to cope with a mass of acutely injured patients as well as the usual workload.

'I'm not even going to ask if you've got anything for me, Fi. But thanks for holding off on the pager; I've been suturing down in A and E.'

'I knew you wouldn't be hiding. First things first—have you eaten?'

'I have. How about you? And what are you doing here anyway? Aren't you supposed to be on nights again?'

'I still am. I came in when I heard the news on the radio. Luckily I'm coming back after days off so I'm pretty fresh. I'm heading off for a few hours' sleep and then I'll come on about eleven. Rowena is going to stay back late for me.'

'Sounds wonderful,' Alice said enviously. 'Maisy kept me up most of last night. Cripes! The one thing I haven't done is check up on Maisy. I'm just going to make the quickest call in history and then I'm all yours.'

Maisy, of course, was fine. 'We've been watching it on the news,' Mavis said. 'Jeremy rang as soon as he got to work, frantically asking what bus you would be on.'

'Oh.' It had never even entered her head that Jeremy would have been concerned she might have been involved, but there hadn't exactly been much time for introspection. 'I took the tram, Mavis. Have you spoken to him since?'

'No, but I didn't really expect to unless, of course, he hadn't seen you. I'm sure he's too busy to ring his old mum for a gossip.'

Alice laughed. 'You're hardly that, Mavis. He has been

really busy. He's been great,' she added, not even bothering to keep the note of admiration out of her voice.

'Well, if you see him, make sure he eats something. An army marches on its stomach.'

'I will,' Alice assured her, though with the breakfast Mavis had served him she was sure Jeremy had enough in reserve to last the month out.

Replacing the receiver, she turned to a waiting Fi. 'I'm all yours now.'

The experience Alice gained during that on call was like a condensed version of her full three months and would stand her in good stead for years to come. With the more senior doctors unavailable and tied up in Theatre, Alice made more decisions and judgements that day and felt the weight of a doctor's responsibility more heavily than she ever had before. And yet, far from being fazed by it, she actually revelled in it—well, most of it.

Doing a post-op check on Kim Earl, Alice felt an over-whelming sadness as she looked at the bed cradle holding the sheets and blankets away from the newly fashioned stump. Kim was too out of it to understand what had happened in Theatre but her red-eyed parents sitting stunned by the bedside told the whole story.

'How is she doing, Doctor?'

Alice looked up from the charts. 'She's stable. Her observations have been good since she returned to the ward. I've just got her haemoglobin level back from the lab and it's still low, despite the transfusion in Theatre, so I'm going to order her a further two units of packed cells. Has she spoken at all?'

'Just a few words,' Bill replied. 'Sister Fi said she wouldn't make much sense for a few hours with all the morphine and everything.'

'That's right,' Alice agreed. 'She's had a lot of sedation.'

'She asked where Ted was.' Bill said, his voice suddenly bitter. 'I didn't know what to say.'

Alice looked around. 'Has he gone to the canteen?'

'The pub, more like. He couldn't get out quick enough when Mr Khan told us about her leg.'

'You don't know that, Bill,' Sheila interjected. 'He's upset. We all are. Anyway, there's not much he could do right now.'

But Bill wasn't going to be brushed off. 'He could be here,' he retorted smartly. 'He could be here for her, loving her—that would be enough. Isn't that what it's supposed to be about?' His voice was thick with tears, and Alice listened as this bearded, tattooed man spoke with empathy and passion. 'Sure, sometimes you can't change what's happened—we'd all like a magic wand to make the past disappear—but that's not going to happen. He should stand by her now when she needs him most. What's Kim got now?' And then he broke down, his wide shoulder slumping as he put his head in his hands and cried. Cried for his beautiful daughter, and what she had lost.

'She's got you,' Alice said gently. 'And from where I'm standing, that's going to be more than enough.'

CHAPTER TEN

BY TWO a.m. exhaustion was definitely starting to set in. Drug chart, IV charts, a pile of sticky notes attached to her worksheet—they all blurred in front of Alice's eyes. She ached to see Jeremy, longed to see how he was coping, how the day's events had taken their toll on him.

'A and E just rang up. There's going to be a debriefing at nine for all staff who were on in A and E—they'll do the wards after. Will you go?' Fi asked.

Alice nodded without looking up. 'I guess. Hopefully they'll put on a decent spread.'

'You cynic, you. Don't you think it helps?'

Alice signed off the drug sheet she had written up, leant back in her chair and swivelled to face Fi. 'I'm not sure. I don't know if I'm into all this dissecting things, analysing how we felt, how we reacted. Sometimes I think it can only make things worse. I'll be far more interested in the medical debriefing when Samuel Donovan goes over all the data and histories. There's something to be gained from analysing that, but as for the rest of it…'

'Maybe you're right,' Fi said, stifling a yawn. 'Dragging it all up doesn't change what happened. I guess you either cope with it or you don't.'

The call bell interrupted the rather deep conversation, and as Fi got up to answer it Alice carried on with her work. She hadn't been strictly truthful with Fi. The only debrief she was interested in was with Jeremy. Knowing how he'd coped, how he'd reacted—with him she knew she could have shown her feelings.

'How's it all going?'

There Jeremy was, his tired eyes looking down at her. She ached for him to put his hands on her shoulders, to lean back against him and let him massage away the horrors of the day, but instead she carried on writing.

'Getting there. How about you?'

'Alice?' Fi appeared, looking a bit anxious. 'Kim Earl's awake. She's extremely distressed. It's just hit her that she's lost her leg. She's not due for any more analgesia yet but I wondered if a stat dose of Valium might be in order?'

Alice took the drug sheet Fi was holding. 'Maybe. I'd better have a look at her first, though.'

'I'll do it.'

Fi and Alice looked on in surprise as Jeremy took the drug sheet. 'Will you come with me, Alice? She might recognise you from when she came in. A familiar face can only help.'

Kim's sobs could be heard down the ward as they made their way to her bedside.

'Kim.' The fact he had used her first name was something of a rarity, but Kim was oblivious as she lay there, sobbing hysterically. 'Kim.' His voice was sharper in an attempt to gain a response. 'I'm Mr Foster, Jeremy Foster. I operated on you this morning.'

'Are you responsible for this?' Yanking back the sheet with strength born from hysteria and fear, Kim started to scream as she saw the dressing covering what used to be her leg. 'Are you the doctor that chopped it off?'

She raised her hand, so deranged with grief Alice knew she was about to hit him. A more pitiful sight she couldn't imagine—the battered body of Kim, her arms laden with drips and equipment, attempting to take a swipe at the man who had saved her. Thankfully Jeremy was too quick for her. Grabbing her wrist before it met its target, he held onto her. 'Kim, that's not going to help anyone.' His words somehow got through and, utterly defeated, Kim slumped back on the pillow, the fight seeping out of her, her tears agonising, rasping but rational now.

'Did you chop it off?' she asked again.

Alice watched as Jeremy stood there, his hand still holding Kim's arm, but gently now, more comforting than controlling. 'No, it wasn't me. It was the orthopaedic consultant who made the final decision. Kim, I don't know if what I'm going to say now will be any help, or if you can take it in, but I'm going to tell you anyway. The orthopaedic consultant didn't amputate your leg. It was already practically amputated by the time you arrived here.' Alice winced at the brutality of his words but stood quietly, trusting in his experience. 'Mr Khan did his absolute best to re-attach it, but he couldn't. Now, somewhere down the track you're going to wonder whether on a different day with a different doctor your leg might have been saved. Well, I'm going to answer that for you. Mr Khan did everything—and I mean *everything* he could with every piece of the latest technology available, and there was nothing that could be done.'

'What did you do?' Kim's eyes were searching Jeremy's.

'You had a large tear in your liver—which, I might add, was incredibly difficult to stop bleeding—and you also had a perforated bowel. At one point it looked as if you might have to have a colostomy fashioned. Do you know what that is?'

Kim nodded. 'Where you have to wear a bag on your stomach.'

'That's right—to get rid of effluent. Well, we didn't want to land too much on you—I reckoned losing your leg was enough to be going on with—so we soldiered on. There's no guarantees. The next few days will be telling but hopefully we've saved you from that. If it does become necessary, though, it will only be temporary.'

Amazingly Kim seemed to cope well with his honesty. 'Alice said you were good.'

His eyes left Kim for a moment and travelled over to hers. 'Did she now?' he said softly.

'I know I should be grateful, I know you've all saved my life, it's just… It was my *leg*. What am I going to be like? What's Ted going to think? He's never going to want me now.' She started to cry and Alice could hear the note of hysteria creeping in again.

'Of course he'll want you.'

'You haven't met him. He likes me to look good, and I like looking good—I'm a model for heaven's sake…' She glared at Jeremy as if he were responsible for all mankind. 'Would *you* want me? Be honest, would you still want me?'

It was the ranting of fear, of morphine and desperation, and Jeremy had absolutely no need to answer, no need to reduce this conversation to a personal level—he had never done so before. But Alice watched in stunned silence as his hand left Kim's arm and he held her hand. Pulling a chair over, he lowered himself slowly.

'Ah, now, that's a question. Well, put it this way—just over a year ago I'd have been out that door without a second glance. Hell, I've chucked girlfriends for having their hair too short.' Alice felt her breathing quicken. He had been so good—surely he wasn't going to mess it up now? 'And then, like you, I was involved in an accident. OK, I didn't lose my leg, but I just about lost my life. My brain was so swollen I was unconscious for three weeks. My left kidney was torn from the abdominal wall and had to be reattached, and my back was broken. I was the lucky one, but I tell you it didn't feel like it at the time. Lying in traction for three months, not knowing if I'd ever really walk again, having to be spoon-fed, learning to talk and walk and go to the bathroom all over again. But I did it, and so can you, because we are the lucky ones. And if you don't believe me, there's a mortuary full of kids and grown-ups tonight who I can only imagine would love to be in your shoes.'

'Or shoe.'

Alice had to stop herself from gasping out loud as she heard the attempt at a joke escape from Kim's pale lips.

'Kim, I was as vain as a man can be—probably a bit like your Ted. Looks mattered, money mattered, image mattered. Or so I thought. My accident served as a huge wake-up call and, although I never want to be there again, I'm glad it happened, and I can say that honestly. And with the right attitude maybe some day so can you. Stare at the ceiling for the next week, cry your eyes out and mourn what you've lost. You deserve that. Then get on with it. Pick yourself up, dust yourself off and get on with living—and while you're at it, decide who's coming on the journey with you. Because, let me tell you, with what you're about to go through you need the best, and if Ted's not up to the job then it's time to say goodbye.'

Kim's eyes were heavy now. The morphine was kicking in again. Her head lolled on the pillow. 'But you got there in the end? You're happy now?'

Hot tears were trickling down Alice's cheek. She hardly dared move to wipe them in case she broke the moment and, more pointedly, in case she didn't hear Jeremy's answer.

'Not yet,' he answered with a simple honesty that tore at Alice's heart. 'But I'm working on it, and at least I can sleep at night now.' Again he looked at Alice and gave a tiny smile. 'At least, most nights.'

Fi crept in, apologising for being so long. 'I got stuck with bed four. Here's the Valium.'

'It's all right, Fi,' Jeremy said, his voice a dry whisper. 'Looks like she's settled.'

'Good. Look, I'm sorry, Jeremy, Intensive Care just rang—they need you.'

I need you, Alice wanted to shout as he made his way out through the curtains, but he was already gone—and, anyway, she had left it too late. Suddenly it hit her with a certainty beyond question that she had let go of the best thing that had ever happened to her and Maisy.

Needing some fresh air and a moment to herself to take it all in, she headed outside to stand in the staff car park.

'Don't tell Dianne.'

Shocked that anyone else was out here, Alice swung around in time to see Josh hastily stubbing out a cigarette.

Alice managed a thin laugh. 'Have you got any left?' But her attempt at laughter caught in her throat and she started to cry in earnest. 'Oh, Josh, I've messed everything up.'

He was over in a flash. 'Hey, Alice, what are you talking about? There's nothing that can't be fixed.'

But she was inconsolable. 'We were so much in love. I know it could have worked but at the time I was so scared it just seemed so impossible.'

Josh's arms were comforting around her, like the big brother she had never had. 'I assume we're talking about our mutual boss, though technically that could also qualify as Linda. You're not about to give me a coronary, are you? I haven't got things that wrong?'

Thumping his chest as he held her, Alice laughed through her tears. 'Can't you be serious for once?'

'For you, Alice, yes.' And for once Josh was serious. Steadying her, he sat her down. Pulling a packet of cigarettes out of his pocket, he offered her one but she shook her head. 'Now, how about you tell me about it, and we'll see if there's anything that can be done?'

'I don't really know how it started,' Alice began. 'I knew all about him—his reputation, I mean—and I never even considered he'd like me. Well, not that way. But as the days went on, we just...well, you know. I had a confrontation with Marcus, Jeremy was there, it ended up in bed—not straight away,' she added hastily, glancing over to check Josh's reaction, but he stood there non-judgementally, puffing away. 'Then the pregnancy really took a dive. I know it wasn't his fault but I started to blame him. Then once Maisy came along…' she started to cry in earnest '…I just couldn't believe he could still want me. I was feeling pretty low, I can't really explain it, then Linda came to visit.'

'To brighten up your day.'

It was the first time Josh had interrupted.

'Josh, she didn't mean to hurt me. She told me about her friend.'

'Linda hasn't got any friends.'

'Are you going to listen?'

Josh threw his butt onto the ground and stepped on it, his jaw tensing as she continued. 'She was really nice. She didn't know everything that had gone on. She told me about her friend, another single parent, and how it had been for her. Up in front of the family law courts, trying to explain away her latest boyfriend and fighting for custody of her own child. Marcus is getting married to a kindergarten teacher, for heaven's sake. What chance would I have? Anyway, Linda let it slip—and it *was* an accident, Josh— that they weren't on call that night, although Jeremy had told me he was. I even rang the switchboard to confirm it. Linda said he was up to his old tricks, pulling everyone in sight, saying anything to get them into bed.'

'And you believed her?' Josh's voice was deadly quiet.

'She wasn't to know what had gone on.'

Josh stood up then, his eyes blazing. It was the first time ever Alice had seen him angry. 'Of course she knew. I told you never to trust her. She knew, Alice, we all knew.'

'But how?' she begged, utterly bewildered.

'Linda and I were walking to work the day you were

admitted with Maisy, and you and Jeremy were in his car. As for the mix-up with the on-call, Jeremy specifically swapped with Mr Taylor so he could be there for you on your first night home with Maisy. You know Switchboard only goes by the roster in front of them.'

'Then when she came to see me…' Suddenly the jigsaw was beginning to fall into place.

'She was fully prepared to do a hatchet job, and the state you were in unfortunately made it all too easy. Alice, you've been so down on yourself, so wrapped up in doing things right for Maisy, you've failed to see how good Jeremy really is. Don't you think you'd look better in the family courts—and it's doubtful that it will ever come to that—in a happy stable relationship with a guy who loves you and who's been through it all with you? And, as much as Linda goes on that Jeremy would sleep with anyone, she conveniently forgets she was someone he'd rejected.

'I never told you this, it never really seemed relevant. A few nights before Jeremy had his accident there was a surgeons' ball. Linda made a big play for him. I lied today—it was the second time I've seen her wearing lipstick. It was awful. She had too much to drink. I know Jeremy can be a bastard at times but he tried to let her down gently. She just wouldn't take the hint. It got really embarrassing. In the end he turned around and in that dry snobby voice he's perfected so well he said to her, "Madam, please, control yourself." Everyone cracked up laughing, and in fairness to Jeremy it was entirely merited, but it was awful just the same. Linda turned to stone. She didn't see him again till the day he came back, the day you started.'

Alice raked her fingers through her limp hair. 'Oh, poor Linda, no wonder she hates me. It must have been awful for her, seeing that Jeremy fancied me.'

'He doesn't fancy you, Alice, he *loves* you. All that poor guy has ever done is love you. We've all got a past—me,

Jeremy, and even you. Hell, yours is two months old and sprouting teeth. We can't change our pasts but there's a hell of a lot we can all do about our future.'

She clutched her fists to her head, battling with the self-directed anger inside. 'What if I've left it too late?' she wailed. 'What can I say to him now, after the way I've been?'

'I'm sure you'll think of something. At the end of the day you could always resort to bit of honesty.' A glint appeared in Josh's eyes. 'But do us a favour, Alice, make it soon, for all our sakes. I'm starting to hope that I'm rostered for Theatre with Linda! It's enough to make a guy question his own sexuality.'

But 'soon' would have to wait. There were patients waiting, and later, as the sun rose and the curtains were drawn back on the wards for the six a.m. obs, Jeremy was called to Theatre and Alice was stuck on the wards. She didn't see him again until the ward round, her longing intensified as she saw the dark circles under his beautiful blue eyes, the dark blond stubble on his strong chin. That day would go down in history, Fi remarked, as the first ward round without Jeremy in a suit.

It would go down in history for other reasons as well. Arriving breathless at the apartment, Alice collided with Mavis on her way to the child health centre.

'You made it.'

'Only just. How has she been?'

Mavis gazed fondly down at the baby. 'She's been golden. You'd better take a brolly; the radio said there was a chance of rain.'

Alice looked up at the blue sky. 'They never get it right.'

'Got your gumboots all packed?' June asked as she weighed Maisy. 'I'll give you a letter to take to your new maternal and child health nurse.' She tutted a couple of times. 'Silly me, you won't have one of them where you're off to. I'd better address it to your new GP. Are you starting to get excited?' she asked, handing back Maisy.

'I'm not sure,' Alice mumbled, horrified at the thought of leaving for the country but not yet ready to burn her bridges.

June gave her a questioning look but didn't push. 'Well, we'd better fill in Maisy's progress book. You think you'll never forget the milestones, but by the time you've had a couple more it all starts to blur a bit.' She opened the yellow folder that contained Maisy's details—her length, her weight, her head circumference. Turning to the back, she started to ask Alice some questions.

'When did she start to follow your face with her eyes?'

Alice thought for a moment. 'After a couple of weeks.'

'Good.' June filled in the blank. 'How about her reaction to sound, a door banging perhaps or a hand clap. Does it startle Maisy?'

Alice nodded. 'Absolutely. There's rather a lot of door banging in the flat upstairs, unfortunately.'

'And how about her first smile?'

Alice gave a soft laugh. 'Well, Jeremy, my...' she hesitated '...my friend. He swears she smiled at him the day she was born, but I'd be more inclined to say since she was about four or five weeks old.'

June looked up from the book, pulling off her glasses, her bossy, no-nonsense exterior seeming to vanish for a moment. 'Then I'd say Jeremy's a lucky man. Their first smile is always something special, he was lucky to witness it. However, we'll write five weeks in the book, shall we?' Pulling on her glasses again, she picked up her pen.

It was a short, almost inconsequential conversation, but to Alice it was a revelation. Jeremy had sworn he'd seen Maisy's first smile, and there would be other firsts too that he would witness if only she would let him. Maisy and Jeremy had already shared so much. So he wasn't her biological father—he was the one who had been there when it had mattered, who had held her when she was born, showed her the moon and the stars.'

'Right, then, I'd better do this letter.'

Alice stood up, grabbing Maisy's nappy bag. 'June, there's somewhere I have to be. Look, could you hold off on the letter for now? I'll give you a call later in the week.' She paused. 'If I still need it.'

June gave her a wide smile. 'Or to make a further appointment. Good luck, Alice.'

Mavis had been right. Melbourne was known for its four seasons in one day. The blue sky had darkened and huge raindrops were starting to pelt from the dark grey sky, gaining in momentum. They would get drenched. About to turn back into the centre to ring for a taxi, she caught sight of a silver car. For a second her heart seemed to stop for there was Jeremy, waiting for her, ready to help her just as he always had been. Catching her eye, he ran out of the car. Throwing his coat over Maisy's carrycot, he ran with her the short distance to his car.

'Get in. I'll take care of Maisy.'

As she sat there in the warmth, watching as he diligently strapped her baby in, Alice realised that she wasn't really surprised to see him. After all, hadn't he always been there for them both when he was needed?

Slipping into the car beside her, he gave her a tired, cautious smile. 'Mum said you'd gone out without an umbrella, so I thought I'd better come when it started raining. He looked over at Maisy. 'How did she go?'

'She's put on another 300 grams.'

'That's good.' He looked utterly spent. He should have been in a bath, soaking away the pain and horrors of the last twenty-four hours, but instead he managed to turn and give Maisy a tender smile. 'You're catching up fast, aren't you, little lady?' As he reached forward to turn on the heater Alice's hand caught his.

'Thank you, Jeremy, for being there.'

'No problem. I didn't want her getting wet.'

'I mean for always being there, not just today.' She stared at her hand coiled tightly around his and she could feel his searching eyes questioning her movement, sense his uncertainty as to her sudden change. 'What would you say if I told you that saying goodbye to you was the biggest mistake of my life?'

For what seemed like an eternity he didn't answer, his eyes never for a second leaving her face. 'I'd be inclined to agree with you.'

'And what would you say if I told you I don't want to go to the country. I want to be here with you.' A sob escaped her lips as she finally admitted the truth.

'Hey, Alice.' He turned to face her. Gently disengaging is hand, he cupped her face with his palms. 'You don't have to stay here to have me. If you think things will be better for Maisy in the country then that's where we'll go.'

In stunned wonder she gazed at him through her tears. 'You'd do that for us? You'd give up your job?'

'In an instant. Alice, forget what I said about never living in a tent. If that's what it will take to keep you two, I'd pack up my backpack here and now. Admittedly I'd have to buy one first.'

She managed the tiniest laugh, then the tears came again. 'You don't have to leave your job. I only wanted to go to the country to give Maisy some security. I can't believe you'd do all this for me when I've been so awful, so doubting. How can you still love me?'

'Because I do, and that's all you need to know. Alice, you've had the most terrible time, you've been through so much. You were right to be doubtful—even I shudder at my past, and at the end of the day you had Maisy to think of. I know you had to be sure, and though I'm not going to deny it hurt I can understand it. You're a mother now, you had to put your child first—if anything I love you all the more for it.'

His lips met hers, his chin rough and unshaven scratching against her tears-soaked cheeks, his lips warm and full, quieting the sobs from her trembling mouth. And as Maisy drifted off to dream milky dreams he kissed Alice slowly and swore he'd never let her go again.

Finally, when the rain had stopped and the windows had long since misted over, he started the engine. Turning, he smiled, all traces of tiredness gone now. 'Where to, ladies?'

She glanced into the back, where Maisy slept on peacefully, and then her gaze drifted to Jeremy, the other love of her life, and Alice knew without a shadow of doubt that she was the luckiest woman alive. 'Take us home, Jeremy,' she said softly. 'Take us home.'

EPILOGUE

ALICE knew she should have been resting, but with the apartment to herself for once she had taken the opportunity of filling yet another photo album and making entries in Maisy's milestone book. Hearing the key in the lock, she let her eyes linger for a second longer on Maisy's adoption certificate, which certified Jeremy as her father. No matter how many times she gazed at the simple piece of paper, taking pride of place in Maisy's 'first year' book, it never failed to move her.

'Feeling better?' Jeremy asked as he staggered through the door, clutching a sleeping Maisy and the never-ending paraphernalia that seemed to accompany her.

'Much. I just needed a couple of hours. A and E was really busy last night.'

'Well, forget about work for now. Neither of us have to be back until Monday.'

He was right. The whole weekend lay before them and Alice stretched luxuriously on the bed. 'Was it a good party?'

Jeremy grinned. 'Well, not as wild as some I've been to, but it was certainly as noisy. Maisy had a ball. I'd better put her down, she's out of it.'

'How were the twins?' Alice asked as he returned. 'It's hard to believe that they're one already.'

'You'd better believe it. They're as cheeky and corrupt as their father. I caught Eamon stuffing ice-cream cake into poor little Maisy.'

Alice didn't believe him for a moment, knowing Jeremy was more than likely to have been the culprit there.

'Here, I got you a present.' He thrust a brown paper bag onto the bed. 'I'm becoming quite a celebrity at the local chemist. I think they officially class me as a "sensitive guy" now. How much more caring can you get—buying a pregnancy test kit with Maisy in a carry sling? I shall have to grow a beard and start eating lentils.' He was rambling now, unsure of her reaction.

So he'd noticed she'd missed her period! Opening the bag in silence, Alice finally found her voice. 'Actually, Jeremy, I beat you to it.' Padding through to the *en suite* bathroom, she handed him the indicator. 'I was going to tell you this evening.'

He didn't say anything for a moment, just stared at the tiny faint line which meant they were going to have another baby. 'We'll have two babies under two,' she said with a slight tremble in her voice. 'I'm going to get huge again.'

'Alice!' The rapture in Jeremy's voice said it all. 'Two babies will be wonderful, and Mum will always help out. And as for your size…as if that's going to worry me. You were huge when I met you!' Picking her up in his arms, he carried her the short distance to the bed. 'Now, young lady, it's back to bed with you. You should take the opportunity while Maisy's asleep.'

'But I'm not tired…' Alice protested.

Placing her gently down, he climbed on the bed beside her and kissed her slowly, deeply, leaving her in no doubt he was as delighted with the news as she was. 'That's good,' he said, coming up for air. 'Who said anything about sleeping?'

EMERGENCY: MOTHER WANTED

by

Sarah Morgan

PROLOGUE

'SAY that name again?'

Zach Jordan paused with a coffee-mug halfway to his lips, his blue eyes suddenly watchful.

'Which name?' His colleague Sean Nicholson, the senior consultant in the accident and emergency department, glanced down at the list he'd been reading aloud. 'Um…Keely Thompson?'

Keely…

Zach put his coffee-mug back on the table, untouched.

'What's the matter? Do you know her?' Sean frowned and Zach's eyes narrowed as he did the calculation in his head. Could it be her? Had that much time passed? Could she really be one of the new senior house officers?

'I think I might do,' he said finally. 'You interviewed her—can you remember what she looked like?'

Sean nodded and tossed the file of papers he was holding onto the table. 'I certainly can. Small and delicate, short blonde hair…a bit urchin like—massive blue eyes, the biggest smile I've ever seen…' He broke off and gave an appreciative grin. 'In fact, I have to admit that she was absolutely gorgeous, but don't tell Ally I said that.'

Zach gave an absent smile, knowing that Sean adored his pretty wife and their three children. 'Bouncy? Bubbly personality?'

'That's her.' Sean picked up his coffee and took a sip. 'She's the daughter of *the* Professor Thompson from St Mark's. I suppose we should count ourselves lucky she's here. With that sort of pedigree I don't expect she'll be

5

hanging around the Lake District for long. She'll be aiming for a job in one of the hot seats of academic learning.'

Would she? Zach gave a slight frown. That didn't seem like the Keely he'd known as a child. She'd been gentle and caring and totally lacking in ambition. In fact, there had been times when he'd wondered how on earth the Prof had managed to produce a child like Keely—she was so very different from the rest of them. But if she was following in the family footsteps and carving a high-profile career for herself then she'd obviously changed.

He sat back in his chair, wondering what she'd be like now. Last time he'd seen her she'd been a typical teenager, worrying about school and arguing with her mother. It was pretty hard to accept that she'd become a fully qualified doctor.

Sean was looking at him curiously. 'So how do you know her?'

'I trained with her older brother and sister.' Zach leaned forward and retrieved his coffee. 'They're twins. And one of my first surgical jobs was with the Prof. I used to go and stay with them sometimes. They had this fabulous house in the Cotswolds. That was where I met Keely.'

'She was the youngest?'

'Yes.' Zach gave a slow nod. 'The baby of the family. I wonder what she's doing up here in the Lake District?' If she was so ambitious, why hadn't she stayed in London? 'Can I look at her CV?'

He held out a hand and Sean passed it over. 'It's pretty impressive. Top grades all the way through.'

Zach studied it carefully. 'So did she say why she wanted to come here?' The hospital had a good reputation but it was hardly the most high profile in the country. Why hadn't she stayed in London?

Sean gave a shrug. 'I didn't really ask her that. Why

shouldn't she come here? It's a great place. We love it. Why shouldn't other people?'

'It is a great place,' Zach agreed, frowning thoughtfully. 'But it's hardly the best springboard for a fast-track medical career.'

'You seem to know rather a lot about her.' Sean gave him a keen look. 'Did you have an affair with her?'

Zach choked on his coffee. 'For goodness' sake, Sean! She was sixteen years old and I was twenty-four! What sort of man do you think I am?'

Sean grinned. 'A woman's dream—if the gossip is to be believed. According to the nurses, you're now top of the list of the most eligible bachelors in Cumbria.'

'Oh, for Pete's sake, Sean!' Zach shot him an impatient look and put his mug down on the table with a thump. 'Since when did you start listening to women's gossip?'

'Since I lived with three of them,' Sean said ruefully. 'I'm decidedly outnumbered in my home and work life so I've decided to give in gracefully and adopt some of their habits.'

'Well, whatever gossip says, rest assured that I have more self-control and decency than to seduce sixteen-year-olds.' Zach was careful not to reveal the slight uneasiness Sean's words had prompted.

If it had been left to little Keely, they most certainly *would* have had an affair. She'd had a massive teenage crush on him.

A ghost of a smile hovered around his firm mouth as he remembered the night she'd proposed to him. Turning her down without hurting her fragile ego had been one of the hardest experiences of his adult life.

What would she be like now? And would she have recovered from her teenage crush on him? If she hadn't then they were going to be in trouble.

Zach gave a short laugh, picked up the mug and finished

his coffee. Of course she would have recovered. That was years ago, for goodness' sake, and he hadn't seen her since that night. He'd kept away—more for her sake than his. He'd decided that the sooner he removed himself from her life, the sooner she'd get over him and start fancying boys her own age. Which was probably what she'd been doing ever since.

'So come on, Mr Eligible Bachelor, bring me up to date.' Sean leaned back in his chair, a slow smile spreading across his face. 'Who's the lucky woman at the moment?'

'I thought you were one of the few people I could trust not to interfere with my love life,' Zach growled, irritation sizzling through his veins. This was one topic of conversation guaranteed to ruin his day. 'I have enough of it from your wife and the nurses in this department, without getting it from you, too.'

Sean looked at him calmly. 'Ally thinks it's time you got married.'

Zach closed his eyes and counted to ten. He loved Sean's wife dearly but he wished she'd stop trying to arrange his life. 'For the record, I am perfectly satisfied with my love life.'

'From what I've heard, you don't have a love life,' Sean said bluntly, 'just a sex life.'

'And since when was that any of your business?' Zach's blue eyes flashed a warning and Sean must have heard the threatening note in his voice because he gave a lopsided smile and lifted a hand.

'All right, all right. Calm down. I'm just saying that sooner or later you're going to have to take a risk and get back into a proper relationship.'

Sean was as direct as ever and Zach felt his hackles rise. Why did everyone feel they knew what was best for him?

'I have no intention of doing anything of the sort. I like my life as it is.'

There was a slight pause. 'It wasn't your life I was thinking of,' Sean said gruffly, not quite meeting his eyes. 'It was Phoebe's.'

Zach swore under his breath and stood up suddenly, the chair scraping on the floor as he pushed it away. 'Phoebe is fine.'

'Zach, she's not even three years old,' Sean said quietly. 'She needs a mother.'

Zach closed his eyes and the breath hissed through his teeth. Damn. Why did it still hurt so much? *Why?* It had been more than a year now. Were his battered emotions ever going to recover?

Sean gave a sigh and rubbed his forehead with long fingers. 'Look, tell me if I'm out of line, but—'

'You're out of line,' Zach said coldly, dropping his empty mug into the washing-up bowl. 'And, please, tell Ally I don't need her advice on my love life. And I certainly don't intend to get married again. There are some things you only do once in a lifetime.'

Sean studied his coffee. 'You say that now because you don't think you'll ever meet anyone again, but you will. Perhaps sooner than you think.'

Zach rolled his eyes. 'And I suppose this is the part where you tell me that you and Ally are having some people to dinner and I'm the available single man?'

Sean shook his head and grinned. 'I know when I'm beaten. I'm just going to let nature take its course. Once you meet Keely I'm sure you'll revise your opinion on romance.'

'Keely?' Zach blinked, thrown by the change of subject. 'What on earth has she got to do with this? Keely's a child, Sean.'

Why were they talking about Keely all of a sudden?

'A *child*?' Sean lifted an eyebrow and a ghost of a smile played around his mouth. 'She might have been a child when you last saw her but, believe me, that was no child that I interviewed. Your ''child'' has grown into a woman. And a very beautiful woman.'

Zach scowled. 'You shouldn't be making sexist comments about the doctors who are coming to work for you.'

'I wouldn't dream of making a sexist comment when I'm working,' Sean defended himself smoothly, 'but you and I are off duty at the moment and as your friend I'm just telling you that your little Keely is a knockout. Sweet, sexy and honest as the day is long.'

'Then I'm sure she'll make some lucky man very happy,' Zach said shortly, 'but it isn't going to be me.'

Firstly, whatever Sean said to the contrary, he couldn't think of Keely as anything other than a child and, secondly, he knew he would never, ever find another woman he wanted to marry. How could he after Catherine?

CHAPTER ONE

WHAT *had she done to deserve it?*

Keely Thompson stared in disbelief at the man standing at the front of the lecture theatre.

She always helped old ladies across the road, she fed the birds in winter, she donated time and money to a charity for the homeless, she never told lies and she rang her mother regularly.

All in all she was a pretty responsible citizen and she definitely—*most definitely*—didn't deserve to bump into Zach Jordan again. Which proved that people didn't always get what they deserved, she thought gloomily, shrinking down in her seat and staring at her notepad. They got what they were given, and she'd been given Zach Jordan. Out of the blue, with no warning, and as her boss. Well, not exactly as her boss, but as a senior colleague, which was almost as bad.

When he'd walked through that door to deliver the lecture she'd felt as though she'd been hit by an express train. She'd been expecting one of the junior consultants from the accident and emergency department. She certainly hadn't expected Zach.

But it *was* Zach. And as it looked as though she was going to be a senior house officer in the same department as him, she had to come to terms with the fact that he was going to be under her nose. On a daily basis.

She stifled a groan and leaned her forehead on her hand so that he wouldn't be able to see her face.

So much for her escape plan. She'd chosen the Lake District because it was far away from home. And, most

11

importantly, far away from people who knew her family. She'd needed space. Space and time. Time to think about what she really wanted to do with her life. She hadn't known that Zach would be here.

Zach, who knew her family almost as well as she did, and on top of that had been present, if not responsible, for the single most humiliating moment of her life. She'd been sixteen and he'd been twenty-four...

What was she going to say to him? How on earth did you greet someone you used to have a massive teenage crush on and hadn't seen for eight years?

She moved her head slightly and peeped cautiously at the tall, broad-shouldered man standing at the front of the lecture theatre, totally at ease in front of his audience, his presentation style confident and relaxed.

Satisfied that he wasn't looking in her direction, Keely rested her chin in her palm and allowed herself the luxury of one long look at him. Over the years she'd decided that what she'd felt for Zachary Jordan had just been part of a teenage fantasy, but looking at him now all she could think was that she'd had impeccable taste when she was younger.

The man was lethally attractive. Smooth dark hair swept back from his forehead, sexy blue eyes, a permanently darkened jaw and a body that made women drool. Zach Jordan was a real man in every sense of the word and at sixteen his looks had left her breathless. No other member of the opposite sex had affected her in the same way. She'd spent every minute of every day dreaming about how it would feel to be kissed by him.

He was the stuff of fantasies...

Obviously she wasn't the only one who thought so if the soft sigh from the female doctor sitting next to her was anything to go by.

'Wow! I thought doctors only looked like that in

American movies. Tell me I'm not going to be working with him every day. I'll never be able to concentrate. I'm Fiona, by the way.'

Keely quickly introduced herself and picked up her pen. She wouldn't be able to concentrate either.

She shrank further into her seat as she remembered the way she'd behaved towards him as a teenager. The things she'd said to him. Like the night she'd proposed—

She suppressed a whimper of horror as she recalled that night. How *totally* humiliating. How on earth was she going to convince him that she wasn't a dippy teenager any more?

At least she *looked* different. Her blonde hair was shorter and somewhere along the road she'd grown a chest. And she was twenty-four now, for goodness' sake. Hardly the child who'd thrown herself at him all those years before. Maybe he would have forgotten all about it.

Staring at Zach was making her insides feel strange so she stared down at her lined pad instead and decided that the thing to do was to concentrate on making notes. It was certainly a better alternative than looking at Zach's broad shoulders—not that it was guaranteed to keep her mind on her work. There had been at least four occasions at school when she'd been given detention for scribbling 'Keely loves Zach' all over her notebook instead of paying attention.

Keely loves Zach…

Only she hadn't loved Zach, she told herself firmly, tapping her pen on the page as if to emphasise the point to herself. Not really. She'd just been a vulnerable, impressionable teenager and he'd been drop-dead gorgeous and very kind to her. A recipe for emotional disaster when you were sixteen.

She gave herself a mental shake and a sharp talking-to. She didn't have anything to worry about. She was a completely different person now. A grown woman and a fully qualified doctor about to take up her position as casualty officer in the accident and emergency department. She was long past the age of suffering from childish crushes. All she had to do was keep their relationship professional and prove to him that she was an excellent doctor.

With a determined expression on her delicate features she concentrated hard on that deep, sexy voice, making notes as he spoke about the medico-legal aspects of working in the A and E department, the importance of good note-taking and liaison with GPs.

He was a good speaker, using just enough humour to keep their attention and just enough drama to make his talk interesting. Everyone was paying attention. Especially the women.

'He's unbelievable. I don't think I can work next to that man every day without throwing myself at him,' Fiona said dreamily, and Keely gave a wry smile. If her brother and sister were to be believed, women had been making fools of themselves over Zach since the minute he'd arrived at medical school, and probably long before that.

And hadn't she done exactly the same thing herself?

With a sigh her mouth softened into a smile and she remembered the first time her brother had brought Zach home to stay.

It had been love at first sight. On her part at least. Not on Zach's, of course. By all accounts he'd been used to cool, sophisticated women, and she'd been a smiley, chatty schoolgirl. He wouldn't have even *thought* of her in those terms. But still they'd been friends. And maybe they could be friends again—

She pulled herself together to find everyone in the lecture theatre staring at her expectantly.

'Dr Thompson?'

Oh, help! He'd asked her a question and she'd missed

it. She'd been so intent on planning how to make him see her as a mature, qualified doctor that she hadn't been listening.

Her face heated and her palms were suddenly sweaty. So much for wanting him to take her seriously.

'I asked you to tell us where you worked last, Dr Thompson.' He repeated the question calmly and she swallowed.

'Medical,' she said breathlessly, glancing round with a self-conscious smile, relieved when he turned his attention to another of the new SHOs.

'I bet he's fantastic in bed,' Fiona said in an undertone. 'Look at those shoulders, those muscles, those legs—I feel faint just thinking about it.'

Keely felt faint, too, but for different reasons. This was never going to work. Zach was going to treat her the same way everyone else back in London had. As just another member of the Thompson clan, instead of as an individual. All the usual pressures would be there, the expectations— only with Zach it would be even worse because he was bound to remember her as a scatty teenager.

Was he going to think she wasn't up to the job?

With a long sigh she stared hard at her pad. Unlike her companion, she didn't want to look at Zach's body. She already knew how good it looked and the only way she was going to be able to work with Zach was if she *didn't* look at his body.

Suddenly she realised that everyone was standing up and shuffling papers. The lecture was over. It was time to start work. And Zach Jordan was walking towards her…

She stood up and clutched her notepad to her chest, aware that her new colleagues were melting discreetly into the background.

'Hello, Keely.' The tone of his deep voice told her immediately that he knew exactly who she was and she felt hideously self-conscious. What on earth should she say? *Sorry I wasn't listening when you asked me a question. Sorry I proposed to you last time I saw you.*

'Hello, Dr Jordan—I mean Mr Jordan.' She'd suddenly remembered that he was a surgeon and corrected herself hastily.

A smile touched his mouth. 'Just Zach will do fine,' he murmured. 'We're very informal in A and E.'

'Right—well, what a surprise to see you.' She stroked a strand of blonde hair behind her ear and smiled brightly, wondering what it was about those blue eyes that made her revert to a stammering teenager. 'I had no idea that you'd be working here.'

'And is that a problem?' He gave a quizzical smile which made her knees feel weak and her heart misbehave.

'Problem?' Her voice squeaked slightly and she cleared her throat. 'No—of course it's not a problem. Why would it be a problem?'

She could think of a hundred reasons, starting with the physical effect he had on her. Just being in the same room as him brought her close to physiological meltdown.

'So what are you doing here?' He tilted his head speculatively. 'You're a long way from home, Keely Thompson.'

That had been the general idea when she'd chosen the Lake District.

'After six years in London I needed a change,' she said quickly, 'and I love mountains.'

She flushed under his steady regard, remembering that he'd always been perceptive. Could he read her mind? Did he know the real reason she was here? Had he guessed that she'd needed some space to make her own decisions, away from the influence of her family?

'Right.' He continued to watch her thoughtfully. 'And how are Prof and the twins?'

The inevitable question.

'Oh, you know,' Keely pinned a smile on her face, her response automatic. 'Fine. They're fine. Doing very well as usual.'

'I lost touch with Stephen,' Zach confessed, his blue eyes disconcertingly sharp as he looked at her. 'Doubtless he's made it to the top?'

Of course. Where else was there for her family?

'Professor of Immunology,' Keely muttered, still managing to maintain the smile. Just.

'And Eleanor?'

'Consultant Oncologist in London.' The smile was slipping but he didn't seem to notice.

'And the Prof? Is he retired?'

'Dad?' Keely's cheek muscles were aching and she gave up smiling. 'Oh, come on, Zach! Dad will never retire. His whole life revolves round being a professor.'

'I suppose it does.' Zach's voice was suddenly soft. 'And what about you, Keely? What's your chosen career path?'

Did she tell him the truth? That she didn't know? That the whole question of her future was driving her mad—

No, of course she couldn't tell him that! Zach was exactly like the other members of her family—clever, ambitious and totally driven. A born leader who had probably never known a moment of self doubt in his life. He was hardly likely to understand or sympathise with her plight, would he? She could hardly confess that she wasn't entirely sure what she wanted to do with her career—could hardly confide that she wasn't totally enchanted at the prospect of a career as a hospital doctor.

'Well, I'm doing six months of A and E before I commit myself,' she said finally, trying to sound suitably enthusiastic, 'but I'm thinking of doing cardiology. It's always fascinated me and we haven't got a cardiologist in the family.'

'I see.' He spoke quietly, his expression thoughtful, and for a moment she wondered whether he'd guessed that she wasn't being entirely honest.

'And do you think you'll enjoy A and E?'

She swallowed. Did he think she wasn't up to it? He'd already said he hadn't got used to the fact that she'd grown up.

'I know I'll love it,' she said firmly.

'Right.' Those blue eyes fixed on hers a moment longer. 'Well, if you have any problems—any worries at all—I want you to come to me.'

Oh, bother, he definitely didn't think she was up to it.

'I'll be just fine,' she said, a determined expression on her face. 'I'm really looking forward to A and E. It's going to be brilliant. I know I'll love it.'

He seemed amused by her enthusiastic outburst. 'It's nice to see you haven't changed.'

Well! Talk about tactless! Keely gaped at him. Did the man have problems with his eyesight?

'Of course I've changed!' She hoped that none of her new colleagues were listening to this conversation. How embarrassing! Being told she hadn't changed since she was sixteen was hardly flattering. 'Last time you saw me I had a flat chest, long hair and spots.'

He threw his head back and laughed. 'Actually, I wasn't talking about your physical appearance, I was talking about your personality. You always were smiley and good-natured.' His grin faded. 'I just hope you don't find A and E too stressful.'

'Zach, stop treating me like a child!' Keely was still put out by the fact that he didn't think she'd changed. She liked to think of herself as a cool cat. He made her sound more like a fluffy kitten. 'Of course I won't find it too stressful. I'm a doctor now! I'm not some child that needs to be nurtured.'

'I know that.' His voice was a slow drawl and he smiled again, obviously amused by her defensiveness. 'It's just going to take me a bit of time to get used to the idea.'

Oh, great. Then this was going to be every bit as bad as she'd feared when she'd first seen him stride into the lecture theatre.

She clutched her notepad harder and changed the subject. 'So, how long have you been working here?'

'In this department? Two years. I've been a consultant for a year.'

He was young for the post but, then, that was no surprise. He was every bit as bright as her siblings. In fact, she remembered Stephen sulking because Zach had beaten him in several exams.

'Well...' She broke off and cleared her throat. 'I don't suppose we'll see that much of each other, will we? I mean, there are four consultants in the department.'

'True.' His eyes gleamed. 'But we each work with three SHOs and you're on my team. We'll see plenty of each other, Keely.'

Her heart tumbled in her chest. How was she going to work with him every day without making a fool of herself? Just five minutes in his company had been enough to show her that the man still had a powerful effect on her. And what did *he* think of *her*? He'd admitted that he needed time to get used to the idea she was grown up. Did he think of her as the schoolgirl who'd proposed to him all those years ago?

She chewed her lower lip and decided she had to get things into the open.

'Listen, Zach...' She coloured furiously and glanced around quickly to check that no one was listening. 'About what happened when I was sixteen...'

His face was impassive but she thought she detected a brief twinkle in his eyes.

'I don't remember anything happening when you were sixteen.'

He was turning a blind eye to the fact that she'd made a total fool of herself over him.

'You're very kind, but I *want* to apologise. I've wanted to for a long time.' She pressed on, determined to have her say. She couldn't work with him otherwise.

'There's really nothing to apologise for,' he said quietly, and she flushed.

'How can you say that when I—when I—' She broke off, totally swamped with embarrassment, and his face was unbelievably gentle.

'Had a crush on me? There's nothing to apologise for, Keely. These things happen.'

'Are you sure?' She looked up at him anxiously. 'You're not cross? You don't think it's going to be a problem between us?'

One dark eyebrow lifted. 'Why should it be? Unless you're planning to develop another wild crush on me.'

She was beginning to think it was entirely possible but she managed a laugh that she hoped sounded convincing.

'Goodness, no! I think I'm a bit beyond childish crushes now, Zach.'

And even if she wasn't, there was no way he was going to find out about it this time!

His eyes locked with hers. 'Good. Well, in that case we're not going to have a problem, and we won't mention it again.' He held out his hand. 'Welcome to A and E, Dr Thompson.'

With that he turned on his heel and left the room, leaving her staring after him. If he'd been handsome at twenty-four—and he certainly had been—then at thirty-two he was devastating.

Not that she was going to think about him in those terms, she told herself hastily. She had made a complete fool of herself over Zach all those years ago and once in a lifetime was more than enough for anyone. This time she was keeping a strict control over her hormones.

She was *not* going to fall in love with Zach Jordan again…

Zach walked out of the lecture theatre and made his way back to the A and E department, his thoughts full of Keely.

He still couldn't believe it was her.

Last time he'd seen her she'd been little more than a child—and a very engaging child at that. He'd never been able to understand how her family had managed to produce a child like Keely. She was so totally different from the rest of them. Eleanor and Stephen were both like their parents—academic, emotionally reserved and totally driven.

But Keely… Zach gave a slight smile as he thought of how she'd been—Keely was warm, affectionate and slightly scatty. Unfortunately those qualities hadn't been valued enough by her family and he remembered several occasions when Eleanor and Stephen had given their little sister a hard time.

He frowned as he pushed open his office door and put the slides from his lecture back in the cupboard. But somewhere along the line she'd obviously changed if her career plans were anything to go by. Funny really. He wouldn't have thought she was the sort to be happy in a high-powered hospital career. But he was obviously wrong.

He flicked on his computer, checked his messages and then glanced out of the window towards the mountains. This late in January the fells were always topped with snow and the views from the hospital were breathtaking. He loved it here, but would Keely?

Zach frowned slightly as he remembered her breathless enthusiasm for her new job, her transparent embarrassment at seeing him again and her sweet concern that he'd still see her as a child.

Was she right?

Was that how he saw her?

To be honest, he wasn't really sure. Certainly it was hard to imagine her as a doctor and, frankly, he was distinctly uncomfortable about exposing her to some of the horrors that they saw in A and E. But was that because he saw her as a child? He didn't think so. It was more to do with her personality. Keely had a vulnerability about her that brought out all his protective instincts.

He could see immediately why Sean had found her attractive. It wasn't just that she was pretty, although she was. Very pretty. But her appeal went much deeper than just her looks. She had the widest, most compelling smile he'd ever seen, an infectious laugh and a warmth that wrapped itself around you like a blanket from the moment you met her.

And privately he thought she was going to find A and E work emotionally draining. Keely felt things too deeply to be able to successfully shrug off some of the incidents that burst through their doors on a daily basis. Which meant that he needed to keep a close eye on her. A very close eye on her indeed.

By the end of the week Keely was at screaming pitch.

He was driving her mad. Whereas her colleagues were left to their own devices until they shouted for help, every time she turned round Zach was breathing down her neck. It was doing absolutely nothing for her confidence.

She could do the job—she *knew* she could. But not if her every move was being watched.

She was going to have to say something. The trouble

was, when? Working in A and E was fast-paced to say the least. So far they'd had very little time for cosy chats. Maybe today she'd pluck up courage...

Before she could work out how to tackle the subject without sounding defensive, the paramedics brought in an emergency and she and Adam, one of the other new casualty officers, were called to the resuscitation room.

Seconds later Zach slammed open the swing doors of Resus and joined them at the trolley.

'OK, what have we got?'

'Twenty-five-year-old male, overdose—we don't know what he's taken. He was brought in unconscious.' Nicky Roberts, one of the A and E sisters, briefed him quickly as they all swung into action. 'One of his friends found him. Said he'd been depressed lately but didn't know if he'd been taking any drugs. The ambulance crew put in an airway.'

'OK.' Stethoscope looped round his neck, Zach started to examine the man, his movements swift and methodical. 'No gag reflex. Someone bleep the anaesthetist and let's give him some oxygen.'

Keely tried not to be impressed by the speed and confidence with which he worked as he took charge of the situation.

'He's got dilated pupils, a divergent squint and increased muscle tone and reflexes.' His eyes flickered past Keely and rested on Adam. 'Does that give you any clues as to what he might have taken?'

Keely ground her teeth. *He was doing it again.* Ignoring her and asking Adam the questions. Why hadn't he asked her? Why wasn't he treating her the same way he was treating the others?

Did he think she didn't know the answer?

She gave Adam a moment to speak but when he hesitated, clearly unsure, she stepped forward, her small chin lifting slightly as she spoke.

'Could it be tricyclics?'

Zach's gaze swivelled to her and she saw the flicker of surprise in his blue eyes. 'It could be.' He looked at her for a long moment, obviously unsure whether to question her further.

Keely took the matter in her own hands. 'Obviously you'll want certain tests done,' she said crisply. 'In my opinion he needs a drug screen and a blood glucose, BMG, ABG and U and Es.' She listed the necessary investigations and then held her breath, waiting for his response. Would he give her a row for interrupting when he'd asked Adam the question?

There was a long silence and then a ghost of a smile played around his firm mouth.

'Then you'd better get a line in and send off those tests.' He shifted his sharp gaze to one of the student nurses. 'Pulse and BP?'

Keely felt a rush of relief and reached for an IV cannula.

'Pulse is 110 and his blood pressure is 70 over 50,' the student nurse said quickly, flushing slightly as that hard gaze shifted in her direction. 'Wh-what are tricyclics, Mr Jordan?'

Zach jerked his head towards Keely. 'Dr Thompson will tell you.'

Was he testing her? Keely taped the cannula in place. 'It's a type of antidepressant. Unfortunately it's quite serious in overdose.'

'He's tachycardic and hypotensive,' Zach muttered, his eyes moving back to Nicky. 'And his skin is dry and hot. Check his temperature, please. I'm sure Keely's right and it's tricyclics. What do you think?'

Nicky shrugged and picked up a thermometer. 'You're the doctor, Zach.'

'That's never stopped you giving an opinion before.' Zach's tone was dry as he returned his attention to the patient. 'OK, is that line in? Well done, Keely. Let's give him a plasma expander—500 mils gelatin. Do we have a name for him yet? Address?'

'The friend was giving his details to Reception. We'll check,' Nicky said quickly, despatching another nurse to talk to the receptionist.

Zach drew breath and wiped his forehead on his sleeve. 'Someone contact the GP, please—find out what he's taking, if anything.' He glanced up as the anaesthetist strode into the room. 'Hi, Doug.'

His colleague gave a brief smile of acknowledgement. 'What's the story?'

'Overdose,' Zach said briefly. 'Don't know what yet. We're working on it, but we're guessing tricyclics.'

The anaesthetist rolled his eyes and snapped open the laryngoscope. 'Bloody antidepressants.'

'Quite.' Zach's gaze returned to his patient. 'He's got no gag reflex. I want to wash him out. We need to intubate him with a cuffed tube.'

'By ''we'' I assume you mean me,' the anaesthetist said dryly, and Zach grinned.

'I do indeed. I'm not rummaging around in someone's vocal cords unless I have to.'

The anaesthetist frowned and reached for an endotracheal tube. 'Isn't it a bit late for gastric lavage? When did he take them?'

'His friends saw him two hours ago and he was fine,' Zach said calmly. 'I want to try it and I want to give him some charcoal.'

'You're the boss.' The anaesthetist shrugged and intubated the patient quickly, using a cuffed endotracheal tube designed to prevent liquid accidentally entering the lungs.

'Great.' Zach lifted his eyes to Nicky. 'Let's wash him out. Keep 20 mils of the aspirate for a drug screen. Then I want 50 grams of activated charcoal down the tube. And let's do an ECG.'

His steady stream of instructions left Keely's head reeling and she watched in awe as he and Nicky worked together, their smooth teamwork a result of years of experience. Nicky seemed to anticipate Zach's every move without being asked and he was so calm and relaxed that Keely's admiration quickly turned to gloom. Would *she* ever be as confident as that?

'He's in urinary retention,' Nicky said quietly, and Zach nodded.

'That's common after a tricyclic overdose. Try suprapubic pressure. If that doesn't work then let's put in a catheter. How's that ECG?'

He leaned over her shoulder, frowning as he saw the trace. 'Well, that pretty much confirms Keely's diagnosis.'

As if to prove the point the student nurse came back in at that point. 'I've spoken to the GP. He *was* taking tricyclics. Amitriptyline.'

'Well done, Keely.'

Zach's quiet words of praise brought a faint colour to her cheeks and she suddenly felt deliciously warm inside. Maybe she would be as confident as him one day. He was the consultant after all.

Zach lifted the ECG trace and stared down at it. 'All right, Keely, you're the one who wants to be a cardiologist. Take a look at that and tell me what you see?'

He handed her the ECG trace and waited while she looked at it.

'Prolonged PR interval and QRS widening.'

'Right.' Zach took the trace back. 'Consistent with a

tricyclic overdose. Let's give him 8.4 per cent sodium bicarbonate.'

Nicky turned away to do as he'd instructed and Zach turned back to Adam. 'He needs to be admitted to CCU for cardiac monitoring. Can you bleep the medical reg and I'll have a word with him?'

Half an hour later the man was stabilised and had been admitted by the medical team.

'Will he live?' The student nurse stared at Zach, her eyes wide and slightly stunned.

'Probably. And he'll probably do it again,' Zach said calmly, folding the ECG trace and putting it carefully in the notes.

'You were amazing, Mr Jordan. You knew exactly what to do. You saved his life.' She stared at him with a mixture of awe and reverence and Keely felt some empathy with the girl. Watching Zach in action was a humbling experience. Not only was he clearly a skilled doctor but his cool self-confidence had transmitted itself to the rest of the staff. There was no panic with Zach around.

The student nurse was still round eyed with admiration and Keely saw Zach frown slightly as he registered her longing gaze.

How would he react? Would he demolish the girl? No, that wasn't his style. Look how kind he'd been to *her* for a start.

But she sensed that his style had changed over the years. The easy charm was still there on the surface but underneath she sensed a cynicism, a hard edge that hadn't been part of the Zach that she'd known all those years ago. Was it just maturity? Or something else? Had something happened to change him?

'Saving lives is what we do in A and E.' His tone was matter-of-fact and a touch impatient as he addressed the student nurse. 'It's the job. Any of the doctors here would have done the same.'

Keely could tell by the look on the young nurse's face that she didn't believe him, that she'd suddenly turned Zach into some sort of god with supernatural powers.

Nicky had obviously noticed, too, because she dealt with the situation quickly.

'You're needed in the dressing clinic, Bella,' the A and E sister said hastily, ushering the young student nurse out of the room before she could say anything else.

Zach made no reference to the incident, instead thanking them all for their help and issuing a few final instructions to Nicky before striding out of the room to talk to the patient's friends who were waiting in the relatives' room.

Keely exchanged looks with Nicky. 'Does he have that effect on everyone?'

Nicky nodded as she started to clear up the debris in the room.

'Everyone female. They soon get over it when they realise he isn't interested.'

Keely threw some rubbish in the bin and tried to sound casual. 'Isn't he?'

'Never.' Nicky glanced up and shook her head slowly as she looked at her. 'Oh, no. Not you, too.'

Keely stiffened. 'What do you mean?'

'I recognise that expression on your face. I've seen it too many times before not to. Don't fall for him, Keely,' Nicky warned, lowering her voice as she spoke. 'It's a quick route to a broken heart.'

Keely licked dry lips. 'Do lots of women fall for him?'

'What do you think?' Nicky pulled a face and tilted her head to one side. 'Zach Jordan is so good-looking he can't walk down a street without women getting neck ache as they stare at him. He's clever—very clever—and on top of that he's got this air of calm confidence that women find irresistible. Pretty devastating combination of qualities. Of course lots of women fall for him.'

'Is he married?'

Now, why on earth had she asked that question?

Nicky's expression was suddenly remote and discouraging. 'I can't discuss Zach's private life—it wouldn't be right. But take it from me, he's not available.'

Keely frowned slightly, wondering why Nicky hadn't just answered her question.

'Forget him, Keely. He's a colleague and nothing more.' Nicky opened a laryngoscope to check the bulb. 'I know he's good-looking but, like I said, falling for Zach is a quick route to a broken heart.'

Unfortunately her warning was about eight years too late, Keely thought gloomily as she ripped off her gloves and tossed them in the bin. She'd fallen heavily for Zach when she'd first met him and she had a nasty feeling that nothing much had changed. He still had the power to turn her insides to jelly.

CHAPTER TWO

'FANCY a drink?' Nicky opened her locker and pulled out her coat and bag. 'There's a lovely pub just across the road. Log fire, nice staff, dishy barman...'

Keely grinned. 'In that case, definitely.'

It had been a long and stressful day so maybe a drink was just what she needed. A drink and the chance to stare at a dishy man who wasn't Zach. With any luck she'd fall madly in love with the barman.

'I'll just give Fiona and Adam a shout,' Nicky said, fastening her locker and putting on her coat. 'They're both off now, too.'

Keely took a deep breath. 'And Zach?'

Nicky shook her head. 'Not Zach. Zach never joins us and anyway...' she frowned at Keely '...I've already warned you.'

'I know.' Keely wrapped a wool scarf around her neck and smiled brightly 'Just being sociable, that's all. He *is* one of the team.'

'At work, yes,' Nicky agreed, walking across the staffroom and tugging open the door, 'but out of work—no. Zach keeps himself to himself.'

Did he? Why?

Keely followed her down the corridor, waited while she hassled the two SHOs into joining them and then walked out into the bitterly cold January night and across to the pub.

The pub was warm and cosy and a welcome alternative to her chilly flat.

'I need to find somewhere decent to live.' Keely sipped

her orange juice and passed her crisps to Nicky. 'Because I was living and working in London until last week, I didn't have much time to hunt around so I took the first thing I saw. Believe me, it's less than exciting and, frankly, the landlord gives me the creeps.'

'My wife and I are renting a house in Ambleside until we decide where we're going to settle,' Adam told them, savouring his beer with obvious enjoyment. 'What about you Fiona?'

'Oh, I've got an aunt who lives about ten minutes from the hospital, so I'm staying with her for now. She's great fun, actually.' Fiona ripped open another packet of crisps. 'Where do the rest of the staff live?'

Nicky settled back in her chair and stretched out her hands towards the log fire. 'Well, the senior consultant, Sean, lives about fifteen minutes' drive away in a converted barn with his wife and three utterly delectable children. Zoe, the staff nurse you probably met today, lives with her boyfriend in Ambleside and I live with my husband in a cottage about ten minutes away towards the Langdales.'

'Nice. I want to live somewhere more rural. At the moment I'm stuck in a tiny flat in the middle of town.' Keely pulled a face. 'What I really wanted was to live in a rural retreat. You know, views of the fells, sheep at the bottom of my garden and an appalling trip to work every time it snows.'

Nicky laughed. 'In other words, somewhere totally impractical.'

'That's me.' Keely beamed at her. 'I came up here to escape from the city. If I wanted the city I'd still be living in London.'

'So why the Lakes?'

Keely shrugged and took a sip of her drink. 'Because

this unit has a good reputation and because I love walking.'

And because it was sufficiently far away from her totally
oppressive family to give her some much needed breathing
space.

'I like walking.' Nicky munched at the crisps. 'So does
Sean. He was in the army before he trained as a doctor so
he's a real expert at climbing and things. And Zach loves
the outdoors too.'

That explained the athletic body…

'Well, I'm going to go and see some rental properties
as soon as I get a free moment,' Keely muttered, pushing
thoughts of Zach's body away and glancing at her watch.
'I suppose I'd better be going. I've got some serious studying to do.'

Fiona lifted an eyebrow. 'Studying?'

'Yes, studying.' Keely gave a wry smile, deciding to
confess. Even though they'd only worked together for a
week, she already liked her new colleagues enormously.
'The last time I saw Zach I was sixteen years old and he
obviously still sees me that way. I need to impress him.'

'Sixteen?' Nicky put her drink on the table with a thump
and stared at her in amazement. 'How did you come to
meet Zach at the tender age of sixteen?'

'He trained with my brother,' Keely said, carefully missing out that he'd also worked for her father. The less people knew about her family the better. 'He used to come
and stay sometimes.'

'Wow.' Fiona gave her a saucy wink. 'I bet he played
havoc with your hormones at sixteen.'

Keely managed a weak laugh. He was playing havoc
with her hormones at twenty-four, too.

'Anyway, I clearly have to work harder to impress him
than everyone else.'

Nicky frowned. 'I don't think that's true. You impressed

him yesterday—you told him that the man had taken tricyclics.'

'Yes—and I was the one who didn't know the answer,' Adam reminded them with a sheepish grin. 'If anyone needs to go home to study it's me.'

'No.' Keely stared into her now empty glass. 'Zach doesn't see you as a teenager.'

Nicky wiggled her toes in front of the fire. 'If I were you I'd just be yourself. From what I've seen today you're going to make a great casualty officer. You're good humoured, you don't panic in an emergency, you're friendly to everyone and you're nice with the patients. Zach will see that for himself soon enough.'

Would he?

Keely wasn't so sure. After the way he'd reacted this week it was fairly obvious to her that Zach thought he needed to keep an eye on her.

She'd give it a few more days and then she'd have to have a word with him.

'There's been a pile-up on the motorway. Six cars. They've asked for a medical team. Zach, I'd like you to go.' Sean Nicholson glanced at the other cas. officers. 'And Keely.'

Keely felt a rush of excitement which died immediately when she heard Zach contradict him sharply.

'Not Keely. I'll take Adam.'

Adam?

Keely opened her mouth to protest and then shut it again, glancing instead towards Sean. Surely he'd object?

But he didn't. He merely gave a brisk nod. 'Fine. Nicky and I will get things ready here. Nicky, which of your nursing staff do you want to send?'

'Liz,' Nicky said promptly, and immediately everyone swung into action.

Seething with fury, Keely helped prepare Resus for a large influx of casualties and she liaised with Ambulance Control and the wards.

By the time the patients had been admitted and dealt with her shift was almost over, but she was determined to have a word with Zach. She thought she knew why he hadn't sent her out with the medical team, but she wanted to hear it from his lips.

'May I talk to you?'

He looked slightly surprised but he gave a nod and they walked towards his office.

'Were there any fatalities?' It was small talk but she didn't want to tackle her problem in the corridor with the whole department listening.

'Two. Trapped inside one of the vehicles. It was the usual story—everyone driving too close together, bunched up in the fog.'

He opened the door to his office and she followed him inside and closed the door firmly behind them.

His eyes drifted quizzically to her hands which were still holding the door handle. 'So what's the matter, Keely?'

She took a deep breath. 'You're the matter. Or rather, the way you treat me is the matter. Why are you doing it, Zach?'

He looked at her warily. 'Why am I doing what?'

She gave him an impatient look. 'You don't ask me any questions, you don't let me see any complicated patients, you hang over me like a nursemaid and now you just refused to let me go out as part of an emergency team even though Sean obviously thought I was capable of it.' She ticked the reasons off one by one on her fingers. 'I know you don't trust me but I think you should at least give me a chance.'

There was a long silence and then he turned and walked

over to his window, staring out into the darkness towards the fells. 'I do trust you.'

'No, you don't!' She walked over to him, determined to make him look at her. 'You never let me work the way you let the other doctors work.'

'That isn't because I don't trust you,' he muttered, raking long fingers through his already ruffled hair.

Keely frowned, baffled by his response. 'Why, then? If you trust me then why aren't you just throwing me in the deep end along with everyone else? Why wouldn't you let me go out as part of the emergency team? It's obvious that you don't trust my clinical judgement—'

'That's not true.' He frowned sharply, as if the thought hadn't occurred to him. 'From what I've seen, your clinical judgement is spot on.'

'So why…?'

He turned to look at her, his blue eyes suddenly hard. 'Because sometimes these pile-ups are dangerous and the medical team ends up operating in lethal conditions. You could have been sitting in a squashed car giving pain relief to some poor chap who was going to be trapped for hours, you could have been dealing with someone who'd been thrown through the windscreen…'

She swallowed, taken aback by his grim expression and by the harsh tone of his voice. 'But you sent Adam.'

He closed his eyes briefly and gave a sigh. 'Yes. I sent Adam.'

'Because he's a man?' Keely frowned. 'Because you don't think I can handle the stress? Why can Adam handle the stress better than me? I didn't think you were a chauvinist, Zach.'

He muttered something under his breath. 'I am not a chauvinist.'

'Then why did you choose not to send a woman into that situation?'

'I didn't choose not to send a woman.' His jaw was rigid with tension. 'I chose not to send *you*.'

'Me?' Keely stared at him. 'So you're saying you would have sent another woman, but not me.'

He held her gaze. 'Maybe.'

She felt bemused and frustrated. 'Because you think I'm a child?'

'No.' He shook his head impatiently. 'This is nothing to do with your age. More your personality.'

Keely's heart was thudding and her lips felt stiff. 'What's wrong with my personality?'

'Nothing's wrong with it!' He lifted a hand and rubbed his fingers along his forehead. 'You've got a lovely personality.'

'But?'

'But nothing,' he said quietly, sitting on the edge of his desk and watching her steadily. 'I just know how sensitive you are.'

Keely gave an outraged gasp. 'That is not fair! You don't know me at all—you're just remembering how I was as a teenager. I'm trying to learn and be part of a team, and you're stopping me. Anyway, why should it bother you if I *do* get upset? It's *my* problem, not yours.'

He held her gaze without flinching. 'It bothers me because I feel responsible for you.'

'Responsible for me?' She gaped at him. 'Why are you responsible for me?'

'Because you're miles away from your family—'

Her eyes widened. 'I'm a grown woman, Zach! Believe it or not, I don't need to keep running to Daddy!'

'Keely, I just don't want you hurt.'

She stared at him, touched and frustrated at the same time. 'But you weren't worried about Adam?'

'Of course not!' He gave a short laugh. 'Adam can take care of himself.'

'And so can I,' Keely said softly. '*So can I*, Zach. Whatever you may think of me, whatever your memory tells you, I'm completely grown up now. I don't need your protection, however well meaning.'

His expression was bleak. 'We see some hideous things in Casualty.'

'Then I'll see them, too,' Keely said firmly, pushing her blonde hair behind one ear. 'Please, Zach, this is ridiculous. All week you've been hanging over my shoulder, asking everyone questions except me, treating me like the teenager I used to be. I am not a teenager any more. This isn't even my first job. You're driving me mad.'

Zach winced and had the grace to look guilty. 'Have I been that bad?'

'Worse!' Keely scowled and then grinned, her natural good nature reasserting itself. 'But I'll forgive you if you stop policing my every movement.'

Zach walked towards her and stopped dead, his eyes scanning her face as if he was trying to see her for who she was and not for who he remembered her to be.

'I just don't want you hurt,' he said gruffly. 'I know Prof would want me to keep an eye on you.'

'He certainly would,' Keely agreed sweetly, 'but you never did what Prof wanted when you worked for him, so don't use that as an excuse. I distinctly remember him saying that you were the brightest, most frustrating doctor he'd ever worked with. You questioned everything and you took risks that made his hair stand on end. And those risks usually paid off.'

'OK. I take your point.' He spoke slowly, a wry smile playing around his firm mouth. 'You have a right to spread your wings, too. I'll stop treating you as a child. On one condition.'

'Which is?'

His voice was soft. 'If you have a tough day, you come

and talk to me. As a friend. We all need someone to turn to in this department. I want to be sure that you won't bottle anything up just to because you're trying to prove yourself.'

'I never bottle anything up—you of all people should know that.' She coloured slightly but decided that she might as well clear the air once and for all. 'If I was any good at hiding my emotions, Zach, I wouldn't have yelled at you just now and I wouldn't have proposed to you all those years ago.'

The corners of his mouth twitched and his blue eyes gleamed. 'I thought we weren't going to mention that again.'

She gave a groan. 'I know. You've been so discreet and I can hardly bear to think about it, it's so embarrassing. But I still feel that I haven't really apologised properly.'

'I've already told you you don't need to apologise.'

'Zach, *I proposed to you*!'

His blue eyes twinkled. 'It was a leap year, sweetheart. You were allowed to propose to me. I was very flattered.'

Sweetheart. The way he said it made her insides melt even though she knew it hadn't been meant in *that* way.

Keely pulled herself together and cleared her throat. 'Anyway, I apologise for behaving like such an idiot and embarrassing you.'

'You didn't embarrass me.' His gaze was steady on hers and for a moment she stared at him, her pulse picking up as she looked at the broad shoulders and the dark hair. He was seriously gorgeous…

She suppressed a whimper. Why did he have such a powerful effect on her. Why? She wasn't a teenager any more, but when she was with him she certainly felt like one.

No!

She wasn't making that mistake again.

She was *not* going to fall for Zach a second time.

'So that's agreed, then.' She made an effort to ignore the effect he had on her. 'You'll treat me like an adult and forget the fact that I once had pigtails and proposed to you.'

'It's a deal,' he said softly. 'Oh, and by the way—you look considerably better without the pigtails.'

For a moment their eyes held and she immediately forgot all her resolutions and allowed herself the luxury of one brief fantasy. *Zach looking deep into her eyes and telling her that he loved her...*

Oh, help! She was going mad.

'Right, then.' She backed away, forcing herself to break the spell. 'I'd better get back to work.'

As she closed his office door behind her she gave a low groan.

Working with the man was going to be a nightmare! She may have grown up but the reaction of her hormones was exactly the same as it had been when she was sixteen. The truth was that she couldn't be in the same room as Zachary Jordan without wanting him. Which meant that she had a very big problem.

She couldn't see a fracture.

Keely stared hard at the X-ray, half expecting something to suddenly appear, but it looked clear. Which didn't fit with what she'd discovered on examination. All her instincts told her that the wrist was broken.

So why was the X-ray clear?

Bother.

She was going to have to ask Zach's advice.

Which was a nuisance because she'd been successfully avoiding him all week. Although he was the senior doctor on her shift, she'd managed to deal with almost everything without his help.

She found him in Resus, talking to Nicky.

'Problems?' He lifted a dark eyebrow and she felt her heart stumble. Why did he have to be so good-looking? It was very distracting. If she was going to last six months in A and E she was going to have to develop survival strategies. Like looking over his shoulder when she talked to him rather than at his face.

'I need your advice.' She raked slim fingers through her jagged blonde hair and gave him a brief smile. 'I've got this lady in cubicle one I'm not sure about. She fell on her wrist and all the signs are that she's fractured her scaphoid, but I can't see anything on the X-ray.'

'Scaphoid fractures are notoriously easy to miss on X-ray so you're right to ask for help,' he said quietly. 'What did you find on examination?'

'Swelling, pain on wrist movements, tenderness on direct pressure two centimetres distal to Lister's tubercle of the radius and on proximal pressure on the extended thumb or index finger.' Keely listed everything briskly and he nodded.

'What X-rays did you request?'

'AP, lateral and scaphoid views—was that wrong?' She felt a stab of anxiety. 'Did I miss something?'

'No, you did well.' There was a glimmer of surprise and admiration in his eyes. 'Better than most. Come on, I'll check the X-rays for you.'

Keely followed him down the corridor, struggling to keep up with his long stride.

He squinted at each of the X-rays in turn. 'Well, you're right. They're all negative. Let's examine her.'

He introduced himself to the patient, examined her thoroughly and then nodded at Keely.

'It's a scaphoid fracture. I agree with you. Well done for trusting your instincts.'

As usual his quiet words of praise made her feel as though she could have walked on water.

'But why are the X-rays clear?'

Whenever she was in doubt about a patient she took every opportunity to pick his brains and was rapidly finding out that Zach Jordan was a first-class teacher.

'The fracture isn't always visible,' he told her. 'Put her in a scaphoid plaster and refer her to the next fracture clinic. They'll X-ray again and it might be visible by then.'

She remembered her father saying that Zach Jordan was one of the most talented doctors he'd ever worked with and now she was seeing it at first hand. He was fast and confident, never doubting himself and always ready to do his best for each patient. She just wished she didn't find him so disturbing.

'He's married.'

Fiona, the doctor who'd sat next to her in the lecture theatre on that first morning, flopped into a chair in the staffroom, a gloomy expression on her face. 'Why are the good ones always married?'

'Who's married?' Keely stirred her coffee, her mind still on a nasty road traffic accident that had come in earlier.

'Zach Jordan.'

'Zach?' Her hand suddenly shook and hot coffee sloshed over the side of the mug. 'Oh, no!'

She stood up and fetched a cloth only to find Fiona watching her with a knowing expression.

'You, too…'

Keely walked back to the table. 'What do you mean— "you, too"?'

'You're obviously just as smitten as the rest of us.'

'Fiona, I just spilled my coffee,' Keely said calmly, carefully mopping up the mess she'd made. 'Why does that make me smitten?'

Fiona gave a wry smile. 'Because he has that effect on women. My entire body shakes when he comes into a room. Believe me, I can't hold anything hot within a hundred yards of the man.'

Keely laughed. 'Fiona, you're awful.'

'Well, all I can say is that she must be an amazing woman.'

Keely rinsed out the cloth and put it back by the sink. 'Who must be?'

'His wife.' Fiona curled her legs underneath her and settled herself more comfortably in the chair. 'Imagine marrying a man like that. Not only does he have the most luscious body I've ever seen but he's strong and cool-headed and a brilliant doctor. And so-o sexy. What a man!'

Keely frowned. Was Zach really married? And why should it bother her if he was?

A man like Zach was bound to be involved with someone. And it was really none of her business. It wasn't as if she had feelings for him. Not really. She was just struggling with the remnants of a powerful teenage crush.

'He called her sweetheart,' Fiona said dreamily. 'I heard him on the phone. And then he said he loved her. Can you imagine? Isn't that romantic? He didn't care who was listening, he loves her so much he just wanted to tell her. If you ask me, she's a very lucky woman.'

A lucky woman indeed. Whoever she was.

Keely had heard enough. She emptied the remains of her coffee down the sink, made a limp excuse to Fiona and left the room.

Why did hearing about Zach's love life bother her so much?

She frowned again. Her reaction didn't make sense. So she'd once had a crush on him. So what? That wasn't enough to make her feel as though she'd just had major surgery to her insides. Her emotions were just confused, that was all.

She walked back to the main area of Casualty and picked up a set of notes. Work, that was the answer. Bury herself in work and forget about Zach. He wasn't hers and he never had been. And she didn't want him to be, she told herself firmly. OK, so she found him attractive. But so would any woman with a pulse. It didn't *mean* anything.

'So, have you found somewhere to live yet?' Nicky flicked the switch on the kettle and turned to glance at Keely. 'You've been here three weeks and you're still living in that awful flat.'

'Awful?' Zach walked into the room in time to hear the last remark. 'What's awful about Keely's flat?'

'It's fine,' Keely lied, 'just not in the nicest position. I wanted to live in the middle of the country with a view of the fells.'

'Your flat is not fine,' Nicky said firmly, ignoring the looks that Keely was giving her. 'There's damp on the living-room walls and your landlord is decidedly creepy. And he's bothering you, you know he is.'

Keely glared at Nicky but it was too late. Zach was suddenly still, his eyes watchful.

'In what way is he bothering you, Keely?' His soft tone didn't deceive anyone and there was a sudden silence in the common room.

'He isn't,' Keely said hastily. 'Not really. Nicky's exaggerating.'

'That's not true.' Nicky spoke up again and Keely closed her eyes.

She was going to kill Nicky when she got her alone!

'He keeps knocking on her door at all sorts of weird hours,' Nicky told them, oblivious to the furious glances that Keely was sending in her direction. 'I'm really worried about her. She needs to move out of that place.'

Zach's expression was grim. 'Keely? Is it true?'

Keely suppressed a groan. Oh, no. Now he'd get all protective again, and he'd just started to treat her like an adult.

'I think he's just a bit lonely,' she said lamely, and his mouth tightened.

'I'll get you a room in the medical block until you can find somewhere else.'

Without waiting for her reply he paced over to the phone and spoke to the accommodation officer. Judging from Zach's tone, they were less than helpful and when he finally replaced the receiver his expression was black.

'They haven't got anything at the moment—apparently they had a burst pipe last week and it's taking for ever to fix. We'll have to think of something else.'

'It's all right,' Keely said mildly. 'I've got two flats to look at on Friday when I'm not working. Thanks for trying but I'm taking care of it.'

He hesitated, his dark jaw tense. 'I'm not happy with you staying there—'

'It's fine, Zach,' Keely repeated firmly, conscious that Nicky and two of the other doctors were watching them curiously. And no wonder. Why was he making such a fuss?

'Well, if those flats don't come to anything, let me know. If you're stuck you can sleep in the doctors' room.'

They had a room where doctors could sleep if they were on duty at night, but it was rarely used.

'Thanks.'

Zach turned and walked out, and Nicky let out a long breath.

'Well, who's protective, then?'

Keely rolled her eyes. 'To Zach, I'm still sixteen and I probably always will be.'

With that she stood up and left them to speculate.

She was checking an X-ray later in the day when she heard Nicky shout from the corridor.

'Keely, I need a doctor—*now*!'

Keely was there in an instant, her heart pounding as she saw the toddler in the arms of a paramedic.

'She's fitting,' Nicky said quickly. 'It may be a febrile convulsion. Get her into Resus and I'll bleep Paeds.' A febrile convulsion was a fit brought on by a high temperature and was quite common in very young children.

'Are the parents here?' Keely took charge of the toddler's airway and gave her some oxygen.

'Not yet.' Nicky turned to one of the student nurses, her expression grim. 'Call Zach. Call Zach *now*!'

Keely glanced up in surprise. Why was Nicky in such a panic? It wasn't like her at all and everything was under control.

'It's OK,' she said calmly. 'I can handle this without Zach.'

'I know you can handle it,' came the reply. 'I don't need Zach for his medical skills.'

Keely didn't have time to question Nicky further.

'Let's give her some oxygen, please, and some diazepam rectally,' she ordered. 'Do we have any details? What's her name?'

There was a brief silence and then Nicky cleared her throat.

'Her name is Phoebe.'

Keely glanced up expectantly.

'Phoebe what?'

Nicky hesitated. 'Jordan,' she said finally. 'Phoebe Jordan. She's Zach's daughter.'

Zach had a daughter?

Oh, dear God.

Keely turned her attention back to the sick child, her heart thumping. 'OK, what's her temperature? Let's strip her off, give her some paracetamol and get a line in.'

Nicky looked doubtful. 'Should we wait for Zach?'

'No way.' Keely was adamant. 'We need to cool her down and find out what's causing her temperature. Can someone get a fan, please?'

Luckily Keely found a vein easily and secured a butterfly onto the tiny hand.

Only seconds later the doors to Resus slammed open and Zach strode into the room.

'What's the problem?'

His eyes fastened on the limp figure on the trolley and his face blanched.

'Phoebe?' He elbowed Nicky out of the way and bent over his daughter. 'Phoebe?' He glanced from one to the other. 'What the hell's happened?'

It was the first time that Keely had ever seen him near to losing his cool.

'It looks like a febrile convulsion, Zach,' she said quietly. 'We've checked her blood glucose and that's fine. Her temperature's 40.5. I've given her diazepam and paracetamol.'

Zach's expression was tortured. 'We need to get a line in—damn, I don't think I can do it to her.'

He gritted his teeth and Nicky put a hand on his arm.

'It's OK,' she told him. 'Keely's already done it with no problem. She was brilliant.'

'I need to take some blood for U and Es and FBCs and I think we should try and get an MSU.' Keely hesitated, knowing that she was increasing his anxiety. 'And maybe a lumbar puncture. We've bleeped Paeds but we need to find out what's causing the temperature. Was she ill this morning?'

'I didn't see her this morning. I was working here last night.' Zach took a deep breath and then bent over the trolley, his powerful body in stark contrast to the tiny toddler. 'Daddy's here, sweetheart.'

The rough, protective tone of his voice made Keely's heart melt.

'Who was with her last night, Zach? We need to know if she's been unwell.'

Zach straightened, his expression grim. 'Her nanny. Speaking of which, where is she?'

Nicky licked her lips. 'It wasn't the nanny that brought her in…'

Zach went totally still, his voice lethally soft. 'So who brought her in?'

'An ambulance crew, and they were called by the staff of the crèche.'

'Crèche?' Zach's voice was like a pistol crack. 'What crèche?'

Even Nicky flinched under his biting tone. 'The crèche at the leisure centre. One of the staff came in with her. They're in Reception.'

'What the *hell* was she doing in a crèche?' Zach took a juddering breath, checked that his daughter was stable and then looked at Keely. 'Look after her.' With that he strode out of the room towards Reception.

'Ouch.' Nicky pulled a face. 'I think the nanny's in trouble.'

'Her temperature's coming down.' Keely checked the reading and nodded with relief, turning back to the little girl with a gentle expression on her face. 'Good girl. Hello, sweetheart.'

She stroked the blonde head gently and felt her heart twist. The child was gorgeous. Long, feathery lashes drifted against her smooth cheeks and her skin was baby perfect.

Right on cue the eyes opened—two blue replicas of Zach's—and Phoebe started to grizzle.

'Want Daddy.'

'I know you do. Daddy's coming in a minute.' Keely examined her quickly, looking in her ears and her throat. 'Hello—what have we here? One very red throat and a pair of very red ears.'

She put the auriscope back on the trolley. 'That's probably what's causing it.'

Nicky looked anxious. 'You don't think its meningitis, do you?'

Keely shook her head. 'I don't think so but they'll take a look at her in Paeds and do a lumbar puncture if they're in doubt. In my opinion she's got an ear and throat infection. Come and have a cuddle with your Aunty Keely.'

She swept the fractious toddler into her arms and cuddled her close, walking across Resus towards a little mobile that they had hanging from the ceiling.

'Here—look at this...' She was spinning the mobile when Zach strode back into the room, the strain showing on his handsome face.

'How is she?'

'Want Daddy.' Phoebe held out her arms and he took her instantly, holding her tightly against him, his eyes on Keely. 'Temperature?'

'It's come down a bit. Thirty-nine degrees,' she told him. 'We've given her some ibuprofen as well as the paracetamol.'

'Good.' He nodded. 'So what do you think?'

Keely was touched that he was asking her opinion on his daughter.

'Her ears and throat are red,' she said quickly. 'I think we should start her on some antibiotics, keep up the paracetamol, monitor her temperature and admit her overnight. But I suppose we need a paediatric opinion.'

'That's me.' A voice came from behind them and they both turned, Zach's face showing visible relief.

'Tony—thanks for coming yourself. It's my daughter…'

'No problem.' Tony put a hand on Zach's shoulder and it was obvious from the sympathetic expression on his face that the two men were friends. 'History?'

Zach breathed out heavily and rubbed the back of his neck. 'She was fine when I left yesterday lunchtime. I didn't go home last night—I was working—but I called the nanny this morning and she said that everything was fine. But it seems that she's been taking the child to a crèche when I've been at work so that she can use the gym—'

'Ouch.' Tony pulled a face and Zach's eyes were icy cold.

'Precisely. The nursery nurse who looked after Phoebe in the crèche said that she was fretful and hot this afternoon—they tried to call the nanny but apparently they couldn't get hold of her. Then the child fitted and they called the ambulance.'

'Right.' Tony nodded. 'So it seems as though we have a history consistent with a febrile convulsion.'

'That's what Keely thought.' Zach suddenly remembered Keely and turned to her with an apologetic frown. 'Sorry. You haven't met, have you? This is Tony Maxwell, one of the paediatric consultants.'

Keely gave him a smile, described her findings and then watched while Tony examined the little girl himself. Zach settled himself on a chair and held Phoebe while Tony looked in her throat and ears and listened to her chest.

'I agree with Keely. It's her ears and throat, Zach. I'd say admit her for observation overnight and we'll see how she is in the morning.'

Zach frowned. 'You want her to stay in?'

'Only because you'll be stressed out by the responsibility of having her at home,' Tony said quietly. 'It's hard to think rationally when it's your own—believe me, I know. I've got two and I'm a nervous wreck when either of them are ill.'

Phoebe whimpered slightly and Zach held her closer. 'Can I stay the night with her?'

Tony shrugged. 'Of course. We've got a spare side room at the moment. You can go in there with her. I'll go back now and tell them.'

Nicky followed him out of Resus and Keely was left alone with Zach.

Zach dropped a kiss on his daughter's blonde head and looked at Keely. 'Will you do me a favour?'

She swallowed. 'Of course…'

Anything…

'Once I've settled her on the ward, will you sit with her until I've sorted out the nanny?' His expression was grim but Keely felt no sympathy for the woman. She deserved everything that was coming to her.

'Of course I will.' She felt suddenly awkward. Surely she wasn't the right person to be staying with his daughter. 'Do you want me to call your wife or something? I expect Phoebe will want to see her mother.'

Frankly she was amazed that the little girl hadn't already asked for her mother.

Zach stood up, his features stiff and cold. 'I don't have a wife, Keely. She died a year ago.'

CHAPTER THREE

THE only light in the room was a gentle glow from a lamp placed on the locker beside the cot.

Outside the wind howled and wrapped itself around the hospital, a sharp reminder of the cold winter weather which had suddenly descended on them.

Phoebe lay in the cot, dressed in just a nappy and covered in a cotton sheet, her breathing steady and even.

Keely sat next to her, head resting against the bars of the cot, waiting for Zach to return. At least the child was more peaceful now. Her temperature was down and she was sleeping deeply.

In the quiet of the room, with nothing but a sleeping child for company, Keely had plenty of time to think. And all she could think about was Zach and what he'd told her down in Resus.

His wife had died? Phoebe's mother had died?

Dear God, why? How?

Her heart twisted as she imagined just how hard it must be for Zach. Not only had he lost the woman he'd loved but his precious daughter had been left without a mother.

Instinctively she reached a hand over the side of the cot and stroked the soft blonde hair. The little girl felt cooler, thank goodness, and Keely reached out a hand and switched the fan off.

'How is she?'

Keely jumped as Zach's voice came from behind her, catching her by surprise.

'Oh—she's doing well, I think.' She fought the urge to

fling her arms round him and hold him close. Crazy! As if a hug from a friend could even begin to make up for the loss of a loved one. 'She's cooler. More peaceful. Her breathing is better. Tony came a few minutes ago and checked her again. He doesn't think they need to do a lumbar puncture unless you disagree.'

Zach shook his head. 'No. I've just spoken to the nanny and she says that Phoebe was up in the night with a temperature.' He touched his daughter gently, feeling her skin, his eyes alert for any change. 'She's claiming that she didn't tell me this morning because she didn't want to worry me.'

'Well, that may be true,' Keely said softly, but Zach gave a cynical laugh.

'You think so? I'm afraid I don't have your faith in human nature. I think the reason she didn't tell me that Phoebe was ill was because she knew I'd be checking up on her during the day and that I'd find out she'd been putting her in the crèche.'

That had been puzzling her and she frowned slightly as she stared at him. 'I'm surprised the staff in the crèche were prepared to take her.'

'They had a letter.' Zach leaned his forearms on the cot and watched the little girl, his tone menacing. 'It was written on hospital notepaper and signed by me, giving full permission for Phoebe to be left with them.'

Keely gasped. 'She forged your signature?'

Zach nodded. 'That's right. Charming, isn't it?'

'What are you going to do?'

'I've already done it,' he said grimly, stroking a strand of blonde hair out of Phoebe's eyes. 'She's clearing her things out of my house as we speak.'

'Well, at least Phoebe looks as though she's going to be OK,' Keely said soothingly. 'That's the main thing.'

He was silent for a moment and then some of the anger seemed to drain away and a wry smile played around his mouth. 'You always manage to see the important things in life, don't you? That's what I always loved about you as a child. You were totally different from everyone else. While your family were clawing their way up the career ladder, you were skipping school to help out in the local children's home.'

Keely's eyes widened. 'How did you know about that?'

'Your horrified family told me.' He gave a short laugh. 'You were the first person in the family to see that there was more to life than studying, and it came as a big shock for them.'

She grinned. 'I was in big trouble.'

'I know.' His eyes glittered in the semi-darkness. 'You were for ever in trouble about something. But you always had your priorities right.'

'I don't know about that.' She blushed and stared down into the cot, a lump building in her throat. She didn't want to think about her priorities. She wasn't even sure what they were any more. 'She's beautiful, Zach. You're very lucky to have her.'

'I know that.' He gave a short laugh. 'But being a male single parent is no picnic I can assure you. Take now, for instance. I've got myself a sick child, no child care and a demanding job. I'm not quite sure how they're going to fit together.'

'It will work out,' Keely said softly, leaning her cheek against the cot. 'And, anyway, she's the thing that matters most—not your job. She's gorgeous.'

Zach smiled, the first real smile for hours. 'Actually, she's a total minx,' he said dryly. 'The only time she's quiet is when she's ill. I suppose it was only a matter of time until the nanny left, if I'm honest.' He gave a long sigh and shook his head. 'Phoebe can be pretty difficult. You know what children of this age are like.'

'I certainly do.' Keely looked up and returned his smile. 'Is there anyone who can help you with child care?'

He gave a shrug. 'Sean's wife Ally helps me out in an emergency but she works part time as a GP so she can't offer more than the occasional day or two. I suppose my housekeeper Barbara could do the days.' He frowned, obviously thinking it through in his head. 'She's a real grandmother figure and Phoebe adores her, but the problem is the nights when I'm working. I suppose I'll just have to advertise again, but the thought of trusting anyone with her horrifies me.'

Keely's brain was working overtime. 'I could do it,' she said impulsively, leaning forward in her chair and lowering her voice so that she didn't wake the sleeping child. 'You can put me on different night shifts to you so that one of us will be at home with her.'

'You?' Zach looked startled by the suggestion. 'Why would *you* want to do it?'

Because she could make his life easier. She couldn't make up for his terrible loss. Maybe no one would ever do that. But she could help him with the practical problems. All she had to do was convince him that it was a good idea.

'Why would I want to help? Loads of reasons.' Keely's eyes drifted back to the cot longingly. 'Firstly because I love children at this age and I know she and I would have fun together—'

His eyes were watchful. 'And secondly?'

'Secondly…' She paused and took a deep breath. It must be such a sensitive subject. Would he hate her mentioning it? 'Secondly, because I'm so, so sorry that you lost your wife.' She faltered slightly as she spoke, nervous that she might upset him. 'You must be feeling so awful. The last thing you need is to battle with practical problems. I can't bring your wife back, Zach, but I can try to make life easier for you and Phoebe. If you'll let me.'

She broke off and bit her lip, waiting anxiously for his response.

'You always were a sucker for a sob story, Keely Thompson.' He gave a long sigh and rubbed long fingers over his forehead. 'And what would we offer you in return?'

'Accommodation,' she said promptly. 'My landlord is giving me grief. I need somewhere to live.'

It wasn't anything she couldn't handle but she hoped that it would be enough to make Zach accept her offer to help.

He was silent, indecision showing on his handsome face. 'She isn't easy. She locked the nanny out of the house last week.'

Keely grinned, sensing weakness. 'How enterprising. And how stupid of the nanny to put the front door between herself and a toddler.'

Zach still wasn't convinced. 'She climbs everywhere—she's lethal—'

'Zach, I know what a child is capable of,' Keely said gently, and he breathed out heavily and shook his head slowly.

'I just think it's an imposition—'

'It's not an imposition. I'd love to do it if you'd trust me.'

'Trust you?' His brows locked together in a deep frown. 'Of course I trust you.'

'Well, that's settled, then,' Keely said in a cheerful

whisper. 'After work tomorrow I'll pick up some things and move into the nanny's room. I don't know where you live so you'll have to draw me a map.'

'I live in the middle of nowhere,' he told her in a low voice. 'Are you scared of being on your own in the house?'

She shot him an exasperated look.

'Zach, you're doing it again! I *am* the babysitter,' she reminded him dryly. 'I'm not the one that *needs* the babysitter, remember?'

He raised his hands in the air and gave her an apologetic smile. 'Sorry. In that case, thanks for the offer. I accept gratefully, although I don't know why you're doing it so any time you start to regret it, please, say. I'll draw you a map and leave a key for you in A and E, and you can come over any time you like tomorrow. I've cleared it with Sean that I'm taking a few days off.'

'Good.' Keely nodded and stood up. 'And now I'll go and find you a cup of coffee and a sandwich. You look exhausted.'

'I am.' He sank into the chair she'd just vacated and stared at his daughter. 'Oh, and, Keely…'

She stopped on her way to the door and turned. 'What?'

'Thanks. For everything.'

For a long moment their eyes locked and suddenly she found it hard to breathe. Was it her imagination or was he looking at her differently—almost as if he was seeing her properly for the first time?

With a supreme effort she dragged her gaze away. She was imagining things. Deluding herself as usual. Only this time she had her emotions well in hand. Zach needed her help and Keely wanted to do everything she could to make his life easier. After all, that was what friends were for.

*   *   *

Zach's house was a gorgeous stone cottage nestling at the bottom of the mountains with nothing but sheep for neighbours.

Keely looked at the keys in her hand but decided to use the bell instead. Instantly there was a thunder of feet and then a crash and noisy crying. Keely winced. Obviously a poorly, fractious toddler. Zach had sent a message down to her earlier, telling her that they were discharging Phoebe and that he'd be at home, so it wasn't a surprise to find them there.

The door opened and she grinned at Zach. 'The cavalry has arrived.'

'Well, am I glad to hear that,' he muttered, his eyes showing how tired he was. 'She's lost her favourite bear and I can't find the damn thing anywhere.'

Keely frowned. The man hadn't been to bed for almost three days if her calculations were correct. Which just showed how tough Zach was—a lesser mortal would have collapsed by now and all he had to show for it was some fine lines around those gorgeous eyes.

'Go upstairs and run yourself a hot bath,' she suggested, plopping herself down on the hall floor next to Phoebe, who was still screaming and drumming her heels. 'And then go to bed. If I need help I'll yell.'

Zach hesitated. Keely knew that he wasn't going to leave his daughter without some evidence that she could cope with the situation, so she reached into her pocket and pulled out one of the toys she'd had the foresight to buy in the hospital shop.

She didn't say anything to the toddler, just started playing with the car herself, exaggerating the engine noises and giggling just to show what fun it was. Sure enough, the screaming ceased almost instantly and a tear-stained face lifted itself from the carpet to stare at her.

'Brrmmm…' Keely pushed the car towards the wall and was gratified when Phoebe knelt up and held out a hand.

'Phoebe's turn.'

'Great idea.' Keely passed her the car, and when the little girl started to play she glanced up at Zach. 'You see? We're fine. Now, go and have that bath. Then go to bed and get some sleep. If I need you, I'll call.'

He hesitated, obviously still unsure about leaving her in charge. 'She's a pretty difficult child to handle…'

Keely gave him a gentle smile. 'Sick toddlers are always difficult. Go to bed.'

'All right, if you're sure.' He paused, still reluctant to leave her. 'If you need me—'

'I'll call,' she finished quickly, rescuing the car which had become entangled in the hall curtain. 'Goodnight, Zach.'

She pushed the car back to Phoebe and Zach gave her a tired smile.

'I haven't got the energy to argue. She needs more paracetamol in two hours. Thanks, Keely.'

Keely watched him go and then got stuck into the task of occupying a very fractious toddler. Zach hadn't been joking, she thought wryly as she coaxed and cajoled the little girl into playing with her.

Two hours later she was exhausted and running out of ideas.

'Want Daddy,' Phoebe said flatly, plopping down on the floor of the playroom which Keely had discovered at the back of the house.

'Oh, Phoebe, look, is this the bear you lost?' Looking round frantically for a distraction, she scooped up a large brown bear and handed it over with a flourish, relieved to see a smile light up the little girl's face. Thank goodness. Another crisis averted.

She quickly assembled a few other toys which she thought might be useful and then found the kitchen and made some tea for the child.

'No!!' Phoebe flung the toast onto the kitchen floor and Keely picked it up calmly and put it in the bin.

'Aren't you hungry? Don't you want anything at all?' She could see another tantrum brewing and searched quickly for another diversion. Fortunately, at that moment a cat jumped onto the window-sill and Keely silently blessed it.

'Look, Phoebe. Cat. What does the cat say?'

Phoebe looked doubtfully at the cat and her face started to crumple. 'Daddy. Want Daddy.'

'That isn't what the cat says!' Keely scooped her out of the high chair and gave her a hug. 'Cat says meow.'

Phoebe rubbed her eyes. 'Want Daddy.'

'I know you do, sausage,' Keely murmured, 'so here's what we'll do. We'll put you to bed, and later on Daddy will come in and see you.'

The poor mite was obviously still feeling poorly and upset by her trip to hospital.

Keely whisked her upstairs, bathed her and settled her in a fresh cotton T-shirt. She didn't want to put too much clothing on her in case she spiked a temperature again, and with that in mind she made herself a little bed on the sofa in Phoebe's room. Zach was too tired to listen out for the little girl tonight and at least she'd had *some* sleep the night before.

After two stories Phoebe snuggled into her bed, stuck her thumb in her mouth and promptly fell asleep.

Keely breathed a sigh of relief and tiptoed out of the room. Thank goodness for that! She cleared the debris from the bathroom and quietly pushed open Zach's bedroom door. Was he OK? Had he managed to get to sleep?

He was sprawled on his back on the bed, one arm across his forehead, his breathing even. Keely's heart twisted. The man hadn't even had the energy to get under the sheets. His dressing gown had fallen open, exposing a broad muscular chest covered in curling dark hairs.

He was going to catch cold.

Keely's mouth dried as she reached out a hand to pull his dressing gown over him. Her fingers lightly brushed his warm skin and she pulled away as if she'd been scorched. The urge to touch him was so powerful it shocked her, and she curled her fingers into fists, curbing the temptation. She wasn't going to fall for Zach again, she reminded herself firmly. She was here to help him, not to make a fool of herself all over again. That sort of behaviour was in the past.

Gingerly she lifted the edge of the duvet and tried to fold it over him, but it was trapped under his powerful body and wouldn't budge.

Maybe she could find a blanket in one of the other rooms.

Averting her eyes from his hard jaw, dark with stubble, she backed out of the room, searched the bedrooms and eventually found a spare duvet which she placed over him.

Then she checked Phoebe again, cleared the kitchen and went to bed herself. Ridiculously early, of course, but she was sure that the little girl would need her in the night so she wanted to sleep while she could.

She was in his child's room.

Zach stood in the doorway, his eyes resting on the slim figure of the woman asleep on the sofa.

When he'd woken up he'd gone straight to Phoebe's

room to check on her and then searched the house for Keely. He hadn't even noticed her asleep on the sofa in his daughter's room. He just hadn't expected her to be there. Why would she do a thing like that?

Why hadn't she just made herself comfortable in the guest room and left him to listen out for his daughter? And why had she bothered to cover him with a duvet when he was asleep?

Because that was the sort of person she was. Warm and giving. A real nurturer.

Zach gave a sigh and allowed himself the luxury of looking at Keely. She was gorgeous. That blonde hair, cut in a jagged, modern style that suited her so well, and those long, slim legs curled up on the sofa cushions. And she was even smiling in her sleep. She looked very young and very vulnerable and she was right when she accused him of treating her as a child. He *was* treating her like a child. He had to. Because if he didn't treat her as a child, he'd treat her as a woman—and if he treated her as a woman...

Damn.

He shouldn't be thinking that way about Keely.

As he stood in the doorway she stirred and then gave a gasp of fright as she saw him.

'Oh, Zach, you made me jump!' Her soft whisper made him smile and he walked over and crouched down by the sofa.

'Keely, you don't have to sleep in here. That sofa will give you backache. Go and sleep in the guest room.'

She rubbed her eyes like a sleepy child and stifled a yawn. 'What time is it?'

'One o'clock, and thanks to you I've had eight hours' uninterrupted sleep so it's your turn to get some rest.'

She shook her head. 'I'm fine. Honestly. And so's Phoebe. She had paracetamol before she went to sleep, she drank some milk and seemed fine. She hasn't woken up once. I took her duvet off and gave her blankets instead because I didn't want her to overheat.'

She'd thought of everything.

Zach felt an unfamiliar sensation tug at his insides. He lifted a hand and stroked the tempting strands of honey blonde hair that fell in a tousled mass around her pretty face, telling himself firmly that what he felt towards her was just gratitude.

She froze under his touch and stared at him like a rabbit in a trap. 'Zach?'

Her hair felt incredible. Soft and sensual, a silky curtain of temptation that he wanted to touch for ever.

Still groggy from lack of sleep, she looked totally adorable, her huge blue eyes bemused and unfocused as she looked up at him.

Driven by an impulse outside his control and beyond his understanding, he bent his head, his mouth hovering only a breath away from hers while he made a final valiant attempt to resist temptation and listen to common sense.

He saw her eyes widen, saw the question in them and then he was kissing her. Really kissing her, the way a man was meant to kiss a woman.

And she *was* a woman.

He knew that now.

There was no way he could pretend otherwise.

There was nothing childlike in the way she was responding to his kiss.

Nothing childlike in her warm, womanly response which made his guts clench and his heart thunder in his chest. He was drugged by the taste of her, by the seductive touch of her lips, and he deepened the kiss, exploring every inch of her soft mouth.

Kissing Keely.

It was something he'd never even allowed himself to contemplate. She'd always been out of bounds. The baby sister of his classmates.

But she wasn't a baby any more...

Without breaking the kiss, Zach scooped her up in his arms and sat down on the sofa, settling her on his lap so that he could have better access to her body. He felt her shiver with reaction and soothed her gently, one hand stroking her arm, the other locked in her hair, holding her head steady for his kiss.

He felt her hand reach up and part his dressing-gown and then rest tentatively on his hard chest.

Still blocking out common sense, he mirrored her action, slipping his long fingers inside her dressing-gown and touching the soft swell of her breasts. He was surprised by how full she was for such a slight woman, and her body's immediate response to his touch made the blood race through his veins.

'Drink!'

Pheobe's cry was like a cold shower and Keely gave a soft gasp and wriggled off his lap, leaving him to fight for control.

Damn.

What had he been playing at?

He ran a hand over his face and shook his head slightly to clear it.

'She's not hot. She was just thirsty.' Keely didn't look at him and Zach could tell by the dark stain on her cheeks that she didn't know what to say to him. Which was hardly surprising, because he didn't know what to say to her either.

What the hell had come over him?

'I'll sort her out. Go to bed Keely.' His voice sounded

rough. Rougher than he'd intended. 'I'll stay with her now. You need some sleep.'

Why had he done that?

Why had he kissed her when he'd known it was madness?

Because he'd lost control. And he couldn't remember the last time he'd lost control with a woman. He never lost control. Even when he had relationships—and he was becoming more and more choosy as time went on—he always managed to keep himself emotionally detached. In fact, since Catherine's death it was as if his heart had been replaced by a block of ice. He seemed incapable of feeling anything for anyone except Phoebe.

So why had he reacted so strongly to Keely?

Zach gritted his teeth and settled his daughter back in her bed. Maybe if they just ignored what had happened it would go away. They'd both been tired and worried about Phoebe, that was all. It hadn't meant anything. But he'd better make sure she understood that. The last thing he needed was Keely developing another crush on him. She wasn't the sort of woman to settle for a brief affair and he was in no shape to give anything more. He had nothing to offer a woman like Keely.

Keely walked hesitantly down the stairs the next morning and then froze when she heard laughter in the kitchen. She couldn't do it. She didn't know what to say. Turning quickly, she started to go back up the stairs, but it was too late.

'Keely?'

Zach had obviously heard her footsteps. Bother. No escape.

Now what?

What did you say to a man who'd kissed you senseless the night before and then behaved as if it hadn't happened?

'Hi, there.' She flashed him a bright smile that probably looked as false as it felt and walked briskly down the stairs as though passionate kisses in the middle of the night were an everyday occurrence. 'How's the invalid this morning?'

'Come and see for yourself.' He'd pulled on a pair of tracksuit bottoms and a loose-fitting sweatshirt, but he obviously hadn't bothered to shave. He looked breathtakingly handsome and Keely's heart thumped against her chest and threatened to obstruct her breathing.

Oh, help, it was happening all over again. She was falling for him.

No. No. No! She gritted her teeth and told herself firmly that she was doing no such thing. She was bound to find him attractive—what woman wouldn't? But that didn't mean she had real feelings for him.

She followed him into the kitchen and smiled at Phoebe who was sitting in a high chair at the table, demolishing the remains of a boiled egg.

'Hello, cherub.' Keely sat down next to the child and touched her forehead. 'You feel cool. More paracetamol?'

Zach shook his head. 'Not since the dose you gave last night. I think she's getting better.'

'Phoebe poorly,' the little girl said clearly. 'Poor Phoebe.'

Zach grinned. 'Poor Phoebe, indeed.' He ruffled her hair and sliced her toast into fingers. 'At least you're more cheerful this morning.'

Phoebe wrapped her chubby fist around a piece of buttery toast and held out her arms to her father. 'Want cuggle.'

'Cuggle?' Keely frowned and then nodded. 'Oh, I see— she wants a cuddle.'

'Finish your breakfast first,' Zach said firmly, but Phoebe started to whine and grizzle and eventually he scooped the messy toddler onto his knee, ignoring the lumps of butter and egg that attached themselves to his clothing. 'There we are, then. One cuddle coming up.'

Keely swallowed hard and reached for a piece of toast. Just seeing the two of them together turned her insides to marshmallow.

'Awful parenting, I know,' Zach said with a rueful smile, finishing his own toast as he balanced Phoebe on his lap. 'I should have been stern and made her stay in her high chair until she'd finished eating. I over-compensate all the time, I'm afraid.'

'Don't apologise Zach. You're doing a great job,' Keely said quietly, spreading butter on her toast. 'A really great job.'

Zach watched her for a moment and then pushed a mug of tea towards her. 'Here—this is yours. You deserve it after last night.'

'Thanks.'

'It's me who should be thanking you,' he said quietly, and she concentrated on her toast to hide her blush.

What exactly was he thanking her for? Kissing him?

Probably not.

'You're welcome,' she said finally, glancing up and giving Phoebe a smile. Anything rather than look him in the eye. 'Presumably you're not going in today?'

'No.' He shook his head. 'I don't want to leave her with anyone until I know she's better, but I'm going to talk to Barbara, my housekeeper, about looking after Phoebe during the day. I might go in tomorrow if she's all right.'

Keely took a sip of tea. 'I'm off tomorrow, so I'll look after her then if you like. Just to make sure that she really is on the mend before you give her to anyone non-medical.'

Those blue eyes were suddenly wary. 'Keely, there's something I need to say to you…'

Oh, help. She could guess what was coming.

'You want to talk about the kiss,' she said lightly. 'But it's OK, Zach. We were both tired. It didn't mean anything.'

There was a brief silence. 'And you're all right about that?'

'Of course,' she lied bravely. 'Why wouldn't I be?'

He gave a sigh and tilted his head against the back of the chair. 'Because, to put it bluntly, you once had a crush on me and last night I did something I shouldn't have done. I don't want you to get the wrong idea.'

He was obviously afraid she was going to throw herself at him again.

Well, she wasn't.

She'd never make that mistake again. She couldn't stop herself from finding him irresistibly attractive, but she *could* stop herself from showing it.

'Look, it was just a simple kiss,' she pointed out gently, and he gave a short laugh.

'In my experience there's no such thing. I need to spell this out, Keely, and if I hurt you then I'm sorry.' He took a deep breath and his expression was serious. 'I am not in the market for a serious relationship.'

She nodded slowly, her eyes sympathetic. 'Because of your wife?'

His jaw tightened and he stood up quickly, the chair scraping on the kitchen floor. 'Because of Catherine, yes.'

'You don't have to talk about it, Zach.'

'No.' His voice was harsh. 'And, frankly, I don't want

to. Suffice it to say that any relationships since her have been…superficial.'

Superficial?

Presumably he meant just sex.

Suddenly a lump grew in her throat. What was it like to love someone that much? So much that no one could ever take their place.

A muscle worked in his lean jaw. 'Don't fall for me, Keely.'

'Relax. I got over that when I was sixteen.'

He didn't look convinced. 'You're all right about living here? After last night?'

'Why shouldn't I be?' She gave a shrug and reached across the table to give Phoebe some more toast. 'I'm old enough to handle one kiss without falling into a swoon and expecting you to marry me.'

'You're making light of it but I just want to make sure you're clear—'

'I'm clear.' She held his gaze and smiled. 'I understand the main house rules. Residents must *not* fall in love with the master of the house. Any other rules I should know about?'

He visibly relaxed and shook his head. 'No. Aren't you going to be late for work?'

She looked at the kitchen clock. 'Oh, help. Probably! I'd forgotten I had further to drive this morning.' She stood up and waggled her fingers at Phoebe. 'I'll see you later.'

'If you have any problems today, talk to Sean,' Zach told her, frowning slightly as she picked up her bag and keys and flew towards the door.

'Yes, boss.' She grinned and opened the door, letting in a stream of icy cold air. 'See you later.'

She climbed into her little car, trying to ignore the leaden feeling in her stomach. It was all very well telling herself that she wasn't going to fall for Zach, but after that kiss… But it hadn't meant anything, she reminded herself firmly. It might have been breathtaking, and fantastic, and all the things that kisses were meant to be in fairy-tales, but it hadn't actually *meant* anything. There hadn't been any feelings behind it—at least not on Zach's part.

Zach was obviously convinced that he'd never love another woman again, and maybe he was right. Maybe for him there would never be another woman who matched up to his first wife. Certainly he'd just gone to great pains to make sure that she hadn't misunderstood the situation.

And she hadn't.

She understood perfectly.

Falling for Zach would be a quick route to a broken heart, just as Nicky had told her, and she had no intention of putting herself through that twice in a lifetime.

CHAPTER FOUR

'YOU'RE KIDDING!' Nicky stopped dead, her arms full of sterile dressing packs. 'You've *moved in* with him?'

'Why are you so surprised?' Keely caught the dressing packs before her colleague dropped them on the floor.

'Well…because… He never…' Nicky gaped at her, almost speechless, 'Zach never, *ever* lets women stay at his house. In fact, to my knowledge, he's never introduced any woman to his daughter—apart from the nannies, of course.'

Which was exactly what Zach had told her himself.

'Yes, well, that's where I fit in,' Keely said lightly, tossing the packs into the box in the treatment room, ready for the dressing clinic. 'In Zach's eyes I'm somewhere between a child and a nanny.'

Or at least she had been before last night.

'Even so, I cannot believe he's letting you stay with him.' Nicky straightened her uniform and took a deep breath. 'Maybe there's hope after all.'

'Hope for what?'

'Hope for Zach. Hope that he might one day allow himself to get involved with a woman again.' Nicky frowned. 'Frankly, he's so emotionally detached that I didn't think he'd ever let anyone get close to him again.'

'Don't get carried away, Nicky,' Keely said dryly. 'I'm staying in his house to help look after his child, not him. I'd hardly say we were close.'

It was true. Zach might have kissed her but she wasn't any closer to the real Zach than she'd been when she'd arrived. Nicky was right when she described him as emo-

70

tionally detached. He certainly was. But, of course, now she knew the reason. Part of him was locked away after the death of his wife.

Nicky shrugged. 'I still think it's a step in the right direction.'

Keely lowered her voice. 'He—he told me about his wife.'

'Did he?' Nicky sighed. 'Awful, isn't it? I don't know any of the details—it all happened before he came to the Lakes.'

'He must have loved her very much.'

'Yes. He certainly isn't interested in another serious relationship,' Nicky agreed, opening a new box of sterile needles. 'But what about you, Keely? Are you sure you're going to be able to live with the man without falling for him?'

'Honestly?' Keely gave a rueful smile. 'No, I'm not sure. But if I do fall for him I promise not to let it show.'

Nicky shook her head. 'Don't let yourself be hurt, Keely.'

'It's Zach who's hurt,' Keely said simply. 'And if I can make things better by helping out in a practical way then I will. Don't worry about me. I can cope with my feelings.'

At least, she hoped she could.

Zach was bathing Phoebe when he heard Keely's cheerful greeting from the hall.

She was home.

He lifted Phoebe out of the bath and wrapped her in a towel, ruthlessly pushing aside memories of Keely's soft mouth under his. The way she'd felt...the way she'd tasted...

Damn.

He should never have kissed her.

He'd thought of nothing else all day and, despite his

blunt warning to her this morning, he knew that the kiss was gong to cause him no end of problems. She was going to expect something he couldn't ever give a woman again.

He walked into Phoebe's bedroom, slap into Keely who was obviously looking for them.

'Oops. Sorry.' She grinned and steadied herself against the door, leaning forward to kiss Phoebe. 'How is she?'

'Much better, thanks.' Zach moved past her, trying not to notice her flushed cheeks or her happy smile. If he looked at her smile then he'd see her lips, and if he saw her lips he'd want to kiss them again...

What on earth was the matter with him? He never normally had any trouble resisting women. In fact, he'd become something of an expert at keeping them at a distance. Why was Keely proving so much of a temptation? She wasn't even his usual type, if he was honest. Normally he ended up with cool, sophisticated women—like Catherine. But Keely was nothing like Catherine. Maybe that was it. Maybe he was attracted to Keely because she was as unlike his first wife as a woman could possibly have been.

'Why don't I put her to bed?' Keely reached out to take Phoebe from him, but she squirmed away and clung to her father.

'Sorry. Don't take it personally.' Suddenly Zach felt exhausted. 'She's always been quite clingy. She doesn't go to people very easily.'

'Well, that's understandable,' Keely said softly, a sympathetic smile on her face. 'Phoebe, shall we go and look out of your bedroom window? We might see that cat again.'

Phoebe stiffened and looked suspiciously at Keely. 'Cat in garden?'

'Maybe.' Keely nodded and gave the little girl a smile. 'What do you think? Shall we go and look?'

Phoebe hesitated and then nodded and reached out her arms.

Zach hid his surprise and watched as Keely settled his daughter on her hip, still chatting about the cat.

Damn, she was good with children. Incredibly patient and good-humoured. He knew only too well just how difficult Phoebe could be, but Keely didn't seem bothered by her behaviour. Just incredibly understanding. And smart. She always had a distraction ready, something to capture the little girl's interest.

'You could pour yourself a drink and put your feet up.' Her eyes were twinkling at him and he frowned and shook his head.

'You're the one that's been at work all day.'

'And work is nothing compared to looking after a toddler, as we both know,' she said with a laugh. 'Go on. We're going to look for the cat. Pour me a glass of wine while you're there and I'll be down in a minute. White, please.'

But he couldn't move. Seeing his daughter cuddled close to a woman made his insides twist.

'Are you OK?' Keely's voice was soft and her eyes were concerned. 'Zach? Have I done something?'

'No. You haven't done anything,' Zach said roughly, 'and I'm fine.'

Damn.

It wasn't her fault that his emotions were in a mess. But he was going to have to be more careful in the future. He knew what Keely was like—if she guessed just how raw he was inside then she'd be trying to mother him and sort him out. And that was the last thing he wanted.

'Daddy poorly,' Phoebe said emphatically, and Zach gave a wry smile and ruffled her soft blonde hair.

'Daddy's not poorly,' he reassured her gently, stiffening as Keely touched his arm, her expression still worried.

'Do you want to talk about it?'

'Nothing to talk about.' He detached himself from her touch and walked towards the door. 'I'll go and pour the drinks.'

It was typical of Keely to think that talking would solve his problems, typical of her trusting, optimistic approach to life. He most certainly didn't want to discuss his feelings with her and he had no intention of dumping his hurt or bitterness in her lap. He didn't want to use her in that way. She was still young and naïve enough to believe that relationships could end happily ever after. Who was he to disillusion her?

He gave a short laugh. And anyway, if he was honest, talking was the last thing on his mind. What he *really* wanted to do was drag her into his bedroom and have his wicked way with her. Lose himself in that gentle warmth and amazing passion which he'd glimpsed the previous night when he'd kissed her—

Which was out of the question, of course.

Keely wasn't that sort of person. For all he knew, she might even still be a virgin. But whether she was or wasn't, she certainly wasn't the type to go to bed with a man unless she was emotionally attached. And emotional attachment was definitely off the agenda.

Keely hesitated in the doorway of the kitchen, unsure whether Zach would welcome her presence. He'd been very short with her upstairs and she wasn't entirely sure why, although she could guess. Seeing another woman getting close to his daughter must be hard for him, even if she was only a friend.

So what should she say?

Deciding to keep it neutral, she stepped into the kitchen and settled herself at the table.

'Nice smell.' She gave an appreciative sniff and rested

her chin on her palm as she watched him cook. 'What are we having?'

'Nothing exciting.' He reached into the fridge and removed a bag of ready-prepared salad. 'Lasagne OK with you?'

'More than OK. I love it. Is this mine?' She leaned forward and picked up one of the glasses of wine that he'd poured. 'Zach, I don't expect you to cook for me if I'm living here. I can look after myself.'

He shrugged. 'It makes sense to eat together if we're both in.' He threw a smile over his shoulder. 'Don't worry, it's your turn tomorrow.'

'Deal.' She grinned and took a sip of wine. 'I love your house, by the way.'

'Do you?' He put the food on the table and settled himself opposite her. 'I like it, too, but some of the nannies have found it a bit isolated. It's hardly close to the local nightspots.'

She chuckled. 'Are there any?'

'A few.' He handed her a spoon. 'Help yourself.'

Keely helped herself to a generous portion of lasagne. 'So how many nannies have you had?'

'Four in total. It's been a nightmare.' He heaped salad onto his plate and pushed the bowl towards her. 'The first one stayed two months, the second one managed eight months, which was pretty good, the third one stayed one month—that was bad—and the last one, well, you know about her.'

His mouth tightened and Keely pushed his wine towards him.

'Don't think about her,' she advised. 'Why did the others leave?'

'Various reasons. Phoebe was difficult—missing her mother.' His tone was casual but a faint colour touched his hard cheekbones and Keely frowned at him suspiciously.

'And?'

'What?' He took a slug of wine and glanced up at her, his expression remote.

'There must have been more to it than that. A professional nanny should have been able to cope with one little girl, however difficult.' Keely's eyes widened as the penny suddenly dropped. 'It wasn't Phoebe, was it? It was you. They all fell in love with you, didn't they?'

He gave a short laugh. 'I wouldn't exactly put it like that.'

She put her fork down and stared at him. 'Oh, Zach, that must have been the last thing you needed.'

'That's an understatement.' He stabbed his salad with more force than was warranted. 'It certainly made it difficult for Phoebe. Every time she got used to a nanny, I had to get rid of her.'

Ouch. More reasons for him to avoid women.

'Did they cause you real trouble?'

'Yes.'

His economical response made her smile. 'Go on, give me the gory details.'

'You want details?' He sighed and sat back in his chair. 'All right. I found number one lying in my bed, waiting for me, when I came back from the hospital one night. That was tricky.'

Keely gasped and covered her mouth with her hand. 'Oh, Zach! What did you do?'

'Not what she wanted me to do,' he said dryly. 'Number two was slightly more subtle. She made my dinner every night and finally burst into tears and said that she couldn't carry on living with me unless I married her because she was so in love with me.'

'Ouch.' Keely pulled a sympathetic face. 'And number three?'

'Number three was virtually a repeat of number one but slightly more pornographic.'

'Oh, dear.' Keely put her fork down and started to laugh. 'Maybe you should have recruited an older nanny?'

'You think I didn't try that?' He drained his wine and stared into the empty glass. 'Unfortunately they all have their own families and don't want to live in. With the demands of my job, I need someone to live in.'

Keely picked up her fork and started eating again. 'Talking of which, did you manage to speak to your housekeeper today?'

'Barbara?' He nodded. 'Yes. Thankfully she's only too happy to help. She adores Phoebe and really wanted to look after her but couldn't offer before because she couldn't cover the nights.'

Keely's eyes twinkled. 'And will you be safe from your housekeeper or are you likely to find her lying naked in your bed?'

His smile was wry. 'She's fifty-six with two grandchildren of her own, so I think that the only thing she's likely to be doing with my bed is making it.' He cleared his plate and pushed the dish towards her. 'Have some more.'

'Thanks, it's delicious.' She spooned more onto her plate and noticed him watching her curiously. 'What?'

'It's just very refreshing, being with a woman who eats. Normally women pick at their food.'

'Don't remind me. My appetite is my biggest failing,' Keely told him gloomily as he topped up their wineglasses.

'Why? You hardly need to watch your weight—you've got a fabulous figure.'

Her eyes lifted to his and she blushed gently at the reminder that he was fairly intimately acquainted with her figure after the kiss they'd shared the previous night.

They stared at each other for a long moment, awareness sizzling between them. Then Zach stood up abruptly, his chair scraping the floor as he moved away from the table.

Keely took a deep breath and tried to slow her pulse rate. They'd gone from comfortable to awkward in the space of a second.

'Listen, Keely…' He turned to face her and his voice was rough. 'About last night—'

'We already discussed last night, Zach,' she reminded him calmly, 'and you made your position quite clear.'

A muscle worked in his jaw. 'I was wrong to kiss you—'

'Stop worrying,' she said quietly. 'It was just a kiss. This may come as a surprise to you but I have been kissed before. Please, don't think I'm reading anything into it. We were both worried about Phoebe and weird things happen to common sense in the middle of the night.'

He sighed and ran a hand through his hair. 'Maybe, but that's no excuse on my part. I should have shown some self-control.'

She was glad that he hadn't. Which was ridiculous, of course, because that kiss had left her wanting something she knew she couldn't have.

'I don't know why you're worrying. Let's just try and forget it,' she suggested lightly, standing up and loading her plate into the dishwasher.

'Can you do that?'

She looked him straight in the eye and summoned up her best acting skills. 'Of course. I've already told you that I've moved beyond the stage of childish crushes.'

It was a half-truth. She'd definitely moved beyond childish crushes. *But what about the more adult version?*

He hesitated, his eyes searching hers. 'Keely, if you want to move out I'll understand.'

'Move out?' Her eyes widened. 'Do you want me to move out?'

'Of course I don't. You're fantastic with Phoebe, even when she's at her most difficult, and you're helping me out of a very tight spot. I'd have to be mad to want to let you go. But you're making all the sacrifices.'

'I'm helping a friend,' she said gently, touching his arm. 'And I'll carry on helping for just as long as you need me. Now, are you going to relax and make us both some coffee or are you going to continue scowling at me?'

She busied herself tidying up the kitchen, hoping that he'd drop the subject. She didn't want to be forced to examine her feelings for him too closely. She had a feeling that what she might find would scare her even more than Zach.

The rest of the week passed quickly and on Friday Keely was snatching a well-deserved cup of coffee in the staff common room when Adam came into the room.

'OK, who's the best with screaming toddlers?' He flopped into one of the chairs and pulled a face. 'I've totally failed, I'm afraid. I can't get near the child.'

Nicky grinned. 'I thought you had children of your own.'

'I have.' Adam looked sheepish. 'My wife deals with the difficult bits. Tantrums are her department.'

Keely took pity on him and stood up. 'What's the story?'

'Head injury and, frankly, it's heading fast for another one if it doesn't stop flinging itself on the ground.'

'You'd probably strike up a better relationship if you didn't refer to the child as "it",' Keely said dryly, walking towards the door and looking towards Nicky. 'Any help on offer?'

'Zoe is already down in the paediatric area,' Nicky said hurriedly. 'And she's a qualified paediatric nurse. Much better with toddlers than I am.'

Keely glanced round at her colleagues in frustration. 'You're all hopeless!'

Rolling her eyes and shaking her head, she left the room and walked down the corridor, wincing as she heard the screams. Adam hadn't been exaggerating. The little girl was lying on the floor, ignoring all attempts to soothe and placate her.

Keely gave the A and E staff nurse a smile and walked casually over to the toy box. Then she sat down on the floor and started rummaging through it, careful not to look at the toddler.

'Oh, look at this, Zoe!' She pulled out a brightly coloured train and set it on the floor. 'Have we got any track?'

She rummaged again and managed to find some track.

'You start at that end of the room, Zoe, and I'll meet you in the middle.'

The staff nurse obligingly dropped to her knees and started to assemble the train track. As Keely had hoped, the screaming suddenly stopped and the toddler sat watching them, thumb jammed into her mouth.

'Any carriages?' Keely delved again and found a rather battered carriage. 'Perfect. Now I need someone to fix it to the engine.'

'Em's turn.' The child scrambled unevenly to her feet and tottered over. 'Em's turn.'

'Is that you?' Keely handed her the carriage. 'Are you Em?'

The toddler nodded, thumb still jammed in her mouth.

'Short for Emma—or Emily?'

'Emily,' the mother said quietly. 'But we tend to call her Em because that's what she calls herself.'

'And how old is she?'

'Two and a half.'

'Right.' Keely turned back to the toddler. 'What colour is this train, Em?'

'Wed. Wed and boo.'

'Clever girl.' Keely beamed at her. 'Red and blue. And can you fix it to the carriage for me?'

Em removed her thumb from her mouth and snapped the two toys together with ease.

'Brilliant. Now, can you put them on the track and push them to my friend Zoe?'

The toddler plopped onto the floor and pushed the train along to the nurse.

'Well, she seems quite lucid and she's playing happily,' Keely said, reaching for the notes Zoe had placed on the couch and quickly scanning them. 'What happened, Mrs Barrett?'

'She tripped and banged her head on the coffee-table.'

Was it her imagination or did the woman look nervous?

'And did she cry straight away?'

Mrs Barrett nodded and licked her lips. 'Oh, yes. She was hysterical.'

Keely gave her a sympathetic smile. 'Well, at least we know she wasn't knocked out. Has she been sick or drowsy?'

'No, nothing like that.'

'I just need to take a look in her eyes and examine the bump,' Keely explained, reaching for an ophthalmoscope and a teddy. 'OK, look at this, Em.'

She switched on the ophthalmoscope and pointed it at the teddy, pretending to examine its button eyes.

'Em's turn.' The toddler was by her side in an instant. 'Want torch.'

'Please,' her mother prompted automatically.

'Pees.' The little girl reached out to grab the ophthalmoscope and Keely whipped out a pen torch. 'This one's for Em. Em, look at the teddy and Keely look at Em.'

Quickly, knowing that she didn't have time to waste, she examined the child's eyes.

'Does your head hurt, Em?'

'Em hurt. Rick push Em.'

Keely stopped what she was doing and her eyes met the mother's. 'Someone pushed her?'

'No.' Mrs Barrett swept the toddler into her arms. 'No one pushed her. My boyfriend was walking past and knocked into her, but it was an accident.'

Keely's instincts were on full alert but she knew better than to alienate the mother at this stage.

'That happens so easily with toddlers.' She held out her arms. 'Em come with Keely?'

Em slipped easily into her arms and she strolled up to the trolley and sat her down.

'I just need to finish examining her, Mrs Barrett.'

She slipped the little girl's dress over her head and tickled the child's stomach until she gurgled with laughter.

The mother stared at her suspiciously. 'Why are you undressing her when she banged her head?'

'Because toddlers fall for a number of reasons,' Keely said smoothly. 'Sometimes it's because they're unsteady on their feet and sometimes it could be because they have an infection of some sort which can affect their balance. We always do a full check with a head injury. I'll want to check her ears and throat as well.'

Zoe stepped over, her expression friendly. 'Mrs Barrett, can I just get you to fill out this card for me with Emily's details?'

As the child's mother followed Zoe without question, Keely was able to examine the child thoroughly, which had obviously been the staff nurse's intention. Blessing her quick thinking, Keely examined the child, frowning slightly as she saw the faint yellow bruises on her upper arms.

Her lower legs were covered in bruises, too, but these were less concerning because children of Emily's age fell over so frequently.

Taking a quick look at her back, she saw faint marks that made her feel decidedly uneasy. Could it be what she suspected? It was so difficult to tell in children of this age who were frequently covered in bruises.

'Well done, Em.' She slipped the dress back over the little girl's head and glanced at Zoe.

'I just need to talk to Mr Jordan and then we'll sort out that head.' She turned to the mother with a relaxed smile. 'Mrs Barrett, Emily has a nasty bump on the head and we may well need to admit her to our paediatric ward for twenty-four hours' observation.'

The mother looked uneasy. 'I thought she could go straight home.'

'I don't think so.' Keely wrote carefully on the notes, documenting everything she'd found. 'Head injuries can be deceptive in small children. I just need to talk to one of our consultants.'

She walked briskly down the corridor and found Zach examining a young woman with chest pains.

'Can I see you when you have a minute?'

He gave a nod, finished his examination and then handed over to Adam.

'Problems?' He walked with her into the corridor and she bit her lip.

'Maybe. I've got a two-and-a-half-year-old in Paediatric Casualty with a bang on the head. Mother says she tripped and banged her head on the table but the toddler says she was pushed. I've examined her thoroughly and she has marks consistent with old bruising on her upper arms and back.'

'Children of that age are always covered in bruises,' Zach reminded her, his gaze quizzical. 'Phoebe's the same.'

Keely nodded. 'I know that. But these bruises aren't in the common places.'

Zach rubbed his chin, his expression suddenly watchful. 'And you think it's non accidental?'

'I don't know.' Keely hesitated. 'I don't want to think that, but all my instincts are saying that something isn't right.'

'How does she react to the mother?'

'Fine.' Keely shrugged. 'Mother seems a bit nervous but that could just be because it's hospital, of course.'

'Any sign of Dad?'

Keely shook her head, wishing his gaze wasn't quite so blue or so direct. It made it hard to concentrate. 'No dad. Mother mentioned a boyfriend. The same person that the toddler said pushed her.'

Zach frowned. 'I don't think you can rely on the evidence of a two-and-a-half-year-old, Keely.'

Keely took a deep breath. 'I know that, but will you just look at her?'

'I'll look at her.' For a moment their eyes held and tension sparked between them, then he muttered something under his breath and strode off down the corridor, leaving her feeling weak-kneed.

Quickly she pulled herself together and caught up with him. 'I've warned the mother that we may want to admit her for twenty-four hours' observation.'

Zach paused. 'Have you checked the register?'

Keely shook her head. All the A and E staff had access

to the Child Protection Register which listed children considered to be at risk.

'Check the register and meet me down there.'

Zach strode off and Keely hurried to Reception. There was no record of the child on the register, and by the time she got back to Paediatric Casualty Zach had finished his examination.

He was playing comfortably with Emily and had the mother eating out of his hand.

'Dr Thompson is quite right, Mrs Barrett,' he said smoothly, casting a relaxed smile in Keely's direction. Not by the flicker of an eyelid did he betray that anything was amiss. 'Emily has had a bang on the head so we would like to keep her in overnight. I'll call the paediatricians.'

Mrs Barrett complained a bit but also looked slightly relieved.

'Odd,' Keely said afterwards as she and Zach walked back towards the staffroom. 'It was almost as if she wanted the child to be admitted.'

'So maybe it is the boyfriend and he's out of control.' Zach shrugged and held the door open for her. 'Either way, it's not our problem any more. Paeds can deal with it. If necessary, they'll get an emergency protection order.'

Keely bit her lip. 'But maybe I should contact the health visitor or the GP, or maybe—'

'Keely, this is A and E,' Zach pointed out gently. 'The child has been admitted. Paeds will deal with all that.'

'But—'

'We can't get involved in the small details of people's lives,' Zach reminded her. 'We just repair the surface damage and leave the rest to someone else.'

But that wasn't what she wanted to do. She wanted to see it through. She wanted to make sure that the patients were all right once they got home, that they could cope…

'Three cheers for Keely.' Adam was back in the common room, a big grin on his face. 'What you don't know, Dr Thompson, is that we all sneaked down after you to watch you with that child. We thought we might learn something.'

'Never knew you liked trains so much,' Nicky teased, 'or that you found the floor so comfortable.'

Keely rolled her eyes. 'Pick up any tips?'

'Yes.' Adam gave a broad grin. 'If it's a child, call Keely. I need all the help I can get when it comes to children. I'm the first to admit it. I never know where to start but you were fantastic.'

'You're being ridiculous,' Keely said gruffly, blushing as she walked across to the kettle and flicked the switch. 'I'm no better with children than anyone else is.'

'Yes, you are.' Zach looked at her steadily. 'Adam's right. You're incredibly good with children. You know just what to say and what to do to get the best out of them. You're great at averting tantrums and you seem to be able to coax a smile from the most moody, miserable child.'

She stared at him, stunned by his praise, and then Adam cleared his throat.

'So, on the strength of that reference, Dr Thompson, maybe you should be applying for a job as a paediatrician. What is it you're planning to do when you finish here?'

Keely licked dry lips. 'Cardiology.'

'Well, it's a waste,' Adam said cheerfully. 'You should definitely go into paediatrics. Don't you agree, Zach?'

There was a brief silence while Zach watched her. 'I think she should do whatever she wants to do.'

Keely turned away quickly and busied herself making the coffee. She wished they'd change the subject. She really didn't know what she wanted to do, or how she felt about her career.

She passed Zach a coffee and for a brief moment their eyes meshed. And she knew. Knew without a doubt that there was one thing she *was* sure of. She loved Zach Jordan.

She always had done, and she always would do.

CHAPTER FIVE

IT WAS her turn to cook supper.

Keely let herself into the house, said goodnight to Barbara, who'd been in charge all day, then played a game about body parts with a giggling Phoebe.

'Nose.' Phoebe put a little hand over her nose and then touched Keely's nose.

'Eyes.' Keely pointed to her eyes and then her chin. 'What's this?'

'Chin.' Phoebe clambered onto Keely's lap and buried her face in her chest. 'Bosoms. Nice. Soft.'

Keely's chuckle turned to a blush as she glanced up and saw Zach standing there. 'Oh!' her voice was an embarrassed squeak. 'We didn't hear you.'

He didn't even try and hide his laughter. 'Obviously not.'

Help! Why did he make her feel so hot and bothered? And why, when she was dying to see the man laugh, did it have to be at her expense?

'Well, now you're home you can take over and I'll make supper. You did it last night.' Keely stood up and handed him his daughter, her face still burning with mortification.

'Neck.' Phoebe reached out and wrapped her arms around her father's neck, and Keely slunk out of the room before the child picked out any more embarrassing bits. Next time she'd just play a quiet game of hide and seek.

She concentrated her attentions on the supper and by the time Zach reappeared, having put Phoebe to bed, she had herself under control again.

'Adam was right. You're so good with small children,'

he observed, leaning forward and helping himself to some olives she'd put on the table.

Keely laughed and gave the casserole a stir. 'Don't tell me—you think I should be a paediatrician, too.'

He sat back in his chair. 'What I think doesn't matter—you should be what you want to be.' His tone was even. 'Why do you want to be a cardiologist?'

Her hand froze and for a moment she stopped stirring. The honest answer was that she didn't know that she *did* want to be a cardiologist. But she couldn't tell him that. Zach was like the rest of her family, ferociously intelligent and aiming for the top of his profession. He wouldn't understand her doubts. Wouldn't understand if she confessed that she wasn't sure she wanted any sort of hospital career…

'Why do I want to be a cardiologist?' She started stirring again and fished around in her brain for the sort of plausible answer one might give at an interview. 'All sorts of reasons. I find cardiology fascinating, I like the intellectual challenge, the variety, the research opportunities—loads of things.'

She tasted the casserole, added more salt and then placed it in the centre of the table.

'This smells delicious.' Zach leaned forward and gave an appreciative sniff. 'So, have you applied for anything?'

'Not yet.' She handed him a spoon and watched while he served himself. 'There's a post coming up in London that Dad wants me to apply for. It's with Professor Harding.'

'*The* Professor Harding?' Zach lifted an eyebrow. 'I'm impressed. You're certainly heading for the big time.'

'I didn't say I'd got the post,' Keely reminded him dryly. 'I just said that Dad wants me to apply.'

Zach was suddenly still. 'And are you going to?'

'Probably,' Keely said quietly, carefully hiding just how

unenthusiastic she felt about the whole thing. 'But he gets loads of applicants, of course, so I probably won't even get an interview.'

'You're a clever girl, Keely. I'm sure you'll walk into any job you want.' His jaw was tense. 'So you're definitely planning on going back to London at the end of your six months, then?'

His tone was slightly cool and she frowned slightly, wondering why. Was he checking that she wasn't getting any silly ideas about staying near him? That she wasn't altering her career plans for him? Well, he didn't need to worry on that score. Whatever she decided about her future, she was going to make sure it was well away from Zach. He'd made it crystal clear that he didn't want any sort of relationship with her. Or with any other woman.

She gave a nod. 'Yes, I'm going back to London.'

It would be the best thing for all of them. Obviously what he'd shared with his wife had been too special ever to be repeated. But everyone needed friends and she could be a good friend to him. She'd stay around and help him until he sorted out his child-care arrangements and then she'd move out and try to build a life without him.

The next day they were both working the early shift and it turned into a horrendously busy morning. The weather was freezing, the roads were icy and by nine o'clock they'd had two nasty RTAs—road traffic accidents—admitted to the unit.

They'd only just cleared up and restocked the resus room when a man was admitted with a penetrating chest injury.

'He was stabbed on his way to work. Would you believe it? Broad daylight. What a bloodbath,' Nicky muttered as she applied pressure to the wounds and jerked her head towards a nurse. 'Someone call Zach now! *Move!*'

'What happened?' Zach came into Resus seconds later, took one look at the patient and started scrubbing.

'He was stabbed twice in the chest.' Keely's voice faltered slightly as she struggled to get a line in. Thank goodness Zach was here. For once she was willing to admit that she was totally out of her depth. 'He's got distended neck veins, hypotension and muffled heart sounds. I think he might have a cardiac tamponade.'

A tamponade was bleeding into the sac that surrounded the heart and Keely knew it was potentially life-threatening.

Zach lathered down to his elbows. 'Has he got an output?'

'Yes—I've fast-bleeped the cardiothoracic team but they're in Theatre. They'll be here as soon as possible.'

'OK.' Zach turned the taps off with his elbows. 'Let's give him oxygen, Nicky, and get two lines in. And someone get me a thoracotomy tray just in case.'

'It's on your left,' Nicky said as she glanced at the monitor. 'Damn. He's arrested.'

'OK, we're going to have to open him up.' Zach spoke calmly, as if it were an everyday occurrence. 'Get that pack open, Nicky, and let's get some blood down here fast. I'm going to open his chest.'

He worked with such speed and skill that Keely couldn't keep pace with him.

'Rib retractors!'

Obediently Keely produced the retractors and helped him position them so that he had better access to the chest cavity.

'OK, I can see the heart. Hell, what a mess.' He frowned and reached into the chest while Keely watched in silent admiration. How could he begin to see what he was doing? With a sure movement he cut through the bulging pericardium and evacuated the blood. 'I can see a tear.'

He put his finger over the defect and performed internal cardiac massage by pressing the heart between his hands.

Just then the doors flew open and the cardiothoracic surgeon strode in. 'For Pete's sake, Zach, couldn't you wait?'

'Needed the practice.' Zach grinned and glanced towards Nicky. 'Get the expert some gloves, will you? And some 4/0 prolene sutures.'

Swiftly the team worked together to save the man, and finally Zach glanced up at the monitor. 'All right, I'm stopping massage.'

There was a tense silence in the room while everyone watched the monitor and then Zach muttered under his breath, 'Come on, come on, give me an output.'

As if following his instructions, the ECG machine sprang to life and Keely gasped with delight, as did the rest of the team.

'Good work, folks.' Zach glanced up. 'Let's get a CVP line in and give him some cefuroxime. Then I want an arterial line inserted and a catheter. Keely, recheck his U and E, glucose, FBC and clotting, please. Anything else, David?'

'You've just about covered it,' the cardiothoracic surgeon drawled, lifting an eyebrow. 'Are you after my job?'

'Most definitely not.' Zach stripped off his gloves and gave a wry smile. 'I can't stand the sight of blood.'

The immediate crisis over, Keely treated herself to a long look at Zach. His short hair was slightly dishevelled, his jaw was already showing signs of stubble and his eyes were beginning to show the strain of the past few hours. But she'd never loved him more in her life. Not just because he was so handsome that he made her knees weak, but because he was the cleverest, most impressive man she'd ever met.

Her siblings were clever, but somehow they always

managed to make her feel inferior. Zach never did that. He made everyone feel that their contribution was important. And no matter what came through the doors, Zach never lost his cool. Even when he was operating under pressure, he still found time to involve and praise the staff who worked with him. He'd thanked them as a team for saving the young man's life, but in reality the skill had been *his*.

'Snap out of it.' Nicky's soft voice brought her back to earth sharply and Keely gave a weak smile.

'Sorry. I was dreaming.'

'And no prizes for guessing who you were dreaming about.' Nicky adjusted the IV and put the notes on the trolley, ready for transfer to ITU. 'Mind you, I don't blame you. That was some performance. Impressive, isn't he?'

Keely nodded and glanced across the room to where Zach was standing with the cardiothoracic surgeon. 'How does he do it?' She kept her voice low so that he couldn't hear her. 'How can he stay so calm? All I could see was blood. Why didn't he panic?'

'Zach? Zach never panics,' Nicky said simply. 'Nothing ever throws him. Certainly not blood. But, then, he was a surgeon, of course. I suppose that helps.'

And he'd been a very skilled surgeon if her father's reports were correct.

'Well, that man was jolly lucky he was on duty,' Keely said gruffly, and Nicky gave her a sympathetic smile.

'Oh, dear, you really have got him badly, haven't you?'

Keely opened her mouth to deny it but then decided not to bother. 'Very badly. I can't sleep without dreaming of him and I lose concentration at work if I'm not very, very careful. I'm afraid I'm going to do myself serious internal damage hiding it from him.'

'Never mind that,' Nicky muttered hastily. 'Just make

sure you *do* hide it or you'll find that he also has a reputation for biting impatience with women who drool over him.'

Keely bit her lip and then gave a start as she realised that he'd walked over to her, his blue eyes quizzical.

'Is something wrong?' His voice was quiet.

'Yes. I'm feeling totally incompetent,' she confessed, sliding her fingers through her blonde hair and giving a helpless shrug. 'I was useless back there and I'm really sorry.'

'Useless?' He looked genuinely puzzled. 'When were you useless?'

'With that patient. I didn't have a clue what to do, and I couldn't keep up with you—'

'Keely, the man was stabbed through the heart. I wouldn't have expected you to know what to do.' He frowned and shook his head slightly. 'That sort of emergency happens about once every year or even less in A and E. It's almost impossible to gain experience in that sort of technique.'

'But you knew what to do, Zach.'

And from what she'd seen, he *always* knew what to do.

'I'm a consultant, Keely,' he reminded her gently. 'I'm supposed to know what to do. In another seven years you'll know what to do as well if you choose to stay in this discipline. Don't lose confidence. You're an excellent doctor.'

'Oh.' She blushed slightly, warmed by his praise. 'Had you done that before?'

'Several times.' He gave a wry smile. 'I worked in South Africa for a while and there's no shortage of trauma experience there, I can assure you.'

He stepped to one side to have a final word with the cardiothoracic surgeon, and Keely dragged her eyes away from him with a huge effort.

'Keely, you're doing it again,' Nicky muttered in an undertone. 'Get a grip.'

'Sorry.'

She couldn't help the way she felt about him. She loved him more every day and she loved Phoebe, too. And the more she loved them, the more she wanted to make everything better for them.

Arriving at work the next morning, Keely wondered how much longer she was going to be able to carry on working with Zach without giving herself away. Every time he walked into the room her knees wobbled alarmingly and her pulse rate soared.

At least the department was busy, which helped take her mind off him for some of the time.

She was seeing a woman with an injured wrist when she heard screaming from Resus.

Now what?

Even as she was wondering what was happening one of the student nurses appeared at her elbow.

'Can you come quickly, Dr Thompson?'

Immediately Keely excused herself and hurried into Resus.

'What's the problem?'

'Help!' A young woman was sobbing and yelling, her white-faced husband clutching her hand as she writhed on the trolley.

'How are you at delivering babies?' Nicky asked grimly, wrenching open a delivery pack and addressing the student nurse. 'Call the labour ward now, please—get them down here urgently. Zach's on his way.'

Delivering babies?

Keely felt a twinge of panic. She hadn't done obstetrics yet and although she'd seen a baby delivered as a medical student, she was hardly an expert.

'When's the baby due?'

The woman groaned but her husband glanced up, his face strained. 'Not for another week.'

'And is this your first baby?'

He nodded. 'Yes. I thought first labours were supposed to last a long time.'

'Not always,' Keely murmured, giving them a reassuring smile. 'But don't worry. Everything will be fine. OK.' She took a deep breath. 'Can I have some size-six gloves, please, Nicky, and let's listen to the foetal heart.'

She was washing her hands when Zach arrived, his eyes focusing straight on Keely.

'What's the story?'

'Precipitate labour,' Keely said quickly, relief flooding through her. At least the responsibility wasn't all hers now. Would Zach know what to do?

He did, of course, dragging on a pair of sterile gloves and examining the labouring woman, talking quietly to her all the time.

His voice seemed to calm her and the woman stopped screaming, instead tightening her grip on her husband's hand and fastening her eyes on Zach with a trusting expression on her face.

'It's coming, isn't it?'

'It certainly is.' Zach gave a lopsided grin and then glanced at the notes to check the woman's name. 'Try and remember your breathing, Tina. That's it—good.' He looked at Nicky. 'Let's give her some Entonox, please. Keely? Do you want to…?'

He was asking her if she wanted to deliver the baby and she shook her head vigorously. She didn't have the confidence to deliver a baby.

'No—no, you do it.'

He gave a slight smile and stood on the right of the patient. 'OK, Tina, just keep breathing, that's it…'

'I've rung the labour ward,' Nicky said in an undertone, 'and someone is coming down to help.'

'Well, they're not going to be much help unless they're here in the next two minutes,' Zach said calmly, 'because this baby isn't going to wait. All right, Tina, you're doing well. I can see the baby's head. Let's see if we can get you a bit more upright.'

They helped Tina wriggle into a better position and Zach waited until her next contraction.

'Keely, come a bit closer so that you can see.'

Keely obeyed his instruction, watching with fascination as the baby's head crowned.

'The foetal heart is dipping,' Nicky said quietly, and Zach nodded.

'Pant for me, Tina,' he said quietly. 'Don't push. Good girl, well done. Let's get this baby out.'

Keely watched as he used his left hand to control the rate of escape of the head.

'Excellent.' Having delivered the head, he allowed it to extend and then used his fingers to feel for the cord, slipping it over the baby's neck. 'There we are. Nicky, have you got the ergometrine ready?' He turned back to Tina. 'We're just going to give you something to make your uterus contract once the baby is delivered. It's perfectly normal.'

She nodded and then screwed up her face and yelled as another contraction hit her and the baby shot into Zach's waiting hands.

He placed the baby gently on Tina's stomach. 'A little girl. Congratulations.'

'Oh, Mike!' Tina looked at her husband and tears spilled down her cheeks. 'Mike, she's beautiful.'

'She certainly is.' Her husband bent down and kissed her gently, his eyes damp. 'We're a family now. A real family.'

The baby cried loudly and everyone sniffed and looked decidedly emotional. All except Zach, whose face was strangely devoid of expression.

Keely watched as he clamped the cord and cut it and then examined the vessels.

Something was the matter with him.

Was it seeing the baby born? Was it the husband's comments about being a family? It must be awful for him, seeing other happy couples with children when he—

Damn. She couldn't bear to think about how much he must be hurting.

'Keely.' His voice was slightly sharp, as if he'd guessed what she was thinking. 'Can you remember what to look for?' He was as cool and professional as ever as she moved closer to see what he was doing.

'Two arteries?'

'That's right.' He shifted his position just as a man in theatre greens walked into the room.

Zach looked up. 'You've missed the action, Jed. Sorry.'

The other man grinned and looked down at the woman on the trolley. 'Trying to give everyone a heart attack, were you, Tina?'

The young woman still looked shell-shocked. 'At least she didn't arrive while we were shopping.'

'Yes, let's be thankful for small mercies,' the obstetrician agreed, glancing at Zach. 'Any problems?'

Zach shook his head. 'I'm just delivering the placenta. Do you want to take over?'

'Not especially.' But Jed stayed close by, talking calmly to the couple, keeping an eye on proceedings. Finally he gave Zach a thump on the back.

'Well done. We'll take it from here if that's all right with you.'

'Fine.' Zach stood up and ripped off his gloves, tossing

them in the bin before moving back to the trolley and smiling at Tina. 'Well done.'

'You can have a cuddle if you like,' Tina said, but Zach's smile faded and his expression was suddenly remote.

'Thanks, but I'd better not. The sooner you get up to the ward the better.'

With that he picked up the notes and glanced at Nicky. 'I'll write up the notes in my office. Can one of you take them up to the ward later?'

Nicky nodded. 'Of course.'

Keely watched with concern as he strode out of the room. He was upset. He was definitely upset.

So what should she do about it?

Should she ignore it? Let him bottle it up?

Or should she follow her instincts and see if he needed a friend...?

CHAPTER SIX

KEELY hesitated outside Zach's office and then tapped gently on the door.

He should have finished writing the notes by now but there was no sign of him emerging from his office. And she was worried about him.

She tapped again and gingerly opened the door, stopping dead when she saw him standing with his back to her, his powerful shoulders tense as he stared out of the window at the snow-capped mountains.

'Zach?'

He didn't turn. 'The notes are on the desk.'

Keely closed the door behind her, refusing to be daunted by his discouraging tone.

'I don't want the notes.' On impulse she turned the key in his door and then stood for a moment, wondering how best to break down the barriers he'd built around himself.

He turned to face her, his eyes tired. 'This isn't a good time.'

'I know that.' She hesitated, knotting her fingers together anxiously. 'But I was worried about you'

'I'm fine, Keely.' He looked at her for a moment and then turned back to the window. 'And I need to be on my own.'

She ought to be taking the hint and leaving him to his own thoughts, however painful, but she sensed how much he was hurting and couldn't leave him alone.

'Please.' Her voice was soft. 'I want to help, Zach.'

'How?' He gave a harsh laugh. 'No one can help. Not even you.'

Keely felt her heart twist. There must be *something* she could do—surely just knowing that someone cared must help a little bit?

She closed the gap between them until she was standing so close they were almost touching.

His dark jaw was tense. 'I really don't want to talk about this.'

'Well, you should,' she said bravely, ignoring his curt tone. 'You told me that if things upset me here, I should talk to you. I think it's time you followed some of your own advice, Zach. Tell me why you're upset. Talk to me. Was it the baby being born?'

He swore fluently under his breath and his blue gaze was menacing. 'Keely, I *don't* need to talk. I don't *want* to talk.'

His words throbbed with pain and on impulse she stood on tiptoe and hugged him, the same way she would have hugged Phoebe if she'd been upset.

Standing rigid in her embrace, Zach lifted his hands and gripped her arms tightly, clearly intending to remove them.

'For God's sake, Keely.'

His words were like a shower of cold water.

What on earth was she doing?

'I'm sorry.' She stepped back, mortified, realising that he'd misinterpreted her actions. Bother. It had been a simple hug. Nothing more. But he'd thought... He'd obviously assumed...

She closed her eyes, thoroughly confused and embarrassed. Now what?

'I'm sorry, Zach,' she mumbled finally, not quite meeting his eyes. 'I was just trying to help. I wasn't. Oh, damn.'

'Hush...'

She felt his hands on her shoulders and glanced up awkwardly, preparing herself to apologise again—to explain that she hadn't been throwing herself at him. Instead, the words died in her throat and what she saw in his eyes took her breath away.

'Keely.' He said her name softly, his strong fingers stroking through her blonde hair as he scanned every inch of her face. 'Little Keely. You can't see anyone hurt and not try and help, can you?'

'I'm not little.' She frowned, hurt that he seemed to be dismissing her concern so lightly. 'I'm an adult, remember? I don't—'

'Dammit, I know you're an adult.' He growled the words against her mouth and then suddenly he was kissing her. Kissing her the way he'd kissed her that night in Phoebe's bedroom.

She gave a soft gasp and he took instant advantage, steadying her head with strong hands as he deepened the kiss.

Her heart thudding erratically, she melted into him and with a rough exclamation his arms slid round her, trapping her against his powerful body.

Swamped with need, her knees sagged and without breaking the kiss he propelled her backwards until her shoulders came into contact with the wall, his body hard against hers as he continued to drive them both to a frenzy of need. He seemed to know exactly how to kiss her, exactly what to do to excite her the most.

His breathing harsh, he lifted her skirt, his hands sliding up the warmth of her trembling thighs and cupping her bottom.

'Dear God, Keely…' He muttered the words against her mouth, his strong fingers tightening on her flesh, his touch sending rivers of wild excitement tumbling through her insides.

'Zach…' She was trembling like a leaf in a storm, her whole body consumed by the fire he'd ignited inside her. She felt his fingers tugging at her skimpy pants and gave a soft gasp as he sought access to the very heart of her passion.

She clutched his shoulders and her breath came in tiny pants as her body responded to the touch of his clever fingers. She couldn't believe what was happening, couldn't understand the response that he coaxed from her, and she trembled as she felt the ripples of sensation spread through her body. For a brief moment in time she forgot where she was—she forgot *who* she was—aware only of the sudden explosion within her body. His mouth captured her cries of ecstasy and afterwards she nestled against him, hiding her burning face in the cool fabric of his shirt.

'Oh, Zach…' She whispered his name, not daring to look at him. 'I wasn't— I didn't mean to—'

He gave a soft laugh, his warm breath brushing the top of her head. 'You didn't. I did. If anyone needs to apologise here, it's me.'

She shook her head, her cheeks still burning. *How could she have let him do that? How could she have been so totally shameless?*

'Keely, look at me.'

She ignored his quiet command, her face still buried in his shirt.

'I can't. I'm too embarrassed.'

With a soft curse he slipped a hand under her chin and lifted her face so that she was forced to look at him.

'Zach, I really didn't mean…' She swallowed hard and tried again. 'I don't want you to think— When I hugged you, I wasn't throwing myself at you.'

'I know that.' A ghost of a smile played around his firm mouth. 'You were trying to comfort me, and I'm sorry.'

Her eyes widened. 'Why are *you* sorry?'

'Because I was the one who kissed you. And I shouldn't have done it.' He hesitated and then gave a humourless laugh. 'I always seem to be saying that to you, don't I?'

Keely closed her eyes, still hideously embarrassed. 'Zach, it was my fault, not yours—'

Zach covered her lips with a gentle finger, stopping her in mid-flow. 'It wasn't anyone's fault, Keely. The truth is that you and I can't seem to be within a metre of each other without sparking enough electricity to power the whole of the national grid.' His hand dropped and suddenly he looked weary. 'But it doesn't change the fact that I have nothing to offer any woman at the moment. The truth is that after Catherine I haven't got anything left to give anyone.'

'I know. I understand. Truly I do.' With a massive effort Keely flashed him a smile. 'Let's just forget it. It was just a kiss.'

The way he lifted an eyebrow made her realise how totally ridiculous it was to refer to what they'd shared as 'just a kiss'.

Saying that it was 'just a kiss', was like saying that Everest was just a mountain!

'What I mean,' she said hastily, 'is that you don't need to worry that I'll read anything into it—you know that all I'm interested in at the moment is my career. I'm certainly not looking for permanent attachments. It won't be long before I'm off to London to start a new job.'

Heavens, how could she tell such a lie and sound convincing?

'That's right, so you are.'

His manner suddenly cool, he turned and walked over to his desk, flicking open the notes and scanning them quickly.

Keely felt suddenly confused.

Now what had she said?

Surely her words should have reassured him?

She frowned, but before she could question him there

was a tap on the door and Keely bit back a growl of frustration. Talk about rotten timing!

Zach strode across his office and opened the door, his manner as calm and unperturbed as always.

'Oh, Nicky, you want the notes.' Not by a tremor of his voice did he betray the fact that only a minute or two earlier he and Keely had been locked together with a passion that had nearly singed the paint from the walls. 'Keely's ahead of you. I was just finishing them off.'

'OK.' Nicky gave them a cheerful smile. 'Wasn't it great to have the chance to deliver a baby? It's nice to have something cheerful happening in the department for a change, don't you think?'

'Wonderful.' Zach's tone was even but Keely could see that the tension was back and she wanted to scream with frustration. For a brief moment she'd broken down those barriers that he'd built around himself. He'd let her close to him.

He walked back to his desk, signed the notes and handed them to Keely.

'There we are—all yours.'

His glance was cool and professional, and she sagged with disappointment. What had happened to the passion that had exploded between them? He was so distant that their kiss might never have happened, but she knew that for those few wild moments he'd wanted her as much as she'd wanted him.

But now he'd had time to think, he was backing off again. The death of his wife had hurt him so badly that part of him couldn't let go—couldn't allow him to give himself to a woman again.

The rest of Keely's shift was a nightmare. Every time she looked at Zach she remembered his mouth on hers and his hands touching her body.

Several times he had to repeat instructions, and by the end of the shift she was so jumpy that she thought everyone must have noticed that something was wrong.

She was relieved to climb into her little car, relieved to put some distance between her and Zach. Although not for long, of course. As they were both off duty he'd be under her nose tonight and the whole of tomorrow.

Torture.

When she arrived home she left a note on the kitchen table saying that she needed to get on with some studying and had taken her supper upstairs. At least that way she wouldn't have to spend an evening trying to pretend that she was totally indifferent to the man.

It was all very well telling herself that she wasn't going to throw herself at him, but it was becoming harder, not easier. She couldn't look at him without remembering how it had felt when he'd kissed her, and as for the rest...

She gave a groan and reached for a cardiology textbook. Maybe work would take her mind off Zachary Jordan.

Fortunately it snowed overnight, which at least provided a topic of conversation at the breakfast table.

'Good morning.' Zach strolled into the room and Keely's hands started to shake so badly that she dropped the packet of oats onto the floor.

Bother. Bother. Bother.

Why did he have such a powerful effect on her?

And why did he have to look so good in the morning? One glance in the mirror had been enough to confirm that a sleepless night had done nothing for her own appearance. Her cheeks were pale and her blue eyes were shadowed. Obviously he hadn't suffered a similar fate, she thought dryly, noting how sleek and handsome he looked. But, then, why should he? From his point of view all they'd shared had been a kiss. A very memorable kiss, of course, but nothing that was going to disturb his sleep.

Nothing that came close to what he'd shared with his wife.

'Something wrong, Keely?' One dark eyebrow lifted and she gave a bright smile.

'Nothing at all,' she said as she stooped to retrieve the box of oats. 'Just a little tired. I was reading until very late.'

'Yes. I saw your note.' He poured himself some coffee and gave her a cool smile. 'What were you working on? Anything in particular?'

'I was looking through my cardiology textbook,' she told him, skimming over the fact that she'd barely taken in anything she'd read. Her mind had been well and truly on other things. Him.

'Were you preparing for your interview?'

'Yes.' She made some porridge for Phoebe, careful not to look at Zach. If she didn't look at him she could pretend he wasn't there. And then maybe she'd stop shaking.

Zach glanced out of the window and sipped his coffee. 'There's snow on the fells. How do you fancy taking Phoebe sledging?'

'Yes, yes.' Phoebe bounced happily in her chair. 'Phoebe sledging.'

Sledging.

In the snow.

Snow was cold. If things became too desperate maybe she could push some down the neck of her anorak to cool herself down.

'Good idea.'

She served the porridge, made herself a piece of toast—which she didn't touch—and then busied herself getting things ready for their outing.

By the time they were ready to leave she had Phoebe warmly dressed in an all-in-one skisuit and furry boots.

Zach left his car by the side of the road and the three of them scrambled up the side of the fell until they reached a suitable slope.

'Nice.' Phoebe bent down and tapped the snow with her mitten and then plopped down onto her bottom. 'Phoebe slide.'

'Wait.' Zach laughed and lifted her onto the sledge before climbing on himself and holding onto the ropes. 'OK, off we go.'

They shot down the slope, Phoebe whooping with delight, and Keely watched with a smile and a lump in her throat.

Oh, she loved them both so much.

Then Zach dragged the sledge back up the hill and it was her turn. She settled herself behind the little girl, held her tightly and then shot down the slope so fast that she gasped with fright.

The sledge hit a bump and they both tumbled off into a pile of soft snow.

'More. More.' Phoebe bounced up immediately, totally undaunted by the crash, but Keely lay still for a minute, slightly winded.

'Are you all right?' Zach strode down the slope, scooped his daughter into his arms and then held out a hand to Keely. 'Come on.'

He hauled her upright and she stumbled against him, feeling the hard muscles of his thighs pressing against her.

For a moment their eyes locked and she knew that he was remembering their kiss. Then his jaw seemed to tense and he released her, swinging Phoebe onto his shoulders and jogging back up the slope with her, leaving Keely to drag the sledge after them.

Desperate to relieve the tension between them, Keely

bent down and scooped up an armful of freezing snow and then crept up behind Zach, raised her right arm and aimed the ball of snow with deadly accuracy.

It hit his body with a satisfying, muted thump and he turned, his eyes gleaming as he prepared himself to retaliate.

'Keely, Keely—you really shouldn't have done that.' He was laughing now and she gave a shriek as he lowered Phoebe to the ground and bent to pick up some snow to throw.

'Phoebe, save me!' Keely turned and ran as fast as she could in her cumbersome boots, but he caught her easily, stuffing the snow down the neck of her jacket while she shrieked for mercy.

Phoebe joined in, dancing around with excitement, and soon it was all-out war. By the time they eventually arrived home, all three of them were soaked and laughing.

'You two go and have a shower and I'll make us some hot soup.' Keely walked through to the kitchen, rubbing her damp hair with a towel.

'That was fun.' Zach followed her into the kitchen and dropped their wet things on the floor. 'I haven't seen Phoebe laugh that much for ages. Thanks, Keely.'

'You're very welcome,' she said quietly, rummaging in the cupboard for some cans of soup. 'I had fun, too.'

It was true. She'd really enjoyed herself. She'd even managed to stop thinking about how much she loved Zach for five minutes.

She straightened and met his eyes, and for a moment they stared at each other, tension shimmering between them.

'Keely...' When Zach finally managed to find his voice it sounded gruff, as if his emotions were lodged in his throat.

'Daddy, Daddy—boots stuck.'

Phoebe's shout from the hall interrupted whatever he'd been about to say and he gave a sigh and closed his eyes briefly.

'OK. I'm coming, sweetheart.' He dragged his eyes away from Keely's with a visible effort and walked out of the room to see to his daughter.

Keely dropped onto a chair, feeling as though she'd been caught in the path of a tornado. She felt sure now that he *did* feel something for her, even if it was just a physical thing. But he clearly didn't intend to do anything about it. He was still in love with his wife and he wasn't ready to move on.

It continued to snow and the weather played havoc with the workload of the casualty department.

'Why don't people just stay indoors?' Nicky muttered as she looked at the ever-growing number of people in the waiting room. 'I've lost count of the number of people who have slipped on the ice today. Why don't they just stay in bed?'

The mere mention of bed made Keely think of Zach and brought a hot colour to her cheeks.

Nicky gave her an odd look. 'Are you all right? You're very red all of a sudden—maybe you're catching something.'

'I'm fine,' Keely said quickly, knowing that she'd already caught something. The trouble was, it was called Zach and, as far as she could tell, it was totally incurable. The only answer was work. 'I'd better get going. Do you want me to see the lady that the ambulance crew brought in last?'

Before Nicky could question her further she picked up a set of notes and made her way to one of the cubicles.

A white-haired lady was lying on the trolley covered in

a blanket and a younger woman was hovering anxiously by her side.

'Hello, Mrs Weston. I'm Dr Thompson.' Keely introduced herself and then questioned them both about the injury.

'I was only going to the corner shop for a loaf,' the old lady fretted, and her daughter gave a long-suffering sigh.

'And I would have got that for you, Mum,' she said briskly, rolling her eyes at Keely. 'There was absolutely no need for you to go out at all today.'

'But I wanted to get out, dear,' her mother said placidly. 'If I don't get out, how will I keep these old joints of mine moving?'

The daughter opened her mouth to state the obvious, but caught Keely's look and decided to bite her tongue.

'You're right to try and get some exercise,' Keely said tactfully, examining her carefully, 'but I suppose in future it might be wiser to wait until the pavements aren't so slippery.'

The old lady gave a slight smile. 'Shall I tell you something, dear? It isn't always much fun being wise. Sometimes it's a better idea to just be reckless.'

'Mum!' Her daughter looked horrified but Keely returned the smile that Mrs Weston was giving her.

'You may be right,' she said softly, thinking about Zach. 'You never know what life is going to throw at you, so it's best to live life to the full while you can.'

Her examination revealed that the injured leg was shortened and externally rotated.

'You've fractured your hip, Mrs Weston,' she said quietly, and the daughter tutted.

'Oh, Mum!'

The old lady looked at Keely. 'So what happens now?'

'Well, I'll arrange for you to have a series of X-rays, take some bloods and do a trace of your heart, and then

I'm going to refer you to the orthopaedic team because they're the experts. Would you like something for the pain, Mrs Weston?'

'Yes, please. If it's not too much trouble.'

'It's no trouble,' Keely assured her quickly, popping her head around the door of the cubicle to look for Nicky. 'I just need to find Sister and then we'll give you something.'

She found Nicky, arranged for her to give Mrs Weston something for the pain and then completed the X-ray request form.

No sooner had the old lady been transferred to the ward than another victim of the icy roads was rushed in by ambulance.

This time Zach took charge and there was no doubt in anyone's mind that the young motorcyclist was badly injured. His leathers were badly torn and he was obviously in severe pain.

'OK, let's get his leathers off and see what we've got.' Zach was his usual cool, professional self and Keely found it hard to believe that this was the same man who could kiss a woman senseless. It was as if there were two completely different sides to him. The trouble was, she loved them both. 'Let's give him oxygen and get a line in, please—we need U and Es, FBC and blood sugar, and cross-match four units of blood.'

With the severity of injury it was highly probable that the man was going to need a blood transfusion.

Keely inserted a large-bore intravenous cannula and attached it to an infusion of saline.

Zach glanced up from his examination. 'I'm going to do a femoral nerve block to relieve the pain.'

Anticipating his request, the A and E sister passed him a 21-gauge needle with syringe and Keely watched while Zach palpated the femoral artery and then inserted the femoral nerve block.

'Right, let's sort out this traction—it'll help his pain and his blood loss and make it easier to move him to X-Ray.'

The A and E team splinted the man's leg, checked the pulses in his foot and then transferred him to the orthopaedic team.

'I'm jolly glad I'm not in the orthopaedic team today,' Keely muttered as she helped clear up the mess in Resus. 'They haven't had a moment to breathe since we started work.'

'You should see the fracture clinic,' Nicky agreed, attaching a giving set to a bag of saline in preparation for the next emergency to be brought through the doors. 'I've lost count of the number of Colles' fractures they've seen today. Why do people always put their hands out when they slip?'

'Well, it's either that or they bang their heads,' Zach pointed out dryly, tossing his gloves in the bin. 'They've got to fall on something. At least the wrist is neat and relatively quick to deal with.'

There followed a light-hearted conversation about which bits of the body each of them would like to break most or least and then they were all called away again to deal with a head injury.

By the time Keely arrived home she was totally exhausted and she flopped onto Phoebe's bedroom floor to read her a story.

'Keekee poorly.' Phoebe stroked her head gently and Keely grinned up at her.

'I'm not poorly, minx. I'm just totally exhausted. Partly because thinking about your gorgeous daddy keeps me awake at night and partly because of my job, which wears me out during the day.'

She gave a groan, kicked off her shoes and stretched out on the cushions. 'Right. Which book are we having?'

Phoebe plodded over to her bookcase, stared at the contents and then tugged out a book, sending a shower of other books tumbling over the cheerful blue carpet.

Keely gave a groan but was too exhausted to get up and put all the books back. There was always tomorrow. Instead, she held out her hand and took the book from the mischievous toddler, snuggling the little girl into her lap.

'Mmm, you smell good,' she murmured, burying her face in the blonde hair and breathing in deeply. 'You smell of baths and babies and nice things like that.'

Phoebe frowned and pushed the book into her chest. 'Read,' she said firmly, and Keely saluted quickly.

'Yes, boss.'

She opened the book and started to read, totally absorbed in the wonderful pictures and the clever rhymes.

By the time she'd finished the book Phoebe was yawning, and Keely lifted her up and put her in the cot.

'There we are. Night-night.'

'Tuck me in,' Phoebe pleaded, her eyes huge, and Keely smiled.

'You want me to tuck you in? Of course. Lie down.'

But instead of lying down Phoebe slid her chubby arms round Keely's neck and squeezed.

'Want cuggle.'

'Cuddle. Of course you can have a cuddle.' She lifted the child out of her cot again, loving the way the little legs wound round her waist like bindweed. After a few minutes she gave Phoebe a final squeeze and tried to put her back in her cot, but she was having nothing of it.

'More cuggle.'

'Time for sleep now,' Keely said gently, trying to peel her away from her body, but Phoebe's grip tightened.

'No sleep. Cuggle Keekee. Sleep with Keekee.'

Oh, dear.

Keely was just pondering how to handle the situation

when Zach appeared in the doorway, his top button undone and his jacket slung casually over one shoulder.

'Problems?'

He looked so wickedly handsome that she nearly dropped Phoebe and fell to the floor at his feet.

'She—she just wanted an extra cuddle.'

That sexy mouth, the same mouth that was capable of doing such amazing things to her, curved into a smile.

'And who can blame her?' His eyes met hers briefly and then he turned his attention to his daughter.

'Phoebe come to Daddy.'

'No.' Phoebe's arms tightened around Keely's neck until she felt as though she were trapped in a vice. 'Stay with Keekee.'

Help! Now what? Inspiration struck and she tossed a book that she'd seen earlier into the cot. 'Phoebe, look!' She injected an enormous amount of excitement into her voice. 'Look what's waiting for you in the cot.'

As she'd hoped, the toddler turned, her attention caught by Keely's tone of voice, and she allowed herself to be lifted into the cot.

'Phew.' Keely grinned at Zach. 'For a moment there I thought I'd be sleeping in a cot tonight.'

Zach didn't laugh. Instead, his eyes were fixed on his daughter.

Keely's heart sank as she looked at his tense features. She could read his mind. He was worried that Phoebe was getting too attached to her.

'Go and get changed,' she said quickly, hoping to distract him. 'I'll pour us both a drink.'

He stood frozen to the spot, his eyes still fixed on his daughter, but then he gave a brief nod and turned on his heel, leaving her with a sinking heart.

In the kitchen she tugged open the fridge, poured them both a glass of wine and walked through to the sitting room. Zach had already lit a fire and it crackled and whispered in the hearth, sending a warm glow across the cosy room.

'Is that for me?' He walked up to her and took the wine with a nod of thanks and then strolled over to the fire.

'Zach?' She said his name tentatively, not sure how to broach the subject. 'Look, I know what you're thinking...'

'Do you?' He stared down into his wine glass, unsmiling. 'And what am I thinking?'

She swallowed hard. 'That Phoebe is getting too attached to me.'

There was a long silence and then he gave a short laugh. 'How come you're so good at reading my mind?'

Because I love you, she wanted to say, but managed to stop herself in time.

'I suppose it's a fairly obvious concern,' she said quietly, 'but I'm not going to hurt her, Zach.'

'No? As you rightly said, you're getting close to her. I've never seen her respond to anyone the way she responds to you. What happens when you leave?' His gaze was direct. 'What happens when you take up this cardiology job you keep talking about?'

The cardiology job she wasn't even sure she wanted...

'Well, I'll stay in touch,' she said lamely, and he gave a long sigh and picked up his wine again.

'Try explaining that to a three-year-old.'

This was ridiculous. She didn't want to go anywhere. She wanted to stay with both of them. But there was no way she was telling him that. There was no way she was throwing herself at him again.

'Look, Zach—'

'Forget it, Keely.' His voice was rough. 'It isn't your problem. It's mine. I need to work out what to do for the best. Maybe you moving in wasn't such a good idea after all.'

Her heart thudded heavily in her chest. 'Are you saying you want me to move out?'

She held her breath as she waited for his answer, her fingers coiling into her palms. She couldn't bear to move out.

He stared into the fire, his expression remote. 'No. I'm not saying that. At least, not yet. I'm hoping I can think of another solution.'

She could think of another solution.

Instead of asking her to leave, he could ask her to stay.

But Zach would never do that. He'd loved his wife too much to make a commitment to another woman.

CHAPTER SEVEN

As KEELY walked towards the staffroom the following Monday, Zach waylaid her.

'We've had a dinner invitation,' he said briefly. 'Sean and his wife have invited us over tonight.'

She swallowed. She had to spend a whole evening in Zach's company in front of other people? She'd never be able to do it without giving herself away.

She searched her brain for an excuse.

'Why don't I look after Phoebe for you?'

'She'll come, too.' Zach gave a tired smile and jammed his hands in his pockets. 'I probably ought to warn you that Sean's wife, Ally, is not particularly subtle when it comes to matchmaking attempts. And that's probably what this is. She's heard that you've moved in with me and she's hearing wedding bells.'

The woman obviously had a hearing problem, Keely thought wryly. There were certainly no bells ringing anywhere near Zach. Except maybe alarm bells.

'Right.' Keely gave him an awkward smile, not sure what to say. 'In that case, perhaps it would be best if I didn't come.'

'You've got to come,' Zach said dryly, 'or she'll smell a rat. Our only hope of escaping her well-meaning tendency to pair me up is to prove to her that we find each other totally resistible.'

And how on earth was she going to do that?

'OK.' She smiled with more conviction than she was feeling. 'Well, I'll just talk about going to London. That should convince them.'

'Yes. It certainly should.' Zach's smile faded and he glanced at his watch. 'I'll tell them we'll see them at seven, then.'

Keely watched him move down the corridor away from her and wondered how on earth she was going to spend a whole evening pretending to be indifferent to Zach.

It was a long and difficult day in A and E and by the time she got home she was totally drained. Goodness only knew how Zach would be feeling—he'd born the brunt of the trauma and tragedy they'd had to deal with in just one shift.

The last thing she really felt like doing was going out to dinner, but she didn't see how she could refuse.

She had a quick shower, applied some make-up to hide just how tired she was and on impulse ran Zach a bath.

He arrived home an hour after her with only twenty minutes to spare before they had to leave.

'What a day.' He shrugged his coat off and tossed it over the bannister before taking the stairs two at a time to the bathroom. 'You ran me a bath?'

He frowned and then glanced at her, and she blushed.

Hmm. Maybe she shouldn't have done that. On reflection it had been rather a wifely gesture, but at the time she'd thought it might help relax him after a hard day.

'You don't have to have it,' she said quickly, stroking her hair behind her ear as she always did when she was nervous. 'I just thought you'd had an awful day and I—'

'Hush. Stop apologising.' He put a finger over her lips and gave her a lopsided smile. 'It was a really sweet thought. I just keep forgetting what a truly nice person you are. Give me ten minutes to shave and change and I'll meet you downstairs.'

He was as good as his word and by the time she'd packed a small bag for Phoebe he was ready.

'OK. I'll just get the wine from the fridge...' He went

through to the kitchen and came back holding two bottles. 'You take these and I can carry Phoebe.'

Keely risked a glance at him and then wished she hadn't. He was wearing a black poloneck jumper that emphasised the breadth of his shoulders and a pair of trousers that clung lovingly to his hard thighs. As usual he looked so handsome he took her breath away and she turned away quickly, sure that what she felt must show in her eyes.

They arrived at Sean's just after seven and Keely was immediately absorbed into the noise and warmth of the Nicholson household.

'Come on in and make yourselves comfortable.' Ally had a baby cuddled against her shoulder and a toddler tugging at her leg. 'For goodness' sake, Katy, Mummy's going to trip over you—Sean, I need a hand!'

Sean quickly swept the toddler into his arms, casting a rueful smile at Zach.

'Sorry. It's utter chaos here as usual. They're all meant to be in bed but they wanted to stay up and see you.'

'Don't apologise—we've brought one of our own,' Zach reminded them dryly, shifting Phoebe more comfortably in his arms.

'Why don't you men settle the children while Keely and I make some drinks?' Ally suggested, handing the baby over to Sean. 'Come on, Keely. I'll show you around.'

After Zach's warning, Keely was nervous about what Ally was going to say to her but she dutifully followed her into the kitchen.

'So, Sean tells me you're living with Zach at the moment.' Ally tugged open a cupboard and removed a bottle of gin. 'What can I get you to drink? Gin and tonic? Wine?'

'Just the tonic, please,' Keely said with a smile. 'I'm driving us home.'

'Home.' Ally gave a sigh and her expression was

dreamy. 'That's so romantic. I never thought I'd ever see Zach involved with anyone.'

Oh, help!

'We're not involved,' Keely said hastily, glancing nervously towards the door and hoping that Zach wasn't within earshot. 'I've just moved in to help him out with his child-care crisis. Nothing more than that.'

'Oh.' For a brief moment Ally's face fell but then she smiled. 'All the same, living with each other—well, one thing is bound to lead to another eventually, isn't it?'

'No!' Keely stared at her in consternation. 'It isn't like that—really.'

'Oh, come on, Keely.' Ally reached for a lemon and cut off several slices, which she popped into the glasses. 'You're the envy of the entire female population of Cumbria. Don't try telling me you don't find Zach attractive.'

'Don't you ever give up, Ally?' Zach's mild reproof came from the doorway and Keely blushed scarlet.

How much had he heard? Oh, no, he was going to think they'd been gossiping about him. She took a large slug of her drink, thoroughly embarrassed.

Ally, on the other hand, didn't seem at all embarrassed. She smiled broadly and handed Zach a drink.

'Just worrying about your welfare.' She slipped her arm through his and they walked towards the living room. 'So how's Phoebe been, Zach?'

'She's doing very well—which reminds me.' Zach's eyes flickered to Keely. 'She wanted you to go and give her a goodnight kiss.'

'No problem.' Relieved to have an excuse to get away from Ally's quizzical gaze, Keely hurried off to find Phoebe.

She took much longer than was necessary to settle the

little girl down, curling up on the bed and reading her an extra story.

By the time she rejoined the rest of the adults, they were all seated at the table and Ally was placing an elaborate-looking starter in front of them all.

'It's a new recipe,' she declared with a flourish. 'You're guinea pigs.'

'Great. You really know how to whet someone's appetite.' Sean shook his head in exasperation as he looked at his pretty wife. 'You're not meant to tell the guests they're guinea pigs.'

'So how's general practice,' Zach asked Ally as he tucked into his starter. 'Still seeing all the usual trivia?'

'Trivia?' Ally glared at him and then subsided and smiled when she saw the twinkle in his eye. 'Zach Jordan, you're always winding me up and I fall for it every time. The answer to your question is that general practice is great and, no, I'm not seeing trivia.'

Keely took a sip of wine and looked at her shyly. 'Do you work full time?'

'Yes.' Ally glanced at Sean and laughed. 'But only three days a week in general practice. The rest of the time I'm a general slave and dogsbody.'

'Stop moaning, woman,' Sean growled, but his eyes twinkled and there was no missing the closeness between the couple.

Zach helped himself to a bread roll. 'Don't you ever miss real medicine?'

'No,' Ally said calmly, 'because I'm practising real medicine every day. It's you lot that work in a strange environment. Hospitals are totally alien places. You just treat symptoms there. Never people. In general practice we treat the whole person.'

Sean grinned. 'Since when did you need to treat the whole person to manage an ingrowing toenail?'

'Go ahead. Patronise me,' Ally said loftily, 'but I've lost count of the number of times we've had patients home from hospital—your hospital—with no end of problems that none of you managed to identify. The problem with hospitals is that each consultant just manages the bit he knows about. No one looks at the overall patient. That's what I do.'

Sean gave a smile. 'And you do it very well, angel. Your patients are damned lucky.'

Keely put her fork down, her appetite suddenly gone. Hearing Ally talk had made her realise just how much she didn't want to pursue a career in hospital medicine. She felt exactly the way that Ally did. That there was more to caring for a patient than managing a symptom.

Which wasn't going to make her much of a cardiologist...

'Are you all right, Keely?' Ally was looking at her, suddenly concerned. 'You look as though you've seen a ghost.'

'I'm fine.' Keely smiled at her through stiff lips. 'Tell me more about your job.'

'My job?' Ally shrugged and glanced round at the others. 'Well, why not? It's a quick way to irritate these two and that's always good for a laugh.'

She started to talk, telling them all about the day she'd had in the surgery, about a woman who'd been admitted to hospital with a broken leg, about how they'd had to arrange for all her animals to be cared for.

'The hospital didn't even realise she had animals,' Ally said shortly, clearing the plates and standing up. 'Fortunately one of the neighbours saw the ambulance arrive to pick her up and came haring round here to ask us to sort it out. Which we did, of course.'

She took the plates into the kitchen and returned with the main course, a delicious chicken dish with rice.

'So what about you, Keely?' She served everyone and then looked at Keely curiously. 'Are you staying in A and E or are you doing a GP rotation?'

'Neither.' Keely picked up her fork and tried to summon up an appetite. 'I'm going to be a cardiologist.'

Except that she really, really didn't want to be one. Maybe she should talk to her father. Ask his advice. He was very career orientated but she knew that he loved her dearly. He wouldn't want her to do anything that she wasn't sure about.

'A cardiologist?' Ally glanced up and nodded. 'In Glyn Hughes's team?'

'Not Glyn Hughes's.' Zach's voice was strangely flat. 'Keely's not staying in Cumbria for long. She's going back to London at the end of her six months.'

Ally's face fell. 'You're not staying?' She looked visibly disappointed as she glanced from one to the other. 'But I thought—I assumed—'

'We all know what you assumed, sweetheart, but we'd rather you kept it to yourself,' Sean said gently, topping up her glass and giving her a smile. 'Now, buck up and eat your dinner before it gets cold.'

Ally ignored him, her eyes on Zach. 'I really hoped that—'

'Ally!' This time Sean's voice was sharp and Ally seemed to pull herself together.

'Sorry.' She turned her attention to her dinner. 'Cardiology. You must be a very clever girl, Keely.'

Keely shook her head, embarrassed by the sudden attention. She didn't feel clever. She felt confused. More confused than she'd ever felt in her whole life.

'We went sledging last week.' Zach picked up his wineglass and changed the subject neatly. 'The snow was fantastic.'

'Where did you go?' Sean topped up the rest of the

glasses and they chatted about the snow for a while, swapping stories and anecdotes.

'I must admit it's the first time I've had a snowball thrown at me since I was about ten years old,' Zach said dryly, smiling across at Keely who stared at him, outraged.

'At least mine just hit you on the *outside*! You stuffed yours down my jacket! I nearly had frostbite.'

Ally glanced up, her face brightening. 'So, do you do lots of things together with Phoebe?' she asked casually, and Zach sighed.

'No, Ally. Generally we don't. The whole point of Keely living with me is that she's there to cover when I'm working so it's very rare that we're at home at the same time.'

Ally cleared her plate and put her knife and fork down thoughtfully. 'But Phoebe doesn't go to people very easily, does she, Zach? So she must really have taken to Keely.'

'She has taken to Keely,' Zach said, his smile exasperated. 'Now, drop it Ally. You're like a dog with a bone.'

'She's worse than that. She's embarrassing,' Sean growled, glaring at his wife. 'I'd buy her a bow and arrow for Christmas so that she can play Cupid full time, but her aim is so lousy I dread to think what it would do for our workload in A and E.'

They all laughed and after that the evening improved and Keely found herself relaxing in their company.

By the time they scooped a sleeping Phoebe up from the bed and transferred her to the car, she was sorry to leave. The Nicholsons were a lovely family. And Ally was a lucky woman. Sean was drop-dead gorgeous and clearly very much in love with his pretty, if rather indiscreet wife.

'Thanks for coming.' Ally gave her a warm hug and then turned to Zach and lowered her voice. 'You should marry her, Zach. Snap her up quickly before she goes to London. She'd make a lovely mother for Phoebe.'

Keely sank into the driver's seat, mortified, relieved that she hadn't been able to hear Zach's reply. She could guess what it probably would have been.

He slid in next to her and she drove carefully out of the drive and into the tiny lane that led to the main road.

'I'm sorry about Ally.' Zach settled himself into his seat and closed his eyes. 'I did warn you that she was rather obsessed with pairing me up.'

'Yes.' Keely stared at the road, not daring to look at him. 'It doesn't matter.'

'Did she spoil the evening for you?'

She could feel his gaze on her and her hands tightened on the wheel. 'No. Not at all. I thought she was lovely.'

'She is, actually,' Zach agreed softly, 'just rather meddling.'

And very astute. Keely suspected that the other woman had had no trouble guessing exactly how she felt about Zach.

'Does she always try and pair you up with whoever you take there to dinner?'

'Well, I don't usually take women there to dinner,' he admitted with a wry smile, 'so I suppose in a way it was my fault. Taking you and admitting that you're living in my house is tantamount to putting an ad in *The Times* as far as Ally is concerned.'

'But she's tried matchmaking before?'

'On countless occasions.' He gave a short laugh. 'At one time or another I've been introduced to every one of Sean and Ally's single female friends.'

'How awful for you.' Keely's glance was sympathetic. 'Still, I suppose she means well.'

'She does indeed. And I suspect that her meddling streak makes her a very good GP.' He stifled a yawn. 'She knows everything there is to know about her patients and what makes them tick. What she does is very different to what we do, and whenever we get together we're always teasing each other.'

It certainly was different. And the more she thought about it, the more she thought it might be exactly what she wanted to do. Work in a small, country practice where she could get to know the patients inside out and help them. Not just deal with one crisis and then abandon them.

So what was she going to do?

There was no point in mentioning it to Zach. In fact, there was no way she *could* mention it to Zach. He'd assume that her change of heart was something to do with him. No. She'd have to do some research quietly by herself and then talk to her father.

CHAPTER EIGHT

THEY were working together the following morning when a young girl was brought in who'd collapsed.

Keely helped the ambulance crew move the patient onto the trolley and glanced at the girl's mother who was hovering anxiously in the doorway.

'What happened?'

'I really don't know.' The woman was obviously beside herself with panic. 'She was fine. Absolutely fine. One minute we were in a café together and the next minute she'd collapsed.'

Zach started to examine the girl. 'What were you eating?'

'Sorry?' The girl's mother looked at him blankly.

'What were you eating just before she collapsed?' Zach glanced at Keely. 'Let's get a line in, give her high dose oxygen and attach a cardiac monitor and a pulse oximeter. We need to get her stats above 94 per cent'

'Cake.' The mother looked confused. 'We were eating cake, but I don't see—'

'Is she allergic to anything that you're aware of?'

'Nuts.' The woman went pale. 'But there were no nuts in the cake. I checked.'

'Are you sure?' Zach turned to Nicky. 'She's wheezing badly. I want .3 mils of one in one thousand adrenaline. Give it intramuscularly, please.'

Nicky turned away to the drug trolley and Zach glanced at the mother. 'This is a very severe reaction. I think for the moment we'll have to assume that it was nuts.'

Nicky thrust an ampoule under Zach's nose and he read the label and nodded.

'Fine. And let's give her 200 mg hydrocortisone IV and nebulised salbutamol.'

They worked for half an hour and finally the young girl was stabilised.

'Right.' Zach wiped his forehead with the back of his hand and gave the mother a tired smile. 'I'm going to refer her to the medical team. She needs to be admitted and we need to find out exactly what caused this reaction.'

The girl's mother nodded, obviously still worried.

'Will she be all right?'

Zach glanced at the girl and nodded. 'I think so. She seems stable now but I'm going to play it safe and admit her. It was a nasty reaction.'

They transferred the girl to the medical ward and Zach slumped against the wall, wearily surveying the mess in the room.

'I've got a really, really bad feeling about this week,' he muttered, and Nicky groaned as she tossed a discarded IV bag into the bin.

'Don't say that. Last time you had one of your feelings we were deluged with awful accidents.'

'I know that.' Zach straightened and rubbed a hand over the back of his neck. 'But look at the weather. The roads are like glass and people still insist on driving everywhere.'

No sooner had he said the words than the doors from the ambulance bay flew open and another accident victim was admitted.

After that there was a steady stream of patients and by the time Keely arrived home she was exhausted. So was Zach.

'That,' he said quietly, sinking into a chair in the

kitchen, 'was a very bad day. Let's hope the rest of the week is better.'

It wasn't.

In fact, it got worse.

Every time the doors to A and E opened, drama followed, and by the end of the week Keely felt emotionally drained.

Dealing with critically injured patients was bad enough, but for Keely the worst bit was telling the relatives. Telling someone that their loved one had just died was the hardest thing she'd ever had to do.

'How do you do it?' she asked Zach one afternoon after they'd failed to resuscitate a twenty-year-old motorcyclist. 'How do you cope with telling them that their child is dead?'

Zach poured them both a cup of coffee, his face drawn. 'How do I cope? I suppose I switch off. I treat it as a job to be done. But it doesn't mean I don't feel it.'

He did feel it, Keely knew that. She'd seen the strain on his face after a week of repeated tragedy.

'I almost wanted to lie to those parents,' she admitted quietly, staring down at the coffee he handed her. 'The way they looked at me when I walked into the room, I wanted to tell them that there might be hope.'

'I know the feeling,' Zach said gruffly. 'But you mustn't ever do that. As it is, people find it hard to take in bad news. Harsh though it sounds, the only way to do it is to be blunt early on. And don't use euphemisms. Relatives will try very hard to misunderstand you because they don't want to hear the truth. If the patient is dead then you need to use the word "dead" very early on in the conversation and then use it several times. It's kinder in the long run.'

Keely looked at her coffee without enthusiasm. She

didn't think her stomach would tolerate anything at the moment.

'Well, I'm seriously hoping not to have to use the word "dead" for a long time,' she said gloomily. 'I've used it enough this week to last me a lifetime. Surely we can't have any more tragedy.'

They did.

It was later in the afternoon when the hotline—the phone that connected straight to Ambulance Control—rang.

Nicky picked it up, listened and made notes, asked a few questions and then replaced the receiver.

'They're bringing in a four-year-old with difficulty breathing,' she told Keely quickly. 'I'll check everything in Resus. Will you make sure you're ready when they arrive?'

The doors to the ambulance bay crashed open only minutes later and the crew hurried in with mother and child.

Keely took one look at the child and turned to Nicky.

'I want the paediatric consultant, the ENT guys and an anaesthetist down here now!'

Quickly they took them into Resus and Keely pushed forward a chair.

'Sit down, Mrs Potter. Keep her on your lap.' She glanced at Nicky. 'Let's keep her with her mother so we don't upset her further, and give her some humidified oxygen, please.'

Zoe, the paediatric staff nurse, reached for the oxygen and placed a mask near the child's face, murmuring soothing noises as she did so.

The child looked severely ill, her face pale as she leaned forward on her mother's knee, drooling slightly.

'I need some details from you, Mrs Potter,' Keely said quietly, her eyes never leaving the child as she watched for any change in her condition. 'How long has she been ill?'

'Alice was fine yesterday.' The mother stroked the child's hair. 'I can't believe that she can have got like this so quickly.'

'Has she complained of any pain? Has she been coughing?'

'She said her throat was sore and she stopped eating because she couldn't swallow,' Mrs Potter said, and Keely nodded, her eyes still on little Alice.

The child was ominously quiet and Keely had a very, very bad feeling about her.

'Zoe, let's give her some nebulised adrenaline.' Hopefully that would buy her some time until the team arrived. She turned back to the mother. 'And has she had all her childhood immunisations?'

Mrs Potter suddenly looked wary. 'No. No, she hasn't. I don't believe in all that, I'm afraid. I think children are better off picking up the germs and developing their own immunity.'

Keely swallowed her frustration, reminding herself that everyone had the right to make their own choice about immunisation. The trouble was, she had a strong suspicion that Alice Potter was suffering from a disease that had been virtually eradicated thanks to the success of the vaccination programme.

'Shall I check her BP?' Nicky asked quietly, and Keely shook her head vigorously.

'No. Don't disturb her at all.'

Mrs Potter looked up. 'What's wrong with her?'

Keely took a deep breath. 'I think she has something called epiglottitis,' she said finally, and Mrs Potter frowned.

'I've never even heard of it.'

'It's extremely rare now,' Keely told her quietly, 'because most children are vaccinated when they're babies.'

Mrs Potter went slightly pale. 'But she'll be all right, won't she?'

Keely hesitated. 'She's seriously ill, Mrs Potter—very seriously ill.'

'Are you sure it's not just a bad sore throat?' Mrs Potter became slightly belligerent. 'You haven't even looked in her throat.'

'It could be very dangerous to look in her throat,' Keely explained. 'If she is suffering from epiglottitis, examining her could totally obstruct her airway.'

Even as she watched, the child started to gasp for air and Keely turned to Nicky, her expression urgent.

'Let's get her on the trolley and call Zach quickly. And crash-bleep the paediatrician again. If he doesn't arrive soon I'll have to intubate her, and I'd like Zach here.'

'She's not breathing,' Zoe said quickly and Keely moved to the head of the trolley.

'OK, give me a small endotracheal tube and an introducer.'

While Zoe hurried the mother out of the room, Keely tried to intubate the child.

'It's all too swollen,' she muttered grimly as she tried to insert the tube into the little girl's airway. 'Damn. This is impossible. Give me an IV cannula—where the hell's Zach?'

'I'm right here,' came the calm reply, and she looked up with a sigh of relief.

'She's in respiratory arrest but I can't intubate her because her airway is so swollen. I'm going to do a needle cricothyroidotomy.'

With Zach's reassuring presence by her side she managed to perform the procedure successfully, and his quiet words of praise increased her confidence dramatically.

Then all of a sudden the room was full of people and the paediatricians took over.

'She's arrested.' Tony Maxwell snapped out some instructions and they all worked to save the little girl.

An hour later Tony shook his head, his expression grim. 'I think we should stop now. Does everyone agree?'

'No!' Keely's cry was anguished. 'We've got to keep trying. She's only four years old.'

Zach put a hand on her shoulder and his voice was gruff. 'Keely, she's not responding.'

'But we can't let her die.'

'She's already dead,' Tony said gently, his eyes bleak as he looked down at the tiny figure on the trolley. 'Agonising though it is, I think we have to leave it at that.'

'It needn't have happened.' Keely felt a lump building in her throat and fought for control. Zach already thought she wasn't emotionally tough enough to cope with A and E work. She didn't want to prove him right. 'It's just so unfair...'

'I know.' Tony looked round and then his broad shoulders sagged slightly. 'OK, thanks, everyone.'

Keely took a deep breath. 'I'll tell the mother,' she said quietly, but Zach shook his head.

'Tony should do it, Keely. He's the senior paediatrician.'

Tony nodded, his expression glum. 'I get all the good jobs. Will you come with me, Nicky?'

The A and E sister nodded and Keely noticed a tear shining in the corner of her eye.

So it wasn't just her, then...

'You did well, by the way.' Tony turned to Keely. 'I'm sorry we took so long to get here but we had an arrest in ITU.'

'I didn't manage to intubate her,' Keely mumbled, swamped by feelings of inadequacy. Surely there was something more she could have done? It all seemed so needlessly tragic. 'Maybe if I'd managed we'd have saved her.'

Tony shook his head. 'No one would have been able to intubate her,' he assured her calmly. 'Her airway was almost entirely obstructed. You did brilliantly. Better than most. And your diagnosis was spot on. Don't doubt yourself, Keely. You're a good doctor. A very good doctor.'

So why did she feel like such a failure?

Aware of Zach's scrutiny, Keely mumbled an excuse and walked out of Resus. At least her shift was over. Which meant she could go home and make a fool of herself in peace and quiet.

'Da-addy-y…' Phoebe hurtled out of the playroom and attached herself bodily to Zach's legs as he let himself into the house.

'Hello, trouble.' He stooped to pick her up, smiling at Barbara who'd followed her charge into the hallway. 'Has she been good?'

'Mostly.' Barbara had a twinkle in her eye that made Zach groan.

'Come on. What's she done?'

'She fed her toast into the video,' Barbara said calmly, 'but fortunately she sucked the butter off it first, so there was no long-term damage.'

'And?' There was more. He could tell. Zach braced himself.

'And…' Barbara glanced down at the sheepish toddler and gave her a wink. 'We actually had a small accident with a pen and the sitting-room wall, but it's all sorted out now.'

Zach closed his eyes and muttered something under his breath. 'Anything else I need to know?'

'She managed to dial 999 on the telephone.'

Zach winced. 'Who do I have to call to apologise?'

'I've done it.' Barbara bent down and picked the little girl up. 'The only thing I haven't solved is the problem of last week's copy of the *Lancet*. It was by your bed…'

Zach's eyes narrowed. 'And dare I ask where it is now?'

'In the bath,' Barbara told him cheerfully. 'Or, to be exact, drying on the radiator, having had a wash in the bath. My fault entirely. I turned my back to get a towel.'

Zach groaned. If he lost Barbara he didn't know what he'd do. 'What can I say?'

'Absolutely nothing,' she said firmly. 'I love her to bits. She's very bright and busy. Just as a healthy toddler should be.'

Zach shook his head in disbelief and kissed his daughter's face.

'You're a handful, madam.'

'More kiss.' Phoebe leaned towards him and he grinned and kissed her again, glancing up the stairs as he did so.

'Is Keely home?'

'Yes.' Barbara's smile faded and she gave a worried frown. 'To be honest, I thought she looked a bit upset. She's in the bathroom and she's been in there for ages.'

Zach's mouth tightened. And he could guess what she was doing. Crying her eyes out.

'Don't worry.' He scooped his daughter up and gave the older woman a smile. 'I'll go and see her.'

'Good. I'll be off then.'

Zach loosened his tie and took the stairs two at a time, Phoebe's arms clutched tightly round his neck.

'Keely?' He called her name through the bathroom door but there was no answer and he cursed under his breath.

'Keely!'

He thumped a fist on the door and Phoebe's bottom lip trembled and her arms tightened around his neck.

'Daddy no shout. Daddy noisy. Daddy say sorry.'

Before he could answer he heard Keely's voice, slightly muffled from the bathroom.

'I'm OK, Zach. I'm just having a bath.'

He didn't believe her for a moment, but he was helpless to do much with Phoebe in his arms. He'd put her to bed first and then sort out Keely.

It was half an hour before he returned to the locked bathroom door, and there was still no sign of Keely.

He called her again and finally she opened the door.

She was wrapped in a towel, the ends of her blonde hair damp from the steam and her sweet face blotched with tears.

'Zach!' She scowled at him and tried to brush away the traces of tears, obviously annoyed that he'd caught her crying. 'I just wanted to be alone.'

'I was worried about you.'

'Well, I'm OK.' Conscious of her nakedness beneath the towel, a soft blush touched her cheeks. 'Leave me alone, Zach.'

'No.'

'Why not?'

'Because you're upset,' he said calmly, lifting a hand to brush a blonde strand of hair away from her face. 'And I think you'd feel better if you talked about it.'

She glared at him. 'You never talk about your feelings— why should I?'

She looked so sweet and defensive he could barely keep his hands off her.

Her half-naked body was testing his self-control to the limits, and the sooner he got her dressed the safer it would be for both of them.

'Why don't you come out of the bathroom,' he suggested, 'and we can talk about it downstairs?'

'I don't want to talk about it,' she mumbled. 'I just want to be left in peace.'

'Well, that's one thing I'm not going to do.' He lifted one dark eyebrow in her direction. 'Are you coming out or am I carrying you out?'

The tears welled in her huge eyes and her voice shook. 'She was only four years old, and if her mother had had her immunised it never would have happened...'

Damn.

Zach reached for her, quickly wrapping her in his arms. Keely started to sob into his chest, great tearing sobs that shook her whole body and made him feel totally helpless.

'Hush, sweetheart...' He held her tightly and whispered nonsense into her hair until finally she was too exhausted to sob any longer. Then he lifted her into his arms and sat down on the bathroom chair with her on his lap.

'It's so unfair.' Her words were jerky. 'She didn't have to die. How will that poor mother cope with losing her child?'

'I don't know.'

Zach felt as sad about it as she did. In fact, he almost envied her ability to let her emotions out. Sometimes he wished he could do the same.

'Tell me honestly, Zach.' She wiped her eyes on the back of her hand. 'Was there anything else I could have done? What if I'd given her antibiotics straight away?'

He shook his head and stroked her hair away from her damp cheeks with a gentle hand. 'You did everything absolutely right. It was textbook management of a case of epiglottitis. We were all incredibly impressed that you even recognised it, to be honest. It's very rare these days.'

'But not rare enough,' she said in a quiet voice, leaning her face against his broad chest.

Zach tried not to react, reminding himself that she was just using him for comfort. But unfortunately his body wasn't that discerning and his immediate response to the soft scent of her hair and the warmth of her body made him grit his teeth.

'Let's get you dressed,' he said gruffly, hoping that she'd move before he embarrassed himself, 'or you'll catch cold.'

'No, don't let me go. Not yet.' She snuggled closer and he stifled a groan.

Any minute now she'd realise the effect she was having on him.

'Keely…'

She lifted her head to look at him and her tear-washed eyes and trembling mouth were only inches away from his. And the temptation was just too much…

With a groan he lowered his head and captured her mouth, and the tension that had been building for weeks exploded between them.

Slowly at first, his lips moved over hers, the tip of his tongue seeking entry between her softly parted lips as he savoured the taste of her.

He felt her tremble in his arms and then her tongue touched his as she returned the kiss, her immediate and passionate response to his touch sending desire roaring through him like a runaway train.

Without breaking the kiss, his fingers tugged at the towel, leaving her naked in his lap.

'Zach…' She gasped his name against his mouth and then her tongue licked at his lips again, tantalising and teasing him until he was ready to forget the preliminaries and make love to her on the floor of the bathroom.

But she deserved better than that…

Battling with his instincts, he slipped his arms around her and stood up, intending to take her to the bedroom, but she gave a murmur of protest and tightened her arms round his neck.

'No, Zach.' Her voice was almost a sob. 'Don't let me go.'

Dear God, she was enough to test the will-power of a saint. Zach's fingers tightened into her warm satiny flesh. *He had no intention of letting her go...*

Their mouths fused again and they kissed desperately, biting at each other, trying to get closer—and closer still...

'The bedroom, Keely.' He murmured the words against her mouth but she gave a moan of protest and wriggled out of his arms, sliding down his body until she was on her knees, her fingers shaking as they dealt with his zip.

And then he felt her soft mouth touch him, her tongue and lips tasting and teasing him until he thought he'd explode.

'Keely...' His fractured groan of disbelief brought no response from her as she continued with intimacies that left him stunned and shell-shocked.

Finally, when he could stand it no longer, he lifted her roughly to her feet and backed her against the wall, his mouth devouring hers with a wild hunger that took them both past the point of no return.

In a smooth movement he lifted her and she wrapped her legs around his hips, her breath coming in pants as she felt his hardness brush against her.

'Please, Zach, please...'

She was sobbing with need and her soft gasps and the incredible liquid warmth of her body left him totally unable to control his actions.

His mouth still holding hers, he angled her hips and surged into her, taking her hard and fast, surrendering to the mindless passion that overwhelmed both of them.

He felt her body tighten around his and then she cried out his name, quivering and shaking in his arms, her frantic movements driving him over the edge into ecstasy.

For endless seconds they clung together, breathing

heavily, and then he lowered her gently to the floor, his hands supporting her as her knees buckled.

Stunned by the power of the emotions that had erupted between them, Zach struggled to control his breathing and then bent his head to look at the shiny mass of blonde hair that was buried in his chest.

She was unbelievable. So sweet. *And so incredibly sexy...*

He slipped a gentle hand under Keely's chin and lifted her face, urging her to look at him.

Her cheeks were flushed and there was just a hint of shyness in her eyes, as if she didn't quite know what to say to him. Which was understandable, because he didn't know what to say to her either.

There had been a lack of control about their lovemaking—a primitive edge that had left them both shaken.

Her beautiful blue eyes looked nervous and her voice was no more than a whisper. 'Whatever you're about to say, Zach, please, don't tell me that you regret what we just did...'

The idea was so ridiculous that he almost laughed. How could she possibly think he could regret an experience like that?

'The only thing I regret is not taking more time over it,' he said softly, stroking her tousled blonde hair away from her flushed cheeks with a gentle hand. 'You deserve more than a quickie in my bathroom. Did I hurt you?'

'No. It—it was fantastic.' Her softly whispered words and the deepening flush on her cheeks made his guts clench.

With a slow smile he scooped her up in his arms and bent his head to kiss her gently on the mouth.

'It certainly was. So fantastic we're going to do it again. Only this time we're not rushing it.' He opened the bathroom door and shouldered his way through to the landing. 'This time we're going to take all night.'

Keely lay in the bed, her eyes closed, a deliciously warm feeling spreading over her body.

Zach was an insatiable lover...

After their one, breathtakingly powerful encounter in the bathroom he'd proceeded to make love to her for the entire night in almost every position imaginable.

She blushed slightly when she remembered some of the things she'd allowed him to do to her—things she'd been much too shy to allow anyone else to do before. But, somehow, with Zach everything felt right.

And Fiona had been right on that first day when she'd guessed that Zach would be good in bed. He was better than good. He was incredible. He knew exactly where to touch her—how to touch her—to drive her totally wild with excitement. And his body...

Talking of his body, where was he?

She glanced around the room and decided that he must have gone downstairs. Had she slept that late?

She reached out an arm to grab the clock and gasped. Oh, help. They were both supposed to be working that morning and if she didn't get a move on she'd be late.

Keely showered in record time, pulled on her clothes and made her way down to the kitchen.

Suddenly she felt impossibly shy. What should she say to Zach? How should she react? It was pretty hard to pretend to behave normally after everything they'd shared the night before.

She paused in the doorway and then took a deep breath and walked into the kitchen, her cheeks slightly pink as she glanced at him.

'You should have woken me up.'

'You were totally out for the count.'

His voice was noticeably cool and Keely felt as though she'd been showered with cold water.

Why wasn't he looking at her?

Phoebe was in her high chair, fighting with a plate of food in her usual manner, and Keely sat down next to her.

'Your father rang.' Zach handed her a cup of tea and she stared at him blankly.

Her father?

Why would her father ring?

'D-did he leave a message?'

'Yes.' Zach's tone was even. 'You've got an interview in London in a few weeks. Congratulations.'

Keely looked at him in silence.

Was that all he was going to say? After everything they'd shared—everything they'd done? All he could say was, 'Congratulations'?

'Don't forget to ask Sean for the day off.' He was so matter-of-fact that she wondered whether she'd imagined everything that had happened between them the night before.

Had the whole thing been a dream?

Why wasn't he trying to stop her? Why wasn't he trying to talk her out of going?

Didn't he mind that she might move to London?

Obviously not, she thought dully, staring down at the piece of toast on her plate.

Last night had obviously been nothing more than a diversion for him. Something to briefly take his mind off his wife.

So that was that.

Last night she'd been so sure that he'd felt something for her. So sure.

But he was making it all too clear that he considered

their night together to have been a mistake. He didn't want her and she certainly wasn't throwing herself at him again.

Which meant she may as well go to London.

She couldn't carry on living with Zach after last night. It would be too much to bear.

CHAPTER NINE

'You look awful.' Nicky opened the fridge to get some milk and frowned across at Keely who was sitting slumped in an armchair in the corner of the staffroom.

'Thanks for that.' Keely drained her coffee and stood up, knowing that it wouldn't take Nicky long to guess what was wrong.

And she didn't want to talk about it.

She *couldn't* talk about it.

Not without making a complete and utter fool of herself.

She walked briskly across to the door but Nicky's voice stopped her in her tracks.

'Keely, wait.' Nicky caught up with her and put a hand on her shoulder, her eyes searching. 'I suppose it's Zach?'

Was it that obvious?

Keely opened her mouth to deny it but then decided that she may as well be honest.

'Yes,' she mumbled. 'It's Zach.'

Nicky groaned. 'Oh, Keely, I warned you.'

'I know that,' Keely said, bravely dredging up a smile. 'I should have listened harder.'

'I'll kill Zach,' Nicky muttered, and Keely shook her head and ran a hand through her hair.

'It isn't his fault, Nicky,' she said wearily. 'It's my fault. All my fault. He warned me that he'd never get involved with another woman and I wouldn't listen. I was so crazy about him I just wanted to help him. I thought I could do that without getting hurt myself. But then he—we—' She broke off and Nicky gave a groan.

'You don't have to tell me. I can guess.' There was a

slight pause while Nicky digested what she'd just heard. 'And is it over? Are you sure?'

'Yes.' Keely nodded and managed a wan smile. 'You were right. He just won't ever get involved with another woman after his wife.'

Nicky frowned. 'Has he told you he's not interested?'

'Yes.' Keely paused. 'Well, not lately, I suppose. But after we actually... To be honest, he didn't say anything at all, but it didn't take a genius to work out that he wasn't interested.'

'Why? What did he do?'

Keely frowned and shook her head, still puzzled by it herself. 'He was so cold and distant. I couldn't believe it. We'd been so close, Nicky...' Her eyes filled and she cleared her throat. 'Damn. Sorry. When I woke up he was already downstairs and he was like a different person.'

'Right.' Nicky was looking at her thoughtfully. 'So something happened between him leaving your bed and you coming down for breakfast.'

'Nothing happened.' Keely gave a shrug. 'What could have happened? He got Phoebe up, gave her breakfast and took a phone call from my father. Nothing earth-shattering, I can assure you.'

'A phone call from your father?'

'Yes.' Keely rubbed her aching temples with her fingers. 'He rang to tell me I've got an interview in London in a few weeks.'

'And what did Zach say about that?'

Keely gave a humourless laugh, unable to hide the hurt. 'He said congratulations and reminded me to ask Sean for the time off.'

Nicky stared at her. 'That was it?'

'Yes,' Keely mumbled with a watery smile. 'He wasn't bothered, Nicky. In fact, he's probably pleased. It gets him out of having to tell me he'll never love me as much as his wife.'

'You don't know that.'

'Yes, I do.' Keely's voice was flat. 'Zach isn't interested in making a commitment to another woman. You know that as well as I do.'

Nicky let out a long breath. 'So what happens now?'

'I'm going to have to move out.' Keely made the decision on the spot. 'I can't carry on living there. Not now. It would be too difficult. I'm sure that Barbara will help with Phoebe until he can find someone else.'

Just thinking of little Phoebe made her heart twist. She'd got so used to the wonderful evening routine of bathing the little girl and giving her cuddles while she read a story. Giving that up would be almost as bad as giving up Zach.

Nicky gave her a quick hug. 'If it's any consolation, he's let you closer to Phoebe—and to him—than any other woman.'

'Well, it doesn't feel like a consolation at the moment,' Keely muttered, swallowing down an enormous lump in her throat.

Oh, for goodness' sake!

She was being totally pathetic. He'd been totally straight with her right from the beginning. She had no right to drip around, feeling sorry for herself.

Nicky shrugged helplessly, her expression sympathetic. 'Keely, I don't know what to say…'

'There's nothing you *can* say,' Keely said stoutly, glancing at her watch and deciding that the sooner she buried herself in work the better. 'Just hope I find somewhere to live fast. Before I make a fool of myself in front of him.'

'Well, that's easily solved. You can move in with me if you like,' Nicky said quickly. 'Our cottage isn't large but we've got a nice spare room which you're very welcome to.'

'That's really kind of you...' the lump in her throat grew bigger '...and if I get desperate I might take you up on it but, frankly, I think I'd be better off on my own.'

She felt so utterly miserable about Zach and Phoebe that she knew she'd be lousy company and she didn't want to have to keep putting on a brave face.

Nicky looked concerned. 'Are you sure you'll be all right staying with Zach until you find somewhere?'

'Oh, yes. We're on different shifts this week,' Keely said glumly. 'We overlap at work in the afternoons but we won't be seeing each other at home. I should survive.'

Or at least she hoped she would.

Thankfully they were incredibly busy over the next week, which helped Keely survive the trauma of seeing Zach every day and not being able to touch him.

It was still difficult.

She tried not to look at his familiar dark features, tried not to torture herself with memories of what they'd shared.

As for Zach, he seemed tired. Which didn't really make sense, she mused. To her knowledge he hadn't had any late nights and he hadn't been on call. So why did he have fine lines around his blue eyes and why was he so uncharacteristically impatient with people?

'Ouch,' said Nicky one morning after all of them had been on the receiving end of his biting sarcasm. 'I'm going for a cup of coffee to get out of the line of fire.'

'He's never normally like that,' Adam grumbled, looking quite white after the dressing-down he'd just received from the consultant. 'I don't know what's the matter with him.'

'I do,' Nicky said softly, glancing at Keely and giving her a knowing look. She waited until Adam left the room and then lowered her voice. 'I think you'll find that our handsome consultant isn't finding it as easy to give you up as he thought he might. Hang in there, kiddo, you might just find that this has a happy ending.'

But Keely knew there was no chance of that. If he wanted to have a relationship with her, why didn't he just say so? He must have guessed how she felt about him.

No. The only reasonable explanation was that he really didn't want to pursue anything between them.

At home they were like polite strangers—behaving as if their night of incredible passion had never happened.

If only she didn't have to see him every day, Keely thought glumly. It just reminded her of all the reasons why she'd fallen for him in the first place. He was such a brilliant doctor that watching him in action was enough to make anyone fall for him. And they did. She could hardly fail to notice that most of the nurses cast covert glances in his direction all the time—and some of the female doctors, too!

His skill and intuition as a doctor was brought home to her later that afternoon when a young woman was admitted having fainted in the shops.

'She just collapsed on me,' her husband said, the anxiety showing in his face. 'She's never fainted before to my knowledge. Never.'

'Right, well, let's get her on a trolley and examine her,' Keely said, frowning slightly as she looked at the woman. She was ashen and slightly sweaty and Keely didn't like the look of her at all.

'Nicky, let's get Zach in here, please,' she said in a calm voice and the A and E sister left the room quickly, obviously picking up just how worried Keely was.

Zach was by her side in a matter of minutes, his handsome face serious as he questioned the husband.

The woman moaned softly, opened her eyes and then gave a little shriek and clutched her stomach.

'Oh, help me…'

'Is that where it hurts?' Instantly Zach's eyes flickered to the husband. 'Could I ask you to wait outside, please, while I examine your wife?'

The husband frowned and clutched his wife's hand. 'I'd rather stay.'

'I'll call you back in straight away,' Zach said gently, 'but I just need to take a look at her. I'm sure you understand.'

Nicky took the husband by the arm and led him out of Resus, and Zach immediately turned back to the woman.

'Does it hurt anywhere else?'

'My shoulder,' the woman gasped, and Keely stared at her, baffled. Zach's questioning was obviously aiming in a certain direction but at the moment she couldn't see what it was.

'Is there any possibility that you could be pregnant, Mrs Blythe?' Zach asked quietly, and the woman shook her head vigorously.

'No!' She gave a whimper and clutched her stomach again. 'Ow, it hurts!'

Zach was watching her closely. 'And when was your last period?'

'I don't know.' She avoided his eyes. 'I'm never regular.'

'Can you give me a rough date?'

Keely stepped forward and gave the frightened woman a gentle smile. 'Don't be scared, Mrs Blythe. We have to ask these questions to find out what's wrong with you. Everything you say to us is confidential.'

The woman started to sob. 'I don't know what's wrong. I haven't had a period for eight weeks, but I can't be pregnant.'

'All right.' Zach's blue eyes narrowed slightly. 'I'm just going to examine your stomach, Mrs Blythe. Try and relax for me. What method of contraception do you use?'

'The coil,' she answered, and Keely watched while Zach examined her and then glanced at Nicky, his expression calm.

'Get me two large cannulae—12 or 14 gauge—get her cross-matched for six units of blood and request rhesus status. Nicky, I want a pregnancy test, please, and fast-bleep the gynae team.'

Keely listened to his list of instructions, her eyes fixed on his calm features. Despite his totally cool manner, he was obviously worried. Very worried. He was getting ready to resuscitate a potentially shocked patient—he obviously thought that Mrs Blythe was seriously ill.

Nicky and one of the staff nurses swung into action while Keely gave the woman some oxygen and prepared to take some bloods.

Suzy Blythe stared at them with frightened eyes. 'What's wrong with me?'

'You have a ruptured ectopic pregnancy,' Zach said gently, 'which basically means that the fertilised egg has implanted somewhere other than your uterus—usually one of the tubes that carry it to the uterus. That's what's causing the pain, and that's why you fainted.'

Keely stared at him.

How did he know that? There was no doubt or uncertainty in his voice at all. He was completely confident in his diagnosis.

'I can't be pregnant!'

Zach's gaze rested on the young woman's frightened face. 'Why?'

'Because my husband's been away for the last six months,' she sobbed, her whole body trembling. 'I can't be pregnant. I just can't be.'

Keely held her breath. Was Zach wrong?

'Suzy…' Zach took a deep breath and his voice was incredibly patient. 'Believe me, we're not here to judge

you. We just want to make you well. You have a very
serious condition, which I'm sure is an ectopic pregnancy.'

Suzy's cried harder. 'I don't know what to do.'

Zach's voice was gentle. 'But you could be pregnant?'

There was a long silence, broken only by Suzy's sobs.
'Yes. It was just the once,' she admitted jerkily, her tear-
stained face contorting as another pain hit her. 'Oh, heavens, what am I going to do? What will Rob say?'

'Don't worry about that now.' Keely gave her shoulder
a squeeze, feeling desperately sorry for her.

Zach quickly finished his physical examination. 'Have
you had any vaginal bleeding, Suzy?'

'No. Nothing.'

'The pregnancy test is positive, Mr Jordan,' the staff
nurse said quietly, her eyes fixed adoringly on Zach's face.

Keely gritted her teeth and felt a powerful surge of jealousy, which shocked her. Why should she be jealous? She
had no right to be jealous. He wasn't hers. And she could
hardly blame the nurse for drooling over him. If she found
the man irresistible, why shouldn't everyone else?

'Keely, take bloods for FBC, U and Es, blood sugar and
G and S,' Zach ordered, 'and call the gynae team and tell
them she's going to need to go to Theatre.'

'Will they tell Rob?' the woman whispered, and Zach
gave a sigh.

'I'll have a word with the consultant who'll do the operation. The answer is, I don't know. It depends on what
happens in Theatre.'

Keely helped prepare the woman for transfer to Theatre
for a laparoscopy—an operation which would allow the
surgeons to look inside her abdomen.

When she returned, Zach was making himself a cup of
coffee in the staffroom.

Bother. She'd been hoping to have five minutes by herself. But, still, she could use it as an opportunity to pick Zach's brains. She was still stunned and impressed that he'd known instinctively what the matter was with the woman.

'How did you know it was an ectopic pregnancy?'

Maybe if she kept it professional they'd be able to have a conversation without her wanting to throw herself into his arms.

'I've seen it before,' Zach told her, adding milk to his coffee and stirring it slowly. 'Several times, in fact. She was lucky. She had a stable form. In the unstable form it's often touch and go.'

Keely still didn't understand how he'd reached his diagnosis so quickly. 'But it could have been any number of other things.' She ticked them off on her fingers. 'Appendicitis, a gastrointestinal bleed—'

'True. But the first thing you exclude in a woman of childbearing age suffering from abdominal pain is ectopic pregnancy,' Zach told her, taking a sip of coffee and dropping into one of the armchairs. 'It's important to assess risk factors to see how likely it is.'

Keely was confused. 'But she told you she couldn't be pregnant so it didn't seem likely. Why didn't you believe her? I think I would have just taken her at her word, and then what would have happened? How did you *know*, Zach?'

'How did I know?' He gave a sigh and stretched long muscular legs out in front of him. 'Firstly, because she was of childbearing age and her symptoms suggested it. Secondly, because her body language suggested that she wasn't telling the truth—'

'But how did you know that?'

She would have missed it, she knew she would.

He shrugged. 'Experience.'

Keely's shoulders sagged. 'But I wouldn't have pushed

her like you did. I don't think I would have had the nerve to do a pregnancy test when she'd told me that she couldn't be pregnant.'

'On the contrary, you handled it very well,' Zach said quietly. 'You spotted instantly that her condition could be serious and you called a senior doctor, which was absolutely the right decision. You were kind and approachable and I suspect that if I hadn't forced her to tell me, she would have eventually confided in you.'

'But you knew what was wrong with her,' Keely said gloomily, 'and I didn't have a clue. I haven't got your instincts.'

'You haven't got my experience,' he corrected her gently. 'There's nothing wrong with your instincts. Your instincts are fine. Stop beating yourself up.'

Their eyes locked and awareness sizzled between them.

With a muttered curse Zach thumped his mug down on the table and stood up abruptly. His broad shoulders tensed and his blue eyes were suddenly wary. 'Keely, we need to talk.'

'Yes.' Her voice was little more than a whisper. 'I suppose we do.'

'At home. It's more private.'

'I thought you were working late tonight?'

'Sean swapped with me,' he said smoothly, 'so that I can be home in time to put Phoebe to bed.'

'But I could have done that,' she protested as he walked over to the sink and put his mug on the draining-board.

'Thanks.' He kept his back to her. 'But I'd rather do it myself. It's one of the things I need to talk to you about.'

In other words, he didn't want her near his daughter.

Keely watched him go and felt more miserable than she ever had in her life. If he was going to those lengths to keep her away from his daughter then it was definitely time that she moved out.

* * *

Zach was in the kitchen when she arrived home, and he got straight to the point.

'I'm sorry, but this isn't working out any more Keely.' His eyes were steady on hers. 'You'll be off to London in no time at all. It's time Phoebe got used to not having you around.'

'You want me to move out?'

She'd planned to do just that, so why did it feel so painful when he suggested it?

'She's getting too attached to you.' He ran a hand through his sleek, dark hair, obviously finding the conversation difficult. 'I don't want to see her hurt.'

'Neither do I, Zach.' Did he really think she wanted to hurt his daughter?

'I know you don't, but nevertheless that's what's going to happen when you leave. And it's just going to get harder the longer you stay.'

'Yes. I see that.' Her voice sounded strangely flat. Totally unlike her own. 'I'll start looking for somewhere else to live.'

He rubbed his fingers over his clenched jaw, visibly tense.

'Listen, Keely...' He hesitated, obviously struggling to find the right words. 'We haven't talked about what happened between us but—'

'No.' She held up a hand and interrupted him before he could say any more. 'Don't say it. There isn't anything that needs to be said.'

It was true. What could he say that wouldn't make her feel a million times worse?

She didn't need him to spell out the way he felt.

He looked at her warily. 'I'm really grateful for your help with Phoebe.'

Keely ignored the hurt and gave him a brave smile. 'You're very welcome, Zach. I hope it works out for you both. I'll start looking or somewhere else to live tomorrow. Can I stay here until I find somewhere?'

He frowned. 'Of course, but—'

'Thanks.' She stroked her blonde hair behind her ears and walked towards the door, anxious to put as much distance between them as possible. 'Well, I've got to prepare for my interview so if you'll excuse me I'll go upstairs.'

With that she turned on her heel and took refuge in the sanctuary of her bedroom.

The next two days were frantic and Keely barely had time to breathe, let alone make phone calls about flats.

She arrived at Zach's house at the end of the second day in time for Phoebe's bath and wondered what she was meant to do.

Zach had made it clear that he didn't want her near Phoebe so she'd been avoiding the little girl as much as possible, but if Barbara needed to leave to get home to her own family then surely Zach wouldn't mind if she helped out?

She opened the front door and stopped dead as she saw a stunning blonde woman standing in the hallway.

'Hello?' Keely frowned in confusion and closed the front door behind her. 'I don't think we've met…'

'No.' The woman held out her hand and gave a formal smile. 'I'm Maggie Hillyard. The new nanny.'

The new nanny?

Zach had employed a new nanny?

The man certainly didn't hang around.

'Are you…?' Keely cleared her throat and started again. 'Will you be living in?'

'Oh, yes.' Maggie nodded. 'Zach was quite insistent. He's given me the room at the back until you move out. When you've gone I'll have your room because the view's better. I gather you're looking for somewhere at the moment.'

Keely's lips were so stiff she could barely form the words to reply. 'That's right. So when did you get the job?'

When exactly had Zach decided to employ a new nanny? And what had happened to dear Barbara?

'Mr Jordan interviewed me a few days ago,' the nanny said crisply. 'The poor man was obviously desperate for me to start as soon as possible. He told me that you had to leave in a hurry and that he was looking for a replacement.'

Keely tried not to mind that the description made her sound like an employee. She wasn't an employee. She hadn't cared for Phoebe because it had been part of a job description. Or because she'd been paid. She'd cared for Phoebe because she loved her. With all her heart and soul.

'You're right.' She smiled at the other woman, although the smile felt so unnatural that she thought her skin might crack. 'I do have to leave.'

The hope—the little that she'd managed to hold onto—had drained out of her as the new nanny spoke, and she knew she *did* have to leave. She no longer had a choice. If Zach was prepared to go to these lengths to keep her away from his daughter then it was time she faced facts. And the facts were that Zach Jordan had been so badly hurt that nothing could heal the wounds inside him—no amount of love or devotion would solve his problems. He was never going to change his mind and ask her to stay.

'In fact, I was leaving tonight.' Her decision made, she gave the woman another false smile and took the stairs two at a time, walking briskly to her bedroom, careful not to look in on Phoebe who was asleep. She was going to miss the little girl as much as she'd miss Zach.

In her room, she grabbed her clothes out of the wardrobe and stuffed them untidily into a suitcase, biting back the sobs that threatened to choke her. Not now. She couldn't break down now. Zach could be home at any minute and she just couldn't face him. She really couldn't.

Once the suitcase was full she delved into her bag for her mobile phone and called Nicky to check that her offer of accommodation still stood. Then she walked quickly downstairs and wished the nanny every happiness in her new job.

How long would it take the new nanny to fall for Zach? She walked briskly to her car and unlocked it. How long before Zach had to let her go as he had all the other nannies?

Keely slammed the car door shut and turned the key in the ignition with shaking fingers. Damn the man! Damn the man for making her love him, and for having such a lovely daughter.

Hot tears started to burn her eyes and she angrily dashed them away and reversed the car out of the drive. She held the tears back and drove until she was safely out of sight of Zach's house before pulling into a lay-by and sobbing until she thought her heart would break.

She awoke in Nicky's spare bedroom cuddled under a warm, snug duvet covered in tiny flowers.

Her head throbbed and her eyes felt gritty from crying and lack of sleep.

There was a tap on the door and she struggled into a sitting position as the door opened and Nicky popped her head round the door.

'Are you decent? I've made you a cup of tea. It's six o'clock. You need to get a move on if you're going to work.'

Was she going to work? Going to work meant meeting Zach…

'I don't think I can face him, Nicky,' she croaked, and the other girl sighed and walked into the room.

'Yes, you can,' she said firmly. 'You could have a day in bed, but what good would that do? You'd just cry your eyes out all day and that won't make you feel any better.'

It would feel better than bumping into Zach every other minute.

'I'm going to make a fool of myself—'

'No.' Nicky's voice was quiet. 'It's not you that's the fool in all this, Keely. It's Zach. If he's letting a girl like you go then, believe me, he's the fool. You're the best thing that's ever happened to him and the best thing that's happened to Phoebe, but he's too pig-headed to see it.'

'He's just been very badly hurt,' Keely whispered, reaching for her tea and taking a mouthful. 'And there's nothing I can do about that. I don't think he'll ever get over his wife. And how can I begin to compete with someone who isn't even around any more?'

'Don't think about that now. Have a shower,' Nicky advised. 'A long, hot shower. Wash your face and put some make-up on.'

'Oh, no!' Keely clapped her hand over her mouth in dismay. 'My make-up! I forgot to clear my things out of his bathroom. I was in such a state when I saw the nanny that I just wanted to get out of there as soon as possible. How am I going to cover the blotches on my face?'

'With some of mine.' Nicky picked up the empty mug and walked towards the door. 'My make-up box is on the bathroom shelf. Help yourself to anything you fancy. And there's a new toothbrush in the cupboard above the bath.'

Keely gave her a grateful look. 'What can I say?'

'Say that you're going to go to work.' Nicky's chin lifted slightly. 'And say that you're going to tell Zach how you feel about him.'

'No way.' Keely shook her head. 'I'm not throwing my-self at him again. It's time I learned to take no for an answer.'

By the time she arrived at work she was relatively confident that she'd successfully removed all traces of her distress. She certainly looked pale and tired but, then, so did half of the doctors who worked in A and E. It was a stressful environment.

For the first few hours of the day she only saw Zach from a distance and then, just when she was beginning to relax, she walked into him in the corridor. Literally.

'Careful.' His strong hands gripped her shoulders and steadied her, and she stepped back as if she'd been burned.

'I'm sorry.' Dear God, she needed to get away from him. Fast.

Without saying anything further, she turned on her heel but he was too quick for her, his long fingers biting into her arm and holding her still.

'Wait a minute.' His voice was quiet and he was frowning slightly. 'Maggie tells me that you moved out last night. I didn't think you'd found anywhere yet. You didn't mention that you were leaving. Where did you go, Keely?'

'It really doesn't matter.' She'd rather keep it to herself for now. 'I'm fine, Zach.'

'Keely…'

He looked tortured and suddenly she realised that it didn't matter how *she* felt. She just wanted *him* to be all right. She didn't want to cause him more pain. The man had had enough of that to last him a lifetime. It wasn't his fault that he couldn't love her the way he'd loved his wife.

'Really, truly I'm fine.' On impulse she stood on tiptoe and gave him a kiss on the cheek. 'You take care of yourself and Phoebe. Now, I've got to dash.' She lifted her chin and gave him a bright smile. 'I promised to help Nicky.'

Without waiting for his reply, she turned on her heel, hurrying down the corridor and back into the department before he could stop her.

CHAPTER TEN

SOMEHOW Keely stumbled through the next two weeks, working on autopilot and keeping her emotions firmly in check. By a stroke of luck Sean scheduled her to work nights, so the only contact she had with Zach was the occasional glimpse of his broad shoulders in the distance.

And then suddenly she was back on days again and avoiding him became harder.

'Zach was looking for you earlier—did he find you?' Nicky caught Keely in the corridor as she walked towards the common room late one morning.

'No. Thank goodness.' Keely pulled a face. 'I really can't face any more conversations with him at the moment.'

'Well, in that case come up to the canteen with me for something revolting to eat,' Nicky joked, obviously trying to cheer her up. 'It's just about lunchtime and we're not usually this quiet so we should make the most of it while we can.'

Keely pulled a face. The mere thought of food made her stomach churn. She hadn't eaten properly for days and a seed of worry was starting to grow at the back of her mind.

'No, thanks.' She certainly wasn't going to voice her suspicion to Nicky. 'Sean's given me permission to take a long lunch-break and I'm going to Zach's to pick up the things I left in his bathroom. He's working late tonight so I know there's no chance of running into him. I want to get it over with. I need a clear head for my interview so the sooner I'm out of his life the better.'

'OK.' Nicky gave her a worried smile. 'Well, for goodness' sake, be careful on the roads. They're icy.'

Despite the warning, Keely wasn't careful.

She drove too fast, as if her sudden burst of speed might
help her outrun her problems.

She was only yards from Zach's house when she saw
the smoke.

'Oh, my God, no!'

She slammed on her brakes and left the car at a run,
sprinting the last few yards to Zach's house, her problems
forgotten.

Zach's house was on fire!

Flames licked out of the upper windows and smoke bil-
lowed in huge clouds into the cold blue sky. A crowd of
people had gathered at the end of Zach's path and Keely
elbowed her way through, her heart lifting with relief when
she saw Barbara standing at the end of the garden.

'Barbara—thank goodness you're safe. Were you inside?'

Barbara shook her head, her face pale with shock and
anxiety. 'No. The new nanny was in charge.'

The new nanny?

Keely looked round frantically. Where was she?

'Barbara, have you seen her? The nanny? And where's
Phoebe?'

Her heart was pounding and she felt the panic rise and
threaten to swamp her.

Where was Zach's daughter?

'They're over there, under the tree.'

Keely glanced across and saw the nanny in conversation
with a woman from the village. There was no sign of
Phoebe.

Scanning the front garden frantically, Keely tried to stay
calm. The child was bound to be here somewhere...

'The fire brigade are on their way,' Barbara told her. 'With any luck they'll be able to save Zach's house.'

But Keely wasn't thinking about Zach's house. She was thinking of Zach's daughter.

Where was Phoebe?

Her heart in her mouth, she sprinted over to the nanny, stumbling on the hard, frozen earth. It was so cold that everyone's breath was clouding the wintry air. 'Where's Phoebe?'

The nanny looked startled. 'She's playing under that tree…'

She turned to point her out to Keely and her face blanched. 'Oh, no, she's gone…'

Keely looked round frantically, yelling at the others to find the child.

'She's always wandering off,' the nanny grumbled. 'She'll be here somewhere.'

'It was your job to watch her,' Keely snapped. 'She's not even three years old. They all wander off at that age.'

Fergus, the four-year-old son of the farmer who was Zach's nearest neighbour, stuck his finger out and pointed to the house.

'Feefee in house,' he said firmly, and cold fingers of panic squeezed Keely's heart as she dropped to her knees and looked him straight in the eye.

'Phoebe's gone into the house? Are you sure?' Her voice was hoarse, and Fergus nodded.

'She wanted her teddy. She lost her teddy.'

Oh, dear God, if Phoebe was looking for her teddy then she knew exactly where the child would be.

In the playroom—right at the back of the house.

'I'm sure she isn't in the house,' Maggie said nervously, but Keely shot her a look of pure disdain.

'She's gone back to the house. She must have. Don't you know *never* to take your eye off a toddler?' Worry made her uncharacteristically rude. 'What sort of a nanny are you?'

Without waiting for a reply, she turned to look at Zach's house, which was rapidly becoming an inferno. And little Phoebe was in there, looking for her teddy...

Briefly her eyes closed and then she thrust Fergus into the arms of his mother with curt instructions not to let him go. Without stopping to think about the sense or safety of what she was doing, she sped towards the house, ignoring the shouts from behind her.

In the distance she thought she heard sirens but she knew she had to act immediately. Even a few minutes might be too late to save Phoebe.

Trying to remember what she knew about fires, she took a few big gulps of clean air before dropping to her hands and knees in the smoke-filled hallway. Thank goodness the flames hadn't yet spread to that part of the house.

Stay low, she reminded herself firmly. Smoke rises.

Disorientated by the smoke in the hall, she tried to remember the way to the playroom, feeling her way along the wall, turning into the lounge and crawling rapidly into the extension at the back of the house. All around her bits of furniture crackled as the fire took hold and the smoke was so thick it choked her. Forcing down her fear, she paused and peered through the smoky gloom.

'Phoebe!' Her voice sounded odd above the crackle of the flames and she looked round frantically, feeling as though her lungs were going to burst. Where was she? There was no sign of her. Maybe Fergus had been wrong and she was outside, playing a game of hide and seek...

Overwhelmed by fear for Phoebe, she started to panic, her ability to think dulled by the smothering smoke and the pain in her chest.

And then she saw her.

Lying on the floor in a little ball. Unconscious.

Unconscious or dead?

No. Please, not dead.

Forcing herself not to think about that possibility, Keely battled to keep her rising panic in check. This was no time for even the most basic first aid. The best thing she could do for Phoebe now was get her out. If she didn't get her out, she'd die for sure—in fact, both of them would die...

Choking and coughing, she wriggled up to the body of the child and grabbed a handful of her jumper, dragging her along the floor towards the door. But this time her journey was impeded by the extra weight and the ever-building volume of smoke. She cried out and sobbed as a piece of burning wood fell onto her hand and she collapsed face down on the floor ready to give up.

She was going to die. They were both going to die. And Zach would lose his precious daughter.

First his wife and then his daughter.

No!

The thought of what such a loss would do to the man gave a final boost to her will-power and she drove herself forward, teeth gritted, barely breathing as the smoke grew denser. It felt as though her lungs were on fire and she started to cough and choke as she crawled nearer to the door.

Oh, God, please, let Phoebe live.

She didn't even care if *she* died any more. Her lungs and her hand hurt so much that she was ready to give up and let the smoke get her, but she wanted the little girl to live so badly she pushed herself through the pain barrier.

Keep going, just keep going, she told herself, and then finally, through the flames that were starting to lick their way into the hall, she saw the front door. Nearly there. *So nearly there.* But she couldn't make it. Her lungs were burning and she no longer had enough oxygen to continue, but she pushed Phoebe as hard as she could towards the door, dimly aware of a fireman in breathing apparatus grabbing the child and carrying her to safety.

And then her breath scorched in her lungs and the world went black.

'Burns coming in, Zach,' Nicky said briskly, hanging up the hotline phone and scurrying towards Resus.

'Adult and child.'

Zach nodded, his eyes gritty from lack of sleep. Phoebe had been up all the previous night, fractious and unsettled because of the new nanny. She was missing Keely's gentle warmth and, if he was honest, so was he. He forced the thought aside and tried to concentrate on the job in hand. 'Any details?'

'None.'

The hotline rang again and Nicky frowned. 'Not another one. Don't do this to me,' she muttered, picking the phone up and tucking it under her ear. 'Hello?'

Zach watched idly, waiting to hear whether yet another incident was about to descend on them.

'Oh, Lord, are you sure? Read me the address.' Nicky's voice was little more than a whisper and her face visibly paled as she swivelled to look at him.

And he knew.

Just by looking at the expression in her eyes, he knew without a shadow of a doubt that the fire was in his house.

Which meant that the child was—

'Phoebe!'

The ambulance siren shrieked outside the department and Zach was in the ambulance bay and dragging open the doors before they'd turned the engine off.

'Calm down, Zach.' Pete, one of the paramedics, gave his shoulder a quick squeeze. 'She seems OK. Maybe some minor smoke inhalation, but her resps have been fine and she's got no obvious burns.'

'Thank God.'

'It isn't God you should be thanking,' Pete said roughly. 'It's Keely. She ran into your house after the child and saved her life. If it hadn't been for Keely, Phoebe would definitely be dead, Zach. The girl's a bloody heroine.'

Keely?

Zach felt shell-shocked, his gaze shifting from the still form of his daughter to the other body on the stretcher in the ambulance. He hadn't even see that there was another person in the ambulance, he'd been so worried about his daughter.

'She had signs of laryngeal oedema so we've intubated her,' Pete told him. 'And she had morphine at the scene.'

Keely or Phoebe?

For a moment he couldn't take in what was being said. He couldn't think straight and he felt an unfamiliar panic grip him. Dragging a deep breath into his lungs, he forced himself to ignore the fact that it was Keely lying there, and that his precious daughter was injured, too. They needed his skills and he couldn't be objective unless he could switch off.

'OK.' He cleared his throat and pulled himself together, his expression grim. 'Let's get both of them into Resus.'

He scrambled out of the ambulance and sprinted back into the department. 'Nicky—get Tony Maxwell down here now and fast-bleep the first-on anaesthetist.'

He needed someone he trusted to look after his daughter while he concentrated on Keely. No way was he going to let her die. No way.

'Get her connected to an ECG monitor now—if she's inhaled smoke she might have arrhythmias, and let's measure carboxyhaemoglobin.' His instructions were terse. 'And get a line in, Adam. Move!'

Adam worked quickly and Sean Nicholson strode over to the trolley, his expression serious.

'I just heard. What do you want me to do?'

'Check on my daughter,' Zach said through gritted teeth. 'The paramedics told me they thought she was OK so I'm letting someone else deal with her.'

'I'll see to it,' Sean said quickly, moving across Resus to the other trolley.

'OK, Adam.' Zach looked up. 'Let's give her the highest possible concentration of humidified oxygen and get an IV up—we need to maintain circulating blood volume.'

'She's got a nasty burn on her hand,' Nicky said. 'Shall I dress it?'

'Let's get her stable first,' Zach said shortly. 'How are her vital signs?'

'She's doing well,' Adam said quickly. 'Her ECG is normal and her pulse and BP are stable.'

'Phoebe is going to be fine.' Sean appeared by Zach's shoulder. 'No sign of smoke inhalation or burns. I suspect she breathed in and then fell to the ground and that probably saved her. Keely obviously got her out before any lasting damage was done.'

She'd saved his daughter.

Zach pushed the thought away. He couldn't think about that now. He was too busy saving her.

Sean moved closer. 'How's she doing?'

'All right, I think. I want to do a chest X-ray. We've sent off bloods and we need to sort out her hand.'

Sean took a quick look. 'It isn't too bad. Smother it in silver sulphadiazine cream, Nicky, and put it inside a sterile plastic bag.'

Nicky scurried to do as he'd instructed and Zach and Adam finished all the necessary investigations and management before transferring Keely to the ward.

Only once he was satisfied that Keely was stable did Zach return to comfort his daughter, and it was then that it hit him.

He'd nearly lost both of them...

*   *   *

Her chest hurt.

Keely opened her eyes and blinked several times, her vision blurred as she looked round the sterile hospital room.

'Zach…' Her voice barely functioned, little more than a hoarse croak coming from her lips as she tried to speak.

'I'm right here.' He was by her side in an instant and she felt a rush of panic.

'Phoebe?'

'Alive and well.' A muscle worked in his jaw. 'Thanks to you.'

'Oh, thank God…' She closed her eyes and swallowed hard. 'I really thought…'

She didn't want to tell him what she'd thought, but he read her mind and sat down on the edge of her bed, his hand covering her uninjured one.

'I can imagine what you thought. And I can't thank you enough, Keely.' He rubbed his forehead and shook his head slowly. 'I don't know what to say to you. I don't know how to even begin to thank you.'

'You don't have to thank me. I'm just glad she's all right. I was so worried.' Her voice was getting stronger and she didn't feel anywhere near as bad as she thought she should. 'My throat's sore, Zach.'

'It will be.' He nodded. 'You were intubated.'

Her eyes widened. 'Really?'

'Really.' He gave a tired smile. 'For a while back there it was touch and go. You gave me a fright.'

She closed her eyes and breathed out. 'You poor thing. You must have been so worried about little Phoebe.'

'I was equally worried about you,' he said quietly, his eyes fixed on her face. 'Whatever possessed you to take such a risk, Keely? To go into a burning house? You could have been killed.'

A vivid picture of the heat and the flames filled her mind and she shuddered.

'Don't talk about it—I've never been so scared in my life.'

His jaw tightened. 'But you still did it…'

'I had to find Phoebe.' Her face was serious.

'How did you know she was in there? Barbara said that no one had actually seen her enter the house. You could have been risking your life for nothing.'

'I knew she was in there.' Keely smiled weakly. 'She lost her bear again and she's always dropping it in the playroom. I didn't really have a choice. What if I hadn't gone in, Zach? By the time the fire engines arrived she'd have—'

'Don't!' He interrupted her roughly and shook his head, obviously unable to contemplate such an awful scenario. 'I just can't believe you took such a risk for my daughter.'

'I love her, Zach.'

His eyes locked with hers. 'I owe you so much.'

She shook her head and her eyes filled with tears. 'You don't owe me anything, Zach. I'm just glad she's OK. Where is she now?'

'On the ward. They're keeping her in for observation.'

'I'll pop down and see her later.' Keely looked hesitantly at Zach. 'That's if you don't mind, of course…'

Was he still anxious to keep her away from his daughter?

'Keely, don't!' Zach's voice was gruff and his grip on her hand tightened. 'Don't remind me what a total idiot I've been. Will you ever forgive me?'

He thought he'd been an idiot? What did that mean? What was he saying?

He looked at her steadily, his blue eyes searching every inch of her pale face.

'This really isn't the time or the place, but there's something I need to say to you.' His voice was rough and his grip on her hand tightened.

'Mr Jordan?' The ward sister interrupted them, her expression serious. 'I'm sorry to disturb you but Paeds are on the phone. Your daughter is asking for you—and A and E have phoned twice while you've been up here. There's been a pile-up on the motorway and they're desperate for your help.'

Zach tipped his head back and muttered under his breath while Keely carefully hid her frustration. Obviously she was going to have to wait to find out what he wanted to say to her. The man was being pulled in different directions as usual.

The ward sister looked apologetic. 'What shall I tell Paeds?'

Keely struggled into a sitting position. 'Tell them to bring Phoebe up here. I'll keep her company until her daddy has finished in A and E.' She glanced nervously at Zach. 'If that's OK with you, of course.'

What would he say?

Would he refuse?

Was he still trying to keep her away from his daughter?

'You're not well enough to entertain a toddler.' He frowned at her and she sank back onto her pillows.

'I'll be fine. I want to see her, Zach. The staff here will help—'

'Well, of course we will.' The sister rose to the challenge and gave Keely a wink. 'I've got a niece and nephew of the same age so I'm sure I can cope with your daughter on my ward.'

Zach and Keely exchanged smiles. The woman had no idea of Phoebe's capacity for mischief.

'If you're sure you're up to it...' He leaned forward and

brushed his lips against her forehead, a look of frustration crossing his handsome features. 'There's so much I want to say to you but it's obviously going to have to wait. Tell Phoebe I'll be up to see her when I've finished downstairs.'

She stared up at him, her eyes feasting on his firm mouth and his dark jaw. His calm strength surrounded her and she felt deliciously warm and safe after the horrors of the fire.

What did he want to say to her?

Keely watched him go and then closed her eyes, forcing herself not to hope for something that wasn't going to happen. In the meantime, she needed to talk to the doctor. In private. There was something she needed to ask him…

It was several hours later when Zach took the stairs two at a time and pushed open the door to the ward. He'd been in A and E longer than he'd planned and he was worried about Keely.

'Oh, Mr Jordan.' The ward sister intercepted him, catching his arm and stopping him in mid-stride. 'I'm going to have to ask you to be quiet, I'm afraid. They're both asleep.'

'Asleep?' His brows met in a deep frown and he glanced towards Keely's room. 'My daughter's asleep, too? Did you put another bed in the room?'

The ward sister sighed and gave a rueful smile. 'I'm afraid not. It's against all the rules, of course, but your daughter was fretting so we overlooked it on this occasion. She's asleep in Dr Thompson's bed.'

Zach walked quietly to the side ward and paused in the doorway, something squeezing his heart as he stared at his daughter who was fast asleep, her sweet little body cuddled against Keely.

And Keely was asleep, too, each of them holding the other tightly.

'Phoebe's a very lucky girl, Mr Jordan,' the ward sister said softly, her eyes resting on the pair in the bed. 'To have someone who loves her as much as that. Dr Thompson's in a great deal of pain but she insisted on reading to your daughter and cuddling her in the bed. When she heard that you were still busy downstairs she was determined that the child would sleep with her until you were available.'

For the first time in his adult life Zach felt a lump building in his throat, and gave a cough to clear it.

'You're right, of course,' he said gruffly. 'Phoebe is lucky.'

Totally exhausted from the events of the day, he gave a nod of thanks to the ward sister and stepped quietly into the darkened room.

He wanted to make sure that he was there when they both woke up.

Still half-asleep Keely suddenly realised that she was hot and then bit back a gasp of pain as a little body wriggled onto her burnt arm.

'OK, young lady...' Zach's deep voice came from right beside her and almost immediately Phoebe was lifted out of the bed. 'Sorry about that. I was waiting for her to wake up but I must have drifted off. Are you all right?'

Keely winced and managed a smile. 'I'm great,' she lied, trying to ignore the pain in her throat, her chest and her hand.

'Keekee hurt,' Phoebe said solemnly, her thumb in her mouth. 'Keekee poorly. Daddy cuggle Keekee.'

Keely met Zach's piercing gaze and immediately looked away, a hot flush spreading over her cheeks. Help. She didn't need the matchmaking attempts of a toddler, that was for sure!

'Daddy cuggle,' Phoebe said firmly, and Zach gave a grin and sat down on the edge of the bed, his daughter on his lap.

'Everyone seems to be matchmaking, don't they? First Ally and now Phoebe. Maybe it's time we listened to them.' He put his fingers under her chin and forced her to look at him. 'There's something I want to say to you and I need to do it quickly before A and E or some other wretched department rings and tries to drag me away.'

Her heart started to thump. 'Wh-what?'

'I want to tell you about Catherine. It's time you knew the truth.' Zach's expression was grim and he lifted his daughter off the bed in an easy movement. 'You, young lady, are going to play with the nurses for five minutes while I talk to Keely.'

Keely watched him leave the room, her brain totally jumbled. *What was he going to say?* She wasn't sure she could stand hearing him tell her just how much he'd loved his wife. She just wasn't up to it.

He returned a few minutes later without Phoebe and closed the door firmly behind him.

Instead of sitting on the bed, he walked over to the window, his body tense as he looked out over the mountains.

'I don't really know where to start, except to say that what I'm going to tell you now is between you and me.' His voice was low and she had to strain to hear him. 'I've never said this to anyone else and I don't ever want Phoebe to find out the truth.'

Keely stared at him. *Find out what?* What didn't he want Phoebe to find out about? What was the man talking about?

'After I finished my surgical job with your father I took another surgical job in a different London hospital, and that's where I met Catherine.' There was a slight pause. 'She was an orthopaedic surgeon and a very good one. In fact, she was brilliant. I admired her work, we went out a few times and then one night we'd both had a bit too much to drink and—well, let's just say that the result was Phoebe. She was a complete accident.'

Keely lay still, wanting to ask questions but not knowing where to start.

'But…I thought you were in love with her?'

'Well, I wasn't.' Zach turned round to face her, his broad shoulders blocking out most of the light in the little room. 'We were just colleagues really. But I respected her and we had plenty in common—or so I thought. I really believed we could make it work.'

'She was pleased to be pregnant?'

'Pleased? Catherine?' Zach gave a laugh that rang with bitterness. 'Catherine was a career-woman, through and through. She'd made up her mind never to have children. She was even considering being sterilised but, of course, I didn't know that when I met her. So, no, she was not pleased when she found out she was pregnant. She wanted a termination.'

Keely gasped, her eyes wide with horror. 'Oh, Zach…'

'I talked her out of it.' Zach's voice was gruff. 'I promised that I'd help, that she could still work, that we could have a nanny for some of the time. I asked her to marry me.'

Keely swallowed. 'And she did…'

'Yes, she did.' Zach sighed and rubbed his fingers over his rough jaw. 'But it was a mistake. I thought that once the baby arrived she'd settle down, but she was back at work two days after Phoebe was born.'

Keely gaped at him, unable to believe what she was hearing. *'Two days?'*

'Shocking, isn't it? She hired a nursery nurse and went

back to work—full time.' Zach's expression was grim and his blue eyes were suddenly hard. 'And when I say full time, I mean full time. She was never at home.'

Keely was finding it hard to grasp. 'But Phoebe…'

Zach gave a derisive laugh. 'She wasn't interested in Phoebe. She didn't want to be with Phoebe. As far as Catherine was concerned, Phoebe was just something that could ruin her career. Catherine wasn't there when she took her first step or when she said her first word—and she didn't care.'

'Zach, I'm so sorry.' Keely's voice was soft. She found it impossible to imagine anyone not being interested in their child. 'So what happened?'

He shrugged. 'Catherine spent less and less time at home so I spent more time at home to compensate. In the end I gave up on a career in surgery and switched to A and E because the hours were better. It meant that on most days I could be home to bath Phoebe and we had most weekends together.'

'And what happened to Catherine?'

Zach's jaw tightened. 'We muddled along for a while and then she accepted a job in the States—'

'The States? You mean *America*?' Keely's voice was a horrified squeak and he gave a wry smile.

'Why not? She was offered a plum position in Boston and she decided to move.'

Keely shook her head, unable to believe what she was hearing. 'And leave her family?'

He shrugged. 'As far as Catherine was concerned, she didn't have a family. We were just a hindrance. By then our marriage had totally disintegrated and we barely saw each other. Even when she wasn't working she spent most of her time at the hospital.'

'So she moved to America?'

'No.' He shook his head. 'A week before she was due

to go she was called out to a major accident on the motorway. She crashed in the fog. And that was it.'

Keely closed her eyes. 'Oh, Zach…'

'And do you know the hardest thing of all?' Zach's voice was conversational, as if he were talking about the weather, not the death of his wife. 'The fact that everyone felt sorry for me. They all assumed I must be devastated. And I wasn't. It was a tragedy of course—for her. But for us?' He paused and shook his head slowly. 'It sounds callous, I know, but in a way her death made it easier for me and for Phoebe. But, of course, no one knew that.'

'No. They couldn't possibly have understood.' She lifted her eyes to his, knowing that everything she felt for him was there for him to see. 'But I understand. Telling Phoebe that her mother died when she was little is going to be so much easier than telling her that her mother never wanted her and had moved to the other side of the world.'

His eyes locked with hers. 'Precisely.'

She took a deep breath. It was almost too much to take in.

He hadn't loved Catherine.

'We did all assume that you were devastated because you lost your wife,' she said, struggling to sit more upright in the bed. 'We all assumed you loved her so much you could never love another woman again.'

'I know what people assumed.' He gave a shrug. 'And I let them carry on with their false assumptions. It protected Phoebe from the truth. That our marriage was a sham and her mother didn't want her.'

Keely was still confused. 'But you told me that you had nothing left to give any woman after Catherine,' she asked quietly. 'I don't understand. If you weren't grieving for your wife, what was stopping you having a relationship with someone else?'

'A lack of trust. After everything that happened with

Catherine I wasn't in a hurry to trust another woman again. Phoebe's happiness was at stake.' Zach paced across the room, his hands thrust deep into his pockets. 'And I suppose the truth was that I never met anyone I was remotely interested in.' He stopped dead and lifted his head to look at her. 'Until you came back into my life.'

Suddenly the room went very still and Keely forgot to breathe.

What was he saying?

'I tried to keep you at a distance but the chemistry between us is so strong it was impossible…' His voice was hoarse and his eyes burned into hers. 'Let's be honest for a moment. There was always something between us, Keely. Always. Even when you were young, we connected. When I came to stay in your house it was *you* that I enjoyed spending time with.'

She gave an awkward laugh. 'I was an irritating teenager—'

'No.' He shook his head and walked towards her. 'You were never that. You were smiley and enthusiastic and ridiculously caring about everything and everyone around you. When you proposed to me that night I suddenly realised that you were growing up fast. Frighteningly fast.'

'I should never have said what I said.' She blushed. 'I can't even begin to imagine what you must have thought of me.'

His eyes were warm. 'I thought you were gorgeous and I was flattered.'

'But you never visited us again…'

There was a long silence. 'Because I didn't trust myself,' he said finally. 'You were at a very dangerous age. You weren't a child any more and I knew that you needed space to spread your wings. So I kept my distance. I never thought you'd come back into my life.'

'But I did.'

'You did, indeed. And you kept trying to prove to me how grown up you were.'

'I had to. You thought I was a child,' Keely reminded him and he shook his head with a smile.

'Oh, no, I didn't. From the moment I saw you sitting in the lecture theatre, hiding your face behind your hand, I knew that you were all woman. And, believe me, keeping my hands off you nearly drove me crazy.'

He'd wanted her all along?

'So why did you keep saying that you couldn't get involved with me?'

There was a long silence and a muscle worked in his lean jaw. 'I didn't want to get involved with another career-woman.'

She stared at him, taking in what he'd just said.

And suddenly everything fell into place.

Dear Lord, he'd thought she was like Catherine.

No wonder he'd wanted to keep her at a distance.

Now was the time to confess.

'Zach, about my career—this cardiology job…' She hesitated and he sat down on the bed.

'Don't worry about it. I think it's great that you want to be a cardiologist.' His voice was gruff. 'Career or no career, you're nothing like Catherine and I should have realised that straight away. But I suppose I was carrying too much hurt and bitterness to be able to see things objectively.'

Keely licked her lips. 'Zach, I should have talked to you about my career earlier—'

'Your career isn't what matters,' he said quietly, taking her hand in his and stroking her blonde hair away from her face. 'What really matters is the way I feel about you. And the way I think you feel about me. I love you, Keely. I love you with all my heart. I want you to marry me. I want you to be my wife and Phoebe's mother.'

She couldn't believe what she was hearing. Couldn't believe that he meant it.

Tears filled her eyes and spilled out onto her cheeks. 'Oh, Zach…'

'Don't cry!' He gave a low curse and brushed the tears away with his thumb. 'Dammit, sweetheart, I can't bear to see you cry.'

'I'm crying because I'm happy.' She sniffed, rubbing her cheeks with the palm of her hand. 'I can't believe you're really saying this. You'd better pinch me so that I can be sure I'm not dreaming.'

'I think your poor body has suffered enough trauma in the last twenty-four hours without me pinching you,' Zach said dryly, the corners of his mouth lifting slightly. 'I'm in suspense here, Keely. Can I take it that the answer is yes?'

She nodded, the tears starting again. 'Of course it's yes. I've loved you since I was sixteen. You know that. I just can't believe that you really love me, too. That night we— you know…' She broke off, embarrassed, and he gave her a sexy grin that made her insides melt.

'I do know.'

'I couldn't believe it when you didn't mention it the next morning. Then you asked me to move out—'

'I know.' His smile faded and his voice was suddenly serious. 'I must have hurt you very badly. But you have to try and understand what I was thinking. After that incredible night I came downstairs and the first person I spoke to was your father, telling me that you'd got an interview and how clever you were. All of a sudden it was Catherine all over again.'

Keely stared at him, horrified. 'You *do* think I'm like Catherine?'

He gave a lopsided smile. 'No. I know you're nothing like Catherine. You're gentle, warm and kind with wonderful values and a fantastic way with children. But you're also very clever. Cleverer than you realise. You could go far, Keely. You could do whatever you wanted to do.'

Her eyes filled again. 'What I really want is for you to tell me you love me again. You didn't convince me the first time.'

'Then I'd better try harder.' He reached for a tissue. 'Keely Thompson, I love you. Madly. With all my heart and soul. But, please, stop crying or they'll throw me out for upsetting a patient.'

She wanted him to carry on telling her that he loved her…

'But, Zach…' A thought had suddenly struck her and she gasped. 'What about your home? Where will we live?'

Had his house burned to the ground? She hadn't even asked about his lovely house.

He shrugged. 'I love the Lakes, I can't pretend I don't. But I accept that you'll be happier in London, so that's where we'll go. But I'd like to keep the house here, too. For weekends and holidays.'

Her eyes widened and a smile touched her full mouth. 'The house is OK? It didn't burn down?'

He shook his head. 'It'll be fine once the builders have spent some time there.'

'That's great. Because I don't just want to use it for weekends and holidays.' She looked him in the eye. 'I love it here, too. I want to stay here. I want to live in your house.'

He stared at her and his hand tightened on hers. 'I can't ask you to do that—'

'You don't have to,' she said simply. 'I don't want to move to London. And I don't want to be a cardiologist. I had doubts right from the beginning. That was why I came up here. I needed to escape from the pressure of my family. They mean well but they're so forceful that I'd lost sight of what I really wanted to do. I was so swept along with what everyone else wanted that I'd lost track of what makes me happy.'

'But why the hell didn't you say something?' He stared at her, astounded. 'To be honest, I thought it was an odd choice of career for you. Why didn't you tell me how you felt?'

'Lots of reasons.' She gave him a sheepish smile. 'Because I thought you liked career-women. Because I wanted to prove to you that I was an adult and that seemed like a pretty good way, and because—' She broke off and his eyes narrowed.

'Because what?'

She blushed at his gentle prompt. 'Because I knew that I was in love with you right from the start, and I thought that if I kept telling you that I was going to London I'd throw you off the scent.'

'You certainly did that!' He groaned and shook his head. 'What a pair of idiots! I guessed you were in love with me—you're not that great at hiding your feelings, my love—but I assumed that your career was so important you wanted to go to London anyway.'

She shook her head. 'I really, really don't want to go to London. I know exactly what I want to do, and it's not cardiology.'

'Go on.' His voice was hoarse and she smiled, knowing how pleased he'd be by what she had to tell him.

'I want to be a GP, Zach. I decided that night we had dinner with Ally. I loved hearing about what she did and I knew that I wanted to do it, too. You know I'm no good at just dealing with patients for a short time. I'm too interested in them. I want to be involved in their lives and know everything there is to know about them.'

Zach stroked a hand across his face and let out a long

breath. 'You're really sure you want to be a GP? You don't want to go to London?'

'No.' She shook her head. 'I don't want to go anywhere. I just want to stay here with you and Phoebe.'

There was a long silence while he digested what she'd just said and his eyes searched hers.

'I don't want you to accuse me of ruining a brilliant career.'

'What's brilliant about it if it's something I don't want to do? I don't want that sort of career,' she assured him. 'I've got everything I want right here.'

A slow smile spread across his handsome face. 'In that case, I'll make some calls and get you on the GP rotation here as soon as possible.'

'Ah.' He hadn't heard *all* her news yet. 'I'm not sure about that, Zach.'

He frowned. 'But you said—'

'I know what I said.' She looked at him calmly, enjoying teasing him just a little. 'But there are things I have to do first.'

'Like what?'

'Like be a mother to Phoebe,' she said quietly, taking his hand and looking deep into his eyes. 'No more nannies, Zach. Not for a while anyway. I want to be there for her—get to know her.'

'But that would mean giving up work.' He looked at her, clearly stunned and touched by her proposition. 'Are you saying you want to give up work to look after my daughter?'

'*Our* daughter, Zach. She's our daughter now,' Keely reminded him, searching for the right way to say what she had to say. 'And I want to have some time on my own with her before—well, I'll be giving up work pretty soon anyway, so I thought I may as well do it now, when my time in A and E comes to an end.'

There was a long silence.

'Giving up work?' His voice cracked slightly. 'Why will you be giving up work?'

Keely glanced towards the door to make sure that no one could hear them and then gave him a shy smile. 'Because, Mr Jordan, thanks to the overwhelming chemistry between us, we were a little careless one night...'

Zach stared at her, stunned into silence. 'Are you trying to tell me that you're *pregnant*?'

She nodded and then her happy smile faltered slightly. 'Is it—? You don't mind—do you?'

'Mind?'

He looked totally shocked.

'Zach, for goodness' sake!' She stared at him anxiously. 'I know we didn't plan this, but...'

Finally he seemed to stir himself, his eyes clouded with worry.

'Are you all right? I mean, the fire—'

'Everything's fine, Zach,' she reassured him quickly. 'I talked to the doctor and he's examined me.'

'Thank God.' Zach let out a long breath and shook his head. 'A baby...'

'You're not angry?'

'Angry? It's the best thing that could have happened,' he said softly, leaning forward and kissing her gently on the mouth. 'I can't believe this. I was so carried away that night I wasn't even thinking straight.'

'Nor me. But I'm thinking straight now, and I don't want to start my GP rotation yet. I want to be at home for now, Zach, if that's all right with you. There's plenty of time to go back to work when they're older. What do you think?'

'What do I think?' He brushed her hair away from Keely's face with gentle fingers, everything he felt for her showing in his eyes. 'I think you are the most wonderful woman in the world. And I'm the luckiest man on the planet. All of a sudden I seem to have acquired another child and a wife. My perfect family.'

'And a mother for Phoebe,' Keely reminded him with a smile.

'Yes.' His mouth tilted into an answering smile and he nodded slowly. 'And a mother for Phoebe.'

THE SURGEON'S
LOVE-CHILD

by

Lilian Darcy

CHAPTER ONE

HE WAS holding up a sign with her name on it, but he wasn't Terry Davis.

Definitely not.

Terry wouldn't have needed a sign. He and Candace had known each other, on and off, for years. She would have recognised his weatherbeaten face at once, and he would have seen her coming towards him through the milling crowd of arrivals at Sydney's international airport. He would have smiled.

This man wasn't smiling. He hadn't seen her yet. He hadn't realised that Candace had spotted her name, scrawled quickly by hand in black felt-tip pen on a makeshift rectangle of cardboard, and that she was zeroing in on it.

This man looked much younger than Terry. Early thirties, tall and fit and medium dark, with a body that somehow managed to be both solid and lean at the same time. He was wearing jeans and a navy T-shirt that hugged his form closely. In contrast, Terry was well past fifty, and had always looked his age. He never wore jeans.

Candace herself—DR CANDACE FLETCHER, as the sign correctly stated—was thirty-eight years old and intensely conscious of the fact. She had been for months and was, suddenly, particularly conscious of it now. It had been twenty-four hours since she had left Boston. She must look like a dog's breakfast, despite a recent freshening in the unappealing cubicle of the aircraft toilet.

She reached the stranger and his sign, and was tempted to wave a hand in front of his face. Hell-o-o-o! I'm here! He was still scanning the crowd with a frown etched across

5

his high, squarish forehead. Apparently, she didn't look like her name.

'Are you waiting for me?'

The frown cleared at once. 'With insufficient vigilance, obviously, Dr Fletcher. You sneaked up on me.'

'I did think about waving.'

'Probably not what you expected. I should have been Terry.'

'Mmm.'

She almost blurted out that not much in her life had gone according to expectations over the past year and more, but managed to keep the words back. Dear God, it would be so easy to get emotional!

'I'll explain as we head to the car,' he said.

'Sounds good.'

Unobtrusively, he took control of the luggage cart and began to wheel it towards the exit. She walked beside him, matching his pace.

'I'm Steve, by the way. Steve Colton. You'll be seeing me in Theatre fairly regularly. I'm often rostered to handle the anaesthesia. Terry's wife is…not well. That's why he couldn't make it.'

'Oh, no!' Candace said. 'That's too bad! It isn't serious, I hope.'

'So do I,' he answered soberly. 'But I'm actually her GP, so I can't really talk about it. Is this all of your luggage?'

'This is it,' she confirmed. Three suitcases and a box, for a one-year stay. 'My mother helped me pack, and she's very strict.'

'Travels light?'

'Arrives light. Leaves heavy. She's convinced that Australia will have glorious shopping possibilities, thanks to the state of your dollar.'

'She's right, if you can find anything you want to buy. Terry told you Narralee's not a big place, I hope. Not exactly a shopper's heaven.'

'Yes, but my mother has a bloodhound's nose for good places to spend money. And Terry also told me Sydney makes a great weekend getaway, only a three-and-a-half-hour drive. Oh! Which means you're making a seven-hour round trip to pick me up,' she realised aloud, 'and I haven't thanked you yet.'

'Plenty of time for that.'

'Three and a half hours, in fact.'

They both laughed.

He seemed nice, Candace decided. The kind of well-mannered yet easygoing Australian male she'd heard good things about and seen—in somewhat exaggerated form—in various movies over the years. Three and a half hours, plus a stop for a snack, maybe. This shouldn't be any kind of a penance...

And it wasn't. Far from it.

They talked for a while, about the obvious things. Her journey. The city of Sydney. She commented on its red-tiled roofs, bright in the March morning sunlight, and all the aqua blue ovals and rectangles of the swimming pools she'd seen from above in the sprawl of suburban back yards as the plane had come in to land.

Then they left human habitation behind and crossed the wild, wind-scoured terrain of a national park. Steve Colton stopped asking questions and giving out helpful tourist information. Candace pretended to sleep.

She had been doing a lot of that lately—lying in bed with her brain buzzing and the shrill whistle of tinnitus in her ears, totally exhausted, miles from sleep and not fooling herself for a second.

Todd was sleeping with Brittany for six months and I never knew.

He said our marriage was empty long before that. Was he right? If there hadn't been that electrical problem at the hospital that day, and they hadn't cancelled elective surgery... If I hadn't actually walked in on them, naked together in our marital bed... How long before I'd have found out? How long before he would have drummed up the courage to leave? Coming home to find them in bed was bad enough, but having them announce Brittany's pregnancy before our divorce was even finalised was even worse.

I guess in a way I'm glad Maddy decided not to come to Australia with me—although that hurts, too, to think she's so positive that she'll be fine without her mother—because at least, out there, I'll be able to be alone. I won't have to pretend.

And here she was, pretending already.

Much easier to pretend to a newly met male colleague than to an emotional fifteen-year-old daughter, however. By hook or by crook, Candace *wasn't* going to ruin Maddy's relationship with her father. She had no right to do that—to deprive her daughter of something very precious and necessary in Maddy's life purely in order to enact revenge on Todd, when maybe...probably...the blame wasn't all on his side. She had to behave rationally, not let Maddy see quite how deeply ran her sense of betrayal.

But, oh, that huge, glowing and healthily advanced pregnancy of Brittany's *hurt*! She was due in just a few weeks...

The car slowed. It stopped. Then there was silence. She opened her eyes. Dr Colton was watching her. No, *Steve*. She couldn't possibly call him Dr Colton! He had to be a good five or six years younger than she was, and she had been told that Australians were informal people.

'Are we here?' she asked vaguely. She had no idea how long her mind had been churning while her eyes had flickered behind their closed lids.

'No,' he said, 'But I thought it was probably hours since they gave you breakfast on the plane. It was a toss-up between letting you sleep and getting you fed. Did I pick the right one?'

'I wasn't asleep,' she admitted, finding it easier to be honest with him than she had expected. 'Just thinking.'

'That can give you an appetite.'

She smiled. 'It has. Or something has.'

'Rightio, then.'

Rightio? Weird word! Cute, actually. The difference, the newness of it in his easy accent, blew across the raw-burned surface of her soul like a gentle puff of wind, and she was still smiling as she got out of the car.

He hadn't gone so far as to open the door for her. She might have mistrusted that degree of chivalry. But he was standing there waiting, and he reached out a hand to steady her as she stood up.

The kerb was unexpectedly high. She held onto him, closing her fingers around a forearm that was bare and warm and ropy with muscle, while his hand remained cupped beneath her elbow.

'Oh-h! The sidewalk is going up and down,' she said.

'Having your own personal earthquake?'

'No, it's more gentle than that. A kind of quavery undulation.'

He laughed. 'It's that long flight, and the beginnings of jet-lag. What time is it now in Boston?'

'Um...'

'Let's see...'

They both began a mental calculation.

'Sydney is sixteen hours ahead,' she supplied. 'Which means...'

He got there first. 'Yesterday evening, then. Around sevenish. You probably *are* hungry in that case, and an empty stomach wouldn't be helping.'

'No,' she agreed, although this wobbly sidewalk was probably more the result of months of stress and inadequate sleep than a mere sixteen-hour time difference and a few hours without food.

'Shall I let go?' he asked cheerfully.

'Not yet.'

It seemed like a long time since she'd had a man's physical support, and it felt better than she could have imagined. He wasn't in a hurry. He didn't have an agenda. He was polite and steady, and she felt very safe.

'OK,' he said, tightening his grip a little.

Their eyes met and held for a moment before they both looked away. He was very good-looking. She hadn't taken in this fact until now. It was in the shape of his face—the square forehead, the strong cheekbones and chin. It was in his easy, even smile, too, and in what that smile did to his blue eyes. They twinkled and softened, and looked a little wicked.

But this wasn't just about looks, she realised. This was about—

Dear heaven, we're going to have an affair!

The thought sliced into her mind without a shadow of warning, leaving her breathless. She could almost see it— the alluring progression of it—laid out before her like the squares on a life-sized Monopoly board, improbably perfect. A sizzlingly hot, totally heedless, carefree, life-affirming, fabulous affair, which would come to a painless, mutually-agreed-upon end some time before she was due to head home to that much chillier place called Real Life.

She dropped his delicious, masculine forearm like a live snake, her heart pounding.

This doesn't happen to me. The whole idea is ridiculous. I don't have intuitions like this. I'm scared. Would I really want something like that? No! Surely I wouldn't! And surely I'm wrong! Of course I'm wrong!

'I'm starving,' she said aloud.

Wow.

Say it again.

Wow.

Don't let it show on your face, Steve.

This woman is… No, she's not gorgeous. Not even pretty. Something much better, and much more interesting. She's magnetic, womanly, responsive.

He hadn't felt it at first. He had been too busy thinking about the last time he'd been at Sydney airport, several months ago, seeing Agnetha off on her flight back home to Sweden.

The memory was like a splinter in his thumb. Yes, sure, he knew it wasn't a major wound, but that didn't stop it from hurting. And it had preoccupied him more than he'd wanted it to, during his wait for the visiting American doctor.

Did I even *consider* getting serious, asking Agnetha to marry me? No!

If she'd asked me to go to Sweden with her, would I have gone? No!

So what's my problem?

One of sheer, bloody male ego, perhaps. He was… *miffed*…that Agnetha had apparently viewed him the same way she'd viewed the second-hand surfboard she'd bought at the surf shop in Narralee. Something to be enjoyed during her stay, but not something to take home with her, except in a photo or two. The surfboard was still in the back shed, beside his own. Agnetha had smiled as she'd waved goodbye. Five months down the track, she hadn't even sent a postcard.

Now, here was another visitor from the northern hemisphere, equipped with what was known as special needs registration so that she could work here in a rural hospital in her surgical specialty. She was about fifteen years older than Agnetha. She had a long, thick, satisfying rope of honey-gold hair, bound back in a braid, instead of a fine thatch of short, Scandinavian blonde.

She had skin that would probably freckle like bits of melted milk chocolate under the Australian sun, while Agnetha's skin had remained a perfect pale gold. Candace had almond-shaped eyes like brown pebbles, polished by the sea, while Agnetha's were blue and clear and round. She had a ripe, luscious figure, with exquisitely full breasts and rounded hips, instead of a lean, almost boyish slimness.

And she had a lot more *living* evident in her face.

Terry had told him that Dr Fletcher had been divorced last year, and that she had a fifteen-year-old daughter. Well, it showed. Some of the sadness and complexity showed, around her tawny eyes and her generous mouth. For some reason, it actually added to the quiet richness of her unconventional beauty.

There was one thing that Candace Fletcher and Agnetha Thorhus had in common, however. With both of them, Steve had recognised within an hour or two of meeting them that there was a definite, undeniable and very bewitching spark. In this case, he wasn't yet sure what he intended to do about it.

He took Candace to the café that was housed in the little town's former bank. The place had a lot of charm, and excellent Devonshire teas.

'My stomach is suddenly saying dinner, very loudly, at eleven-thirty in the morning,' Candace confessed, so she began with a bowl of pumpkin soup, some salad and a hot, buttered roll. Then she moved on to scones with strawberry jam and whipped cream.

Not particularly hungry himself, Steve drank black coffee while he sat back and watched her eat. She was good at it. Just the right combination of fastidiousness and relish. Her response to the whipped cream was particularly appealing, and when she had finished there was a tiny beauty spot of white froth left just beyond the corner of her mouth.

Knowing that it wasn't just a casual gesture, he leaned forward and used the tip of one finger to wipe it off. She didn't object. Didn't even look startled.

She knows, he thought, and felt an odd little flutter inside his chest which he didn't have a name for.

She knows, too, just the way I do. She knows that something could happen between us. Whether it will or not, neither of us has decided yet...

It was a very pretty drive, Candace decided.

Dairy country, according to Steve. To the right, cliff-like escarpments rose above thick forests of eucalypts, but as the steepness of the terrain shelved away, the forest gave way to fenced farmland that was lush and green. To the left, in the distance, Candace glimpsed the sea. It twinkled in the sun like Steve Colton's eyes.

And I'll be looking at this sight every single day for the next year...

Looking at the sea, not the eyes.

Terry had arranged the rental of a furnished beach cottage for her, sending details, including photographs, of three or four for her to choose from. Narralee wasn't quite on the coast but a mile or two inland, built on the banks of a river's coastal estuary.

She hadn't wanted the tameness and tranquillity of a river, no matter how pretty it was. She'd wanted the sea, fresh and wild and as solitary as possible, and the place she'd selected was in a little seaside community called Taylor's Beach, about ten minutes' drive away.

Steve had the address, and the keys. As soon as he pulled into the short driveway, she knew that the house and its setting were going to go way beyond her expectations. The house was built high, with the utilitarian parts beneath—carport, laundry, storage. On top, with magnificent views of the sea, were the living areas. There were other houses close by but, with tangles of bushland garden surrounding them, they didn't impinge.

Steve helped Candace carry her luggage inside, then watched with a grin on his face as she simply wandered from room to room, uttering incoherent exclamations of pleasure.

'You like it, then?' he asked finally, when she returned to stand, woolly-witted, in front of the French windows that opened onto a shaded deck.

'It's perfect!'

'I told Terry you'd pick this one if you were any good at reading photographs.'

'They didn't do it justice.'

'How about my descriptions?'

'Oh, it was you who wrote those?'

'I tried to be objective, but probably didn't succeed. I'm incurably biased. Couldn't imagine why anyone *wouldn't* want to live along this stretch of beach.'

'So where do you live?'

'Five doors down.'

'Right.' She nodded, and looked quickly out at the ocean again before their eyes could meet. Five doors down. That had the potential to be very convenient. 'Um, I like the interior, too, as well as the setting and the views,' she added, speaking too fast.

The house wasn't elaborate or huge. There was an open-plan lounge and dining room, a modern kitchen, a generous bathroom and two airy bedrooms, one furnished with twin beds, one with a queen-size. But with a whole world of sand and ocean and sky out there, she didn't need interior space. The rooms were decorated in summery blues and yellows, with light, casual touches of good taste in the occasional piece of ceramic work or glassware.

Steve opened the French windows, and a sea breeze combed through the outer screens and puffed air into the full-length blue and yellow curtains, which were pulled back on their tracks to reveal the view. Candace went out onto the deck, willing him not to follow her. She could smell the fresh salt in the air at once.

Here on the deck, the outdoor furniture was made of cane. It didn't normally appeal to her, but fitted in this setting. Yes, she would eat here at this little cane and glass table and watch the ocean, every chance she got...

'I think Linda was planning to pick up some basic supplies for you,' Steve said behind her, just inside. 'Shall I check the fridge?'

'Thanks.'

'Then I ought to head off. I have appointments at my practice, starting at two.'

'You've been terrific.' She stepped back into the cool living room.

They were both being very neutral and polite with each other now.

'Terry wants me to bring you into the hospital tomorrow morning, to meet everyone and get you orientated a little before you start in earnest on Monday. We've had to send a lot of our general surgery patients further north since before Christmas, when Dr Elphick retired. Quite a few people chose to postpone their operations, though, so you'll be busy straight away.'

'Yes, I was going to ask about all that. And about the other two hospitals I'm covering as well.'

'Better talk to Terry. Is it all right if I pick you up at eight-thirty?'

'I'll be ready.'

She watched as he opened the fridge and the pantry. He confirmed, 'Yes, Linda's been here.'

'Should I know about Linda?'

'Linda Gardner, our local ob. You're sharing professional rooms with her. Terry arranged it. With luck you'll meet her tomorrow. Looks like she's decided you'll have eggs for dinner. Unless you phone out for take-away.'

'The phone's connected, then?' She was pleased to hear it.

'Yep. Of course, you'll want to ring home, won't you?'

Another odd word. Ring, instead of call. Quaint. Cute.

'Um, where is it, I wonder? I can't see it.'

'Think I noticed it by the bed.'

'Thanks. I won't keep you.'

'See you tomorrow, then.'

Seconds later, he was loping down the steps at the side of the house to his car.

Alone. Candace was alone, the way she had craved to be for months. Finding a plastic pitcher of iced water in the fridge, she poured herself a glass. Saw the eggs Steve had mentioned and decided that, yes, they'd be fine for her evening meal. If she lasted that long. The floor of the house was rocking up and down like the deck of a boat. Glass in hand, she went back through the French doors and onto the deck to watch the sea.

Just me, with the ocean for company.

It felt different to what she had expected. It was a happier, zestier feeling. She had more than half expected to zero right in on that comfortable-looking bed, covered in an intricately pieced patchwork quilt, and sob her eyes out.

In fact, she'd actually *planned* to indulge in the painfully luxurious release of being able to cry for hours, as stormily as she wanted to, without the possibility of interruption.

But, no, she didn't want to cry now after all.

Mom was the one who had suggested this whole thing. Mom, the redoubtable, loving Elaine West.

'Couldn't you go away, darling?' she had said five months ago, when Candace had gone to her with the blind pain of a wounded animal, freshly ripped apart by the news of Brittany's pregnancy.

'I don't know if I can stand it, Mom,' she had gasped, barely able to speak. 'She's radiant, while he's... oh...already shopping for cigars. Not literally, but—'

'I know what you mean, Candy.'

'They had prenatal testing and they already know it's a boy. Suddenly it turns out that Todd has "always wanted a son". To me, he spent years arguing that one child was enough. Expensive enough. Sacrifice enough. Career-threatening enough. For his sake, I gave away the bassinet and the baby clothes. I told myself he was right. That Maddy was enough. But, oh, I wanted another baby! And now—'

'Couldn't you go away?' Elaine said.

'Away?'

'Some kind of professional fellowship or exchange. Or a temporary position. In Alaska, or somewhere.'

'*Alaska?*'

'You don't need them on your doorstep, Candy.' Her mother was the only person in the world who was ever permitted to call her Candy, and even then only at times, when she needed to feel six years old again, nourishing her soul with a mother's wisdom. 'You don't need to run into Brittany at the gym—'

'Ha! As if I still go to the gym!'

Eighteen months ago, Todd had taken out a family membership, saying they both needed to get fitter. Brittany, aged twenty-five to Todd's forty-four, taught aerobics there. Todd had quickly become very fit indeed. End of story. Candace felt personally insulted that the whole thing was such a cliché.

'Or at the hospital.'

'The *hospital*?'

'Prenatal check-ups. Your OB/GYN has her practice in the hospital's adjoining professional building, doesn't she?'

'Of course, you're right. I know I'll see her. Todd and I have a daughter together, remember? Occasionally we actually pass her back and forth at his place, instead of on safe, neutral terrain like school or the mall. Occasionally we even speak to each other.' The words were hard with bitterness.

'Maybe Maddy would like to get away, too?' Elaine had suggested.

But when Candace had remembered Terry Davis's comment, at a recent international medical conference, that rural Australia was chronically short of medical specialists, and had teed up this temporary appointment, Maddy had elected to stay behind with her father.

It hadn't been in any sense a rejection of Candace. She knew that. It was about friends and routine, not about choosing one parent over the other, but it still hurt all the same.

She's growing up. I'll miss her more than she misses me. But Mom was right. This was probably the best thing I could have done.

After finishing her iced water, she found the phone by the bed. Called Maddy first. Heard Brittany's perky voice, which quickly crystallised into glassy, high-pitched politeness when she realised who was on the other end of the line.

Candace had a brief conversation with Maddy, then called her mother, who said 'See!' in a very satisfied voice when she heard about the beachfront cottage and the acres of sea and sky. 'Have you explored?'

'I haven't even unpacked!'

'Dr Davis met you on time?'

'Uh, no, he had to delegate to a colleague, but it worked out fine.'

And I managed to avoid mentioning Steve's name, which I'm relieved about, and I know exactly why I didn't want to mention it, which is unsettling me like anything...

When Candace had put down the phone, she looked at the suitcases and the box, stuck her tongue out at them and said in her best new millennium teen-speak, 'You think I'm gonna unpack you right now, when there's that beach out there? Like, as if!'

She walked the length of the beach twice, breathing the air and letting the cool water froth around her ankles. Then she unpacked, showered, made and ate scrambled eggs on toast, and conked out at seven in the evening in the big, comfortable bed with the sound of the sea in her ears.

She fell asleep as suddenly as if someone had opened up a panel in her back and removed the batteries.

CHAPTER TWO

IT WAS the best night's sleep Candace had had in months, and it lasted until almost five the next morning. This meant she had plenty of time to iron a skirt and blouse, have another shower and eat breakfast on the deck, watching the sun rise over the sea. She was ready for Steve Colton at eight-thirty.

He was prompt, and if she'd had any sort of a theory overnight that yesterday's intuitive sense of chemistry had been only a product of her jet-lagged disorientation, that theory was knocked on the head at once.

The chemistry was still there, invisible, intangible, lighter than air, yet as real as a third person with them in the room. Neither of them acknowledged it in any way. They didn't get close enough to touch. Any eye contact they chanced to make was snapped apart again in milliseconds.

But, oh, it was there, and she was convinced he felt it, too.

She spent half an hour with Terry at the Narralee District Hospital. He had earned a certain seniority, having been a visiting medical officer in general surgery here for over twenty-five years, but in fact there wasn't the official hierarchy of medical staff that Candace was used to.

There wasn't very much that she was used to at all! It was quite a contrast to come from a 600-bed high-rise American city hospital to this low, rambling, red-brick building, which housed a mere fifty beds.

'And six of those are political,' Terry said darkly.

'Political?'

'They're not beds at all, in most people's definition. We

20

have six reclining chairs where day-surgery patients recover until we're satisfied that fluids are going in one end and coming out the other. But those six chairs make the numbers look better, so beds they've become and beds they'll remain.'

He sounded tired and tense, and Candace longed to urge him, Go. Someone else can show me around.

Steve Colton, maybe? He'd muttered something about 'errands' after he'd deposited her into Terry's care, and then he had disappeared. She was disturbed to realise that she was wondering, in the back of her mind, when she'd see him again.

She wanted to tell Terry, The tour can wait. I know you're anxious to be on your way.

Terry was taking his wife, Myrna, up to Sydney today for a consultation with a top oncologist. The result of her second mammogram and fine-needle aspiration had come back yesterday afternoon, and there was no longer any doubt about the diagnosis. It was breast cancer.

They could only hope that it had been caught early, and Terry was clearly racked with worry. He was also behaving stubbornly in his insistence on a tour and a talk. He must feel as if he had let Candace down by not meeting her at the airport yesterday, and was determined to make up for it.

Accepting that she would only delay his departure if she kept apologising for her bad timing, Candace tried to ask a few intelligent questions and keep the pace brisk.

'No full-time doctors here at all?'

'No, we manage purely with Visiting Medical Officers. The local GPs cover the emergency department and the on-call roster, assist with surgery and handle anaesthesia. Steve probably mentioned that.'

'Yes, he did, but not in any detail.'

'Then there are about half a dozen of us who handle various specialities, travelling between several small hospitals in the region, as you'll be doing. You can work out your own timetable, within certain constraints. Linda Gardner has space in her rooms, and will share her staff with you.'

'Yes, Steve told me. Thanks for arranging it. I'm looking forward to meeting her.'

'You'll like her, I think. She's married with two teenagers.'

'We'll have something in common in that area, then!'

'Basically, you'll probably want to operate one day a week here in Narralee, and a day every fortnight at Harpoon Bay and Shoalwater.'

'A slower pace than I'm used to.'

'Enjoy it!'

'Oh, I intend to.'

The hospital had already created a pleasing impression. Its red-tiled roof had pale green lichen growing on it, attesting to its comfortable age. Above what must once have been the main entrance, the date '1936' was carved. Mature eucalyptus trees shaded thick couch-grass lawns, and windows tinted with a gold reflective film ran all along one side of the building.

Most of the windows were open, providing a volume of fresh, mild air that was unheard of in Candace's experience. In Boston, winters were arctic, summers were steamy and hospitals had air-conditioning.

With its pink walls and mottled linoleum floors, the place was too clean and cheerful to be called shabby, and there was an atmosphere of peace, underlaid by a low buzz of unhurried activity which suggested that hospitals didn't have to be nearly as dramatic and hectic as they always seemed on prime-time television.

Terry doggedly tramped the building from one end to the other on their tour. He showed Candace the eight-bed maternity unit, which opened onto a shaded veranda. He took her through the four-bed high-dependency unit, the aged-care rehab beds, day surgery, the pharmacy, Emergency and Physio. He even took her past the tiny chapel and even tinier kiosk, which was open for just one hour each day. Finally, he pointed out the electrical plant room.

It was a relief to both of them when he finally announced, 'And now I must pick up Myrna. She'll be packed and waiting. Steve should be back before too long. Find someone to make you a coffee, and—'

'I can do coffee on my own, Terry,' Candace said gently. Several strands of his grey hair had fallen onto the wrong side of his parting, and he was rubbing his stomach as if he had heartburn. 'Just give Myrna my very best and have a safe trip.' She almost pushed Terry out through the administration entrance.

She had no trouble over the coffee. Found the nursing staffroom and was at once invited in. She hadn't finished her mug of unremarkable instant by the time Steve appeared in the doorway ten minutes later, but it didn't matter.

'Now, what do you need to get done?' he asked. 'Because I'm not seeing patients today, and you know Terry will have my guts for garters when he gets back if I haven't been looking after you.'

'He'll have your…what?'

'Guts for garters.' He grinned.

'That sounds violent.'

'So you'd better let me look after you, then, hadn't you?'

'Apparently!'

'Good decision.'

'Right, well, I need to get groceries, open a bank account and buy a car,' she announced.

Steve raised his eyebrows and grinned, appreciating the way she'd ticked off each item on her finger with such assurance. Perhaps he shouldn't have teased her with that piece of colourful Australian idiom just now. She didn't need him to entertain her so deliberately.

'Need to learn how to drive on the wrong side of the road, too?' he suggested.

'Well, yes.' Now she looked less confident, but the effect was just as attractive.

His expectations for the day notched themselves a little higher, and he was aware that they'd been high enough to begin with.

'I'll give you a driving lesson,' he offered.

OK, now she looked quite panicky. She gave a shriek, but she was smiling as widely as he was. 'This is going to be a treat for my fellow road-users!'

'Is that where we should start?' he asked. 'With the driving lesson? I can take you somewhere quiet first off then, when you've got some confidence, you can do the shuttling round to the bank and the supermarket. I'll just sit in the passenger seat and give a terrified hiss every now and then...'

'And slam your foot onto an imaginary brake pedal on the floor. I get the picture. Is it an automatic?'

'Yes, it is.'

'And is it insured?'

'Comprehensively.'

'OK, let's do it before I start thinking of excuses. How's the public transport around here?'

'Not good enough for commuting between three hospitals more than fifty kilometres apart, every week.'

'Thought not.'

So he gave her a driving lesson, and it wasn't nearly as hair-raising as either of them had feared.

I'm not flirting with her, Steve realised. Why is that? I'd planned to.

He had acquired some skill in this area over the years. He was nearly thirty-three, now. His brother Matt, three years his senior and married since the age of twenty-five, kept telling him, 'Get serious. Don't miss the boat. Stop going after women who have a use-by date.'

'Use-by date?'

'Like Agnetha. Women that you know are going to leave and let you off the hook. There was that other girl from Perth, too. Agnetha wasn't the first. Settle down!'

And he always found himself thinking, Yeah, obviously. Of course I will... I'm not a hardened bachelor. But not yet. Don't think I've quite come to grips with the married man's job description yet. When he took on a responsibility—and he was in no doubt that marriage was that—he liked to be sure it was one he was fully equipped to handle.

To prove to himself, and perhaps to Matt as well, that he hadn't missed the boat, be it kayak or cruise ship or ferry, he flirted with a variety of women. Mutually enjoyable. Nothing heavy-handed. Not threatening to anyone.

He kept it very light, never trespassed into the sorts of overtly sexual references and double meanings that he, along with most women, would have considered sleazy. He conceded that there was probably some truth to Matt's observation about women with a use-by date as well, although he didn't like the way his brother had worded it.

Candace Fletcher was only here for a year, and he was fully aware of the fact.

So perhaps this *is* flirting, he decided. We're laughing. Teasing each other a little. Only it's even lighter than usual, so I'm calling it something else.

Why?

Because I don't want to scare her off.

There was something in her eyes, something in the way she held that full, sensitive mouth. Coupled with the fact of her divorce, he was pretty certain that she would want a man to take things carefully, no matter how sudden and strong the spark was between them, no matter that she was leaving after a year.

Perhaps the spark was a little deceptive, too. They might both feel it, but that didn't mean acting on it would be a good idea. Some instinct told him to tread carefully, and to think before he acted in this case.

I didn't think twice with Agnetha, and neither did she...

The thought flashed through his mind and disappeared again.

They spent an hour on the quiet roads of Narralee's newest housing development before Candace announced that she was ready for downtown.

'Yes, I know you don't call it that,' she added.

'Just town will do.'

'Tell me how to get there.'

She parked without difficulty in the car park behind the bank and opened her account, then he showed her the supermarket nearest to Taylor's Beach and they tooled down the aisles with a big metal shopping trolley, which she filled to the brim.

Always an instructive experience, shopping with a woman for the first time. What secret vices did she display in the confectionery aisle? Did she actually cook, or merely reheat in the microwave? Agnetha had lived on rabbit food, Steve considered. Celery and nuts and carrots. Horse food, too. Various flaky things that looked and tasted like chaff.

Candace's diet held more promise and less obsessiveness. She smelled a rock melon—'canteloupe' she called it—with her eyes closed and a heaven-sent expression on her face. Then she put two of them in the trolley, right on top of the frozen chocolate cheesecake. She selected some delicate lamb cutlets and a medallion of pork, and they ended up lying next to the five-pack of lurid yellow chicken-flavoured two-minute noodle soups. She apparently drank hot chocolate, tea, three kinds of juice and four kinds of coffee.

He thought he'd been reasonably subtle in his analysis of her purchases, but he was wrong. When they stood waiting at the checkout, she tilted her head to one side and demanded, 'So, Doctor, how many points did I lose? About fifty for the cheesecake and the cookies, obviously, but I believe I do have all the food groups represented in reasonable proportion.'

'I wasn't—'

'You were, too! Silently analysing everything that went in the cart. Comparing me to—well, to whoever.'

Agnetha. He almost said it, but managed to stop himself. Felt colour rising into his neck and thought in disbelief, My God, I'm *blushing*!

'I thought so!' said Candace under her breath.

It was a type of audition. She teetered on the edge of resenting it. He had no right to judge and draw conclusions like that!

Then, with more honesty and less bluster, she decided that she was doing exactly the same thing herself. Auditioning him for this imaginary, unlikely affair she couldn't get out of her head.

So far, he seemed like exactly the right candidate for such a thing, if she was going to consider the question in such cold-blooded terms. He would be easygoing, physical, fun to be with. He'd also possess certain shared understandings that didn't need talking about, because they worked in the same profession.

Yes, quite definitely an ideal candidate for an affair.

Is this what Mom was thinking about when she told me to go away? That I'd meet someone and have a crazy fling, get my socks sizzled off and come home as revitalised as if I'd been to a health spa for three months? That I'd be over Todd and Brittany? Dear God, *over* it. That it wouldn't hurt any more, and twist me up inside with bitterness and resentment and regret…?

The idea was both terrifying and dangerously alluring.

With her breathing shallower than usual, she asked, 'Are you sure there isn't anything else you need to do today? This is taking a long time.'

'My schedule's clear, so don't worry about it. Shall we

take this lot home to your place and unpack it, then grab some lunch before we do the car?'

'Sandwiches? We have the makings for them now.'

'Yep. Great.'

They got to the first car dealership at two, after a lunch so quick and casual Candace might have been sharing it with Maddy. The salesman then spent half an hour addressing himself exclusively to Steve, even when it ought to have been quite clear to him that Candace was the prospective buyer.

'Do you think he realises why he didn't make a sale?' Steve asked her when they left.

She laughed. 'I handled it. In fact, it was useful. He talked to you while I had an uninterrupted chance to think about whether I really wanted the car.'

'I take it you didn't?'

She waggled her hand from side to side. 'Probably not. Let's keep looking.'

At the second and third dealerships, she test-drove two vehicles and finally decided on a compact European model, with very low mileage on the odometer. She felt exhilarated and slightly queasy at having parted with so much money so quickly. Still, it didn't make sense to delay. She was only here for a year. She needed to get organised, get her life sorted out, hit the ground running.

Did this apply to arranging a quick, therapeutic fling as well?

'Now you just have to drive it home,' Steve said, reminding her that in all spheres of life, actions had consequences.

'I don't know the way,' she answered.

'Which is why you'll follow me.'

By the time they reached home, it was late afternoon. Steve suggested an evening meal at a local Chinese restaurant, and that sounded fine.

Sounded fine.

In reality, it was harder. When someone was seated a yard away and facing in your direction, it wasn't as easy to avoid eye contact as it had been during driving lessons and grocery shopping. Candace drank a glass of red wine and regretted it. Jet-lag swamped her again, and the lighting in the restaurant was warm, inviting and intimate. She felt woozy, smily, relaxed and far too conscious of him.

When their eyes did meet, it was like tugging on a cord. She was a marionette and he was controlling the strings. He was making her nod and smile and listen with her chin cushioned in her palm and her elbow resting on the table.

'Hey, are you falling asleep?'

'No...'

'You will be soon. I'd better take you home.'

'You're making my decisions for me,' she retorted.

'Only tonight,' he said softly. 'Promise you, the rest of the decisions will be all yours.'

Perhaps he hadn't meant it to sound like such an intimate threat, but Candace panicked anyway. Her sleepiness vanished and she pulled herself to her feet, grating the legs of the chair on the restaurant's scratchy carpeting.

'Damn right they will!' she said, and saw his startled expression.

'Candace, I didn't mean— I *meant* it, OK?'

'I—I know. I'm sure you did.'

She turned away from him, felt his fingers slide in a quick, feather-light caress from her shoulder to her wrist, and was absolutely positive that she'd end up in his arms tonight. The idea was so breathtakingly terrifying that she didn't wait for him to pay for their meal. She simply stumbled out of the restaurant, hurried along the sidewalk and stood by the driver's side door of her new car until he caught up to her.

Steve didn't say anything about it. Not then. Not for the next few days. And he didn't kiss her.

He had more than one opportunity. Terry and his wife

were still away, but the rest of Narralee's small medical community gathered to welcome her at a barbecue at Linda and Rob Gardner's on Saturday evening. She enjoyed meeting everyone, and laid some tentative foundations of friendship.

As Terry had predicted, Linda was going to be nice. She had a no-nonsense haircut, a chunky build, a throaty laugh and a wicked sense of humour. She was down to earth in her opinions, happy with her career and open in her love for her children and her even more down-to-earth husband.

Getting over her jet-lag, Candace stayed until ten o'clock and drove herself home, then saw Steve's car breeze past her house as she stood on the deck, watching the moonlight over the water.

He glanced across, saw her there, slowed down and waved. She almost wondered if he would come over. They'd had a long conversation at the barbecue. Lots of laughs in it, and some quiet moments, too. If he did come, she would offer him tea or coffee, while secretly quaking in her shoes...

But, no, he didn't show up.

The next morning, they met on the beach. Candace hadn't swum in the ocean in years, but loved it again at once. Taylor's Beach was patrolled and flagged in the Lifesaving Association's colours of red and yellow, so she felt very safe swimming between the flags. Had no desire to go out as far as those surfers, though, in their slick black wetsuits.

One of the surfers was Steve.

She didn't recognise him until he came to shore with his creamy fibreglass board tucked under one arm, and he didn't see her until he'd put the board down, pulled his wetsuit to his waist and towelled himself.

He did this with rough energy, like a dog shaking off the water, then he caught sight of her, slung his towel over his shoulder and came over. Dropping her gaze, she was treated to the sight of his bare, tanned legs still dripping with water from the knees down, and his feet, lean and smooth and brown, covered with sand.

'Hi,' he said.

'You're not afraid of sharks out there?'

'Only when I see a fin.'

'You're joking, right?'

'We get dolphins here sometimes. They like surfing, too.'

'Now you're definitely joking!'

'No! Their bodies are perfect for it. They catch fish around here, too.'

'I'm going to look out for them. Still don't quite believe you...'

'You'll see them,' he predicted. 'If you spend any time on these beaches. The shape of their fin is different to a shark's, and so is the way they move in the water, but when you first glimpse one, before you've had time to work out whether it's shark or dolphin every hair stands up the way it does on a cornered cat. I tell you!' He laughed and shook his head. 'Yes, a couple of times I've been damned scared!'

He was still a little breathless. His hair stood on end and looked darker than it did when it was dry. The coarse plastic teeth of the zip on his wetsuit had pulled apart to just below his navel. She could tell by his six-pack of stomach muscles that he kept himself fit, and by his tan that he didn't always surf in his wetsuit.

My God, he's gorgeous! she thought, her insides twisting. Who am I kidding, that he'd want an affair? With *me*? Sitting here in my plain black suit. He'd probably flirt like this with my grandmother. Oh, I mean, was it even flirting? It was only friendliness. He was making me welcome very nicely, as Terry would have done, and I—Oh, lord, I'm so *raw*, right now, I actually felt nourished by it. *Totally* misunderstood it, obviously.

A girl in an extremely small orange bikini wandered past. She was as blonde as natural silk, sported a tan the colour

of fresh nutmeg and looked about twenty-five. For one
crazy moment, Candace was tempted to reach out, haul her
across by a bikini strap and park her right in front of Steve.

Here you go. Much more suitable. My apologies for tres-
passing on your personal space by even *contemplating* that
you and I might have—

'Ready for another dip?' he said. He had taken no notice
of the orange bikini, or the body inside it, and now the girl
had gone past.

'Um. Yes. Lovely.' Oh, hell! 'That would be really nice.'
She tried again, and managed a more natural tone. 'I've
been pretty timid on my own, but it'd be great to get out
beyond the point where every wave dumps a bucket of sand
down my front.'

He laughed. 'OK, let's go.'

Then he reached for the plastic zipper and peeled the
wetsuit down even further.

He was wearing a swimsuit, of course. Board shorts, in
fact. Black, with a blue panel on each side. Beneath the
wetsuit, they'd ridden down below his hips. He had his
back to her now, and she could see the shallow hollow just
above the base of his spine. Like the rest of him, it was
tanned to a warm bronze, and was dappled with tiny, sun-
bleached hairs.

A moment later, he had hauled casually on the waistband
and pulled the board shorts back to where they belonged.

They swam together for an hour, then she went home for
lunch and he put his wetsuit back on and returned to the
outer boundaries of the surf. She didn't see him when she
went back to the beach for a walk late in the afternoon,
didn't see him when she walked past his house on the return
trip, although his car was in the driveway and a sprinkler
was spinning round on the lawn.

Definitely, he was just being friendly.

And I appreciate that, she realised. Maybe that's the

problem. I appreciate it, and I need it too much at the moment. I'd better get the rest of it under control.

Candace didn't see Steve again until Tuesday, when she had her first surgical list, consisting of three patients. Steve was scheduled to handle the anaesthesia.

She'd seen each of her patients the day before for a brief chat, and had gone through their reports from the pre-admission clinic. No danger signals. Chest X-rays and cardiograms all normal. Blood pressures within the acceptable range.

First was a scheduled gall-bladder removal on a fifty-three-year-old woman, followed by two straightforward hernia repairs, both on older men. Blood had been cross-matched for the gall-bladder patient as there was a higher risk of bleeding during this operation. All three of the patients were here on a day-patient basis. After the surgery, they'd make use of the 'political beds'—those reclining chairs that Terry had been so cynical about.

Preparing for surgery was like coming home. The OR—Theatre One, which sounded odd to her ears—was a place in which she was used to possessing undisputed control. She loved this environment, and the way everything was geared towards a single focus. One patient, one operation and six people who knew exactly what they were doing.

The scrub sinks were different—old-fashioned porcelain, with long levers on the faucets which you flicked on and off with a quick touch. She was used to stainless steel, and foot pedals. Theatre One had washable vinyl walls and the hard, antistatic floors which she knew only too well. They were murder on backs and legs after you'd been standing there for more than a couple of hours.

Candace was the last to scrub, and everything was ready to go now that she had arrived. She briefly greeted the other staff and the patient. Mrs Allenby looked a little nervous, of course. Years ago, Candace had had to fight the instinct to give her patients a reassuring pat, but now it was second nature to keep her gloved hands back.

There was music playing on a black compact disc player set up on a shelf. Something classical. Beethoven, Candace recognised. Not that it made any difference.

'Could we have that off, please?' she said.

The scout nurse, whose name badge was hidden beneath a green surgical gown, immediately went across and pressed a button on the player, bringing silence.

'Would you like something else, Dr Fletcher?' she offered. Her name was Pat, Candace found out a little later.

'No, thanks,' she answered, calm and polite. 'I can't operate with music.'

She registered one or two slightly surprised looks above pale green disposable masks, but didn't take the time to explain. This was her space now. All surgeons had their quirks, and she wasn't going to apologise for hers, now or later. She never swore or threw things or yelled at the nurses; she didn't practise her golf swing to warm up her hands; she was consistent in her preference of cat-gut length and instrument size.

But she liked silence. It helped her sense of focus. No music. A minimum of chatter. No jokes or ribbing. Absolutely no disparaging comments about the patient.

'OK, we're looking good at this end,' Steve said a few minutes later.

'Thanks, Dr Colton.'

Her gaze tangled with his as he looked briefly away from his monitors, and she could tell he was still thinking about the 'no music' thing. Maybe he'd chosen the Beethoven himself. Well, he could listen to Beethoven at home.

'All right, are we ready for the gas?' she asked, and began the operation.

She'd done it hundreds of times, probably.

Several litres of carbon dioxide were injected into the abdomen to provide a space to work in between the outer layers of tissue and the internal organs. A tiny incision allowed the passage of a laparoscope with an equally tiny camera on the end of it, manipulated by the assistant surgeon, Peter Moody. What the camera saw was then screened like a video, allowing Candace to guide her instruments. The lumpy, disorientating appearance of the human abdominal cavity on the screen was a familiar sight to her now.

This patient's symptoms suggested the need for a cholangiogram, which would confirm or rule out the presence of stones in the bile duct. In this case, the X-ray-type scan showed that, yes, there were three small stones present. Candace decided to remove them immediately, rather than bring Mrs Allenby back for a second procedure at a later date.

The monitors indicated that she was handling the anaesthesia well. Candace had no trouble in removing the stones successfully.

'If I know Mrs Allenby, she'll want to see those later,' Steve said.

'She's your patient?' Candace asked.

'Since I started here four years ago. And she's got a very enquiring mind, haven't you Mrs A.?' Under anaesthesia, Mrs Allenby's conscious mind was almost certain to be unaware, but there was strong evidence that many patients could retain a memory of what happened during surgery. 'She wanted to know last week—' Steve began.

'Could we save it until later?' Candace cut in.

'Sure.' He gave a brief nod and a shrug.

Again, there was a moment of tension and adjustment amongst the other staff. Candace ignored it and kept going. She used tiny metal clips to close off the bile duct at the base of the gall bladder, as well as the vessel which provided its blood supply. Next, she used a cautery to detach the gall bladder from the liver, once again working through tiny incisions.

She brought the organ to the incision in Mrs Allenby's navel and emptied its contents through a drain. The gall bladder was limp now, and slid easily through the incision. She checked the area for bleeding and satisfied herself that all was looking good, then the patient's abdomen was drained of gas, the incisions were covered in small bandages, Steve reversed the anaesthesia and the operation was over.

Easy to describe, but it had still taken over two hours, and there was more work yet to be done. The two nurses chanted in chorus as they counted up instruments, sponges and gauze to make sure nothing was missing. Forceps and retractors clattered into metal bowls. Surgical drapes were bundled into linen bins. Mrs Allenby was wheeled, still unconscious, into the recovery annexe where two more nurses would monitor her breathing, consciousness, behaviour, blood pressure and pain as she emerged from anaesthesia.

The two hernia operations which came next were simpler and shorter. Both were of the type known as a direct inguinal hernia, which resulted from a weakness in the muscles in the groin area. A short incision just above the crease between thigh and abdomen on each patient allowed Candace to slip the bulging sac of internal tissue back into the abdominal cavity.

The first patient's abdominal wall had quite a large area of weakness, and Candace asked for a sheet of synthetic mesh to strengthen it. The second patient, several years younger, needed only a series of sutures in the abdominal tissue itself. Each incision was closed with sutures, and both patients would rest on the reclining chairs in the day-surgery room after their first hour or two of close monitoring in the recovery annexe.

She would check on them as soon as she had showered, Candace decided. You never came out of surgery feeling clean.

The shower beckoned strongly as she pulled off her gloves and mask just outside the door of Theatre One. Behind her, Steve and the other staff were preparing for a Caesarean, and Candace crossed paths with Linda Gardner. The obstetrician was about to squeeze in a lunch-break while Theatre One was tidied and replenished with equipment, ready for her to take over.

'Quiet in here today,' Linda commented.

'They'll probably appreciate a request for rock and roll, I expect,' Candace answered.

'So you're the culprit? You like reverent silence?'

'Reverence isn't a requirement,' she returned quickly. 'Silence is.'

'No one gave you a hard time?' Linda asked with a curious smile.

'In surgery, I don't give anyone the opportunity.' She softened the statement with a smile in return, then went and answered the clamouring of her aching back with a long, hot shower.

She emerged in a skirt, blouse and white coat twenty minutes later to find Theatre Two up and running and ready for her.

'All the symptoms of appendicitis, admitted through Emergency,' on-call theatre sister Lynn Baxter explained.

'Give me five minutes,' Candace said.

'And turn off the music?'

'Word travels fast around here. Thanks very much, yes.'

As usual, she didn't go on at length. Didn't admit either that the unexpected extension of her list today was almost as unwelcome as the discovery that the last leg of a long flight home would be indefinitely delayed. She considered it her responsibility to each patient and to the rest of the surgical team never to talk about how she felt.

No complaints, no explanations. Her aching back and feet were private—*her* problem. So were hunger, thirst and an itchy nose or a throbbing head.

And as for the inner turmoil she'd felt during each agonising step between her discovery of Todd's affair and their outwardly businesslike divorce... She had said nothing about it at all until the final papers had been signed and their marital assets divided. Then she had simply made an announcement in the doctors' change-room at the end of a Friday list with a three-day weekend coming up. She had asked those present to pass the word around.

Most of her colleagues had been stunned, she knew, but they had three days to get used to the idea and to recognise the signals she was sending out. They knew her professional style by this time. Comments had been sympathetic and heartfelt, but mercifully brief...

Theatre Two was the exact twin of Theatre One, with all equipment and supplies set out in exactly the same way. This patient, a thirty-five-year-old woman with an uncomplicated medical history, had been given a pre-med through her drip and was already drowsy and relaxed, her considerable pain masked by the medication.

The appendix was notorious for sending out mixed signals, so Candace kept her mind open as she prepared to make the incision. You could open someone up and find nothing at all, even when a patient's white cell count was up and all his or her symptoms slotted into place. Or you could find—

'Good grief!' she said.

She'd spotted it before anyone else. There was a tumour wrapped around the appendix, turning this operation from a routine excision into a complex feat of surgical technique.

'It's huge,' muttered on-call assistant surgeon Mark Daley.

'But still potentially benign,' Candace said. 'We'll take it out straight away to send to Pathology, then explore a bit to see if there's any obvious spread to other organs.'

She excised both appendix and tumour, then looked at the ovaries, which were the most likely sites for a primary tumour in a woman of this age. Fortunately, they looked healthy and normal. Neither was there any evidence of metastasis to the liver.

'We're looking pretty hopeful on this one,' she concluded, and there was a sense of relief all round.

It was after three by the time Candace emerged from Theatre, and her stomach was aching sharply with hunger. She took another brief shower, grabbed a packet of potato chips from the vending machine in the emergency department, gulped some coffee and went straight in to check on the recovery of her day patients.

Mrs Allenby had eaten a sandwich and drunk some juice and tea, voided her bladder and shown a return of bowel sounds. She could manage a strong cough, her lungs were clear and she'd walked up and down the corridor a couple of times to assist her circulation.

'But my shoulder is hurting,' she said.

'Your right shoulder?'

'Yes.'

'Strangely enough, that's normal. Quite a common symptom. It's called referred pain, and that's really all you need to know about it, Mrs Allenby. It should go away on its own by the end of the day. You'll probably notice some discomfort from gas as well. Your stomach doesn't like being manhandled, and it may take a couple of days to settle down. But the surgery went very well, and I'm not anticipating any problems. Dr Colton would like to see you in his rooms in about a week to check on how you're doing.'

'I'll make an appointment.'

'Meanwhile, you can go home as soon as you're ready. You have someone to pick you up?'

'My husband's waiting.'

'Great! All the best, then. You were special, you know— my first patient in Australia.'

'Oh, how nice!'

Mrs Allenby went to the patients' change-room to dress, while Candace checked on her two hernia patients, who were both progressing normally but still too groggy to leave. As she slid her stethoscope around her neck, Candace heard Mrs Allenby say to a nurse, 'All right, I'm ready. Do I get my stones now?'

She hid a smile as she crossed to the three-bed recovery annexe where Andrea Johnson was just emerging from her anaesthesia. Steve had predicted his patient's interest in 'her stones'. In a relatively small community like this one, where a patient's GP could also be present during surgery, there would be more examples of this kind of knowledge. As Mrs Allenby had said in a different context, it was 'nice'. A difference for Candace to enjoy while she was here.

Andrea Johnson was still very sleepy and disorientated. She was lying on a wheeled hospital bed a few metres from the other patient in Recovery, the Caesarean delivery from Theatre One.

'Hurts,' was all she wanted to say. 'Feels awful.'

Candace ordered some additional pain relief, and out of the patient's earshot said to the recovery annexe sister, 'She's not ready to hear about what we found and what we did.'

'Wait until she goes upstairs?' Robyn Wallace suggested.

'Definitely. My notes are pretty clear, I think. I'll follow up in the morning and answer any questions she's come up with. If she seems too groggy to be told tonight, it can wait. And, of course, there'll be a wait anyway for the pathology results. Does she have family here?'

'No, she's single apparently. Drove herself in.'

'There must be *someone* to tell. Could you try and find out?'

'She was probably in too much pain to think about next of kin before.'

'That's usually when people want family or a friend around.'

'True.' Sister Wallace nodded.

'What have we got here? Two for the price of one?' said a new voice just behind them.

It was Steve. As anaesthetist, he was technically responsible for any complications in patients for the first twenty-four hours following their surgery, and he'd be taking a look at the two hernia patients as well as the Caesarean delivery he'd just been involved with.

Candace didn't understand his comment about two for the price of one. She assumed it was another Australian joke, but Sister Wallace looked blank as well.

'They're both my patients,' he explained. 'Sisters. And there's a whole posse of other Johnson and Calvert relatives upstairs, waiting to see Carina and the baby. Should probably warn you,' he added quietly to Sister Wallace, 'sparks will fly if they each realise the other is here. Andrea and Carina don't get on. Andrea seems to have cut herself off a bit lately.'

'I'll keep that in mind, and pull a curtain across,' Sister Wallace drawled.

'Speaking of getting on,' Candace said lightly, 'I'm heading *off*. It's been an interesting first day, but I'm done now.'

She should have known it wouldn't be that easy. Steve caught up to her as she reached her car.

'Heading straight home?'

'Yes, thanks to the existence of the frozen meals we picked up the other day, I don't need to stop for anything.'

'Frozen meals! Yum!' he drawled. 'How about steak instead?'

'Too hungry to wait for steak.'

'I'll get it on the grill as soon as I get home. Walk down to my place when you're ready, and we can call it a late lunch.'

'You don't have to.'

'I know. If I *had* to, I'd be chafing by now. Terry said, "Look after her till Monday."'

'Ah, so he *did* say that?'

She felt the severity in her expression. Couldn't always relax straight after surgery. He would probably think she was tight and humourless and no fun at all. From experience, however, she knew it would be worse to force a more laid-back mood. Wait until she got out of these cruel pantihose and unwound the stethoscope from her neck. She'd be far more relaxed then.

'Yes, he *did* say that,' Steve echoed steadily. 'But it's Tuesday now. This one's pleasure, not duty. And I'm such a crash-hot GP I can tell just by looking at you that your iron stores are low.'

Unexpectedly, she laughed. 'They probably are.'

'You need steak. And a swim.'

'The swim I won't argue with.'

'Neither will I, as long as it's *after* the steak.'

'All right...'

'Then, when we're sitting on the beach, I think we've got to talk about why you hesitated even for a second before you said yes to this,' he finished.

Casual tone. Meaningful after-shock.

It was a threat. Candace was in no doubt about that. And it was a threat which sent twin curls of panic and dizzy need spiralling wildly through her blood. She stalled the car three times on the way home.

CHAPTER THREE

THEY lay side by side on their towels in silence, soaking up some late afternoon sun and digesting what couldn't possibly have been called a late lunch.

Barbecued steak, a microwaved jacket potato and salad, dished up at a quarter to five? Not lunch. Delicious and satisfying, though. Steve Colton cooked steak very well.

He was going to ask me something, but I've forgotten what it was, Candace thought hazily.

She was too busy thinking about signals. Yes, *those* signals! The ones men sent to women, and the ones women, in their different way, sent back to men.

It's been so long... So long since I had to decide if I was imagining it or not. If I wanted it or not. If a man really meant it or not. I was so sure about all those questions the other day, but now...

Some men had flirted with her, had given off signals, during her marriage to Todd. They had been signals she had casually interpreted as meaning, *If you weren't attached, I'd be interested.* The key attitude on her part, of course, was 'casually'. She had never needed to test out her perceptions, to work out whether she was right or wrong.

Because of Todd, because of her marriage, it just hadn't *mattered*. She'd never had the remotest intention of responding to the possible, or probable, signals in any way. She'd never been tempted into an affair.

This time, it was different. A part of her craved the heady therapy of a successful fling. Another part of her was cynical, sceptical and just plain terrified. *If I'm wrong... If I'm right, and it doesn't work...*

If I'm sure I'm right, and I throw myself at him, and he laughs, or he's *kind*, or he tells me very carefully, Oh, but I'm married. Didn't you know? My wife is away visiting her parents for a week in Woggabiggabolliga—which seemed to be the name of at least half of the towns people mentioned around here, as far as she could work out.

Candace had to suppress a gulp of hysterical laughter at this point. Am I going crazy? Who knew that betrayal and divorce could do this to a person?

'You're different in surgery, aren't you?' Steve said suddenly, sitting up cross-legged on his towel and resting his elbows on his knees.

Candace immediately sat up, too. She didn't bother to argue his perception. 'Enough to be worthy of comment, apparently.'

'I didn't—'

'No, go ahead. It's OK.'

'I guess I thought you'd be more touchy-feely.'

'And instead I'm...?'

'You really give the impression that you know what you're doing and you know what you want.'

'Of course I do! I was doing this when you were still dissecting frogs, Steve!'

His abrupt launch into probing questions rattled her, especially the way it followed on from her own jittery train of thought.

'Don't,' he said.

'Don't what?'

'Don't pull rank.'

'Why not?' she retorted. 'I must be at least five years older than you.'

'Six, I think.'

'You've been checking?'

'Terry said you were thirty-nine.'

'Well, Terry is wrong! I'm only thirty-eight, and my birthday's not until July!'

They looked at each other and both laughed at the absurdity of her objection.

'Hey, can we start this again?' he said.

'Start what again?'

'Now you're being deliberately obtuse. This conversation. I hadn't intended it to get confrontational. I wanted to say that in surgery you were...' He hesitated.

'A royal pain about the music?'

'Yes, and it was great. I really liked the way you handled it. I *liked* you in surgery, Candace. I liked your focus and your confidence in the fact that it was your right to dictate the mood. But you were quiet about it. Polite.'

'I'm well brought up.'

'So well brought up that normally you're probably like most women and apologise when someone else steps on your toes, right?'

She laughed again, recognising the arrow-like accuracy of his observation. 'In my private life, yes. In surgery, Dr Colton, you'd better damn well apologise to *me*!'

He grinned and his blue eyes sparkled like the sun on the sea. 'Yep. I liked that. It was good,' he said, then repeated even more lazily, 'It was good.'

Seconds later, he was on his feet and reaching down to pull her up as well. 'Want to?' he said.

'A swim? Yes, I do.'

The surf was bigger today. 'Dumpers,' Steve told her. 'Be careful. They can flip you over pretty hard.'

He kept a careful eye on her and on the waves as they swam, and told her a couple of times, 'Not this one.'

After a while, she could feel the difference in the waves for herself. They didn't curl and pause and fold smoothly over today, but broke abruptly, like hands crashing on piano keys. If you caught them at the wrong moment, they sent you tumbling so that you emerged disorientated, with wrenched muscles.

'Where are the flags today?' she asked Steve.

'They don't patrol Taylor's Beach during the week, out-side school holidays,' he said. 'We can stop, if you like.'

'No, I'm enjoying it.' And she felt very safe beside him, sensed that he really knew what he was doing in the water.

'Jump!' he interrupted, and they managed to keep their heads above water as a wave boiled around them. 'They're breaking all over the place. We'd have to go out a long way to avoid them.'

'No, thanks!'

They stuck it out for a little longer, then Candace got dumped again and came up with sand all through her hair and down her classic black one-piece swimsuit. Salt stung in her nose.

'Let's stop,' Steve suggested again, and this time she didn't argue.

They towelled themselves dry, and he slipped into a white T-shirt, while she wrapped a cotton skirt in tropical ocean colours around her waist, still enjoying the sun on the scooped back of her suit. They went for a walk, and explored the rock pools at the tide-level shelf jutting out from the headland at the southern end of the beach.

He showed her crimson and white anemones, glistening brown sea squirts and pinky-purple crabs. The late after-noon sun slanted golden on the water. A little later, a glo-rious sunset painted a palette of colour in the west, a mix of fiery orange, salmon pink and storm purple as clouds began to move across the sky. The clouds hastened the onset of darkness and they turned back.

'I'll walk you home,' he said, and when they got there, he added helpfully, on a careless drawl, 'You can invite me in, if you like.'

'Are you hungry again?' she teased.

'We could have a drink on your deck.'

'You have a perfectly good deck of your own, Dr Colton.'

This time, he just looked at her. Silent. Patient. His blue

eyes glinted and his mouth was tucked in at the corners. They both knew exactly what the other was thinking. It was a delicious yet stomach-churning feeling.

She sighed. 'Wine, beer, tea, coffee or juice?'

'Iced water?'

Out on the deck a few minutes later, he noticed her scratching her head. 'Hair still full of sand?'

'Yes, and when I try to get it loose, it runs down into my suit. Ugh!'

'We can do something about that, I think.'

He put down his clinking glass and disappeared inside, to emerge in a few moments flourishing her hairbrush. 'You were in a hurry this morning, weren't you?' he said.

'That's right. I left it on the table.'

'I noticed it earlier. Stand up and bend forward.'

'Um…'

'Let me. Please!' The teasing, knowing tone had gone from his voice suddenly, to be replaced by a husky note that was new. 'Please, let me. I'd really like to do it, Candace.'

She nodded, her throat too dry for speech. Time had slowed. There was an almost tangible sense of expectation hanging in the air. With her hands pressed on slightly bent knees, she faced him, then felt the light touch of his fingers on the back of her neck. A tingle flooded her spine.

Steve stroked the brush through her hair, his touch rhythmic and careful and slow. Cool, dry sand showered silently down onto her feet. Steve was silent, too. Only his fingers seemed to speak to her as they threaded a stray strand over her ear, then moved the thick mass to one side to brush in a different place. She was hypnotised by the gentleness of it, by the warmth of his touch and by the faint sound of his breathing. Could have let it go on forever.

'Now sit down,' he instructed her softly, 'And lean your head back.'

Her hair was like a cloud now, and the bristles of the

brush tickled her temples and her scalp as he resumed his steady strokes. She closed her eyes and felt their lids flicker. She felt more vulnerable this way. The swimsuit wasn't outrageously revealing, but when she sat at this angle her breasts were thrust forward and she could feel the imprint of the cooling air pressing deep into the cleft between them. A shudder vibrated through her.

'You're cold,' he said. 'And I should stop. Don't want to.' He held her thick mass of hair in his hands like a rope. 'Could do this for ages.'

She opened her eyes and heard the brush clatter onto the glass-topped cane table. He knelt beside her. 'Your hair is gorgeous, and hidden underneath it are these stretches of soft skin I just want to kiss, Candace.'

He was doing it before he even finished talking about it, nuzzling her behind her ear, whispering his lips across her neck to reach her jawline, wrapping her hair loosely around his hands and using it to pull her close and find her mouth.

She gasped at the firmness and confidence and nutty sweetness of his lips. He released her hair so that it streamed over her shoulders and down her back, then brought his hands across her collarbone and down to brush lightly across her full breasts. They already ached.

Now he was pulling her to her feet and she went without hesitation, needing his strength against her body.

'Steve,' she murmured incoherently. 'Steve…'

'Mmm, you taste like the sea.'

'So do you. Salted peanuts, or something.'

'I could lick it off every inch of you.'

His hands rested lightly on her shoulders and his mouth tangled with hers, tongue and teeth and lips and tongue again. She felt as if this had been building between them for weeks or months instead of days, knew that her legs and mouth and hands were trembling.

'Every single inch,' he repeated, and slid the straps of

her swimsuit from her shoulders, nuzzling at the salt on her neck as he peeled the straps lower with aching slowness.

Soon, soon, he would touch her breasts and feel just what this was doing to her. *Soon*...except that she couldn't wait another second. She arched her back and heard him groan with need as her fullness spilled into his hands.

He held her breasts almost reverently, lifted their generous weight in his hands then touched his lips to the swollen curves, drifting lower until he reached one throbbing nipple then moving across to the other. She flung her head to one side and gasped again, could have let it go on and on.

A car swished past on the road and a ragged thought entered her mind that anyone could have seen them here. Anyone could *still* see them. It was dark, cloudy now after that magnificent sunset, but all the same, if someone came along the sidewalk, looked up and saw their two shadowy figures and the tell-tale paleness of her bared flesh, that person would be in no doubt about what was happening up here on this open deck.

'Come inside,' Steve whispered. 'There are things I want to do to you that definitely aren't for public consumption.'

'I think you've already—'

'I know. It was so good. It's...' He broke off and his gaze swept down from her face to the pale, rounded shapes of her bared breasts, still heavy with need and tight against the chill of the air. 'Still very, very good.'

His hands drifted lightly up from her waist once more, whispered across her thrusting, pebble-hard nipples and came to rest on her shoulders. She was throbbing, on fire, desperate to touch him, too, in all the places that had drawn her unwilling gaze over the past few days. The hollow at the small of his back, his tanned shoulders, delicious backside, square jaw, steady mouth. But his touch on her sensitive skin seemed to paralyse her, and she couldn't find the will to move.

'Come inside now, *please*...' he whispered.

He didn't wait for her assent, just scooped one arm around her thighs and lifted her a step or two, then set her down again, locked her in his arms and almost dragged her to the bedroom.

Not that she was reluctant. Oh, no! But her legs were still shaky and half-numb. Her head just kept coming down to rest on his shoulder so she could press her mouth into the pad of muscle there, and taste the warring scents of salt and male skin.

The bedroom seemed too far away to wait for. There was a charge like an electric current between them and she wanted to pull off his clothes and wrap herself around him, claim him with her hands, feel his heat, hold him and never let go.

They barely made it to the bed, and were both far too impatient to take it slowly. He had come prepared for this. He had brought protection, and she didn't resent it. Of course he had come prepared! If she'd been a man she would have done the same. If she'd been a woman with more confidence in her own perceptions about their chemistry, she would have thought ahead and considered the issue herself.

So she was grateful for his forethought, in the twelve seconds she managed to give to the question, and then all of it—everything else in the entire world—became meaningless against the flood tide of their shared release.

They made love twice more that night. Candace was astonished at how rapidly their need for each other moved from being thoroughly sated to building to a conflagration once more. After the second time, they ate supper in bed—tall glasses of cold milk and that frozen chocolate cheesecake he had eyed in her shopping cart the previous week.

Then they went out and sprawled in each other's arms in the cane lounging chair on the deck for half an hour and talked. Silly stuff, not worth remembering or repeating.

After midnight, after making love, it was hard to manage earth-shattering conversation.

It was lovely, though. Just…quietly…lovely. She wore nothing but a simple sarong knotted across her breasts and he had slipped back into his dry swim shorts. It became too cold eventually, so they had a giggly shower together to warm themselves up, and it led inevitably back to square one.

Finally, then, they slept until morning.

Morning.

The clouds had disappeared again overnight, and the day was already bright, even before seven. Candace had forgotten how strong the morning light was in this country. Glorious, she'd thought on other mornings. Today it seemed cruelly bright, and it hid nothing.

It probably didn't matter to Steve. He was still asleep, his body flung out in her bed as trusting as a child's. Almost as flawless as a child's, too. No crow's feet. No scars. No sags…

Candace fled to the bathroom for another shower and couldn't help pausing before the big mirror to take a merciless inventory of all she saw there. Hair like a bush. Creases around her mouth. And there was a mark on her left breast, a tiny bruise.

No, a love bite.

Hesitantly, she touched the spot with her fingers and remembered how Steve's lips and teeth had lingered there, and elsewhere, making her writhe. Today, it just looked like a bruise. Her breasts, with their nipples still darkened by the friction of Steve's mouth, seemed too heavy and large, too womanly, too pale. Hips and thighs as well.

'Lord, I need to lose weight!' she muttered, then laughed at herself. A few pounds, maybe, but that wasn't the problem.

The problem was that this body of hers was thirty-eight

years old, not twenty-five, and the harsh Australian light would never let her forget it.

A rap sounded on the bathroom door, like someone casually tossing a handful of pebbles.

'Steve?' she questioned, cupping her hands instinctively over her breasts.

As if it could be anyone else! And as if there was any point in hiding this small segment of her nakedness from him!

'Can I open?'

'Uh…yes, fine.' She darted into the clear glass shower enclosure and turned the water on. It hid nothing.

'Hi…' he thwarted any attempt at concealment straight away, opening the glass door and gazing at her '…gorgeous.'

Was that a nickname or a commentary? Whatever it was, she blushed darkly, happy and on edge at the same time.

'I have to head off,' he continued. 'I'm rostered to the emergency department today, and I've just been paged. Not totally urgent, but I'll have to cancel the full American breakfast.'

'Was I offering a full American…?'

'Sort of hoped you were,' he murmured, on a huskily suggestive note. 'But I'll see you tonight, OK?'

He reached confidently into the shower enclosure and pulled her close enough to kiss her wet face.

'No!'

The vehemence of it surprised both of them. Candace wrenched off the faucets, although most of her body was barely wet. She stepped quickly past him and reached for a towel. Lapping it around her body and holding it tightly in place, she left the bathroom. He followed her.

'Hey! Last night was great, wasn't it?' he said.

'Yes. Yes, it was.'

'Then what's the problem…hey, Candace?' The last two words were soft, sweet, like the way he'd spoken—those incoherent snatches of words—as they'd made love last night.

'You're m-making too many assumptions,' she stammered. 'Way too many. I'm not— We need to think about— If this is anything, it's just an affair, OK? And I don't want to take it—'

'Maybe I should just kiss you again, or something? That seemed to work pretty well yesterday.'

'*Work*? As a technique, you mean? A strategy for getting me to—?'

'*No!*'

It was his turn to rebel, and he did it more effectively than she had. He gripped her shoulders, tilted his head, brought his mouth to within an inch or two of hers. 'No, Candee,' he said softly.

'I *hate* that!'

'Candy?'

'Yes.'

'Not when I say it like this. Candee. Spelled double E. It's so sweet, can't you hear? And I mean it. Sweet Candee. Let me kiss you…'

'Mmm.' She turned her head away, pressed her mouth shut, but she was still in his arms and they were tight now, holding her, inviting her to lean on him. She could feel his heat, the elastic hardness of his muscles, the strong length of his bones beneath the fragrant skin she'd explored so thoroughly with her mouth and hands last night. The towel began to slip and, heaven help her, she no longer cared.

'Tell me it wasn't one of the best nights of your life,' he went on, his voice low. Its caressing lilt brought back flashes of memory—the intimate touch of his tongue, the power of his hips—making her shudder. 'Tell me we didn't light bonfires and set off rockets and make orchestras burst into symphony.'

'Yes, and it's wrong!' she retorted. 'I don't do that. I

don't leap into bed with people...men...younger men...when I've only known them a week.'

'Less,' he pointed out.

'Less,' she agreed.

'So maybe it's time you did. Not *all* younger men, by any means. But me, definitely.'

'Why? *Why?*'

'Because it's good,' he said simply. He ran a finger lazily down from her throat to the top of the towel, which had slipped another three inches. Sensation stabbed deep within her. 'I thought it would be, and it is. I have to go.'

'Mmm.'

'Think about it, OK?'

She did. All day.

She thought about it in between seeing several of Terry's patients, as he was still in Sydney with Myrna. Terry's wife had had surgery yesterday—a lumpectomy and removal of the lymph nodes. She thought about it driving south on a winding highway through fragrant eucalyptus forests to Harpoon Bay. She had a surgical list scheduled there on Friday morning and wanted to make sure she knew the route and the hospital and staff a little. She thought about it driving north to Narralee again.

By the time Steve rang at six that evening, she was able to say at once, 'I'm sorry.'

'That's all right.'

'You see, I was married for nearly seventeen years and I didn't get a lot of practice at this and...' She stumbled to a halt.

'Am I seeing you, then?' he asked, as if this was all that mattered.

Maybe it was.

She took a deep breath. 'Yes. I'd like that. As long as there are no expectations. And as long as we keep it to ourselves. Strictly to ourselves.'

She didn't want anyone else judging or making assumptions.

'Yeah, I was going to say that, too. There are…reasons for that to be a good idea, aren't there?'

'Not that it's something I particularly—'

'Hey, let's not analyse it, Candace,' he said, his voice low. 'Not yet, anyway. Come over, and we'll have fish and chips on the beach.'

'Are you going to be at the hospital today?' Steve heard, at the other end of the phone. He recognized his brother Matt's voice.

It was seven on a Tuesday morning, a week after his first fabulous night with Candace. On Friday, she'd received the pathology report on Andrea Johnson's tumour and had phoned him to ask, 'Would you like to tell her, since she's your patient? It was benign. She should have no further problems at all.'

'That's great news, Candace! Yes, I'll tell her. Thanks for letting me know.'

'Well, you know, it's a real hardship for me to have to call you, Steve!' He loved that low suggestive note in her voice.

'Is that why we've both been doing it at least twice a day for the past forty-eight hours?' he'd answered her softly.

And, in fact, he'd expected this call to be Candace. To be honest, he was slightly irritable in his disappointment that it wasn't her voice he'd heard. Seven was early for his brother to be phoning.

'Yes, I'm rostered for surgery,' he answered Matt shortly, still not quite awake.

He could still smell Candace's sweet scent on his body. She hadn't stayed last night. Had left his place at one in the morning, with the imprint of her head on his pillow and his sheets tangled from the way she writhed at his touch.

'I really *have* to get some sleep, Steve!' she'd said, her voice low and husky with regret.

Just thinking about her—her responsiveness, the way her eyes went so wide and dark, the erotic charge that hit him every time he had his face in her hair, or touched the creases at the tops of her thighs, or held those fabulous breasts—made him throb with need. He wasn't yet trying to work out where this was going—Candace had mentioned the word 'affair' and he hadn't felt any need to challenge it—but he sure liked where it was at the moment!

'Might see you,' Matt said his voice a study in casual intonation.

Finally Steve woke up properly and the penny dropped.

'Hey, Helen's had the baby!' Steve's focus shifted at once, with a head-spinning wrench.

'No, not yet, but she's in serious labor, and it's pretty full on. Won't be long. We're heading for the car now. Her mother has just arrived to look after the big kids.'

Matt and Helen had a six-year-old son and twin daughters aged three, but still considered parenting a breeze and were ready for more.

'I'll try and drop in to see you, if things are quiet,' Steve promised.

'They won't be quiet at our end,' Matt answered. 'Helen's doubling up every two minutes now.'

'Get going, then, and I'll see you.'

He shook off the last vestiges of sleep—definitely hadn't been getting enough of it over the past few days, Candace was quite right—dived into his clothes, downed his cereal, skipped coffee altogether and left the house. Candace had a short list this morning, followed by Linda Gardner who had a couple of scheduled gynae procedures.

Sometimes there was a cancellation. A patient's pre-admission check-up might reveal a problem which made the surgery unsafe. Occasionally, some patients just didn't show up and had to be rescheduled for a later date. This morning, Steve found himself hoping that something like this would happen.

Helen didn't have long labours, and he would be an uncle again before the scheduled list was completed. The sight of a sister-in-law he was very fond of and a brother he'd always been close to holding their much-wanted newborn baby was a pleasure he didn't want to put off for too long.

First, though, surgery with Candace at the helm...

I'm nervous, Candace realised as she scrubbed. When am I ever nervous before surgery? We're doing two vasectomies and stripping some varicose veins. Quick, simple procedures that I could do in my sleep. When am I *ever* nervous?

When the man I'm sleeping with—no, staying *awake* with, while we cling to each other and make all that wildness and ecstasy together—is behind one of those masks... That's when I'm nervous.

It had never happened to her before. Todd was a lawyer, her first and only sexual partner until last week, and their love-making had long since settled into the safe and predictable, well before his adultery with Brittany.

I can't bring this into the operating theatre with me. I hate distractions.

Even during the process of her separation and divorce, at least she'd never actually had to face Todd over the operating table. What if it was impossible?

Steve was already inside, gowned, capped and masked. All she could see were his eyes. So blue, so hot, so knowing. The patient was on the table, chattering and joking.

More nervous than I am? I don't think so!

'Hi,' Steve said to her. His tone was a caress, under the cover of some instructions from nurse to patient.

'Help me, OK?' Candace said. 'I'm—'

'You're fine. Come on.'

That was all. He just muttered the words, not even looking at her.

But at the familiar sound of his voice something clicked and shifted and she realised inwardly, Yes, of course I'm fine. I'm manufacturing a problem out of thin air, and there's no reason for it.

After this, the floor felt solid under her feet, the surgical instruments seemed to mould themselves to fit her hand and all three procedures ran as smooth as silk. She finished ahead of schedule. Linda's first gynae patient wasn't prepped yet, and Linda herself wasn't here.

'Great!' Steve announced to everyone. 'Because there's some action going on in the delivery suite today that I'm pretty interested in. My sister-in-law went into labour early this morning.'

There was a chorus of questions, but he shook his head. 'I'll tell you all about it when I get back, OK?'

The nurses, two friendly women in their fifties named Doreen Malvern and Pat Lister, began to prepare Theatre One for Linda's first procedure, while the previous patient was set up in Recovery with Robyn Wallace and Sue Smith. Candace filled in her notes and made a couple of phone calls, then Linda's patient arrived, drowsy from her pre-med and surrounded by snowy pillows.

'OK, now, one more lucky last time,' Doreen said. 'Janine, can you tell us your full name?'

'Janine Marie Prowse.'

'And your date of birth?'

'April the 18th, 1965.'

'And what are you having done here today?'

'My tubes tied.'

'Where's Dr Colton?' Candace heard Pat ask the anaesthesia nurse, Netta Robertson.

'Not back. I guess he's cluckier than we thought. But Linda's not here yet either.'

'On her way.' Robyn Wallace had just put down the phone. 'Five minutes, she says.'

'We'll start getting you set up, Janine, OK?'

'Where'd he go?' asked Joe Sheddin, the theatre orderly.

'Dr Colton? Up to Maternity. His brother's wife is having a baby.'

'Some drama was happening up there a little while ago,' Joe offered cheerfully.

'Yes, Helen Colton was having a baby,' Sister Wallace retorted.

She worked hard at keeping Joe in his place. Candace liked him, though. He wore his royal blue disposable cap like a pirate's head-scarf, low on his forehead, tilted slightly and knotted at the back, and he approached his job with unswerving good humour.

Cup of tea here or across the road? Candace mused to herself. She had some follow-up to do in the professional rooms she shared with Linda Gardner in the building across the street. No, I won't wait any longer here, she decided. I'll go across. I'm seeing Steve tonight anyway, so I'll hear all about the birth then.

She took a quick shower and changed, emerging to find Linda there, Steve still not back and everyone getting edgy. Then the heavy plastic swing doors that guarded the entrance to the theatre suite flapped open and there he was.

Grey-faced. Mouth like a thin chalk line.

'Steve…?' Linda began.

He just shook his head, grabbed some fresh shoe covers, a cap and a mask, all without a word. The phone on the desk in the recovery annexe rang.

'For you,' Sister Wallace said to Candace.

It was the receptionist at her rooms. 'Mrs Halligan has cancelled,' Gillian Thompson said. 'But there's a new referral on the waiting list. Shall I fit him in? He'll take longer than Mrs Halligan.'

'Remind me,' Candace said. 'Who's Mrs Halligan? And can you read me the referral letter?'

The new patient's medical problems were distracting and important enough to get her out of the hospital, and she spent a difficult afternoon in her rooms, her mind returning to Steve's pale face and his agonised silence every time she had a moment to spare. Finishing at half past four, she went straight home and left a stilted message on his machine.

'Am I still seeing you tonight? Obviously something's wrong. I'm praying it's not the baby, Steve.'

Then she cooked Bolognese sauce in case he hadn't eaten, and a chicken and rice soup because cooking the bolognese hadn't taken long enough. Foolish, probably. She didn't even know if he *liked* chicken soup.

He came up her front stairs at ten past six. Her heart jumped like a living creature inside her chest when she heard the rhythm of his footsteps on the resonant wooden treads. They went straight into each other's arms.

'What is it, Steve?'

'The baby died.'

'Oh, dear God…'

'It…he…it was a boy. He was born half an hour before I got there. Everything had been going fine, apparently. Helen didn't want a doctor, and there was no reason for her to have one. The midwife had it all under control. Then, when he was born… He had very severe Down's, and a malformed heart which just…didn't give anyone a chance. I'm thinking, you know, a hot-shot specialist and high-tech equipment but, no, realistically, no. Wouldn't have made any difference. He only lived a few minutes.' His voice cracked. 'Poor Helen and Matt.'

He buried his face in her hair as if seeking nourishment and physical support.

'They must be devastated,' she whispered.

'Her mum brought the older kids in just now, while I was there. I went back as soon as Linda's list was done. I think that helped. The kids, I mean. They took photographs of him with everyone. They had him with them for quite a while. He looked…different, you know?'

'Yes…'

'But the twins didn't notice. They kissed him and talked to him and—Oh, God!'

He broke off and covered his face with his hands. Candace held him against her heart, and they talked about it for a long time. Helen hadn't had any prenatal tests, which was why no problem had been detected.

'She's a bit of an earth mother, and she's not thirty-five for another few months. There was no huge reason for her to have tests. The odds were in her favour,' Steve said. 'She's strong. Wonderful. They'll get through this.'

'Did you eat?'

'No. I mean, breakfast, a bit, but—'

'Do you want to?'

'I feel like I should be on hand, but they told me to go. Well, Matt and Helen need some time, just the two of them. The big kids have gone home with Helen's mother. Helen will go home tomorrow. Matt has to get back to work. He's an accountant…'

'Do you want to eat, Steve?'

'Hmm?'

'Let's eat, then go for a walk or something.' She was worried about how pale he still was, and if he hadn't eaten since breakfast…

He focused at last, let go of her, let out a huge sigh. 'Yeah… Yes, OK. Yes.'

'There's home-made chicken soup, or spaghetti Bolognese, or both.'

'You cooked?'

'I thought— You know— I knew something was wrong. Wanted to…' she spread her hands '…make chicken soup for you.'

'That's nice.' He smiled at last. 'I'll have chicken soup. Not all that hungry.'

After they'd eaten and talked some more, they both needed some air. Candace wasn't planning to leave Steve alone tonight until he asked her to.

The beach, in the darkness, felt good. They both left their shoes at home and just strode along the sand to the headland, with the incoming tide teasing at their bare feet. Didn't say much. Not until they rounded the headland and went even further, to reach a tiny curve of sheltered beach.

Steve stopped and looked at it. It was deserted, lit faintly by moonlight, out of sight of any houses, with vistas stretching on down the coast, wild and beautiful.

'Do you know what?' he said, his tone grim and hungry and restless. 'I'm going to go for a swim.'

CHAPTER FOUR

STEVE began to pull his shirt over his head before Candace could even reply. The ocean scared her a little at night, despite the way the moon silvered the white foam so prettily.

'I'm coming, too.' The words broke from her lips before she could think twice about saying them.

He turned back to her and grinned. 'I hoped you would.'

He peeled down his baggy shorts, taking his underwear with them.

'Oh, like that?'

'Or we'll have to walk back wet,' he pointed out. 'And we haven't got towels.'

'True.'

'A couple of other advantages I can think of as well...'

He watched her as she slipped her sea-blue washable silk shell blouse over her head, unfastened her gauzy sarong and unclipped a black lace bra. Their clothing littered the sand, and she felt a flutter of vulnerability. About her nakedness. About his gaze.

It soon disappeared. He took her hand and pulled her towards the water. The waves were gentle tonight, like sheets of silver fabric slipping in and out. It was cold at first, but Steve wouldn't let her take things slowly.

He ran, still dragging on her hand, and she knew he needed the release of a sudden plunge so she went with him until she lost her footing at waist depth.

They jumped and dived, undulating like dolphins, floated on their backs, trod water, let the waves sweep them closer to shore and then waded out again, past their thighs. Hardly spoke at all. It must have been ten minutes or more before he took her in his arms, his face dark and serious.

'Thank you,' he said. 'I needed you tonight.'

He pulled her close, so that she could feel the sea-chilled wall of his chest against her breasts and, a moment later, his mouth on hers. Her response was as immediate and powerful as ever. As they kissed, her hands curved on his hips and slid back to his taut behind, anchoring his growing arousal against her. He groaned, dragged his mouth from hers and buried his face in her neck.

She arched her back convulsively, her body openly begging for the touch of his lips on her throat and her nipples. The ocean washed around them, contrasting the coolness of its caress with their own increasing heat.

'Can we go home?' he muttered at last.

'That far?' Her arms were wrapped around his neck now. 'The dry sand is only a few metres away. No one's here. We could find a hollow between those small dunes...'

Candace was shocked at the words the moment she'd uttered them. She had never conceived of anything so impulsive, impatient and wild.

Steve's hands trembled as his arms wrapped tightly around her once more. 'Oh, lord, Candace, I'd love to,' he breathed, warming her neck. 'I'd *love* to!'

They clung to each other as they stumbled up the sand, stopping several times to kiss, each time with greater need. The low dunes just ahead seemed expressly shaped for what they wanted.

'Wait until we're dry,' Steve said wickedly, and kept her on her feet, driving her rapidly mad with longing as he caressed her.

Finally, they sank into the cupped hand of the hollow and pushed each other over the edge of explosive release within minutes.

The sand was cool. A little scratchy, too, a little sticky.

It didn't seem to matter. They lay there, listening to the ocean, listening to the beat of each other's hearts.

'I've never done this before,' Steve said.

'No?' She lifted herself onto her elbows, her face betraying her surprise as she leaned over his body and looked into his eyes.

'Why, have you?' he asked.

'No, I haven't, but…that's different. I've only lived near this beach for ten days.'

'Implying that I've lost a lifetime of opportunity?'

'No, I'm glad it was a first for you, too, Steve,' she replied almost shyly. 'Very glad. Because it was…'

'Incredible, wasn't it?' He sounded shy about it, too.

'Mmm, incredible.'

'Totally…' He kissed her softly, caressed her a little, then dragged his hands reluctantly from her body. 'Twice, though, would be a bit too sandy.'

'Mmm, I think so.'

He sat up, grabbed her hand and began to stand. 'Let's get our— Ah, *shoot*!'

'What?' She followed his gaze towards the water, just in time to see the faint dark shape of a piece of clothing sweep up the beach on the lacy edge of a wave and come to rest on the sand. 'Oh, no! Our clothes!'

'Tide's coming in,' he agreed. He had already started down the beach. 'I can see one, two…only two things. Hell, I hope one of them's my shorts, because my keys are in the pocket!'

He broke into a run, seized the sandy, sodden garment, then lunged for another one several yards off. 'My keys are still there, and this is your skirt.'

'Surely we can find the rest if we look,' she said. 'My bra, and—'

'Hang on.' He lunged for another dark shape in the water, and pulled up a skein of seaweed.

'Well, I'm not wearing that!'

Suddenly, they were both laughing.

'This is so crazy!' he said.

'Keep looking!'

'I think you'd look pretty good in seaweed.'

'Yeah, right!' she drawled.

'Seriously, like a mermaid. Your hair is rippling all down your back. Knot that sarong at your waist like a mermaid's tail, and—'

'OK, so where does the seaweed go?'

'Across your breasts, draped like a scarf and offering tantalising glimpses of—'

'*Keep looking*, Steve!'

But it was no use. They looked, stooped down and felt around in the moving water for several more minutes, found two more bunches of seaweed but nothing made of fabric, and finally accepted that the rest of their clothing was lost to the depths of the Pacific.

'Could be worse,' Steve pointed out.

'Could be,' she agreed cautiously. 'You'll be quite decent, for a man. Easier for men!'

'And my mermaid fantasy will come true.'

'Read my lips. I am *not* wearing the seaweed!'

'Spoilsport! OK, let's see what we can do instead.'

He took the gauzy sarong, squeezed out as much water as he could and wrapped the clinging garment around her, knotting it above her breasts. His knuckles grazed Candace's cold-hardened nipples through the wet fabric as he completed the task. The garment clung like a second skin and hid little.

'Steve, I can't...!'

'No choice, sweetheart.'

'What am I going to do?'

'You mean, what am *I* going to do? Put my arms around you to keep you warm. One around your shoulders, like this, and one across your body, like this, and even if we do meet an unexpected crowd of midnight life-savers or something, no one will see a thing...'

My heaven, if Todd could see me now! she thought, as they wandered past the dark, rocky headland together and back to a deserted Taylor's Beach. Walking in a wet, near-transparent sarong along a beach late at night with my handsome lover's body shielding and warming mine, after we've pleasured each other in the dunes beneath the moonlight.

I wish he *could* see it! Oh, damn, I *wish* he could see me *right now*! came the bitter inner realisation.

All those things he accused me of in the weeks before he finally left. That I was stale. Not that our marriage was stale, but *me*. That I was stifling him, boring him, dragging him down, making him feel old, so that the whole thing became my fault and it was clear he didn't even want to *try* and save what we once had. What I *thought* we once had.

Well, I'm not 'stale'. It wasn't just me, and my fault, and if he could see this now... Oh, if he could see it...

'There, you see,' Steve said softly, holding her close in his arms just outside her front door. The wet fabric had chilled her, despite the shelter he had given her, and she shivered. 'Quite safe. No one saw a thing, and I got to hold you against me all that way.'

'Mmm, it was nice,' she agreed.

'Much better than nice.'

'Do you...uh...want to come in?' She bent down and got her key out from beneath a flower-pot.

'I won't,' he said soberly. 'I'm going to drop in at the hospital, have a talk to the night sister in Maternity and hear how Helen's been doing. Matt will be at home now, probably. He would have wanted to help Helen's mother with Jake and the girls. If Helen's still awake I might sit with her for a bit, too, if she wants some company.'

Candace nodded silently and Steve made a gesture of

helplessness. It was clear that he wished there was more he could do.

'You're close to Matt, aren't you?' she observed softly.

'To Helen and Matt,' he agreed. 'Especially since our parents died. But…you know…Aussie males.'

'I'm beginning to…'

'We're not— We don't talk to each other about the real stuff much. I was all prepared to go in there today and punch him in the arm and make some stupid joke about breaking out the cigars. With this, all I can think of is being there, giving them some of my time.'

'That's more important than words, Steve. I'd offer to come with you, only I'm sure she doesn't need any more strangers.'

She opened the front door and stepped inside.

Leaning against the doorjamb, he murmured, 'Let me kiss you one more time?'

And she couldn't help leaning forward to meet the brush of his lips. 'Tell Helen and Matt that my thoughts and prayers are with them.'

'I will.' He nodded. 'Night, Candee.'

'Night, Steve.'

In the shower a few minutes later, washing off the sand and salt, she felt exhausted and churned up inside. Happy, confused, sad about Steve's tiny nephew, physically sated yet miles from sleep.

Miles from sleep. She went to bed at eleven-thirty, was still awake at one, then finally dropped into a dark, heavy slumber a little later, only to be shattered into wakefulness again by the sound of the phone when her bedside alarm read 2.05.

Her first thought was Steve, then Helen, the baby, the beach, their missing clothes… Finally, reality crystallised into focus as she recognised her daughter's voice.

'Mom? You sound like you were *asleep*!'

'I was,' she croaked. 'It's two in the morning here.'

'No, it isn't! It's supposed to be six in the evening. Grammy and I worked it out.'

'Oh, you're at Grammy's?'

'Yeah, and she said the time in Australia was sixteen hours behind.'

Typical of Elaine West, founder of West Interiors, one of the most successful interior design firms in Massachusetts. It wouldn't occur to her that Boston could be behind anyone in anything.

'We're sixteen hours *ahead* here, honey,' Candace sighed. 'I promise you, it's two in the morning. How come you're at Grammy's on a school day?' Mom usually saved Maddy's frequent overnight visits for weekends.

'Dad said I could cut classes today. He dropped me off on the way to the hospital. Brittany's had the baby, a week early. Six o'clock this morning. Dad just called, and he wanted me to let you know. Everything went perfect, yada, yada. Weighed eight and a half pounds, and they've named him Luke.'

'You don't sound too thrilled,' Candace said cautiously.

'Oh, I will be when I see him.' Maddy's prediction was blithe. 'I'll go nuts over him. My baby brother! But I mean, like, it's kind of complicated, you know? Brittany…just kills me most of the time.'

There was an uneasy pause, then Maddy retreated quickly to safer ground. 'I'm real sorry I woke you up, Mom.'

'It doesn't matter.' Candace made a huge effort. 'Tell me how everything else is going.'

They talked for ten minutes, then Elaine came on the line to threaten, 'I'm not buying a gift for that baby! I'll send flowers and a card on your behalf—since I *know* you'll feel it's the right thing.'

'It is the right thing, Mom. Like it or not, this is Maddy's brother.'

'You're right. It is,' Elaine agreed. 'You're too generous

for your own good. I've brought you up very well.' The
contradiction between these two adjacent statements didn't
seem to trouble her.

'You know, I'm surprisingly fond of you, you strange
creature,' Candace interposed, after a short laugh.

'But I will *not* send a gift of my own!'

'No one is saying you have to, Mother.'

'No, well, in case you were planning on telling me I had
to, I'm getting in first and telling you I'm not!'

'Thank you for your support.'

'Are you handling it, darling?'

'Yes, I'm—' Candace broke off to control a jerky breath.
'I'm handling it. Something—'

She stopped again.

Something else happened today. Another baby was born,
and didn't live.

A thought…a wish, so dark and horrible that she didn't
even frame it into words, flooded her mind, and she felt
sick. She gave a strangled sound.

'I beg your pardon, Candy?'

'Nothing,' she said quickly. 'I…should go. I need to get
back to sleep.'

'I just can't believe that. You're really sure you're
ahead?'

'I'm quite sure, Mother, dear!'

But when she put down the phone, she didn't even try
to sleep again straight away. Got restlessly out of bed instead, wrapped herself in a heavy cotton kimono and went
out onto the deck, needing the air and the darkness.

Did I really think it, even for a second? That it should
have been Todd's baby that died…? That it would serve
him and Brittany right for their betrayal? Oh, lord, what's
happening to me?

She buried her face in her hands and recalled that night's
earlier thoughts about Todd with stark clarity as well.

I wanted him to know that Steve and I had made love

on the beach. I wanted to throw it in his face like a handful of sand and watch him grimace in pain and jealousy. That's *wrong*!

Maybe it was human and normal, but it was still wrong, for more reasons than she could get straight in her head right now.

It underlined her vulnerability, for a start. She wasn't over Todd, if she could fantasise about punishing him like that. Could a new relationship hasten the healing process or, more likely, would it only deepen the wound that the end of her marriage had made?

How realistic was it to believe that she wouldn't get hurt again? Steve was a young, good-looking man who might be the town's most notorious womanizer, for all she knew. Telling herself that she only wanted an affair—and meaning it—wasn't necessarily a protection.

And, finally, feeling like this about Todd was impossibly unfair to Steve.

Images of her ex-husband taunted her. Memories of how he'd held Maddy as a newborn, how he'd whispered his pride to Candace, spoiled her with presents and flowers, champagne and chocolates and jewellery. He'd been smug about his virility, and she'd found that endearing at the time.

Now, at this very moment, on the far side of the world, he was lavishing all these things—and more—on another woman and her newborn son.

It's so, so unfair to Steve. I'm using him. Like a weapon. A revenge strategy. A knife in Todd's back. Which is laughable, because Todd will never even know.

Taking Todd out of the equation, then, she was left with herself and Steve. His needs, and hers. His feelings, her vulnerability.

I can't go on with this. My motives are too ugly, and I don't like to feel them in myself. I'm scared. I'm not ready.

I'll have to tell him. I should have realised it and fought this whole thing much harder from the beginning.

Candace didn't tell Steve of her decision for some days, hanging back out of consideration for Helen and Matt, and Steve's involvement in their tragedy.

Little Robbie's funeral took place on Thursday morning, and Steve took six-year-old Jake and the three-year-old twins, Claire and Annabelle, for the rest of the day to give their grieving parents some time alone.

On Friday the family went for a picnic, while Steve and Helen's mother, Barbara, boxed away the baby clothes, the little plastic bath, the bassinet and the snowy pile of nappies.

Candace knew all this because Steve came over on Friday evening and told her, pacing her living room restlessly, his sentences jagged and broken. They discussed a couple of patients as well, over a beer and a bowl of corn chips, but when he leaned against the doorway to the deck and started talking about going somewhere for a meal and then back to his place, she knew it was time to speak.

'I can't, Steve. I—It's best not.'

'Not?' He looked up, startled, his blue eyes suddenly bright with suspicion.

'Best that we don't go on with this.'

Silence, then, 'That's a…development, let's say.'

He circled closer, bringing his gorgeous body into the range of her awareness. She was distracted by it. He must have showered before coming here, because the hair at the back of his head, just touching his neck, was still damp.

She wanted to thread her fingers through it and fluff it dry. His T-shirt was untucked a little, bunched near that hollow in the small of his back which she loved to caress.

She felt a tightness clamp around her throat, and a pull like a magnet between them. Awkwardly, she stepped sideways to stand behind the two-seater couch. It created a barrier which she needed.

What can I say? What excuses can I come up with?

The truth. That was the only fair thing. There had been such honesty in the way they had responded to each other. Honesty in every touch of skin on skin, and in the tumultuous climaxes they'd shared. She couldn't start lying to him now.

'I realised...that this was too much about my feelings towards Todd,' she said carefully. 'It was about showing him that he wasn't the only one who could launch into some wild, sizzling—'

'You *told* him about us?'

'No!' She wrung her hands. 'Of course not! The showing-him thing was all in my head. You know, "Success is the best revenge." Who said that?' she demanded distractedly.

'Ivana Trump, I think,' he drawled, his tone careful and hard to read.

She gave a short laugh. 'There! Exactly! Another wife who lost her husband to a younger woman. I can't—I'm not going to do it. Not to you. Not to myself. We both deserve better.'

'Better? I thought the other night on the beach was pretty good,' he said, deadpan.

'Yes. It was. It was fabulous. And all the way home, I kept thinking that I wished I had *photographs*. *Proof* of how good it was. So that maybe one day when I went back, I could carelessly leave them lying around on my coffee-table. Oh, nothing flagrant. Not really pictures of what happened in the dunes. But just of you and me standing on the beach in the sun, in our swimsuits, with our arms around each other, laughing.'

'I'll go home and get my camera right now...'

She ignored him. 'And Todd would find them. Or

Brittany.' She pressed her palms against her eyes. 'That's…just horrible.'

He was silent, and she blurted after a moment, 'See!'

'See what?'

'See, you're repulsed.'

'I'm not.'

'You *should* be!'

'You didn't do it, though, did you?' he pointed out. He was still watching her carefully. 'And you don't intend to do it. Not really. You just fantasised about it. There's an awful long way to travel between the two.'

'I *wanted* to do it.'

'And then you thought better of it.'

'I was using you,' she insisted.

She heard the hiss of his breath between his clenched teeth and an impatient mutter, low in his throat, that she couldn't understand. There was another beat of silence, then he said, his voice rising, 'Yes. OK. Maybe you were.'

He was still moving restlessly through the room, but his body was far more angular now. She was aware of his strength, the full force of his personality, the driving certainty of his mind.

'What can I say, Candace?' he demanded. 'That I liked being used? That you should feel free to use me that way any time you like? No! It doesn't sit well, does it? You're quite right, there. Or I could argue that there was a lot more to it than that. A hell of a lot more. There *was*, and that's what's important. And I thought you might have had the courage to see it.'

'Courage? This is taking courage! To admit the truth to you about my motivations.'

'Part of the truth, Candace. One very small part.'

'Steve—'

'Stop, OK?' His jaw was hard and square. 'Have it the way you want it. It's over. I liked it while it lasted.'

'Yes, yes, so did I,' she agreed, hardly knowing what an admission it was.

Steve's voice softened again. 'The pleasure…and the need…whatever its source…wasn't all on one side by any means, Candace.'

'No. I—I know.'

He watched her for a little longer, and she felt her skin heat up and begin to tingle. 'No hard feelings,' he drawled.

'Thank you,' she answered, while wondering if he really meant it.

'And I'm still here if you need help with anything,' he offered. It was the kind of thing a man like Steve Colton would say, she guessed. Obligation more than anything else. 'I'm on call in emergency this weekend, but—'

'Terry's back this weekend,' she cut in.

'Terry doesn't have quite the same things to offer that I do.'

The threat was blatant, seductive and unwanted, all at the same time. Memories and images of the things he had to offer came flooding into her mind. The things he had offered and that she had accepted, giving them back in double measure, finding a passion within herself that she hadn't known she possessed.

Proving something. Showing off. Lashing out at Todd. Not in control of what was happening at all.

'If you're saying that it isn't over,' she blurted, 'you're wrong.'

This time he didn't argue, just said softly, 'See you around, Dr Fletcher.' And let himself out of her house.

CHAPTER FIVE

'How were they breaking on the weekend, Dr Colton?' Joe Sheddin asked.

He was wheeling in Candace Fletcher's second patient for the morning. It was another Tuesday, and the visiting American surgeon's fourth surgical list at this hospital since she'd started work here.

'They were breaking like a dream, Joe,' Steve answered the orderly. 'But it didn't do me any good. I was on call in A and E, second weekend in a row, and we were pretty busy. Ended up sending a few patients elsewhere, including one to Sydney and two to Canberra.'

He could see Candace through the open doorway of Theatre One. She was on the phone and had a pen in her hand, hovering over some notes. Her hair was folded up onto her head in a thick pile that immediately made him want to thread his fingers through it and pull it down.

Their relationship hung at a balance point that tortured him at the moment. He knew...every nerve-ending in his body knew...that she wanted him as much as he wanted her, and soon, very soon, he planned to challenge her determination to resist his pull on her senses.

Not yet, he'd told himself for days now. Try it too soon, and you'll be back to square one. Another pointless argument about her ex-husband. She's not ready yet. But very soon...

Ending her phone call to a doctor in Harpoon Bay, Candace put down her notes and went to scrub, listening to the conversation between the nurses with half an ear.

'Oh, but I don't swim after the end of March,' Doreen was saying.

'That's crazy! It's the best time of year for swimming, Doreen, really it is!' Pat answered.

Was it Candace's imagination or was everyone getting more chatty? They had gotten used to her, and she had gotten used to the relaxed atmosphere and the friendliness of the staff. Her habit of formality, focus and silence in the OR was beginning to break down.

Or perhaps it's because of Steve...

For various reasons, setting up a regular Tuesday list in Narralee was working well for Candace. She then alternated surgery in Harpoon Bay and Shoalwater on Fridays, leaving the rest of the week clear for pre-admission and follow-up appointments, and the occasional emergency call. Since Steve's regular anaesthesia day was Tuesday, they saw each other in Theatre every week.

Saw each other? That was a very weak phrasing. Their gazes clashed and clung over their masks. Their bodies pulled together like magnets. Even the sound of his clothing shifting against his skin drew the straining attention of her ears. And every casual exchange between them was laced with a golden thread of deeper meaning.

She hadn't expected their working relationship to develop in this direction after she'd put the brakes on their affair. She'd expected tension. Brittle, hostile, unpleasant tension, and lots of it. But it wasn't like that. He had an aura of wicked and knowing awareness about him every time he looked at her or spoke to her and...yes...OK, *that* was why the mood in Theatre had changed.

She found herself chatting to the other staff to break the tautly stretched fibres of her own awareness. She didn't want him to guess how often or how strongly she found herself reliving that night on the beach. Their other nights together, too.

'Can you count for me, Eric?' Steve asked their patient. 'Backwards from a hundred, OK?'

'Right, sure.' Eric nodded. 'A hundred, ninety-nine, ninety-eight, ninety-seven...'

Seconds later, he was out. Steve checked his monitors. Pat wheeled a trolley closer to the table.

This was another gall bladder removal. The patient was forty-eight years old and in good general health. Past abdominal surgery and consequent scarring had made him an unsuitable candidate for laparoscopic surgery, so Candace was taking the traditional route, opening up the abdomen with a long incision.

It would necessitate a longer hospital stay, more painful recovery and more protracted convalescence, but in this case there was no choice.

'Come with me to the sea pool by the harbour one day, Doreen,' Pat said, as the team began its work.

They were still talking about swimming. Mr Kellett's abdomen was already stained a rusty red from its generous swabbing with antiseptic.

'I didn't know there was a sea pool,' Candace came in. 'Scalpel, Doreen. Is it natural, or...?'

She made a clean incision, working with the lines of his previous scarring as far as possible.

'No, it's a proper Olympic-sized pool,' Pat explained. 'But it gets topped up by the incoming tide twice a day, and then it partly drains when the tide goes out, so the water's always fresh.'

'Fresh salt water? Bit of a...what's the word?'

'Oxymoron?' Steve supplied.

'That's it,' Candace agreed. More scarring and adhesions were showing up now that she'd reached the abdominal cavity. He'd had a serious accident several years ago, and some impressive surgery to repair the damage. 'Gauze...no...yes, Peter, thanks, a bit closer, here.'

'Fresh,' Pat repeated firmly. 'Because there's no chlorine. It's lovely.'

'Freezing!' Doreen said, unconvinced.

'You don't notice it after a few minutes.'

They couldn't reach an agreement on the subject, and continued to bat it around as the operation proceeded uneventfully. There was a three-way split between the five locals. Steve and Pat were firm believers in year-round ocean bathing, whether in pool or surf. Doreen and Netta Robertson, assisting Steve with anaesthesia, were unimpressed with the sea pool. Assisting surgeon Peter Moody, holding a retractor in place, admitted that he could be coaxed into it in the right mood, even in July.

'But I wouldn't make a habit of it,' he said.

Candace felt that she didn't have enough data to go on.

'I haven't been here in July,' she said.

OK, here was the gall bladder, right where it should be, and she could feel through the fine latex of her gloves exactly why it needed to come out. Several stones in the common bile duct, and more in the gall bladder itself. If they stayed there, they often didn't cause major problems, but once they moved into the ducts, it was a different story. This patient had complained of pain and nausea, and had recently been treated for an infection. The organ was overdue for removal.

'I'll take you for an early morning dip in the sea pool one day soon,' Steve promised lazily. 'And you can see what you think.'

'And I'll come and watch, wrapped up in a big, thick coat,' Doreen said.

'Yeah, and I'll sneak up behind you and push you in,' he threatened.

Candace laughed…stones were coming out nicely…and felt that syrupy sense of delight that always washed through her when Steve had a smile in his voice.

'We've got his temp climbing a bit here,' he muttered. The smile had gone. 'Thirty-nine point three.'

'OK, thanks,' she replied. The duct was clear now.

'Everything else is fine.'

'I'm tying off the duct. We're making progress.' She continued to work, closing off the duct and the blood vessel at the base of the gall bladder. She wasn't particularly concerned about Steve's report. Her thought train juggled two completely different subjects at once.

Am I going to go for that swim in the sea pool with Steve? Need the cautery for this vessel... It's tempting. That's got it. No more bleeding... He makes me flutter inside, and he knows it. Blood's looking a bit dark.

'Steve, how's his oxygen reading?' she asked casually.

'Good. Normal.' Their eyes met for a fraction of a second above their masks.

Does he think he's just biding his time, or something? Oh, hell, admit it, maybe he is. Yes, he is. I feel like we're both waiting for something to happen, for it all to start up again.

The idea beckoned so powerfully that she was swamped with the sudden heat of desire.

'Temp's over forty, now. That's a steady rise,' Steve said.

'He's getting very sweaty,' Doreen commented.

'Blood pressure, too,' Steve said. 'It was 90/60 a minute or two ago, now it's jumped to 124/85.'

'Dark blood,' Candace said.

'Temp's still coming up, and his heart rate is climbing, too.'

'His hands are mottled.' Another observation from Doreen.

'You've got dantrolene here, right?' Candace demanded urgently. 'Dantrolene sodium? Of course you have!'

Pat went through the swing doors of the operating theatre at a run.

'Malignant hyperthermia?' Steve said. 'Hell, is that what's happening?'

Suddenly, the relaxed atmosphere shattered into a thousand pieces.

'Has to be,' Candace said. 'How's his temp now?'

'Over 41.'

They all knew what malignant hyperthermia was, although it was rare. Most commonly, it was an inherited trait, a susceptibility to certain anaesthetic agents which resulted in rapid temperature elevation and usually hypertonicity—rigid muscle tone—as well. It could also occur in patients with certain other medical conditions or even, as in this case, in someone who'd previously undergone general anaesthesia with no problems.

And it was fatal if not correctly treated in time.

'*Has* to be,' she repeated. 'But I'm in the middle of the procedure. I can't close up yet.'

'I'll start to reverse the anaesthesia, and you'll have time before he comes out of it fully. Just make it quick. I'll hyperventilate him.'

'What's the dose?' Pat demanded. 'I—I've never dealt with this before.'

She had a container rattling with vials. An adult male patient like this could need as much as thirty-six of them before the danger was past.

'One mil per kilo, by rapid infusion,' Candace said, not raising her eyes from the surgical field. 'But I've heard it's hard to mix.'

'I'm shaking it. That's what the instructions say. But it's not— OK, it's mixing, I think it's all right.'

'You can give ten per kilo cumulatively. Check that, because that's from memory, and if I'm wrong… Drain, Doreen.'

'Did you say drain?'

'*Yes!* Peter, your hand's in the way. I need the cautery again, Doreen. Here's the organ. Steve, are you treating the heart problem?'

'Fifteen mils per kilo over ten minutes,' he muttered. 'Yes, and I've reversed the anaesthesia so you're on a clock.'

'IV saline, surface cooling...' she coached. 'Guys, you do it. I'm not talking you through it. I've got my own problems here.'

Like another bleed, and the blood was still looking too dark, showing its lack of oxygen. She needed the cautery again. Should she have picked up on this sooner? In hindsight, that blood had been darker than usual for a while.

While I was thinking about swimming with Steve in the sea pool...

'Temp's not coming down.'

'What is it?'

'Forty-one point six. His body is rigid.'

'Urine's discoloured,' Doreen said.

'I'm closing now,' Candace could report. She'd worked fast. Too fast, probably. She would be keeping an extra close eye on this patient's recovery over the next few days.

'Good. He's lightening, but he's not out,' Steve said.

'Good,' she echoed.

'OK, and we need sodium bicarbonate, IV glucose. Look at those levels!'

It took them another hour to bring Eric Kellett safely out of the crisis, and they all felt shaky, lucky and light-headed with relief when his temperature dropped, his heart rhythm stabilised and his other signs had begun to return to normal.

He was out in Recovery now, still hooked up to monitors and under close observation. He was on two different drugs for maintenance of urine output. His electrolytes, blood gases, central venous pressure and arterial pressure all needed to be carefully watched and adjusted as necessary, as did his potassium level.

The surgical team was back in Theatre, preparing for the next—delayed—procedure in an atmosphere that was still frayed and tensed.

'We nearly lost him. We damn near lost him,' Steve repeated.

'Stop saying that!' Candace snapped. But she was more

angry at herself than at him. 'Have you ever had this happen in surgery before?'

'No,' he shook his head. 'I learned about it during my anaesthesia training but, you know, you tend to get complacent, lulled by the routine.'

'We throw away several dozen vials of this expensive drug every time it gets to its use-by date,' Pat confirmed. 'We never use it. We have it on hand, but in fifteen years here I've never had to use it. When I couldn't get it to mix, I got really scared there for a moment.' She shook her head, reliving the feeling.

'The trouble with a country hospital like this one is that anyone who's likely to have complications during surgery gets shipped out to Canberra or Sydney. And anyway, there were no indicators with this patient. I— No!' Steve shook his head again. 'Those are excuses. I should have been on top of it.'

'We *were* on top of it,' Peter Moody argued. 'We got him out of it.'

'*I* should have been onto it sooner!' Candace retorted. 'I've handled risky patients. People with Duchenne muscular dystrophy or osteogenesis imperfecta. I've done a lot more surgery than you, Steve. Than any of you. And I've seen malignant hyperthermia before. Admittedly, only once, as a resident, but I should have taken that rise in temperature more seriously as soon as you reported it.'

'There were no other symptoms at that stage,' Steve argued.

'There were. His blood was darker than usual. It should have clicked. But we should let it rest now. Let go of it. You're right, Peter, we did get him out of it. Thanks, everyone.' She took a deep breath. 'Who do we have next?'

'Look at the list. Whoever it is, they've had to wait a while!' Pat said.

Candace had to think hard before it came. Was on the point of doing as Pat had suggested and going to look at the list taped to the wall just outside Theatre, then remembered, 'That's right. Gwen Jolimont for a haemorrhoidectomy and vein-stripping. What's her status?'

'She's not down here yet.'

'She was a while ago, but they took her back up,' Doreen offered. 'They were wondering if you'd cancel.'

'I'll phone through to the ward and check for you if they know to bring her down again,' Sister Wallace said, appearing in the open doorway.

'Thanks, Robyn,' Candace said.

Slowly, the atmosphere returned to normal—on the surface at least. But there remained an element of tension which hadn't been there before. No one chatted this time. People jumped to attention every time Candace spoke. She excised the haemorrhoidal tissue and took out the tired veins with such a determination to stay focused that she actually wasn't particularly focused at all.

She'd temporarily lost her easy sense of control and coolheadedness, and realised only once the patient had been wheeled out to Recovery that she'd forgotten to give her a local. How could she have done that? It meant that Mrs Jolimont would be in a lot of pain when she woke up.

Which meant Steve and Robyn had to spend the next hour walking a tightrope with medication and monitors, because Mrs Jolimont's blood pressure was low—just 75/48 at one point—and that meant they couldn't afford to give her an adequate dose of the narcotic pain relief that she needed. Narcotics lowered blood pressure still further.

'The last patient on the list, the vasectomy, Gordon Southwell, has cancelled,' Pat reported. 'He and his wife had second thoughts.'

The news came as a relief.

As she headed for the shower, Candace heard Gwen Jolimont retching into a kidney dish.

'We'll give you something to stop it,' Sister Wallace soothed. 'I'm sorry you're having such a rotten time.'

And eventually the patient's blood pressure began to climb. In the tearoom, Steve was able to report to Candace, 'I'm increasing her pain relief now.'

'I should have given her that local. I *should* have picked up on that dark blood, Steve!'

Blindly, she gripped his forearm and felt its strength at once, as well as the ticklish, silky texture of the mist of dark hair that grew there.

'Steady on,' he said quietly, his head close to hers. 'Why the self-accusation? Those were my monitors. I should have been interpreting the data better, not just reporting it back to you. I mean, hell, we could *all* talk about what we should have done. Pat was panicking, Peter just stood back at first. The fact is, the patient didn't have any history to suggest an increased susceptibility to what is, as we've agreed, a very rare condition. He'd been under general anaesthesia before with no problem. We handled it, and he survived.'

'Too close for comfort.'

'Agreed. But let's put it behind us. Let go of it. You were the one who said it, before Gwen's surgery.'

'Yes, and then I forgot to give her a local because I hadn't put it behind me at all!'

'Let it go!'

Watching her face, Steve saw her tight little nod, and felt the way she was still clinging to his arm. Her touch stoked a glowing fire of satisfaction inside him and he twisted his hand to let his fingers trail along the sensitive skin of her inner arm. Her quick indrawn breath told him once more what he had been sure of all along. So did the way she unconsciously leaned closer, the way her limbs seemed to soften.

It wasn't finished. Whatever she had said to him ten days ago about her ex-husband, whatever the effect of his own angry words, it wasn't finished between them. He'd known it all along, and suddenly he wasn't prepared to bide his time any longer. She must know it, too. She *did* know it, just as he'd meant her to. They had both been holding their breath, waiting for the right moment, and it had come.

'I'll come round at about six,' he told her quietly and confidently. 'Let's go out. There's a nice seafood place on the riverfront. We can talk.'

'About what?'

'Whatever you like.'

He hadn't given her a choice, but he knew Candace wasn't the kind of woman to respond to an order if she didn't want to. Would she choose to be waiting for him tonight? Watching the dark dilation of her pupils and feeling the slight flutter and jerk of her breathing, he felt quite sure that she would be.

Candace *was* waiting.

Well, she wasn't going to absent herself from her own home just because of his threatened arrival! She hadn't changed her clothes, and still wore the loose ecru trousers and matching blouse in a linen-look fabric which she'd changed into after surgery. She was prepared to talk, and that was all. They could talk just as easily here as they could, dressed up to the nines, at an expensive restaurant. *More* easily, in fact.

Steve, however, was dressed for dinner. She hadn't seen him look this sophisticated before, hadn't known that he would carry the more formal look with such relaxed grace. Her reaction to him at her door disturbed her, and she knew that this was going to be harder than she'd been prepared for.

He wore a simple white T-shirt that closely hugged the contours of his chest and a blue-grey suit whose baggy jacket and pants created an impression of deceptive ease in the way he held his body.

'Come in,' she said. 'Tea, or—?'

'Tea?' he snorted. 'You can do better than that, Candace.'

'Better…in what way?'

'A better job of telling me to get lost. If you want me to get lost, show me the door. Don't make some insipid offer of tea that you hope will put me off. Come on, you're braver than that!'

'Am I?'

'Brave enough to make love to me on an open beach. Brave enough to tell me afterwards exactly what was going on…or what you thought was going on…inside your soul when it happened.'

'We've been through this.'

She closed her eyes, felt him closing in on her and opened them again quickly. She walked towards the kitchen in search of iced water or juice. Glasses in their hands would offer at least some faint form of protection.

'I've told you,' she said with her back to him, 'that was all about—'

'It *wasn't* all about Todd!' he cut in angrily, following her. 'I told you that at the time. I've been thinking about it since, and it doesn't make sense. Nothing in the way we made love, the way we responded to each other's bodies so strongly, that night and the other nights, was about proving something to your ex-husband, Candace, and after ten days of cooling off, you can admit it, I think!'

'Admit it to you?'

'Admit it to yourself. You wanted us to become lovers. Every cell in your body wanted it. And you got your wish, and then you back-pedalled as fast as you could. Because you were scared. Not because you were using me. Not because you were proving something. Isn't that the truth?'

Candace was silent.

The truth. She'd told Steve what she'd believed to be the truth ten days ago—that she'd been proving a foolish point to Todd, which her ex-husband would never even know about, and that she'd been coolly using Steve to do it.

Having said that, and having heard Steve's response,

watched him leave her life—or leave her *personal* life, anyway—without more than a token protest, she'd expected
the whole thing to subside into a feeling of uncomfortable
regret. Perhaps even revulsion.

She'd been on the receiving end of confidences from
single female friends more than once. She knew the pattern.
'We slept together twice,' they would say in an agony of
regret, 'and now I can't understand what I ever saw in him.
Why didn't I stop and think before I leapt into bed? There's
no spark at all.'

But she didn't feel anything like that about Steve. Instead, she was all too aware of how easy it would be to let
him back into her life, and into her bed.

And he knew it.

She was still fiddling at the sink, trying to get ice cubes
out of the tray from the freezer, when he came up behind
her, slid his arms around her, just beneath her breasts, and
touched his lips to her neck.

'I like it when you have your hair pleated up like this,'
he said. 'Makes it much easier to kiss you here. And then,
later on, it's so nice to pull down…'

This was the moment to say no, to pull away, to show
him the door, but she didn't do it. Instead, she gave a ragged sigh, turned around, leaned against him and waited for
the onslaught of his mouth.

'You knew this would happen,' she murmured. 'You
knew it…'

'Didn't you?' His lips were soft and slow, and his question was more kiss than language.

'No. I thought… I'd planned to… I tried to…' The
words trailed off as her head fell back, her mouth drowning
beneath his. 'Yes,' she admitted finally, pressing her forehead against his. 'I knew it.'

He kissed her again, then dragged his lips away and
laughed. 'I wonder if you know how great it is that you
can't resist this. The sight of you melting, of the same fire

building in you that's building in me… It's so good to watch, Candace. So good.'

'Stop talking. Don't make me think too much…'

They didn't get to the restaurant until eight o'clock, and didn't leave it until it closed. He stayed all night at her place, and once again they both had to tackle appointment hours on empty stomachs. On the weekend, he took her swimming in the sea pool and for a hike in the bush, and as the days went by they added more activities to the repertoire.

'It all comes under the definition of things we do to fill in time until it's decently permissible to take each other off to bed again,' Steve teased.

She sighed, then smiled. 'Can't argue, can I?'

They talked on the phone about patients a little more than was strictly necessary. Eric Kellett had had no subsequent after-shocks of malignant hyperthermia and was recovering well from his surgery. As planned, Candace was particularly careful to check the site of his operation, but no complications developed. Steve had taken out Andrea Johnson's stitches in his surgery. Gwen Jolimont was pleased with the results of her two concurrent procedures after her difficult few hours in Recovery.

They ate take-out meals and watched movies, walked along the beach at night, watching the waves. Talked about trivial things, and important things. Brought a blanket to the beach at night sometimes, made love in the secret darkness and were careful about where they left their clothes.

They were careful about other things, too.

Firstly, contraception. Only once had this particular caution broken down—the first night they'd found their special hollow in the dunes. Candace received her body's evidence that there were no unintended consequences to that piece of carelessness and electric spontaneity, but she hadn't been particularly worried in any case, as the timing had been wrong.

They were, if anything, even more careful about keeping their affair a secret from any of the staff at the hospital. Candace's focus and economy with conversation in surgery camouflaged their almost unnatural distance when they met at the hospital. The fact that Steve lived just five doors away made concealment easier, too. And there was a reason why they took most of their walks under the cover of darkness.

No one made any comments which suggested they'd guessed. And there was an element of luck as well. This was a small community. There were times they could have run into someone they knew on a hiking trail or in a restaurant. But they were lucky, and they didn't.

About four weeks after the night when they'd resumed their affair—the day of Eric Kellett's surgery—Candace received the first inkling that their caution in one of those two crucial areas hadn't been enough.

Her period was over a week late. Her breasts were swollen and tender. The smell of tomato ketchup made her nauseous, as did the smells of her bathroom cleaner, her moisturiser, the fuel she put in her car and about a dozen other everyday things.

It was impossible, surely. Steve had been very responsible in that area.

I'm imagining this, she decided. I have to be.

But those dates weren't her imagination, and all at once her memory of how she'd felt for the first few months of carrying Maddy, nearly sixteen years ago, was strikingly vivid.

She spent two more days talking herself out of it, refreshing her memory as to the statistical reliability of Steve's protection and coming up with as many rationalisations as she could. She had sensible theories like the fact that this was a new environment, and that she was still emerging from the emotional upheaval of the past couple

of years. She also had ridiculous theories like the difference
in the drinking water and the phases of the moon.

That was why her period was late. That was why she
was feeling so queasy. It wasn't the obvious reason at all.

Yeah, right...

Finally, one Sunday morning, she drove an hour and a
half north on the highway to a town with a pharmacy which
had extended hours. She wanted one where there was no
danger of being recognised at the counter as she paid for a
pregnancy testing kit.

I won't do the test until I get home, she decided.

Ten minutes later, she screeched to a halt beside a small
park, locked herself into one of the cubicles in the surprisingly clean and airy public toilet and began to fiddle about
with the plastic testing wand. The result only took a minute
or two to appear in the little window.

And there was no doubt. It was positive.

'Hey, nice surprise,' Steve said when he found Candace at
his door just after lunch. 'I was heading for the beach. Want
to come?'

'Um, no.'

'No?'

He stopped in the act of slinging his towel around his
neck. The surf was dead flat today, so he wasn't bothering
with wetsuit or board. Looked like he might not even be
getting a swim.

Studying her face more closely, he noted her high colour,
her distracted manner and the firm press of her lips. Felt a
little prickle of apprehension. She wasn't going to have
another try at ending this, was she? He felt selfish about it.

Don't rock the boat, he wanted to say. Don't keep analysing it and asking questions. You said you wanted an
affair. And it's working as it is, isn't it?

Better than 'working'. Lord, he was loving his discovery
of this woman!

He loved the vein of wickedness in her newly unleashed sensuality. A couple of weeks ago, she'd eaten a dessert of fresh raspberries and whipped cream off his chest, making the action of her tongue deliberately erotic until they'd both collapsed in laughter.

He loved the way she worked with such efficiency and focus, loved the things that tickled her sense of humour, loved the impression she sometimes unconsciously gave that she was shedding an old, painful skin now that she was here in Australia, and that she was ready to tackle life in new ways.

He was aware, though, of just how new their connection was. Less than two months. Intuition and chemistry aside, human beings were complex, and there were a lot of things he didn't know about her yet. Had they spent too much time in bed? There was still a strong possibility that this affair could drift into very dangerous waters...

'Uh…Steve, we have something to discuss,' she began.

'*Again?*' The word slipped out before he thought, and he saw her flinch.

'No, this is something new,' she said steadily, then gave a short laugh. '*Extremely* new.'

'Along the same lines of "new" as the raspberries and cream, I hope.'

'Don't.' She took a deep breath. 'Lord, I just have to *say* it, don't I? Steve, I'm pregnant.'

Whump!

That was the sound of his backside hitting the couch with force. He suddenly knew what the expression 'legs turned to jelly' meant, in a way he never had before. Beyond the beating of blood in his head, he had wit enough to understand at once that his first reaction to this news was critical. Still, the only thing he could come up with at first was, 'That's…a surprise.'

'I know.' She nodded. 'I mean, it isn't really. It happens.

We've, um, been doing our best. But, yes, it's a surprise.'
She flushed, then smiled, and that gave him his first clue.

She's thrilled.

He took a deep breath. The frog in his throat doubled in size. 'Congratulations,' he managed, and she beamed.

Then she frowned, pressed her palms to her cheeks and gabbled, 'It's crazy to be happy about it. But I am. I'm sorry, it's— I'm just telling you. I'm not asking for anything. Haven't worked out…well, *anything*. Not yet.'

'What does it mean for us?' he said, suspecting it was probably one of the questions she wanted to ask him herself.

She spread her hands, just as Steve might have done. 'Don't know.'

'I'm not going to turn my back on you,' he promised.

It was vague, he felt, but sincere. God, what *did* you promise? Nothing that might turn out, later, to be unfair. Nothing that she might interpret wrongly, or magnify too much. As he'd thought before, in a slightly different context, he wasn't yet fully certain of the job description here.

'I didn't think you would,' she said.

There was a light shining in her eyes. It panicked him considerably.

'But I'm not going to marry you either,' he said, too abruptly. 'Not out of the blue. It wouldn't be fair. Or sensible.'

Her chin came up. 'I'm not asking you to marry me, Steve. I hadn't expected this sort of a connection between us either. I'm here for a year. This was—'

'A fling, right?' The word didn't taste right. It reminded him of Agnetha, and he didn't like it. He'd stopped comparing Candace with Agnetha a long time ago. 'I mean—'

'No, it's a good word,' she said. 'Let's not… Let's keep this honest. That's been working for us, hasn't it?'

'Yeah, it has.'

'This is going to take some working out.'

'And yet you're thrilled,' he pointed out softly. 'Don't try and deny it, because it's shining like a hundred-watt globe in your face, Candace. Why are you thrilled?'

She laughed. 'Because…'

Then she burst into tears.

His instinct was to go to her, and he did. Privately, though, his panic level was climbing. Just how much of this sort of thing were they both in for? They'd known each other for less than two months They didn't have the foundation for this. Mood swings and nausea, weight gain, aching legs…and *gossip*, for heaven's sake, because eventually people would have to know…

And at the end of all that, a baby. A human being, made from the two of them. Candace's due date would come just a month or two before she was due to return home. Unless she cut short her time here and went back to Boston early. Would he want that? He didn't know.

Oh, yes, and he was panicked all right. He gritted his teeth and willed it not to show, held her, chafed her back lightly with his palms and waited. She controlled herself quickly and apologised. 'Oops! Where did that come from?'

'It's fine,' he said.

'Ah, no, you were terrified.' She smiled, slid out of his arms, wagged a finger at him, grabbed a tissue from the end table and dried her eyes and nose. 'Nine months of hormones ahead. Who wouldn't be terrified?'

'Well…'

'Look, it's simple.'

'Tell me, then.' He tried not to make it sound too desperate. 'I need to hear something simple.'

'I loved having Maddy,' she said. 'I always wanted another baby. My ex-husband convinced me we shouldn't. Now I'm having one, and against all logic—I'm very capable of *recognizing* logical behaviour, Steve, even if I can't produce it right now—I'm thrilled. I'm going to live inside that feeling for a little while, then start making sensible plans when the dust has settled.'

When will that be? he wondered inwardly. I've got dust to settle, too.

'Wanted to tell you straight away,' she went on, 'because—well, because I believe it's your right to know.'

His right to know.

Just that? Or could he claim more than that?

His right to be involved.

At the moment, he sensed, neither of them knew.

CHAPTER SIX

'I CAN'T stand it, Mom. Can you talk to Dad and ask if I can stay with Grammy until school's out? Then I'm going to come and have summer vacation with you,' Maddy announced on the phone, on a Monday morning near the end of May, without pausing for breath.

Candace, in contrast, had to pause for quite a large, long, careful breath before she replied. Almost eight and a half weeks pregnant now, she was feeling very queasy for much of the time.

'Till school's out,' she repeated. 'That's, what, about two weeks from now?'

'Tell Dad you're missing me.'

'It's true. I'm missing you a lot. I knew I would.'

'And you want me there. Tell him to get me a ticket. Brittany's driving me nuts, and the baby cries all the time.'

'I expect that drives *her* nuts.'

'He's adorable when he's not crying. Like, the three minutes per day when he's not crying! She has this pile of baby-care books about six feet high beside her bed, and it's all she ever talks about. How to get him to not cry. I try not to be home. I practically live at Alicia's or Grammy's. In fact, if I could live at Grammy's until you get back next March, it just *might* stop me from going totally insane. I think Brittany's over-feeding him.'

'How would you know that, honey?'

'He's getting fat! She gives him, like, twelve bottles a day. And *that* I know because for some reason it's my job to wash and sterilise them. Figure that out! Suddenly, it's tied to my allowance. Which, admittedly, has been doubled,' she drawled, and Candace had to laugh.

She wanted to say, I love you, but knew the reception these words would receive. Instead, she kept listening.

'And we never eat properly. Dad picks up take-out practically every night. You know, I wouldn't have thought I could get sick of junk food but I'm here to tell you, it's happened. You should be so pleased with me! I want salad, and that casserole you make...'

'OK, enough! I'd love it if you came out.' Which was close to I love you but not quite as bad.

'Then Grammy will come a couple of weeks later, and we'll go home together, because I have to be back for drama camp,' Maddy said happily, betraying the fact that the thing was a done deal before she even picked up the phone.

Both of them! Candace thought. An attack on two fronts. And Elaine and Maddy had always been as thick as thieves.

Her stomach dropped.

'So when exactly will that be, honey?'

'About the end of July. Grammy can only take two weeks.'

I'll be nearly four months pregnant by then, and if this one's the same as Maddy, I'll already be starting to show, to anyone who takes a close look. Mom might easily guess. And a few weeks after that, everyone will.

Candace hadn't faced this inevitable development yet. Hadn't faced a lot of things. Was concentrating, to a large extent, on simply getting through the days without her condition becoming obvious to her colleagues immediately. She felt horribly ill, especially if she ate the wrong foods at the wrong times or if she didn't get enough rest—and that meant at least ten hours' sleep out of every twenty-four.

Her slower work pace, here in Australia, was the only thing that made it possible to keep her pregnancy a secret. She slept late whenever she could, went to bed early, took a nap in the middle of the day at least twice a week, and lived on a steady intake of finger foods like crackers and grapes and toast.

Being pregnant at almost thirty-nine was very different to being pregnant at twenty-two, she found.

It wasn't just her increased fatigue and nausea. There was also the question of prenatal testing. It hadn't been an issue with Maddy. Back then, she'd had every expectation of giving birth to a healthy baby, and she hadn't been disappointed. This time, a decision had to be made, and it was one of many things that she and Steve hadn't talked about.

They were still seeing each other. Nothing had yet given them a reason to end their affair. This had to count as a plus. It was like walking on eggshells, most of the time, however. Not wanting to drag him down, Candace did her best to pretend, when they were together, that she wasn't pregnant at all. She got a lot of practice at this during surgery and office hours, so she was getting rather good at it.

Steve, on the other hand, treated her as if she were made of tissue paper. He probably wouldn't have made love to her at all if she hadn't seduced him every time. When she did, he left her in no doubt that he appreciated the effort, and this began to form a nourishing centre to their fresh young relationship.

Her body was exquisitely sensitive to his touch at the moment, and he was so determined to be gentle that time seemed to stretch and hours would go by...

It couldn't continue this way. They needed to do more than just laze about together.

'I'm starting to know this look,' Steve said to her, greeting her at his front door on the evening of the day that Maddy had called. He tilted his head a little as he studied her. 'Come in, all three of you.'

'All three?'

She frowned as she eased past him into the welcoming, warmly lit interior of his living room. She liked his place. It was relaxed yet cosy, decorated in a simpler and more masculine version of her own rented house nearby. The blues he'd used were a little darker, like the ocean in a storm, and they were offset by cool cream instead of sunny yellow. She was beginning to feel at home here. Too much so, maybe.

'Yes,' he answered her. 'All three. You, the baby and that packet of chips you're hugging. It's almost as big as you are.'

'I was hungry, and I knew if I didn't—'

'Bring the chips and start munching on them at once, you'd throw up. I know. Here, let me help,' he said, taking the packet from its cradled position in her arms and ripping it apart at the top.

He handed the opened packet back to her, then touched her face gently and slid his fingers back over her loosened hair. 'Have you come for dinner?' he asked.

'I've started on dinner already,' she said, crunching down on a huge curvy chip. The salt was heaven, and her stomach lay down obediently. It was a pity that the effect wouldn't last.

'I haven't,' he said. 'Started cooking, that is. So what do you feel like?'

'Nothing.'

'Pasta?'

'Fine. But it can wait.'

He took her in his arms and rocked her to and fro, shifting his weight easily from side to side. 'Poor thing. Sit down, eat your chips, and tell me about that look.'

'The…?'

'The look on your face. A number three, if I'm reading it right. It's the one that says we've got something to talk about.'

'Right. Gosh! You've got a numbering system for my expressions!'

'Sit!'

Gently, he pushed her down onto the couch and sat beside her. There was something immensely comforting about the warm press of his thigh along hers.

Or perhaps it was the chips.

Taking another one, she leaned her head into his shoulder, felt his arm drop around her and decided, no, it isn't either of those things. It's the fact that he can read my expressions. It's nice.

Aloud, she said, 'We need to make a decision about prenatal testing, Steve. A chorionic biopsy is ideally done at about eleven weeks, and I'm already eight and a half.'

'I know,' he said quietly. 'I was going to give you three more days and then bring up the subject myself.'

'Why three more days? You didn't need to wait. You could have brought it up whenever you wanted. Has it been on your mind?'

'On my mind? What do you think?' His voice rose abruptly, and he slid away from her, sprang to his feet and began to pace the room. 'Of course it has, after what happened to Matt and Helen! Good grief, Candace!'

She gasped and stumbled instinctively to stand as well, then had to stop and clutch her stomach, gripped by nausea.

'Oh, hell, I'm sorry,' she muttered through clenched teeth. Her lips were tight and dry, and the nausea was threatening to take over completely. It was an effort to look across at him. 'I'm so sorry. I didn't even think about that…'

This was one of the problems with a secret affair. She hadn't actually met Steve's brother and his wife. It was more than two months since Matt and Helen had lost their baby at birth, and Candace had been feeling so ill and exhausted these past few weeks, with such a struggle to pretend that everything was normal, she hadn't considered the way the issue must resonate for him.

It had been thoughtless of her. She was about to apologise again, but he got in first.

'No, I'm sorry. I shouldn't have yelled at you.'

'No, I want you to yell at me.' She gave a short, wry laugh. 'I deserved it. And I'm not that fragile. You can yell at me whenever you like.'

'Let's forget it. I know you've had…other things to think about. Tell me what you want to do about prenatal testing.'

He pulled an upright chair out from the table in the dining nook and sat in it with his legs straddling the seat and his forearm resting along the back. He studied her gravely, and some strands of his glinting mid-brown hair fell across his forehead.

'It's your decision, too.' She subsided to the couch again, still needing to move cautiously to keep her stomach under control.

He was silent, then said carefully, 'Not necessarily. Your home is in America, Candace. We can't ignore that. Realistically, this child isn't going to be nearly such a huge presence in my life as it is in yours, no matter what we decide about access and that sort of thing. We've made no commitment to each other. We've agreed on that. I can't force my feelings or my beliefs on you.'

'No,' she agreed. 'But I still want to know what they are.'

He nodded. 'Fair enough.' Then he spoke slowly. 'I guess…I'd feel on surer ground if we knew that there was nothing to worry about. The risk of having a Down's baby at your age is about one in 135. People bet on those odds all the time when it's something they want. A problem with the baby is something we don't want.'

Candace nodded, then thought for a minute, aware of him watching her. His strong chin dug into his forearm and his eyes were narrowed and serious. For a man who had such a deep vein of physicality to his make-up—a man who was such an ideal candidate for a fling—Steve Colton had a considerable depth of intellect and sensitivity as well, she was starting to realise.

'If Helen and Matt had had the test done,' she said finally, carefully, 'what would their decision have been?'

'I don't know,' he answered simply. 'I don't know what my decision would be either. Maybe it'd have to happen, I'd have to be *told*, yes, the test has come back showing that the baby has Down's—or one of the other trisomies, which are less likely but can be even more severe in their effects—before I could be certain of what I'd want to do.'

She sat up higher and looked at him. 'Have you been reading my mind or something?'

'Yes, I get a bulletin over the internet every morning,' he teased. 'No, why?'

'I—I think that's what I was going to say, only I hadn't managed to even work it out yet. I want the test, Steve, even if it's only in order to know more about what lies ahead.'

Without a word, he came to the couch, sat beside her and pulled her close. He pressed his forehead against hers, and they sat like that for several minutes. Finally, he kissed her. It was sweet and slow, tender but without erotic demand. Just the kiss she needed.

'Come and help me make pasta,' he said finally. 'What sort of sauce do you feel like?'

'From a jar?'

'Doesn't have to be. I'm very flexible. What do you *feel* like?' he asked again.

She closed her eyes to think, trying hard to get enthusiastic about food in any form. 'Um, something simple and salty. No tomato. No meat. Or I think I'd—'

'I know what you'd do, Candee.'

'Sorry.' She crunched quickly on another chip.

'Leave it to me. I'll invent something with a heavy emphasis on salt.'

It was on the table in fifteen minutes, just a tangle of fettucini coated in bits of olive and garlic, anchovy, fresh parsley and cheese. She would have enjoyed it immensely if anything at all had tasted right at the moment.

'So I've been thinking,' he said as they ate. 'We should go to Sydney for the test.'

'That far?'

'Not very many people choose a chorionic biopsy around here. People don't have testing done at all, or they go for amniocentesis, which is done at around fifteen weeks.'

'I don't want to wait that long.'

'I agree. But if you go with CVS, you need an obstetrician who's experienced with the procedure, and that means Sydney or Canberra. There's the added bonus of privacy,' he went on, after a short pause.

She didn't argue the point. She did consider protesting his assumption that secrecy remained so important. They'd agreed on that two and a half months ago, but maybe it was time this changed.

No. Not yet. Secrecy *was* important still, she revised after a few moments' thought.

She didn't want the pressure of colleagues or friends or, heaven help her, Mom or Maddy asking about their plans. The future stretched a little further ahead in her mind now than it had done an hour ago. It went as far as the chorionic biopsy and the result, which would come around three weeks later once the tissue from the placenta had been cultured.

Beyond that, her life was a fog.

'We can finesse this a bit,' Steve was saying. 'I can write you the referral letter myself. I'd go with Ian Strickland in Sydney. He's very good. We'll make it a Friday, if possible, and stay overnight. Maybe the whole weekend.'

'You keep saying *we*,' she accused lightly.

'Yes.' He looked at her, his blue gaze very direct across the table. 'Of course I'm saying *we*. You don't think I'd let you go through it alone, do you?'

She could have cried at that point. Managed not to.

'Maddy's coming,' she blurted suddenly instead. 'My daughter.'

Why had she added those last words? Of course he knew who Maddy was!

'When?'

'In two or three weeks. She called this morning to see if it was OK, but really she'd already made up her mind, with my mother to back her up. They're natural allies, those two.'

'And *is* it OK?'

'Yes, it's great.' She laughed, and added, 'It's wonderful, and I haven't got the remotest idea how I'm going to handle it.'

'The very first thing you should do is phone her and make sure she doesn't plan an itinerary that clashes with the optimum timing of the test,' he said. 'As to the rest, worry about it later.'

'I'm getting good at worrying about things later. Better than I want to be.' She looked down at her half-eaten plate of pasta, and this time the fight against tears was harder to win.

The landscape on the Saturday morning drive up to Sydney hadn't changed much in three months.

Although it was early winter now, native Australian trees didn't lose their leaves, and the weather wasn't cold enough to make the grass turn brown. If anything, the late autumn rains had made the landscape greener than before. The sky was still blue, and there was even some vegetation that was still in flower.

Curled in the passenger seat of Steve's car with a pillow behind one shoulder and a mohair blanket over her knees, Candace felt dreamy and content as the pretty vistas unfolded. She was exactly at the eleven-week mark now, had begun to feel—cautiously—a little less nauseous, and was looking forward to this weekend away.

Steve had booked the two of them into a bed-and-breakfast place at Cremorne Point on Sydney Harbour's northern shore, and tonight they were going to dinner near the Opera House, followed by a big, splashy musical. Tomorrow they would explore the Harbour and the city, on Monday she was scheduled for the chorionic biopsy with Dr Strickland, and on Tuesday morning Maddy would arrive.

'Dropping off to sleep?' Steve asked as they swept around a wide curve of highway and saw the ocean and a string of coastal settlements in the distance.

'Not really,' she said. 'Sleepy, but the view is too pretty to waste it by closing my eyes.'

'Nice for some,' he teased. 'I have to watch the road.'

'We can swap. You've trusted me at the wheel of your car before.'

'We're not swapping.'

He was still treating her like a fragile porcelain figurine, and since this was how she felt most of the time, she found it easy to give in to it and let him do it.

Maybe that's why I don't want to sleep, she decided. This weekend might be precious—a precious memory—and I don't want to lose any of it...

An hour later, they stopped at a beachside park in one of Sydney's southern suburbs on Botany Bay. Steve had packed a picnic lunch of thick, chewy ham and salad sandwiches on French bread, as well as tea and some buttered buns with lurid frosting of a very thick and sticky pink.

'No, thanks!' Candace said with a shudder, when he offered her one.

'May I have yours, too, then?'

'Honestly, I've tasted these! If you said you needed them as a substitute for rubber cement, maybe, but to *eat*? *Two* of them?'

He grinned. 'Can't call yourself an Australian if you don't like a nice wad of sticky bun on occasion.'

'I *don't* call myself an Australian,' she pointed out.

He shrugged. 'True.'

A huge Qantas 747 jet lumbered down the airport runway, which jutted into Botany Bay less than two kilometres from where they sat at a picnic bench beneath bright green Norfolk pines. It gathered speed, engines screaming, and finally heaved itself off the ground, to rise steeply over the shallow water of the bay and wheel to the north-west, heading across the Pacific.

Where was it going? Home, maybe. To America, where Maddy's bedroom in Boston was probably a mess of half-packed suitcases right at this moment.

This time in two days, she'll be on the plane. This time in three days, she'll be here...

'You can't wait, can you?' Steve said. He had followed her yearning gaze as she tracked the plane.

'Reading my mind again?' she retorted.

'Reading your face.'

'What number look is this?'

'Number two,' he answered in the blink of an eye. 'You think about her a lot, don't you?'

'Of course!'

'Why didn't you bring her with you?'

Because she would have drastically interfered with the launch of my fling with you.

Something told her very firmly not to follow this thought any further. It led into a wilderness of conjecture that was pointless to explore.

'Maddy wanted to stay at home,' she said instead. 'Australia was a place in a movie, as far as she was concerned. Snakes and sharks, little wooden shacks in the middle of a treeless desert and men in crocodile-skin hats.'

'Great!' He laughed. 'Remind me to hunt up my crocodile skin hat as soon as we get back.'

'It wasn't a place to hang out with friends and start dating cute boys and get elected class president. I didn't push it. I *wanted* to. But it wouldn't have been fair. And she's always been pretty independent. Going off to summer camp without a backward glance from when she was eight. Even when she says she's missing me, she's somehow speaking from a position of strength. No, this was…something I needed for me. Getting away like this. For her, too, I guess. I'll be a better mother when I get back.' A self-mocking laugh escaped her lips. 'Not so bitter and twisted—'

She stopped abruptly.

A *better* mother? A completely different mother. A single mother with a newborn baby. It didn't seem real. She couldn't picture it at all. So much so that she'd actually forgotten for a moment, while talking about Maddy, that she was pregnant. With this man's child.

Steve was watching her, his body lazy, his mouth a little crooked and his eyes hard to read.

'OK, what number look is this?' she challenged him, unnerved by his body language and by the movement of her own thoughts.

'Don't know,' he answered casually. 'Haven't seen this one before. Ready to get going?'

'Yes, because I think, actually, when we get to our bed-and-breakfast, I'll take a nap.'

Suddenly she felt exhausted, and she'd had enough of the planes. The sight of them taking off and landing was dramatic and beautiful in this setting, but these big jumbo jets were a constant reminder that the world was a big place. Too big for a woman who was carrying a child with a heritage split in two by the vastness of the Pacific Ocean.

She wasn't sorry when they drove off, went through a tunnel on the highway that actually ran beneath the airport runway and left the planes behind.

Their harbourside bed-and-breakfast turned out to be delightful. Antique furnishings, complimentary drinks and snacks, fluffy towels, fragrant linens and gorgeous water views.

'It'll just be a little nap,' Candace promised when they'd unpacked.

'No worries. I'll go for a walk, explore the Point and watch the ferries going past.'

'Half an hour.'

But she slept for two, and only awoke when he slid into bed beside her, without clothes. 'Couldn't keep away any longer,' he muttered. 'Is that all right?'

'You know it is. It always is.'

'I've been watching you for ten minutes, and you looked so good...'

She turned into his arms and kissed his mouth softly, still unsettled about those planes and that vast ocean. She wanted to drug herself with his love-making and just forget everything else.

He obliged with delicious tenderness, then they showered together and his slippery, soapy hands on her body—'All my favourite places, your hips, your stomach, your breasts...they feel even better these days...you're beginning to ripen, Candace'—seemed to promise that nothing else mattered but this, and now, and the two of them.

They had dinner overlooking the Opera House and the ferry terminal at Circular Quay, then saw the show they had tickets for. It was light and sophisticated and very well done. The next morning, they breakfasted on a glassed-in terrace at their B and B, then caught the ferry across to Circular Quay and back out to Manly, passing huge cargo ships as well as a gleaming white cruise liner and dozens of colourful sailboats.

The ferry crossed the gap between the harbour heads, rocking more in the rougher water, and they caught glimpses of the spectacular houses that fronted the Harbour, as well as wilder sections of rock and vegetation on the northern shore. At Manly they ate Lebanese falafel rolls and ice cream for lunch.

In the afternoon, they explored the steps around the Opera House and the historic Rocks area, with its lingering flavour of the First Fleet's settlement over two hundred years earlier. That evening, they ate in Chinatown, then walked through Darling Harbour and caught a water taxi back to Cremorne Point. It zipped beneath the dark, awe-inspiring metal fretwork of the Harbour Bridge and skirted Kirribilli Point, where the two historic residences of Admiralty House and Kirribilli House sat grandly amidst their lush gardens.

'It has to be the most beautiful harbour in the world,' Candace said, as they alighted from the water taxi at Cremorne Wharf and walked beneath huge Moreton Bay fig trees back to their B and B.

'Sydneysiders certainly think so,' Steve said.

'You think it has some competition?'

'Hong Kong is pretty nice. Vancouver. New York.'

'I didn't realise you'd travelled so much.'

'I like travelling. I'd like to get to the US again pretty soon.'

For a moment, with the mention of her native soil, they both teetered on the edge of pulling this casual conversation in a more important direction. Candace could feel it. She was holding her breath, waiting. The sense of expectancy, the sense that they were both thinking about it, trying to find the right questions, the right words, was almost unbearable.

But then they reached the front door of the B and B, which was locked at this time of night. They couldn't remember which of them had the key, and the moment passed.

At ten the next morning, Candace had her chorionic biopsy at Royal North Shore Hospital.

She hadn't spent much time thinking about the process of the test itself. Obstetrics wasn't her area, and she vaguely thought that it involved going through the opening of the cervix in order to extract a tissue sample from the foetal side of the placenta. She did know that it would be done with the aid of an ultrasound scan, and had to drink and hold an agonising amount of fluid in order to create a clear image. The ultrasound waves bounced better off a full bladder.

Fortunately, Dr Strickland was on time and she was soon lying on the table in the darkened room, next to the sophisticated scanning equipment. The obstetrician ran through some information which both Candace and Steve already understood—that the test could detect any one of hundreds of chromosomal abnormalities, most of them extremely rare.

'Down's syndrome is the real concern,' Dr Strickland explained. 'And at your age...' he checked her notes briefly '...the risk of you miscarrying as a result of this procedure is approximately the same as your risk of carrying a Down's baby. Do you want to consider that risk a little further before you decide to go ahead with the test? Or consider what your decision would be if the test does reveal a problem?'

Candace looked instinctively at Steve. He reached out and took her hand, and she was suddenly flooded with warmth. However uncertain the future might be, with their shared agreement that no commitment to each other had been made, at least he was here with her now, and giving all she could have asked for.

'I think...' she began hesitantly, then was relieved when Steve took up her reply.

'I think we've talked about it enough beforehand,' he said. 'We're both doctors. We're aware of all the issues. But it was good to have it spelled out again.'

'We'll go ahead with the test,' Candace finished.

Dr Strickland's ultrasound technician spread a clear gel on her lower abdomen, established a picture on the black and white monitor and keyed in some details on the keyboard.

'There's the baby,' Dr Strickland murmured, as the technician slid the probe back and forth to find the best position. 'Alive and kicking. Literally!'

Steve and Candace were both silent.

Awed?

She was. Didn't know about Steve. She was watching the monitor intently, but felt the warm pressure of his hand as he gave her rather clammy fingers a squeeze.

The technician took some measurements, expertly manipulating the probe and using the keyboard to change the scale of the image or freeze it.

'The baby's size and development are both consistent with the dates you've given, Dr Fletcher,' Ian Strickland said, then added, 'Jenny, let's take a closer look at the spine, can we?'

There was a silence, broken only by the click of the keyboard and the hum of the machine. 'Freeze that, can you?' the obstetrician said. 'Yes, there.'

'What are we looking at?' Steve said, sounding a little edgy.

Candace was feeling that way, too, now. She'd expected to move more quickly to the biopsy itself, although it was magic to actually see the baby like this. In another couple of months, she'd be able to feel all that kicking and tumbling the tiny foetus was doing. When she'd thought for so many years that she'd never again take part in the miracle of creating a life, it was amazing.

'You said you were both doctors,' the obstetrician said. 'How familiar are you with this area of medicine?'

'Not very,' Steve answered for them both. 'I guess we know the theory.'

Candace's heart had started beating faster. Like Steve,

she might not be an expert on foetal development and pre-natal testing, but she was definitely an expert on the way specialists worded things to their patients when they weren't completely happy about what they saw.

'There's a problem, isn't there?' she demanded.

'Well, no, I wouldn't say that,' the specialist answered carefully.

'Something's not right. Something's ambiguous on the scan,' she insisted, then realised that her protest, in a rising voice tone, was only delaying his explanation. 'I'm sorry,' she said. 'Just tell us.'

'I'm looking at this measurement here,' he said, elbow-ing the technician aside politely and taking control of the keyboard and probe himself. 'The thickness of the skin in the neck area—the nuchal fold. Can you see it?'

'We can see it,' Steve came in quickly. 'What about it? Hell, there is something, isn't there?'

'Thickened skin in the nuchal fold, at this stage of de-velopment, can be an indicator of Down's,' came the blunt words.

Candace's whole body grew hot, then ice-cold. Yes. Yes, she'd known that, but she hadn't thought about it in a per-sonal context.

Dear God!

Her thoughts were ragged, yet crystal clear.

I'll love you anyway... I'll keep you... I couldn't let you go...

'An indicator,' Steve echoed. 'I'm not thinking clearly. Can you go through the facts on it?'

'It's just that,' the obstetrician said. 'An indicator. There's a link. It's not definitive, by any means.'

He gave them some statistics which to Candace were, frankly, total gobbledygook right now. Then he said that if they were in any doubt about having the test, this infor-mation might cement their decision.

'We weren't in any doubt,' Steve said grimly. 'And

we're not now. My brother and his wife had a Down's baby a few months ago and he died shortly after birth.'

'That's tragic for them,' Ian Strickland replied. 'But there's no correlation.'

'On paper,' Steve said. 'I know there isn't. Let me tell you, that feels completely meaningless at the moment! Emotionally, believe me, there's a correlation!'

'I can understand that,' the obstetrician said.

His manner was textbook perfect—controlled yet compassionate. Candace had spoken like that to patients herself when breaking difficult news. She suddenly realised, Lord, people must hate me sometimes! Must hate *all* of us, no matter how hard we try and how genuinely we care. It's in the nature of the job. I *loathe* this guy, and it's not his fault at all.

Candace cleared her throat with difficulty. 'So it's just a matter of having the test and waiting for the result,' she said. 'There's no short cut to getting a more concrete answer on this?'

Oh, for goodness' sake! I know there isn't! Darling baby, bouncing around on the screen, I don't want you to have Down's...

'I'm afraid not,' he answered. 'We'll all have to wait.'

'Can we get on with it, then, please?' Her voice was high.

She felt Steve's hand squeezing hers, harder this time. His was clammy now, too. As a ludicrously mundane counterpoint to the new question mark over the baby's condition, Candace's bladder felt as if it might soon explode.

The actual biopsy passed in a painful blur. Dr Strickland used a swab of numbing agent on the skin of her abdomen, and only then did she realise in some surprise, He's not going through the cervix after all. I'm out of date on that, or else they do it differently here.

Another time, she might have asked about it, but she didn't today.

Using the image on the screen as a guide, he then carefully inserted the hollow needle. She felt pressure and pain as it passed through the firm barrier of the abdominal muscles and the uterus, then a gentle release as it reached the placenta. The needle was visible on the screen as a fine line.

'Everything's very well positioned,' Dr Strickland said. 'The baby's well away from the needle.'

He drew back on the syringe, extracted the cells he needed and withdrew the needle. Placing the sample in a sterile specimen container, he held it up for Candace and Steve to see. It was pinkish-yellow in colour.

'That's a nice sample,' he said. 'We'll get an unequivocal result from it. Now, the main risk of miscarriage comes when we *don't* get a clean insertion of the needle and a good sample on the first try. If I'd hit the wrong spot and had to have a second or third attempt at it, I'd have been concerned. In this case, there was no problem, but you may still feel some cramping for the next twenty-four hours. Take it easy. Bed-rest would be ideal, and would give you more confidence, but it's not essential.'

'We planned on bed-rest,' Candace said.

'Take a few minutes here, too. You don't have to jump up. I don't need the room for a while.'

'Actually, I *do* need to jump up...'

He understood at once. 'Bathroom's just around the corner on the left.'

'Thanks.'

Steve was still sitting in the chair beside the patient's table in the ultrasound room when Candace returned. She entered the room on the tail end of the ultrasound technician, Jenny Sabatini, murmuring, 'Mmm...mmm,' to Steve and nodding sympathetically, with a frown tightly knitting her brows. She was a motherly type, and it sounded as if he'd been having a heart-to-heart with her.

I wonder what he said.

'Going to lie down again?' he asked her, taking her hand to give it a brief squeeze.

'Five minutes. My stomach does feel sore, and I felt the uterus cramp up a bit in the bathroom.'

She massaged the area around her navel. It was too soon to feel the baby there, but her abdomen felt different all the same. The webbing of muscle had started to loosen, ready for its imminent expansion. And there was psychology at work, too. She knew that the uterus had begun to grow, and that there was a fragile new life inside her. It very definitely felt different.

Steve helped her back onto the table and the ultrasound technician left, on a murmured, 'Good luck, both of you.'

'Want to lie on your side?' Steve asked.

'Yes, please.'

'There you go. Take as long as you like.'

He rested his hand on her shoulder, then rubbed it back and forth, the way he might have rubbed a child's bumped knee. Candace said nothing. She felt fragile and heavy and numb.

It wasn't real. They didn't *know* that there was a problem with the baby. It wasn't the same as Helen's and Matt's loss. But they knew that there *might* be—not just an abstract statistical possibility, but a concrete 'indication' in that thicker-than-usual skin at the back of the inch-long foetus's neck.

The news created a kind of grieving that was as real and difficult in its way as the grieving that Helen and Matt must still be dealing with. From the beginning, this pregnancy hadn't been simple, and now it was even less so.

I don't want you to have Down's, little baby…

There was still the faint possibility of miscarriage. There was the agonising wait for the result of the biopsy, and the knowledge of a potential decision to be made then—a painful, huge and life-changing decision which would vitally affect several lives.

In my heart, the decision's made already, but I'm not kidding myself that living with it would be easy...

There was Maddy's imminent arrival, followed in two and a half weeks by the arrival of Maddy's redoubtable grandmother.

With all this, Candace's relationship with Steve—that sizzling, superficial 'fling', which she'd entered into with such high hopes as to its therapeutic value—seemed like it had become lost in the shuffle.

Still lying on her side on the ultrasound table, she felt his arm slide along hers and the press of his chest against her upper back. His cheek brushed her face, still smooth from his shave this morning. It was only eleven o'clock.

'I'm sorry,' he whispered at last. 'I'm so sorry, Candace.'

And that was all.

CHAPTER SEVEN

MADDY got off the plane on schedule at ten to seven the next morning. Her eyelids were creased from lack of sleep, but she seemed energised and excited about being there, and she was a precious and beautiful sight to Candace.

Hugging her daughter tightly, she came out with the most hackneyed line in the world.

'You've grown.'

Maddy rolled her eyes beneath a mess of dark blonde hair and groaned. '*That's* all you can say?'

'For now. Give me time. I'm working on a big speech.' She turned to Maddy's heavily laden baggage cart. 'My lord, you've brought *three* suitcases? For four and a bit weeks?'

Maddy shrugged and grinned, impervious to the criticism. 'Couldn't decide, so I brought everything.'

She chattered about her luggage and the flight as they eased through the crowds towards the exit, and it was some moments before Candace managed to present Steve, who was doing a good job of hovering in the background, despite his height and strong physical presence.

Candace was nervous about the introduction, and wished she'd actually spelled out to him in advance that she didn't want her daughter to know about their affair. Surely he would realise this without her having to put it into words?

The problem was, there was so much else they weren't putting into words at the moment. All yesterday, her voice had been rusty with fear and unshed tears, and he had seemed so withdrawn. He'd put her to bed at their bed-and-breakfast without saying more than a few words when they got back from Royal North Shore.

How could a man be so tender and so distant, both at the same time? He'd brought her lunch on a tray, attractively prepared and set out by the B and B's ultra-professional hosts, Kevin and Joy Bradley. Then he'd left her to rest for the whole afternoon. Hadn't said where he was going.

Shopping, it turned out. He had brought her a gift of jewellery—an exquisite and expensive solid gold bracelet, inlaid with Australian opals that glinted with red, blue and purple fire.

'Steve...' she'd said with tears in her eyes. The colours in the milky stones had seemed to move with the movement of her wrist as she tried it on.

'Don't say anything. I know it's not enough. But I wanted to. Hell, I *needed* to!'

She'd kept it on for the rest of the day and was wearing it again now.

They had eaten take-away Italian food in their room and had watched the television that Joy Bradley had wheeled in during the afternoon. 'What a pity to get sick and spoil your break!' she had said.

This morning, it had been an effort to rise, pack and leave in time to be here at the airport for Maddy's dawn arrival. Neither of them had talked much. Candace had been too busy shovelling in crackers and sipping on bottled water. She hadn't felt this queasy for days.

I should have spelled it out to him, about us. I don't want Maddy to know.

Why? Her instinct on this niggled at her. Is our relationship something I'm ashamed of? Surely it can't be!

'Maddy, this is Dr Colton, who was nice enough to drive me up to meet your flight.' She avoided mentioning the fact that the drive had taken place three days ago, then remembered the evidence of two bulging overnight bags in the trunk of his car, and added, 'He...uh...showed me around Sydney, too.'

'Hi, Dr Colton.'

'Call me Steve.'

'Do I get to see around Sydney as well?'

'I'm afraid not, honey. Not this time. We have to head south.'

Maddy shrugged. 'Maybe when we come to pick up Grammy.' She yawned. 'I guess I need to sleep, anyway.'

She did a good bit of that on the journey south, and they didn't stop to eat or stretch their legs. Reaching Taylor's Beach, she was suddenly wide awake again, and open-mouthed about the location of Candace's house.

'*On* the beach, Mom! That's so cool!' Then her face fell. 'Only it's winter. How can it be winter? It's so warm!'

'People swim here all year round,' Steve offered.

'*Some* people,' Candace stressed, remembering Doreen Malvern's opinion on the issue.

'So cool!' Maddy repeated, and ran straight up the external stairs to check out the house, while Steve brought up her suitcases.

She was out on the ocean-facing deck when he was ready to leave. Candace didn't miss his cautious look in that direction, from his position at the top of the stairs, before he brushed her arm lightly with his fingers.

'When are we going to see each other?' he asked her quietly.

'I…hadn't thought.'

'She'll conk out pretty early tonight, won't she?' he pressed. 'How about if I come round?'

'All right.'

She didn't want to sound too eager, or let that 'number three—we have to talk' look that he teased her about appear on her face. Didn't want to scare him off. Not now. She *needed* him.

'I'll see you tonight, then.'

He craned to take another look through the open-plan living room and out to the deck, and was evidently satisfied that Maddy was still watching the ocean. His kiss came and went quickly, accompanied by the equally brief tangle of his fingers with hers.

Candace was left fighting the need to go after him.

Half to her surprise, she spent a great afternoon and early evening with Maddy. Her daughter was less full of teenage prickles and moods and cagey behaviour than she had been a few months earlier when Candace had left Boston. Perhaps three months of living with Brittany and Todd had made her appreciate her mother's better qualities!

Whatever the reason for it, Candace wallowed unashamedly in the simple joy of her daughter's company. Wished it could always be like this—that they could always have a fresh appreciation of each other.

She spoiled Maddy a little bit, too. They picked up her current food fads from the supermarket, stopped at a fashion boutique and bought her a new bikini and a wide-brimmed hat. Even Candace's comment about the bikini being the tiniest one in the store and yet the most expensive was said half in fun and earned only an unrepentant grin.

Back home, they walked north along the beach to a little convenience store and bought huge, chocolate-coated ice creams, talking all the way.

It was so nice, just so nice, and it brought back memories of so many other wonderful times with Maddy over the fifteen and a half years of her life that Candace found herself thinking, I'd give anything if I could have this again. If I could have another happy, healthy child…

After a simple meal, Maddy was in bed by eight o'clock. Candace waited a discreet half-hour, and was just about to phone Steve when she heard his footsteps—she always knew which ones were his—on the stairs.

'Maddy hasn't been in bed that long,' she warned him, jittery once more about the possibility of discovery.

'I could check that her light was off before I came up,'

Steve reassured her, 'since her room fronts the street. But why are we whispering?'

She shrugged awkwardly. 'You know. Just in case.'

She made tea and he switched on the television, which earned her querying look.

'I don't like unnatural silence,' was his answer.

'Was it unnatural?'

'Bit.'

'I've…uh…got a pretty big list tomorrow,' she said, sounding too bright. 'Haven't done a Wednesday list before. What's Colin Ransome like to work with, do you know?'

'Slow, I gather. Super-cautious. Frustrates the nurses, but you can't fault him for wanting to be a hundred per cent sure of what he's doing. I guess a couple of times he's cancelled patients from my practice when I felt he could have gone ahead in perfect safety but, hey, I was the anaesthetist who ended up with Eric Kellett nearly falling victim to malignant hyperthermia.'

'That wasn't your fault. On what basis would Colin Ransome have decided to cancel surgery in that case? There were no indicators.' It was an effort to manufacture some energy about the issue.

'Is this what we want to talk about?' he said, with a sudden change of tone.

'No, of course not,' she answered. 'I was trying to deal with that unnatural silence.'

'Yeah, OK,' he agreed. 'I'm sorry. It's probably my fault. How are you feeling?'

'How do you think?'

He shook his head.

Silence. Achingly natural this time. There just wasn't anything to say. Nothing that would help.

What would we do if…? How would you feel if…?

He had to be thinking of Helen and Matt, but their situation was very different. Not necessarily easier, or harder. No one could make that kind of comparison. But different.

They already had a commitment to each other which had stood the test of time and the births of three healthy children. They hadn't been faced with the uncertainty of waiting. They hadn't had a decision to make. They'd simply had to grieve. Together.

'Let's watch television,' Steve said finally. It was what they had both been doing, numbly, for fifteen minutes anyway.

He put his arm around her and she rested her head on his shoulder, as quiescent as a sleepy child. She tried to enjoy the simple, in-the-moment pleasure of it, the way she'd enjoyed Maddy's company today, but couldn't do it.

'Kiss me,' he whispered after a while, and bent his face to hers before she could reply. 'Please, kiss me. I'm hungry for you, Candace. I want to drown myself in your body, and not have to think.'

'Mmm...'

The little sound she made against his warm mouth was kittenish and pained at the same time. If their relationship had ever been simple, it wasn't any more. Winding her arms around his neck, she pulled him closer, seeking oblivion.

'Oh!'

The tiny, half-stifled cry came from a sleepy figure standing at the mouth of the short corridor which led to the two bedrooms. In a daze, Candace looked up in time to see Maddy turn on her heel and disappear, her pale, winter cotton nightdress belling around her legs. A moment later, the door of her room shut with a hollow bang.

'Damn!' Steve said succinctly.

'She only saw...' Candace began.

'She saw your blouse unfastened to the waist, my hands all over the place and my eyes closed because you feel too

damned good for me to ever keep them open,' he retorted.
'That's quite a lot. You didn't want this to happen.'

It was a statement, not a question.

'No,' she agreed, and didn't elaborate because he seemed
to understand without her explanation. 'It could have been
worse. She could have seen us—'

'She's fifteen years old, armed with sex education and
an imagination. She didn't need to actually see it,' he
pointed out.

'Yes, look, I'd better—'

'Of course.' He nodded quickly. 'Go and sort it out. Talk
about it. I don't mind what you tell her now. It's your call.'

'Thanks. I—I'll feel my way with it, I think.'

'I'll go, then.' He eased himself from the couch, letting
his fingers trail lightly down her arm. 'Let me know
whether we're…off the hook, or—'

'Off the hook?' she echoed on a taut laugh. 'You have
a strange outlook at times.'

'Do I? What other times have I—?'

'No.' She shook her head. 'Don't take any notice, OK?
It's me. My fault.'

Suddenly, Candace couldn't wait for him to leave, and
was full of remorse that she'd let him come here tonight at
all. This—all of it—everything—was overwhelming at the
moment, and his presence was an additional and very emotional ingredient which didn't help.

'Just go, Steve,' she added. 'Please.'

'Sure.' He nodded. 'Sure, Candee.'

She was knocking on Maddy's door before he'd even
reached the stairs.

'Can I come in, honey?'

There was no answer, but she heard movement and padding footsteps, and a moment later the door pulled open.

'You could have told me you were sleeping with him!'
Maddy accused. Her body blocked the doorway defensively, and her voice was high and hard.

Candace didn't bother to deny the assumption, since it was entirely correct. 'Could I? I mean, *should* I?'

'Why, what was your plan? To have *that* happen?'

I didn't have a plan. I should have, but I didn't. There has been too much else to think about, and I can't tell you any of it yet. Not until I know…

'I'm sorry,' she blurted.

'Like, that's adequate?'

Where was the sunny, confiding friend from this afternoon? Vanished into thin air. And with some justification, perhaps.

'No, it isn't adequate,' Candace said steadily, 'but it happens to be true. I *am* sorry you had to find out about Steve that way.'

'I mean, what is it? Did it just start? You haven't mentioned him in your e-mails or your calls. Is he important, or is it just an affair? Like, a transitional relationship to get over Dad, or something? It has to be, doesn't it? I mean, he's Australian, and you don't actually live here.'

Bombarded with every question she'd asked herself over the past few weeks, spoken in an unflagging tone of accusation, Candace's frayed nerves suddenly snapped.

'Please, don't speak to me that way,' she said crisply.

'Oh, I don't have the right to be told? You'd ask me some pretty pithy questions if you came across me halfnaked in a guy's arms on the couch!'

'You have a right to ask the questions,' Candace conceded, her voice still sharp with anger. 'Just not in that way. And I don't promise that I have the answers. Not all of them.'

'So what answers do you have?'

'Uh…' Candace's silence was a crumbling cliff-edge all around the precarious piece of high ground she had retreated to. She took a deep, jagged breath. 'It didn't just start,' she said. 'It's been happening for a while.'

'What, you went to bed on the first date?'

'That's *enough*! I'm trying to talk to you like a rational human being. At least give me the space to do it! It's been happening for a while, and I don't—I can't tell you where it's going. Maybe it is just a "transitional relationship", as you put it. I was... Well, I was devastated by the way your father handled his departure, and— Look, I still don't know if I'm thinking straight, OK?'

'Is he going to be staying while I'm here?' Maddy ploughed on, ignoring Candace's plea for understanding and her attempt at a coherent, honest explanation. 'Am I going to have to *listen* to the two of you? Whistle or sing or stomp my feet before I enter a room in my own house in case a parent of mine is getting physical in there with their new squeeze? God, I hoped I was getting *away* from that when I came out here!'

'*I—don't—know!*' Candace yelled, and burst into tears.

Maddy swore through her teeth, then held out her arms awkwardly. They hugged. Candace apologised, felt she should be handling all of this better but didn't know how.

'I mean,' Maddy went on, her voice now full of the appeal that betrayed how close she still was to childhood, 'do you really have to get married again, or be in another relationship, or whatever? Grammy never married again.'

'Grammy was sixty-four when your grandfather died,' Candace pointed out gently. 'I think that makes a difference, don't you? And "never" is a big word. It's only been four years.'

'I guess,' Maddy conceded. It was a token. 'Just don't spoil my vacation, OK? I've been so looking forward to this.'

'I won't spoil your vacation,' Candace replied in a tone of controlled patience, then wondered if she had the right to make such a promise when she had no idea how she was going to fulfil it.

*   *   *

'So, how'd it go?' Steve said, without moving his lips.

'Not great... Hi, Marion! You're quiet in here today.' Candace had to switch tone and mood suddenly at the older woman's approach.

'Don't jinx it!' answered Marion Lonergan, the sister in charge of the accident and emergency department at the hospital.

'OK, that's me caught up on notes,' Steve said, dropping his pen on the A and E office desk. 'If they can't get him up to the ward, Marion, let me know, OK?'

He handed a patient file back to Sister Lonergan.

Candace smiled automatically, not taking any of it in. She wasn't interested in this patient, an emergency admission. She just wanted to talk to Steve with a degree of privacy. Perhaps it had been crazy to even attempt it in the middle of the A and E department. He was on call in here today, while she was in between the first and second patients on her own surgical list.

'She was hostile, or what?' Steve asked, returning to the subject that concerned them as soon as Marion Lonergan had left the small office.

'Hostile,' Candace confirmed. 'Selfish. Kind of "Why do I have to be inconvenienced?" sort of thing, but she had a point. Kids of her age find this stuff hugely embarrassing between people over the age of about nineteen. She has to deal with Todd and Brittany at home, and she hates it. She wants to live with my mother when she goes back, and I'm starting to think it's a good idea. She and Mom adore each other. I should have thought about how we were going to handle it, but then the issue of the baby came up and...' She felt a familiar lump swell in her throat.

'Should we take a break, then?' he suggested.

Candace's stomach dropped.

'A break,' she echoed stupidly.

'If you're concerned that it will be difficult for her,' he explained in a helpful tone.

'Right. Yes. I understand.' She leaned her splayed fingers

on the desk and sat down slowly, battled not to betray the way her legs had suddenly drained of strength. 'Yes, I guess that's the easiest thing.'

'I mean, your mother is coming in two weeks and I imagine you might find it even harder to deal with her—'

'Yes,' she repeated, cutting him off. 'I take your point. Yes. Let's take a break.'

'Rather than having to sneak off and make excuses. We've both been doing enough of that as it is, wanting to keep this private from our colleagues.'

'*Yes!* I'm not arguing, am I? It makes sense. Stop bombarding me with reasons, Steve!'

'Sorry.'

'God, why are we always apologising to each other these days?' she hissed in an undertone, lurching to her feet and stumbling for the door.

He didn't follow her. Perhaps he was afraid they'd create too much of a scene. Perhaps he had another reason. She didn't know.

Back outside Theatres, she picked up the phone, pressed some buttons at random, with the heel of her hand holding down the disconnect button—fortunately no one was watching—and said brightly to the dial tone, 'Yes, I'll hold.'

Then she sat with the buzzing phone against her ear and yesterday's newspaper blurring in her vision, simply buying time. Time to regain control enough to go on with surgery. She had three more procedures scheduled this morning. The nurses were still cleaning up Theatre One after the last patient and preparing for the next, but he was here waiting on a stretcher already, and it wouldn't be long before she was needed.

I can't! I didn't want Steve to say that!

Take a break? *Now?* When our baby might have Down's, and I have to suffer through maybe nearly three more weeks before we know? I need Steve. We need each other, don't we? Obviously he doesn't think we do, or he would have bent over backwards to find a way to ride it out together until Maddy and Mom leave.

Lord, I wanted the two of them here so much! I was so thrilled to see Maddy and now, already, I'm wishing she was gone. Counting the days. No! I don't want Maddy gone, I want both of them. Her and Steve.

Damn it, you fool, you've fallen in love with him, haven't you?

The realisation entered her mind as if it had been spoken by someone else.

I'm in love with him.

I wasn't ready for it *at all*, but it's happened anyway. Is it just because I'm carrying his baby? No, it's not. I would have felt it anyway.

And now we're not going to see each other—not in any way that counts—until Mom and Maddy leave.

If then.

Maybe this is his way of breaking it off. He's easing me out of it by talking about taking a break until Maddy leaves, but once that happens, he'll deal the final blow.

All at once, everything in Steve's behaviour over the past few days crystallised into a new, meaningful picture that she hadn't picked up on before. His silence and his aura of preoccupation. The expensive piece of jewellery he had given her.

She wasn't wearing the gold bangle today, because she was operating. It sat in its box in her top drawer at home, lovingly placed there last night when she'd taken it off before bed. She had been so thrilled and warmed about the gift, and only now realised that she'd subconsciously interpreted it as a love token, a sign of their shared tribulation, a symbol of all the things that were too hard, for both of them, to put into words.

But perhaps it wasn't that at all.

Not a love token. A prelude to goodbye. Something to

sweeten the pill, because Steve had realised he couldn't handle it any more. She was going to be on her own...

'You poor thing, are you still on hold?' Robyn Wallace said, coming over to the desk to write up the current recovery patient's chart.

Candace jumped and realised that the dial tone was still buzzing in her ear.

'Oh... Yes... I'll have to try again another time,' she said feebly, and broke the connection.

Her next patient had been wheeled in, and they would be ready for her as soon as she'd scrubbed.

But she had forgotten that this wasn't Steve Colton on anaesthesia today. Steve had been right. Colin Ransome was slow. Used to the anaesthesiologists she worked with in Boston, with many years of specialist expertise under their belts, she had to fight not to snap at him and the atmosphere in Theatre One was much more tense than usual.

'Are you feeling all right?' Doreen asked her at one point.

'Fine. Just tired. I was so thrilled about Maddy arriving, I hardly slept last night,' she lied glibly, then wondered how many more lies she'd have to tell, to how many more people, over the coming weeks.

CHAPTER EIGHT

'So, what can I do for you today, Andrea?' Steve asked.

It was an effort to focus on his work at the moment. He was racked with guilt and longing, and didn't know how to make it go away. A part of him wanted to run a mile.

If this is what Matt means when he tells me I need to 'get serious', he can keep it for himself! If this is part of the job description, then I'm woefully underqualified. Who needs to feel this way, day in and day out? It isn't fun! From the beginning, something told me to tread carefully with this one, only I didn't do it. Not really. Now I'm in deep enough to drown...

To drown in Candace's tired, pain-filled eyes. To drown in her trembling body, in the cool sweetness of her voice, in their rambling, teasing conversations.

And it doesn't feel good. What I'm feeling at the moment just doesn't feel good.

'I'm moving to Sydney,' Andrea Johnson was saying, as he forced himself to focus. 'Just thought that after what happened in March, I should have a thorough check-up first.'

'Yes, that's sensible.' He remembered her emergency surgery for appendicitis, and the benign tumour that had been removed instead. He read the details in Candace's handwriting in Andrea's notes. 'You'll need to find a good GP in Sydney once you're settled. I can recommend a couple of names.'

'I don't know whereabouts I'll be living yet,' she said. 'It's all a bit of a leap in the dark.'

'You don't have a job to go to?'

'No, but with my computer skills it shouldn't be difficult.'

'Let's have a look at you, then.'

He ran through the usual things. Her blood pressure was fine, nice and low at 110 over 70. Chest and heart sounded good. Clear lungs, healthy heart rhythm and pulse. He asked her a couple of general questions, then did a pap smear, and she was a young, confident woman who wasn't put off by his gender, during what some women considered a horribly intimate procedure.

With a patient's lower body concealed behind a sheet and with most of the work done by feel, Steve found pap smears to be just part of the routine. He chatted a little to help her relax, warmed the speculum with his hands and obtained the cell samples without difficulty. Then he dealt with the slide, disposed of his gloves and left the treatment room so that Andrea could get dressed again.

When she reappeared, he said, 'We should just run through a couple more things. You've had no trouble with your incision as it's healed?'

'It itches sometimes, but that's all. My sister Carina says hers does, too. Only, of course, she has a baby to show for her scar, so everyone's a lot more sympathetic and interested!'

She laughed, but it was a rather bitter sound. Steve waited and, sure enough, there was more.

'That's why I'm moving to Sydney,' she went on.

'Because of Carina, and people fussing over the baby?'

'Because I'm sick of putting myself through it. It's my fault. I know that. Carina's OK. She doesn't mean to rub it in my face that she's got a husband and a baby and all that, but...' She trailed off, then shrugged. 'You know, I just want to get away. Go somewhere where I don't have to feel like this.'

'Yeah, I know what you mean.'

Better than you realise. I'd like to go somewhere where I don't have to feel like this, too.

Guessing that she might regret giving away too much, he went on in a different tone, 'Give the front desk a ring early next week for the pap-smear result. Do you have any other health concerns at the moment?'

'No, I feel fighting fit. If this move works out—'

'Yes, good luck with it. Maybe I'll hear from Carina how you're doing.'

After Andrea had gone, Steve worked his way through a steady stream of patients for the rest of the day and left his practice just before six, feeling exhausted. Totally exhausted. Not physically, which he always considered to be a healthy feeling, but mentally. Emotionally. And it was only Monday!

A week since Candace's test. Another two weeks before they could reliably expect the results. Five days since he'd suggested taking a break.

Was that for her or for me? he wondered as he took a jog along the beach in the dark after he reached home to try and pound out some of the frustration. I thought I was thinking of her, but maybe I'm kidding myself. Maybe I just can't handle the guilt...

He hardly felt the cold foam of the waves around his feet and calves, hardly saw the cliffs and the houses, looming against a clear, starry sky, or the pieces of tangled, scrubby bush. He ran until his lungs ached sharply, and his bare ears were almost numbed by the salt wind.

The guilt.

It had been *his* contraceptive which had failed. Should he have told her at the time that he'd sensed something wasn't quite right, that he'd suspected a tear in the paper-thin latex? He hadn't been sure. If it had been a tear, it had been a tiny one. What did you do? Put the thing under a magnifying glass? So early in their relationship, he hadn't wanted to be neurotic about it.

And it was *his* family's recent experience which had cast such a dark cloud over the ambiguous picture of the baby on the scan. Down's syndrome was a challenge to deal with as an abstract possibility, but for many families there was a positive outcome in the end. He knew Helen and Matt would have made it work if their baby had lived. But little Robbie had been too weak to survive, and it brought all those abstract questions into stark focus.

I yelled at her about it, he remembered, when she asked what I thought about testing. I told her of course I was thinking about Matt and Helen and Robbie, made *her* think about them, too.

He slowed to a walk, his chest heaving, and bent forward with his hands on his knees for a moment to catch his breath. His lungs felt half-frozen, and his ears began to ache at once as feeling returned painfully.

Just ahead, the lights of the houses blinked through the gnarled shapes of the banksia trees like the rhythmic blink of the lighthouse on a distant headland to the north. The wind had freshened, and the trees were swaying, cutting back and forth through the beams of warm yellow.

He knew which lights belonged to Candace's house. She was economical about light herself, and kept a room dark if she wasn't in it. Maddy was apparently more careless. Every room was lit up, and the place beckoned like a si-ren's cave.

He might have liked Maddy if he'd had a chance to get to know her. She was at the prickliest of stages, and would remain there for a couple more years before her perspective matured. She was a factor to consider—a factor that Candace was, no doubt, considering obsessively.

He almost went up and hammered on their door, but then

thought better of it. They'd agreed on 'a break'. His word, but he was sorry he'd used it now. Candace hadn't even phoned, and he just wanted to hear her voice. Hell, so badly! It needn't be a long conversation. Just to touch base, say to each other, 'I'm still alive.'

Well, of course, he knew she was still alive! He was seeing her in surgery tomorrow.

But he hadn't meant that to be their only contact. He'd meant taking a break from sleeping together, from spending their time with each other, so that Candace wouldn't have to deal with Maddy's teenage sensitivity on the issue of adult sexuality at a time when she particularly wanted things to run smoothly with her daughter.

Yes, I *was* thinking of her, he realised. But now I'm thinking of me. I miss her far more than I want to…

'I'm going to use mesh. Look, this area on the opposite side is pretty weak, too. That's recent. There's no sense in pushing it back in here only to have it pop out the other side in six months' time. Or six days, when he has a good cough! You're doing fine, Mr Gatto,' Candace told the unconscious patient, 'but we're going to have to talk about your job.'

The patient's weight and habits, too, Steve observed. Arno Gatto had clocked in at 143 kilograms this morning, and Steve was dosing him accordingly. Mr Gatto had taken an unusually long time to close his eyes and sink into the oblivion of the anaesthesia.

He worked at a local lumber yard, in a job that involved frequent lifting, but this didn't mean he was fit or healthy. He was a heavy smoker, and from the smell of his hair, even through his disposable cap, he hadn't completely stopped before the surgery as Candace, his GP, Peter

Moody and Doreen Malvern, during the pre-admission clinic, would all have advised him to do.

'Hang in there, everyone, we'll be taking a little longer than expected,' Candace said.

'What's up?' Peter himself was assisting with surgery, and he seemed a little tense and jumpy, as if he was wondering if the pre-admission check-up on his patient had been thorough enough.

'We have a hernia textbook here,' Candace answered lightly.

'A textbook hernia?'

'No, I said a hernia textbook. What's that line from *Oklahoma!* about "bustin' out all over"?'

Steve grinned, and couldn't wipe the expression off his face. He shook his head and looked back at his monitors. Despite everything that was going on, Tuesday was still the best day of the week as far as he was concerned.

Candace had relaxed in surgery over the past few months. Not too much. Nothing out of character. She still didn't want music or gossip or anything that distracted from her focus, but she made almost every procedure interesting, and there was something almost artistic in the way she moved. Her neat hands, the way she bent her head, the uncurling of her wrist as she reached for an instrument.

The tight, pale gloves emphasised the grace of the gesture, and Steve often caught himself watching her hands far too intently.

'What are you going to do?' Peter was asking.

'I'm going to illustrate the proverb "A stitch in time saves nine" and deal with the weakness on the other side, too. Will he handle it, Steve?'

'On current indications, yes, and that's certainly what pre-admission suggested, isn't it, Doreen? Peter? Strong as an ox, aren't you, Mr Gatto?'

'That's what I told you, Dr Fletcher,' Peter said. 'But I think Mr Gatto takes that a bit too much for granted. He gets away with a lifestyle that would have killed a lot of people years ago, don't you, Mr G.? I wonder if he cut down on his smoking at all?'

'Pat, better tell them outside that we won't be done in here before…' Candace glanced at the clock '…noon, I'd say. Mr Gatto, we're going to give you a nicotine patch and chest physio and extra abdominal support after this. Can't have you coughing all my stitches out, can we? That would give new meaning to what my daughter says about coughing when she has a chest infection.'

'Stop it, Dr Fletcher, you're making me laugh,' Steve growled, and their eyes met for a moment.

He saw the way hers brightened, saw the self-conscious flush in her cheeks as it crept above the top of her mask. She flicked her gaze down again, and said with a change of tone, 'Blood in the surgical field has darkened, Steve. How's his oxygen?'

'OK, a bit low.' He adjusted the level, the calm of his manner a little deceptive.

'Temp?'

'Normal. Heart's normal.'

'Lord, are we still jittery after Eric Kellett?' Doreen voiced the concern they'd all felt for a moment. 'What would those odds be? To have another malignant hyper-thermia crisis so soon?'

'Slim,' Candace agreed.

'Odds don't work that way in medicine,' Steve pointed out.

'Some people win the lottery twice,' Peter agreed. 'Candace, the pre-admission assessment on this patient— *my* assessment, before he even got to the clinic, and his clinic visit as well—wasn't based on his fitness for a double operation.'

'I know,' she said. 'But ultimately it's less stressful this way than putting him under twice. What's it called? An economy of scale, or something? Both sides at once doesn't take nearly as long as two sides separately. I know what I'm doing, and I'll work as efficiently as I can. Steve, if there's the slightest sign that this is too much for him, let me know and we'll bail out, OK? I can schedule a second procedure if I have to.'

'No worries, Dr Fletcher,' he said, then took his usual pleasure in watching the way she worked. Those hands, the angle of her head and her eyes squinting in concentration.

They'd almost reached the end of the procedure when Mr Gatto's heart tracing went haywire, then flattened to nothing, accompanied by the high-pitched monotone of the alarm. They had equipment on hand, and everyone took their assigned roles with a smoothness that would have made Steve feel a little smug about his rural Australian hospital—if he'd had the time to feel anything.

The paddles pressed to Mr Gatto's chest were brutal in their effect. His torso arched up from the operating table, then slumped down heavily, his solid flesh shaking.

'Nothing,' Steve reported through tight lips. 'Let's go again.'

They gave it a bigger charge this time, and inside the cage of those comfortably padded ribs the heart responded at last. The rhythm on the monitor was erratic at first, but quickly settled and steadied.

'OK, I'm breathing again,' Candace muttered.

Steve followed up quickly with drugs to maintain blood pressure and the correct rhythm, and she put her final sutures in place without saying another word.

Out in Recovery, he ached to follow her out to the tearoom. Was that where she'd gone? She wasn't here on the phone, using the space between patients to catch up on other business as she often did. He knew he couldn't go in search of her, though.

He wasn't prepared to leave anything to chance now, and stayed at the patient's side until he was confident that Mr Gatto was emerging from the anaesthesia as he should. His big frame looked like an empty shell, and his recovery would be slow and uncertain.

Is Candace blaming herself? Steve wondered, staring at the ECG monitor that was still tracking Mr Gatto's heart rhythm. She was right to handle it the way she did. These things happen, and she fixed both those hernias in less than the time it would have taken Harry Elphick to do one of them, particularly in those last few years before he retired. Where's she got to, I wonder?

He would have liked to have talked to her. He remembered that other time when they'd got Eric Kellett through his malignant hyperthermia crisis by the skin of their teeth, and she'd then forgotten to give the next patient a local anaesthetic to tide the woman through the first few hours after her painful haemorrhoidectomy and vein-stripping.

Then, Candace had expressed her need for Steve with a clinging touch on his arm and a huge-eyed gaze. This time, during the routine vasectomy that followed, an hour later than scheduled, she didn't even look his way.

He waited at home that night quite deliberately. Listened for the phone while he made scrambled eggs on toast for dinner. Didn't take a shower in case she phoned while he was in there and he didn't hear over the sound of running water.

But when it did ring, a little later, it was only Helen, inviting him for a family dinner at the weekend. After that, he got impatient and angry—with Candace? He went out to a late movie that he didn't particularly want to see, because if Candace hadn't phoned by five past nine, then she probably wasn't going to phone at all, and he was damned if he'd spend the entire evening waiting by the phone like a teenage girl.

If she didn't need him, fine. If his instinct about the strength of what she felt at the moment was wrong, fine. He wasn't enjoying this, anyway.

Like Andrea Johnson yesterday, he was sick of putting himself through it.

Did that mean he was giving up? That he was ready to abandon Candace, their conceived-too-soon baby and their no-strings-attached relationship?

No! No, he *wasn't* giving up, and sooner rather than later Candace needed to know it.

CHAPTER NINE

'I FEEL as if I've let you down terribly by not having you over before this,' Myrna Davis said to Candace. 'After you were so helpful in getting Terry and me settled in during his fellowship stint in Boston all those years ago.'

'Don't be silly, Myrna. You shouldn't have felt that you needed to do it even now.'

They were seated together in a paved area of garden at the back of the Davises' attractive house, overlooking the river estuary. Terry was flourishing an expensive set of barbecue tongs over a smoking grill, and the June sunshine was stronger and warmer than winter sun had any right to be. There were about twenty people present, and they were all enjoying themselves.

'This is one of my good weeks, between cycles,' Myrna said. 'Now that I know the pattern, I can leave my chemotherapy weeks blank and slot things into the times I know I'll be feeling well.'

'That sounds far too sensible, Myrna! Are you looking after yourself properly?'

'No choice in that department.' The older woman laughed. 'I knew that chemo hits a lot of people hard, but somehow hadn't expected to have to cart a bucket and a box of tissues around with me at every step!'

'Oh, heavens, yes, you poor thing!'

Candace's sympathy was coloured by her own current situation. Myrna was trying to be funny about it, and Candace appreciated the other woman's courage in making light of the ongoing threat to her health, but even the wittiest observations on intractable nausea hit far too close to home at the moment.

She'd been feeling worse over the past couple of days than she had felt a week ago, even though she'd reached the thirteen-week mark, when most women began to feel somewhat better as their hormones stabilised.

It was stress and fatigue, Candace knew. She wasn't sleeping well, couldn't relax by day or by night with the test result still likely to be a week away or more. She was trying hard to ensure that Maddy had a good time, but that took effort as well. She didn't always want to go to a movie or to the local shopping mall after work.

Linda Gardner's teenagers were helping enormously, at least. Richard was seventeen and Julia was just a few months younger than Maddy, and Candace had hosted a casual evening of pizza and ice cream the previous weekend, to which both of them had brought friends.

It was surprising how much clearing up there was to do after ten teenagers when you hadn't even cooked for them, but apparently it had been worth the effort. Richard and Julia and a couple of their friends were here at the Davises' today, and Maddy had hardly deigned to talk to anyone else.

One less thing to worry about.

That wasn't necessarily a plus. In her churning mind, Steve Colton quickly stretched out a little further to fill the newly available space.

He was stretching out now, on one of the Davises' outdoor jarrah-wood chairs near the barbecue grill—legs straight at the knee and crossed at the ankles, fingers laced behind his head and elbows pressed back, casual knit shirt hugging tight across his broad chest.

Not a care in the world? she wondered.

His eyes were closed. His face was basking in the sun's gentle caress. He looked like an itinerant surfer, tanned and free and immortal.

Then she looked closer, and saw the frown notched into his forehead, and the way those closed lids narrowed and flickered. He wasn't really relaxing. He was just wishing he could.

Don't get it wrong, she chided herself. He's in this with me at least as far as the baby's health is concerned. He'll help.

How much help can you give from ten thousand miles away?

It's not his fault that I've fallen in love with him. That was never part of the deal. I'm the one who has changed the rules.

Had he felt her watching him? His lids flickered again then opened, and he sat up straight and shielded his eyes with his hand. Her gaze clashed with his, and he gave a quick, covert smile that was too wry and too complicated.

Her heart did a backward somersault inside her chest. Or maybe it was her stomach. Whichever organ was involved in the uncomfortable sensation, it would win a gold medal in gymnastics at the next Olympic Games at this rate. It was certainly training hard!

'Sausages and steaks are up,' Terry announced. 'Satay sticks are about two minutes away. Help yourselves, everyone. Salads on the table, meats over here.'

Candace got up to grab a plate before Myrna could make a fuss over her. She hated feeling like the guest of honour. Everyone must have been hungry, because a line had formed already, with the teenagers at the head of it and several adults hard on their heels.

Coming next, Candace knew it was Steve who stood behind her, without even turning her head to look. A few moments later, they stood side by side at the salad table, and when his bare arm brushed hers as he leaned towards the coleslaw, she knew it was deliberate, a caress that said, I'm still here. I haven't disappeared.

Yes, but only under the terms of the original agreement, she wanted to answer his unworded message. I want so much more than that now.

Did she, though?

She heard Maddy's confident yet still endearingly child-like laugh. 'Richard, that is *so gross*!'

What *do* I want? My life isn't here, it's halfway around the world. That's where I have a career. Status and office staff, an extremely healthy income and a very large house, with Todd's share in it ceded to me under the terms of our divorce. More importantly, *most* importantly, that's where I have friends I feel truly comfortable with, and a mother I love, and a daughter who's the light of my life. Does loving Steve mean that I'd give all that up to stay here if he asked?

Loving Steve...

It was an instinct at the moment. A need. It made perfect, crystal-clear sense of some things, but threw others into total confusion. Little, trivial things such as her entire future.

'Have Terry and Myrna shown you their garden yet?' Steve said to Candace in his 'public' voice, the one he used to her in front of colleagues, or in front of Maddy, or at any time when he thought they might be overheard.

'No, they haven't,' she answered, in her own version of the same thing.

She wondered if hers grated on his nerves as much as his did on hers. Her public voice was too high-pitched, too cooing and polite, while his was exaggeratedly Aussie, like that of some lone wolf Outback type who'd never had a sexual thought about an older woman in his life.

Dear God, the age thing! She hadn't even given a thought to that potential problem for a while, because it seemed so trivial against all the rest. But maybe it counted against both of them, too, counted against any possibility of a long-term future together.

Women matured earlier than men, and had a head start. At least she'd lived and suffered. Suffered through the slow, unnoticed deterioration of a marriage, the bitterness

of betrayal and divorce, the indescribable joys and relent-
less fears of parenthood. Steve was getting a crash course
in the last item, and maybe, at thirty-three, he just wasn't
ready for it.

'Eat your lunch and I'll take you on a tour,' he offered
heartily.

'That sounds lovely…' she squeaked and cooed in reply.

Her appetite had fled, but she downed a small plate of
salad and barbecued meat. Steve poured her some fruit
juice and they wandered off together, glasses in hand, with
Steve uttering loud, helpful comments about the terraced
flower-beds and the native shrubbery. Candace looked back
once, but Maddy hadn't even noticed she'd gone.

'They have a garden bench down here with great views
of the water.'

'I think you can stop now, Steve.'

'I didn't want—' he began.

'I know.' She nodded, meeting him halfway. 'I do it,
too, don't I? It's OK.'

They reached the bench but didn't sit on it. Candace put
her empty glass down on a stone wall and stood awkwardly.
There was a garden lamp just near the bench, and a set of
stone steps running down to a small wooden dock where a
small motorboat was moored.

'Lovely!' she murmured, leaning a hand on the black
metal of the lamppost.

'You haven't phoned,' Steve said abruptly. 'Not once. In
eleven days.'

She turned, taken aback by the accusation and suddenly
hot with feeling. '*I* haven't phoned?'

'It's easier for you.'

His hands were folded across his chest, emphasising the
hard strength of his forearms. She longed to stroke them as
she had done so many times before, loving their raw, unmistakable masculinity. But she could tell he was angry,
and it was like some sci-fi force field, keeping her at bay.

She hadn't seen him like this before. His powerful physical energy had always manifested itself in other ways.

'The timing, I mean,' he went on. 'You know when Maddy won't be around to hear you. And you know I live alone. You're safe ringing my place pretty much any time you want. But you haven't.'

She was still bewildered at his attack, sick with it. 'You talked about taking a break,' she said helplessly. 'I didn't know you wanted me to phone.'

'Taking a break didn't have to mean total silence, did it?' His voice rasped harshly, and his blue eyes blazed. 'Did it? You tell me!'

'Well, it didn't. Not to me, it didn't.'

'I thought that was what you wanted.'

'No.' He swore under his breath.

'Do you think I've found it easy? Going through this alone?' Her voice rose. 'The endless, agonising wait, while I try to make things nice for Maddy and pretend everything's just fine and dandy. I feel like some demented kindergarten teacher, most days. "Whoo-hoo, let's all have fun!" While really I wish I could just crawl away somewhere and go into a deep sleep until this was *over*.' Her voice cracked on the word. 'And the only person who's in this too—you, Steve—has said to me that we're taking a break. I thought it was what you wanted,' she repeated.

'No, Candace. Hell, of course I wanted to keep in contact! I haven't dropped into a black hole.'

'You should have made it clearer.'

'I'm making it clear now.'

'OK...' She nodded thinly.

'Is that good enough?' he demanded.

'If that's what you're offering.'

'I'm still here, and I'm still this baby's father. I thought you understood that.'

'Yes... There's no fathering to be done at this point, is there?'

She didn't fully understand why she was pushing him away like this. Self-defence, maybe. Illogical, certainly. She was still reeling from the suddenness of his attack, although she'd started to understand his reasons now. But to feel herself in his arms now that she knew she loved him would surely be pain more than pleasure.

'What are you saying, Candace?' he growled. 'What do you mean by "at this point"? That baby's just as real to me as it is to you.'

'It isn't,' she argued. 'It can't be. You haven't felt its effect on your body. And you haven't had a child before. At least, not that you've mentioned. Perhaps there is one, tucked away somewhere?'

'Hey!' Steve took a lunging step forward and gripped her arms. His face blazed with anger. 'Hell, what is this?'

'You started it. I "haven't phoned". Like it was a deliberately inflicted wound.'

'I'm sorry. I was too abrupt. But, damn it, Candace…! And you're wrong! Don't you think it might be *harder* for me because I've never had a child, and because it's not a part of my body? I'm at sea. I'm totally powerless. Can't even pat my stomach the way you do, as a statement of love. I can do *nothing*, except stay away, and wait, and hope you'll take the initiative and phone. Do you know what it's like for a man when he has to do *nothing*? And you tell me you've got it hard?'

He shook his head, twisted on his feet, thrust his hands into his pockets and began to pace the little terrace as if he wished it were ten times the size. He didn't look at her. Did he know how closely she was watching him? She blinked back tears, and several painful questions hovered on her lips.

Is this the end? Are we calling it quits? Am I on my own?

Finally he stopped, turned, faced her.

'Are we giving up? Is that what we're saying?' she forced herself to ask.

For such huge questions, her voice was tiny, squeaky with unshed tears. Evidently, they had the power to electrify him into action.

'Giving up?' he echoed. 'Good God, Candee, no!'

He had gathered her against him before she had time to harden herself and fight him off.

They held each other rather desperately. He buried his face in the curve of her neck, and she felt the pleasing roughness of his jaw against her softer skin. She had her hair loosely swept back into a clip today, tumbling down between her shoulder blades. He laced its silky strands through his fingers, then took a ragged breath and began to kiss her hungrily, holding her against him with his hands bracketing her hips.

'Lord, I need this!' he muttered.

As always, it felt so right. It was the place she wanted to be. She needed the way he felt, and the way he smelt. She needed the sound of his voice vibrating in his chest when she pressed against its broad expanse and listened with one ear.

Not anyone else. Him. He was different to any other man. This was different to how she'd ever felt with Todd.

Better. More intense. More magical.

Candace felt the insistence of his arousal nudging against the heat of her groin and the push of her breasts against his chest, and it was so sweet, so *necessary*, when she hadn't touched him for more than ten days, that she could only give in to it, drink it up and hold onto it.

'You sounded very certain just now,' she managed to whisper.

'Of course I'm certain!' he whispered huskily back. 'Do you think I'm going to walk away from this just because we're having a trivial fight?'

'It's not trivial, is it? We both said some harsh things.'

'We're both under a lot of strain.' Steve brushed his nose across hers, then drank hungrily from her lips, closed his eyes and slid his hands up her bare thighs, taking her skirt with him so that its light, billowy folds screened the intimate movements of his fingers against her body.

'And what's "this", Steve? You said you needed "this".'

He stilled, took his hands away. Her skirt fell. 'This,' he said. 'What we have.'

'What do we have?' She took a deep breath, which she willed to be steady.

'Why do I have to answer that?' he returned impatiently. 'And why do I have to answer it *now*? Do you have an answer? We have this intensity, this way of getting on with each other... We have a baby coming, who might need a huge amount of extra care. We have lives in opposite hemispheres.'

'Yes, and—'

'And against all that, we have this. *This!* I don't know what it is! If you have a suggestion, a definition, then I'm all ears.'

'I—I don't,' she admitted.

'So don't expect answers from me! I'm thinking one day—one *hour*—at a time at the moment. I try and think beyond the test result, but I can't. Can you?'

'No. But, Steve, I've made my decision.' There was both defiance and appeal in her voice.

Candace loosed herself from his arms, stepped back and lifted her head, waiting for him to ask what her decision was.

He didn't. He just watched her for a moment and nodded slowly. Following the downward flick of his gaze, she realised that he didn't need to ask. Her body language said it all. Unconsciously, she had flattened one hand across her lower stomach. He'd mentioned the gesture just a few moments ago. She was protecting their child as she would protect it from now on, no matter what.

Would she be protecting it alone? Neither of them knew.

I was crazy to think I'd be able do it, she chided herself. Immerse myself in him the way I did, and still walk away, untouched, when my year was up, taking our memories with me like a stack of photo albums.

Even if I hadn't got pregnant I couldn't have done it. Even if the very worst happens, and the test does show something so seriously and fatally wrong that we do opt for a termination, my awareness of it will always be there. We created a baby together. We suffered through this wait together.

'What you said about not phoning…' she said slowly.

'Probably wasn't fair,' he conceded.

'I guess I've still felt connected to you even when we haven't talked. Because I knew you had to be still thinking about it. When I saw you in surgery on Tuesday, it was obvious your nights have been as sleepless as mine.'

'Next time you're awake at two in the morning, come over and throw some pebbles against my window,' he teased. 'I'll be waiting.'

'Couldn't I just come to the front door?' Her laugh was almost a sob.

'Whatever you want, Candace,' he said. 'I just need you, OK? I'm not defining it, I'm not quantifying it. But I need you.'

So they got through the rest of the barbecue and the rest of the day, and she sneaked out that night when Maddy was asleep and went to Steve's place. They made love in front of some terrible fifty-year-old B movie on late night television, said all the same things they'd said to each other before, drank some hot chocolate and then just held each other.

And the holding was the only thing that really counted.

*   *   *

Elaine West was one of the last passengers off her flight to emerge from Customs the following Friday morning. As always, however, she emerged immaculate in every detail, from her tiny diamond earrings to her Italian leather shoes. At sixty-eight, in black trousers, a silk blouse, an elegant jacket and the perfect scarf, she was, as ever, the best-dressed woman Candace knew.

'No, the flight wasn't horrible at all,' she insisted airily after they'd hugged with greedy pressure. 'It's all common sense. Drink lots of fluids and walk up and down the aisles. Besides, I got an upgrade to first class,' she finished with a guilty smile, just when Candace was about to conclude that her mother really was inhumanly poised and perfect.

'So you really didn't need a weekend in a nice hotel in Sydney to recover before we drive down to Narralee?' Candace enquired deliberately.

An iron grip landed on her wrist.

'Darling, believe me, I need the hotel,' Elaine said. 'And it has to be a *proper* hotel, you know that, don't you? Not one of those ghastly bed-and-breakfasts that you like. I want anonymity and room service, not hand-quilted cushions. I've got those at home.'

Candace grinned. 'Don't worry, it's all taken care of. Maddy and I stayed there last night as well.'

'You'll love it, Grammy, and it's on the nineteenth floor,' Maddy said.

The further from the ground, the better, as far as Elaine was concerned.

'So we can go straight there?'

'Yes.'

'And you can freshen up a little, too.'

A pair of sharp black eyes alighted critically on Candace's worst features. The face that was innocent of make-up, showing its lines of strain starkly. The comfortable jeans she'd worn to drive up here last night, and hadn't bothered to replace with something smarter this morning.

The hair that could have done with much more than a quick, vigorous brush, twist and clip high on the back of her head.

'You look terrible,' Elaine added, just in case her previous comment and her pointed regard had been too subtle.

Candace caught Maddy's startled glance and her sudden frown. Teenagers weren't the most observant people in the world, but they could use their eyes when they were pointed in the right direction, as Elaine had just done.

'I didn't find the pillows very comfortable last night,' Candace lied, and hoped her daughter wouldn't think back and realise that this peaky, strained appearance and casual approach to grooming had been in place for her entire stay.

'Hmm,' Elaine said. 'We'll call Housekeeping as soon as we get to the hotel and ask them to send up a different kind. And you've lost weight.'

'Yes, isn't it great?' Candace parried the accusation by changing the direction of its spin. 'With the beach right out front of my house, I'm getting so fit!'

She waited for a moment, her breath held tight in her chest, then let the air out with controlled relief when, without further comment on the subject, Elaine turned to her single suitcase.

'Maddy, you can get that for me, honey. It isn't heavy. It has another one nesting inside it for when I've shopped. Which we'll do this afternoon, shall we?'

Her beam of anticipation assumed enthusiastic agreement.

And after these first few awkward minutes, everything was fine. Back in their two-bedroom suite at the high-rise hotel, Maddy watched daytime soaps while Candace 'tried out the new pillows' and Elaine unpacked. They ordered an elegant brunch through room service, then embarked upon a serious shopping expedition.

Elaine expected Candace to be an expert on the city's most appealing merchandise but, of course, she wasn't, and in the end she let her mother take control. Translating the price tags into US currency, Elaine considered virtually everything to be a bargain, and they returned to the hotel at four o'clock with so many bags that she would have needed three suitcases nesting inside each other in order to fit everything in on the return flight.

'You can box the rest up for me and mail it back,' she told her daughter.

After two hours of serious rest and freshening up, they went to the revolving restaurant high above the city in Centrepoint Tower for drinks and dinner. Knowing that her mother would expect a high degree of elegance and finish, Candace wore heels and make-up, jewellery glinting here and there and hair in a proper French pleat. For the first time in weeks she actually felt good.

Energised. Optimistic. Safe. There was something about Elaine West's approach to life.

Or perhaps it's just because she's my mother, the one who's never let me down, in all these years...

'I'm so glad you came, Mom,' she whispered in a foggy voice, and put her arms around Elaine in the elevator going up to the restaurant. A subtle waft of cool, faint perfume reached her nostrils as Elaine returned the hug.

'We'll talk later, darling,' she promised. 'And you can tell me all about it.'

Which was almost as good as all those times in Candace's childhood when she'd heard in that same tender voice, 'It's all right, Candy, darling, Mommy will kiss it better.'

Obviously, Elaine knew perfectly well it wasn't just the hotel pillows that were responsible for her daughter's look of fatigue and strain, but this seemed reassuring rather than ominous tonight. For the first time in two months, Candace's appetite was vigorous and food tasted the way it should. So did the lime juice and mineral water she ordered.

Maddy was bouncy and happy and wanted to climb the Harbour Bridge the next day.

'Richard Gardner told me all about it,' she said. 'It takes three hours or something. It's supposed to be incredible.'

'The Harbour Bridge?' Elaine said. 'You mean the big, black one near where we bought the opals? The famous one? You can't be serious!'

'They clip you onto the rails, or a cable, or whatever. You can't possibly fall. They give you windbreakers. Grammy, don't you think it would have to be just totally, like, ba-a-d?'

'Mom...' Candace said. Elaine was looking excited, and that couldn't be good.

'Oh, let's do it, darling! The three girls? It'd be like that fad a few years ago for walking on hot coals. If I can do this, I can do anything, sort of thing.'

'But the bridge...'

'You're not afraid of heights, are you?'

No, I'm pregnant, and even if they do let pregnant women climb the bridge, I'm not sure that I'd feel safe about it...

'I'd want to hold onto the back of Maddy's collar the whole way, like I used to when she was little and liked to balance on things,' she fudged.

'Stay at the hotel, then,' Elaine offered, almost too easily, after a telling beat of silence. 'Or watch us through binoculars from the Opera House. But we're going to do it, aren't we, Maddy?'

'You're great, Grammy.'

'Darling, when it comes to the point I probably will be a teensy bit scared, so you will look after me, won't you?'

I should have known then that she'd guessed everything, Candace would say to herself later. She was playing the part of fun-loving grandmother just a little bit *too* well...

* * *

'I don't know how she can sleep with her hair over her face like that,' Elaine commented in the sitting room of their suite at six-thirty the next morning.

Coming out of her room in a pale blue silk dressing-gown, she had peeked in on Maddy, observed that she was still asleep and quietly closed the door. Candace hadn't bothered to close it behind her when she'd awoken and slipped out of the same room a few minutes ago. She hadn't intended to make any noise.

But Elaine obviously planned to talk, and didn't want to waken her granddaughter. Not just out of concern for the importance of Maddy's beauty sleep either.

'Do you want to start from the beginning, or shall I just ask questions?' she said to Candace.

'That's already a question, isn't it?'

'And shall we order room service? A hot breakfast?'

'That's two more questions!'

'You ought to eat properly. Maddy can choose what she wants later.'

'Actually, yes, I am pretty hungry.'

Starving! Eggs, bacon, sausages, grilled tomatoes, three cups of milky decaf coffee and about six pieces of whole-wheat toast.

She picked up the room-service menu, then felt her mother's calculating look. She flushed.

'Is it what I think?' Elaine asked.

'That entirely depends on what it is that you think, doesn't it?'

'Well, I don't want to say it, in case I'm way off base, but...' She ticked the items off on her fingers. 'You look exhausted, you're drinking decaf coffee, you wouldn't have wine or a cocktail or even a sip of my champagne last night, and then when you said you didn't want to climb that bridge...'

Candace slumped onto the polished cotton of the couch, with the room-service menu on her lap. 'You're not way off base,' she said.

'Who's going to say it first, then?'

'You are, Mom.'

'You're pregnant, aren't you?'

'Yes.' The word was leaden.

'In the queasy stage?'

'No, yesterday I got to the starving stage.'

'Then it must have…?'

'Yes, it *did* happen pretty early on. We weren't being careless, it was just one of those things. A failure of the technology.'

'Are you still seeing him? Maddy would have said something, wouldn't she?'

'It was a sore point for her so we're taking a break. After she goes…and you. I don't know why I kidded myself that you wouldn't guess eventually, but I think you've outdone yourself in clairvoyance this time, Mom!'

'It's not clairvoyance, Candy. I just care about you so I notice what's going on.'

'After you go, I—I'm not sure what will happen.'

'You were supposed to have a wonderful vacation fling while you were here, darling, but—'

'Yes, I sussed that was your plan.'

'*Sussed?*'

Candace shrugged. 'It's a word I've picked up. It's useful. I'm planning to import it to Boston.'

'But you weren't supposed to take it this far,' Elaine accused lightly.

'It wasn't—' Candace began.

'No, of course it wasn't planned, but—'

'I was absolutely thrilled about it at first.'

'Because you were in love with him.'

'No.' Candace shook her head. Twice. 'I mean, I *am* in love with him…'

She stopped. It was the first time she'd said it aloud. And it felt so *necessary* that she said it again, listening to the words, savouring them. 'I'm in love with him, and I'm thrilled, still thrilled, about the baby. I never wanted to stop at one. That was Todd.'

Her mother cut in with an epithet concerning Todd that she would have absolutely forbidden Maddy to use.

'But—Mom—there's a problem. Might be.' She couldn't say it coherently. 'We had a test. It might have Down's.'

'Oh, Candy!'

'Which is—' She broke off. Began again. 'I mean, people manage. It would be hard—but I already love this baby. Only with the distance… Could I make my life here? Does he want me to? It'd be a whole lot more difficult for him to do it the other way around, professionally. I don't even know if he feels the way I do.'

'How could he not? My daughter? Any man with any sense—'

'Thanks, but you're my mother.' She managed a laugh. 'It doesn't count.'

'You said *might* have Down's?'

'We should find out this coming week. There was this ambiguous indicator on the scan.' She sketched the facts briefly.

'And you said "we".'

'He's not going to abandon the baby. He'll at least visit. Send presents. Want photos.'

'But you think he might abandon you? As a lover?'

'I said to him at the very beginning that I just wanted an affair.' She laughed shortly. '*Why* did I say that?'

'And to him that was a plus,' Elaine came in. 'Because he's not looking for a commitment. Only now you've changed your mind.'

'Not promising, is it?'

'Men can change their minds, too, darling,' Elaine said gently. 'Despite the prevailing mythology, it's *not* just a woman's prerogative. If he did change his and ask you to stay would you do it? Do you love him that much?'

'There's Maddy. She's not really happy with Todd and Brittany. There's you.'

'There you are! There's Maddy and there's me. I'd have her to live with me in a New York minute, if that would help.'

'She'd like that. Her father might not.'

'Her father would have to lump it, as far as I'm concerned. Would *you* like it? Leave Maddy and me out of this.'

'My career at home—'

'Leave your career out of it. Will the test result on the baby make a difference? Can you separate the future of this man's relationship with the baby from the future of his relationship with you? And, I repeat, do you love him that much?'

'I—I don't know.'

'Then you've got some thinking to do, haven't you?' came the gentle suggestion.

Candace nodded silently, then watched, still slumped on the slippery couch, while Elaine politely stole the room-service menu from her lap.

CHAPTER TEN

'SHOW me the beach, Maddy,' Elaine said to her grand-daughter on Sunday evening, in her most imperious I'm-a-senior-citizen-so-you-have-to-do-what-I-want voice. 'Your mom's had a long drive. She needs some time by herself.'

'It's getting dark, Grammy.'

'I need some fresh air.'

'OK. I guess it won't kill me.'

'Well, the bridge climb didn't.'

'Oh, Grammy, it was so great, wasn't it? You were right, I'm gonna think back to it and know I can do *anything* now.'

'As long as you run most of those "anythings" past your mother or me first, OK?'

They headed for the door, and Candace phoned Steve as soon as they'd gone, knowing that her mother had got herself and Maddy out of the way for exactly that reason.

'Do you want to come over?' he asked at once.

'Uh, no, it's fine. Just wanted to tell you I'm planning to call Dr Strickland's office first thing tomorrow. Surely he'll have a result by then!'

'Do you want me to be there?'

'I think I do, yes.'

'You think?'

'I do. I know I do. I just don't want—'

'You're not pressuring me, OK?' he insisted. 'Are you going to ring from home or from your office, or where?'

'My office, I guess.'

'Strangely enough, I've suddenly thought of a patient I need to come and consult you about.'

158

'It's all right. Gillian won't ask questions, and Linda's not there on Monday mornings.'

'Sure you don't want me to come over tonight?'

'Mom and Maddy won't be gone long.'

'I'd like to meet your mother.'

'Not tonight, Steve.' Her tension had pushed to breaking point now, and she didn't want to bring the two halves of her universe together tonight, no matter how well behaved everyone was.

Steve arrived at her office the next morning only moments after she'd walked through the door herself, but it was a wasted trip. Dr Strickland wasn't in his rooms, and his receptionist had no information on the test.

'He'll call you when he has the result,' she promised in a voice of professional sympathy.

'Does he have my pager number?' Candace demanded, jittery and sick. 'And the number of the recovery annexe at the hospital?'

'I'll take those down for you,' said the same patient voice. 'He'll phone you as soon as he can.'

'Nothing?' Steve correctly guessed when she'd put down the phone.

'Nothing.' She gave a thin shrug.

'What are you thinking?' he demanded. 'You're frowning.'

'I'm thinking about the intractable, unbridgeable chasm between doctors and patients,' she said. 'Thinking about how many times I've left those sorts of phone calls until the end of the day, even when I've had a result on my desk first thing in the morning, because I've been too flat out with other stuff, blithely ignoring the fact that an extra eight hours of waiting feels like eight weeks to the patient concerned.'

'You're going to reform from now on?'

'I can't!' she answered. 'Realistically, next time it happens I'm going to have another person on hold on the phone while I'm glancing through the pathology reports, I'm going to be running late for surgery, the patient's not going to be picking up the phone if I do squeeze in a call over lunch, and it's going to get left until the end of the day.'

'Sounds like a familiar story.'

'And I know Ian Strickland has fifty other patients he's thinking about today, and some of those patients—infertility cases, people with cancer—would *wish* they were in my position, waiting for my kind of news.'

She gave a laugh that was more like a sob, and he came around the desk to where she sat and wrapped his arms around her from behind, pressing his cheek against hers.

'Don't torture yourself,' he said. 'Do you have all my numbers? Because as soon as Strickland does reach you, I want you to do your damnedest to reach me.'

'I will,' she promised.

'And we're going to see each other tonight whether we have a result or not. Maddy can have a tantrum about it if she likes.'

'She won't. Mom's very good at keeping Maddy's feet on the ground.'

'Come over for dinner, the three of you.'

'No, not that.'

She said it too quickly. Just couldn't face the thought of all those vibes. Mom trying to assess this man who'd made her daughter pregnant. Maddy feeling hostile. Steve pretending everything was fine and normal and easy.

He was silent for a moment, then said, 'She knows, doesn't she? Your mother? About the pregnancy.'

'Gee, you're almost as clairvoyant as she is!'

'What did she say?'

'A fair bit. Most of it pretty good. Gave me some things to think about.'

Another short silence, as if he wanted to ask more. But he didn't. 'I should go,' he said instead.

'I hope you'll hear from me.'

'So do I.'

Dr Strickland phoned at four o'clock. Candace had a patient with her, but had told Gillian that she wanted this particular call put through at once, no matter what.

'Yes, Dr Strickland?' She was dizzy and sick with apprehension, and drenched in clamminess.

'I have the result on your chorionic biopsy in front of me.'

'Yes?'

He didn't waste words. 'Good news, Dr Fletcher.'

'How good?'

'The best. You're carrying a healthy— Did you want to know the sex?'

'No... Yes. *Yes!*'

'It's a boy who's genetically normal in everything we're able to test for. On this occasion, that thickened skin at the nuchal fold which we noted on the scan was insignificant.'

'Th-thank you,' she stammered. '*Thank* you!' Then she gabbled to her elderly patient, Stan Caldecott, 'Will you please excuse me for a moment, Mr Caldecott?'

She fled the office, ignored Gillian's startled look, paced up and down the deserted corridor outside the rooms she shared with Linda, gave several dry, shaky sobs, then had to stand there for several moments, bringing her breathing and her expression under control.

She gave Mr Caldecott his post-surgery check-up on autopilot, deeply thankful that he was the last patient of the day, and the moment he was out the door she closed it and turned to the phone. Tried Steve's rooms. Was told he'd left for the day. Tried his mobile phone. Reached him in the middle of the supermarket.

'It's normal,' she said shakily. 'He's a boy. And he's fine. Completely fine.'

'Lord, I just want to see you!' came Steve's voice, husky and deep, different from usual yet achingly familiar.

'Yes,' she answered. 'Yes!'

'Right now.'

'Yes. I don't think I should drive. I'm—'

'I'll be there, OK? *Don't leave!*'

She didn't, although the minutes dragged until his arrival.

Gillian had obviously noticed Candace's agitation as she wandered out of her consulting room and into the rear office, ran her fingers automatically through a drawer of files and wandered out again. Darting into Candace's consulting room, the receptionist said in a stage whisper, 'Is everything all right?'

'I've just had some good news. Very good news. Family. Private.' She waved a hand. 'I'm…light-headed with relief.'

'That's great, Dr Fletcher. I'll head off, then, shall I?'

'Yes. Fine.'

Gillian left and then Steve arrived, lunged through the waiting room without the slightest pause and took her in his arms. He brushed her mouth with his lips, buried his face in the tendrils of hair that had slipped free of their clip, stroked her back and then squeezed her and lifted her from the ground to whirl her around the room.

'You're crazy!' she accused, laughing. 'Completely!'

They were both a little crazy that night. When they had calmed down enough to think, Candace phoned her mother at the beach house and told her the news.

'You can start living again now,' Elaine said.

'Yes, that's what it feels like. As if my whole life has been on hold these past three weeks. Steve's here and we're going to… Well, I don't know what we're going to do, but I might not be home for a couple of hours, OK?'

'If you get home before midnight, my girl, I'll ground you for a week!' Elaine said.

There was no danger of Candace getting home before

midnight. Steve drove her up to Braidwood for dinner, and it was more than an hour's trip each way.

'I'm sorry. I hope this is all right,' he said as they looped and curved along the forested highway. 'But I need to cover some ground and feel some speed under my wheels.'

'It's fine. I think I'm the same. I'm just so happy for *him*, Steve. That he's going to come into the world now with everything going for him, instead of with such a struggle ahead.'

'I thought maybe we were going to have to step off a cliff-edge today, but we don't. It's good. We're having a boy!'

'Haven't had one of those before.' She laughed with a secret joy and delight that no words could have expressed.

'Smell this forest,' he said a moment later. 'Don't you love this? This is the lungs of the planet.'

She took a deep, appreciative breath of the air coming through the open car window, as he was doing. 'The planet's been sucking on breath mints.'

'No! Gee, Candace, is that how it smells to you? It's so much fresher than that.'

'Australians are so weird about the smell of eucalyptus!'

'And proud of it!'

She humoured the father of her child. 'It's beautiful. The sunset is beautiful, too.'

The little town of Braidwood, with its well-preserved 150-year-old buildings, was chilly but clear-skied. They weren't dressed for fine dining, so chose a quiet little place that served pizzas baked in a wood-fired oven. They were piping hot, crisp, flavourful and delicious.

They didn't linger too long over the meal. Steve bought a bottle of red wine from the hotel bottle-shop and Candace allowed herself the first small half-glass of alcohol she'd drunk since learning of her pregnancy. He had only one glass as well, and they corked up the bottle and brought it with them.

'For next time,' Steve said.

'Good wine doesn't keep for long.'

'Next time won't be long away, will it?'

They wandered around the town, window-shopped in front of a couple of antique and craft shops and indulged in a flight of total fantasy about purchasing and renovating one of the old stone public buildings, set in spacious grounds. They argued about heritage paint colours and about whether to keep the hotchpotch of outbuildings at the back or pull them down. They bought imaginary horses and landscaped a fantasy swimming pool.

They talked about politics and music and travel, enjoying the sheer pleasure of being able to bat a subject back and forth like a ping-pong ball without it all being part of some painful undercurrent of awareness, a way of *not* talking about what really filled their minds—*is the baby all right?*

They didn't have to think that way any more. The baby *was* all right. He was a boy. He was real and normal. The shadow was gone.

Then it became too cold, so they drove back to Narralee, and didn't even talk about where Steve should park the car.

At his place.

'Mom said I wasn't allowed to get home before midnight...' she said as they came up his external stairs.

'That's a challenge I can rise to without any trouble at all.'

He had his arms around her before they were even inside.

It took days for the mood of light-headed happiness to wear off, and what was left behind was something richer—a contentment, though that word didn't seem strong enough, that Candace had never felt before.

She was newly energised, light on her feet, starving hungry...and she could feel the baby now. Her unborn son. No movements yet, but a distinct, slightly rounded hardness in her lower abdomen which she knew would grow daily.

People would soon have to be told. A few weeks ago, this had seemed like a huge hurdle, but it had faded into insignificance against the question of the baby's well-being, and Candace wasn't going to get her priorities wrong any more. It didn't matter if people knew. It didn't matter what they thought.

Only Maddy's feelings mattered. This was the only reason she still hugged the secret of her pregnancy to herself. She needed to find the right time to tell Maddy.

It came on a Sunday night, halfway through Elaine's visit, when Candace had counted off the fifteen-week milestone. Not the right time, but the inevitable time.

Steve had had the three of them to lunch, along with Matt and Helen and their young children, Jake, Claire and Annabelle, and the afternoon had stretched on until Maddy had whispered to Candace, 'Mom, I'm so *bored*! I mean, the kids are cute, but—'

'You can leave if you like.' She had pressed the front-door key into her daughter's hand.

Maddy's departure—managed with acceptable politeness and grace, to Candace's relief—had allowed the adults to enjoy another hour of conversation, and Candace had warmed increasingly to Steve's brother and sister-in-law. When Steve touched her openly a couple of times, she knew that seeds of understanding were sprouting rapidly in Matt's and Helen's minds. Candace and Steve were both laying the groundwork. But for what?

When Candace and her mother got home from Steve's, Maddy was at first sulky, then very vocal over dinner.

'Richard and Julia phoned when I got home. They'd been trying since noon, they said, and, of course, we forgot the cellphone. I could have gone to their place, but no-o-o. Instead, the most boring afternoon of my life. Why did we have to meet those people? Why were you trying so hard to be nice to them?'

'Oh, was I?' Candace was a little startled by this.

More so when her mother confirmed it.

'They won't have noticed, darling,' Elaine reassured her. 'We only did because we know you. You were wearing your best party voice and you'd starched your laugh. Don't you think it's about time you told her?' she added, without the slightest change of tone.

If she was hoping to slip the question past Maddy, she was destined for disappointment.

'Told me what?' came the sharp demand at once. 'I know about Steve. You haven't been sneaking out to meet him. I thought you'd taken my advice and it was over.'

'Whether it's over or not,' Elaine said, 'there's going to be…'

She stopped.

Candace glared at her mother, then immediately wished she *had* let Elaine bite the bullet. Realistically, there was never going to be an easy time for it.

Maddy, I'm pregnant.

'I'm not sure what's going to happen between us in the future, Maddy,' she forced herself to say, as calmly as possible. 'We…haven't talked about that. But there's one sense in which it's never going to be over. It's the same way with your father and me, despite what happened with the divorce. When you have a child with someone, they'll always be a part of your life.'

'You mean…?' Maddy choked, flushed and looked down at Candace's stomach.

'Yes. I'm pregnant.'

'That is just—! That is just—! *How could you?* Brittany was bad enough, but at least she's *young*! God, I'm going to be so embarrassed!'

She stumbled out of the room, her eyes narrowed and burning, her cheeks flushed and her whole gangly yet graceful teenage body looking like one big scowl. The door of her room slammed.

One day she's going to have to think of a more original

punctuation point to her angry exits, Candace thought. The door-slamming is getting old.

The humour was grim, and she kept it to herself.

'That went well,' she said aloud instead, the sarcasm light but deadly.

'You didn't really think it could, did you?'

'No, of course I didn't, Mom. But I thought perhaps she might be concerned about a few issues that are actually *relevant*, like distance and commitment, instead of my age and her embarrassment.'

'Now you're being as selfish as she is.'

'Oh, I am? Oh, thanks!'

'Honey—'

'Maybe I'll slam a door or two as well. Maybe we all should. Just not speak to each other for the rest of your stay.'

'We'll be going in a week,' Elaine reminded her helpfully.

'I know.' Candace paced the room. 'And I'm terrified because I don't know when I'll see you again. I don't know anything.'

'Not even what you want?'

'Not even what I want,' Candace said. 'Or what I have the right to ask. Of you, of Maddy, or of Steve.'

The atmosphere was tense and unsettled between the three of them for the remainder of Elaine's and Maddy's stay, and Candace was weighed down by mixed feelings when she drove them to Sydney for their Saturday afternoon departure. Maddy still hadn't said one pleasant word about the baby. She'd been uncomfortable enough about Brittany's pregnancy, but her feelings seemed even stronger about this one. Totally hostile. She didn't have a moment to spare for Candace's stubborn, illogical joy about the healthy boy growing inside her.

How is she going to be to live with if I go back early,

when I'm sticking out like an extra shelf, and later, when my energy's consumed with a newborn? Can our relationship survive, or will there be permanent damage? Candace wondered.

Whenever she thought about Maddy's feelings, she was torn between anger and an understanding that didn't help her to find solutions.

The anger was selfish in many ways. Elaine had recognised this, and so did Candace herself. The recognition didn't always help in keeping the feeling at bay.

Nothing helped.

In four weeks, she would be halfway through her pregnancy. Three months after that, she would no longer be permitted on an international flight. If she was going to cut her stay here short and have the baby back home, that decision had to be made soon. Handling her own prenatal care, as she had been doing so far, wasn't going to be satisfactory for much longer.

She could check her own blood pressure and blood sugar, check her weight gain and her urine for the presence of protein, but she didn't have much experience of obstetrics, and didn't trust that she'd pick up on a more obscure problem, or that she'd be able to accurately assess the baby's size and growth.

At her age—'Yes, Maddy, thanks for the birthday cake you made me last week, but you're right, thirty-nine *is* old,' she told her daughter in imagination as she drove south from the airport—and after such a long gap in her childbearing, she wanted to see someone with a lot of experience.

She would go to a top Boston obstetrician if she went home, and perhaps to Graeme Boland, down at Harpoon Bay, if she stayed here. He had a good reputation, she knew. Not down-to-earth Linda, although Linda's reputation was good as well. Linda was too close.

At the moment, however, Boston seemed the more likely place.

Why, though?

Steve was waiting for her when she reached home after the drive back from Sydney, as she had half known he would be. There was a note to that effect on her front door.

'Come straight down. I'll be home. I'll leave a message on your machine if I'm called out.'

After checking her machine and finding no message, she went, eager to see him without the stress of knowing that her mother and her daughter were close at hand.

He opened the door before she'd even knocked. His chest was bare and brown and his jeans hung precariously on his hips, as if he didn't particularly want them to stay up. She loved the way that line of hair, black against the light nutmeg brown of his skin, arrowed down the centre of his lower stomach towards his groin.

'Hello, lover,' he said, and the endearment spoke of sex, in the low, caressing tone he used.

It spoke of the passion that lay at the heart of their relationship, and she thought, Yes, I've missed it terribly, just as much as he has.

His hunger for her glittered in his blue eyes, and his impatience showed in his hands. Without another word, he lifted her jaw with the caress of his forefinger and brought his mouth down to ravish hers. Then he touched her. Everywhere, it seemed.

His hands roved across her breasts, stopping only long enough to ensure that they were swollen and ready for him before dropping to her hips to pull her closer. He slid his hands inside the back of her snug-fitting stretch pants to cup her bottom.

'I haven't seen you naked for so long.'

'Two weeks. Less.' The night they'd found out about their healthy son.

'That's long.' He peeled her cotton knit top up beneath

her armpits and skimmed the balls of his thumbs across her tight nipples.

'Yes… Yes, it is.'

She clung to the waistband of his jeans with two sets of curled fingers, like hanging onto the safety rail on a carnival ride. Her knuckles pressed into the warm, tanned skin at his waist, and she flung her head back and closed her eyes, gasping in delight at the continuing onslaught of his hands and his mouth.

'Let me undress you,' he said, sliding her pants down over her hips. 'Let me see you…'

'And you,' she said huskily. 'Not fair if you get all the pleasure.'

They didn't talk properly until afterwards. A long time afterwards. Not until they'd eaten the meal he'd prepared for her and curled up together on the couch with music playing in the background.

'Maddy and your mother got off all right, did they?'

'Yes, fine. I stopped on the way back at that spot where we picnicked, under the Norfolk pines, and watched their plane take off.'

'Silly!'

'Why?'

'I bet you cried.'

'Was that wrong?'

'No, I guess it wasn't,' he answered. 'Of course it wasn't. Just seems like you set yourself up for it, going to that spot where the planes look so dramatic and the sense of distance is so huge.'

'The distance *is* huge.'

An awareness hung in the air. Not of sex, for once, but the awareness of unspoken things. Problems. Decisions.

Candace was swamped with a painful need to have Steve take control of this, of their future.

Ask me to stay. *Please!* No, *tell* me to stay. Fight for me if you want me. Tell me we can work it out with Maddy and everyone else. Tell me nothing else matters but the fact that we love each other. Tell me that love can always find a way.

It was all clamouring so loudly inside her head that she was convinced he must hear it. Couldn't he feel the way her muscles had knotted? Her whole body was pressed against his side, length to length. He must be able to feel it.

But he said nothing. Until finally words came. 'Are you staying tonight?'

His voice sounded creaky, rusty, as if he'd been half-asleep, or something.

'I don't think I will.'

Maybe if she hadn't dressed again earlier. She had thought of just slipping into one of his T-shirts as she'd done once or twice before. There was something so intimate about that, surrounding herself in the cleanness and subtlety of his scent, swimming inside the garment because he was bigger than she was, casually claiming the right to borrow his clothes.

But she hadn't done it tonight. Instead, she was fully dressed, and it was easy to go.

Better to go. She probably needed some time alone anyway—some time to think about the stark fact that, with all that they'd been through, he hadn't said that he loved her.

'Sure?' he queried. 'I'd like you to.'

I'd love you to? I love you? Sorry, no, it didn't even come close! If he felt it, he needed to say it. And if he didn't feel it...

Out of self-preservation, she hardened her heart.

'Best not.'

She eased herself out of his arms and walked towards the door, turning halfway there to face him. 'I need some time to myself, Steve. I've had Maddy for four and a half weeks, and Mom for two. Now I just need to think.'

'Want to think here? Out loud?'

As an offer, it still wasn't nearly good enough. She shook her head.

'OK, then,' he said.

He kept watching her, and she couldn't tear her gaze away.

'Busy tomorrow?' So casual. Surely he cared more than that!

'I'm not sure,' she answered.

'All right, Candace.' He got up, looking restless now. 'Maybe I'll drop over to your place.'

'I'll…' She hesitated. How much of a stand did she want to take? 'I'll leave you a note if I'm going out.'

'Do that,' Steve said.

Then he watched as she let herself out, standing frozen in the middle of his living room. He didn't move from the spot until quite a long while after she'd gone, and even when he did, it was only to pace restlessly out to his deck to let the air clear out his aching head.

He felt like howling at the moon. Instead, he just gave a shuddering groan.

When he'd asked if she was staying, he'd been so painfully tempted to leave off the last word, 'tonight'. So tempted to make it into a bigger question. *The* big question. The one he sensed she was grappling with as well. They were having a baby together, but they lived on opposite sides of the world. He couldn't just ask her to 'stay' as if it was easy.

If this was just about now, he could have said it in a heartbeat. Stay tonight. Stay for a week. Stay as long as you want.

But it wasn't about now, not even a stretchy, open-ended now. It was about forever. Was he arrogant enough to ask her to stay? Was he humble enough to follow her? Forever?

'Stay forever.' He tried the words on his tongue, speaking them quietly into the chilly night, and they frightened him. He tried them again, with a difference. 'I need you. Stay forever.'

It still didn't work. It wasn't fair. If he was going to say, 'Stay forever,' then he had to be damned sure about what he was promising, about the value of what he had to give. He had to be very arrogant indeed, in the face of what he'd be asking her to sacrifice, and he didn't know how to find that certainty and that arrogance to set against the doubts he sensed in her, and the complexities in her life.

'I'll follow you.' That wasn't any easier. Maddy was at a difficult age. Would Candace want her daughter to have a stepfather hanging around, not really quite old enough for the job?

Speaking of hanging around, would one of them stay at home with the baby, or would they both work? Candace's position as an attending surgeon would be considerably senior to anything he could get in the United States for the first few years. It was demanding, too. Not the sort of thing she could tackle part time. He might end up as the one at home. A certain humility on his part would definitely be a requirement. He wasn't a particularly humble person.

They hadn't talked about any of this at all, and he had no idea about what she would want. No idea. It was a problem. He was waiting for her to come up with some answers, trying to be fair to her, and it wasn't working.

Nothing in their relationship was working at all. Damn, he had to take control of this, take the courage and the arrogance to push both of them blindly forward without knowing where it might end.

A fire of rebellion began to build inside him, flaring with incredible speed. What time was it? Ten? Later? He didn't care. He wasn't going to leave this any longer. He'd been wrong to let her go home alone tonight. She didn't have the right to weigh her options and make her decisions alone. They had to do it together.

CHAPTER ELEVEN

INSIDE the house, Steve grabbed a light jacket off a hook on the back of the door, checked his pocket and belt for keys and pager and loped out the door, almost at a run.

He was halfway down the stairs when he felt the buzz of the pager against his hip. It wasn't the first time it had interrupted him when he'd had Candace on his mind…or lying against his heart as they'd made love. They'd had the usual couldn't-have-come-at-a-worse-moment intrusions because of his profession. 'Phonus interruptus' another GP in his practice called it.

This one, he thought, had to take first prize for bad timing.

He checked the code on the readout, and it was the most obvious one—the one that meant, 'Your presence at the hospital is required. Accident and Emergency Department, please.'

He climbed into the car and got there in seven minutes, ready to be peeved—or maybe to explode—if he wasn't really needed. With Candace. That was where he wanted to be. Not here.

He was needed, though. Coming into the emergency department through a side door, he found the place brightly lit. Night Sister Jenny Shearer was pleased to see him so promptly. Behind her, he glimpsed one of the cubicles set up with equipment and a figure making a mound on the bed.

He didn't know this patient, Christine Smith. She wasn't local. Down from chilly Canberra for a winter break in the warmer climate of the coast. She had her husband Neil and two-year-old son Liam with her. She was twenty-nine

174

weeks pregnant and her membrane had torn, leaking a persistent trickle of straw-yellow amniotic fluid and stimulating painful but intermittent contractions.

They could have dealt with the situation here if it had just been a matter of having her on bed-rest. There wasn't a lot that could be or needed to be done. Strict bed-rest, good fluid intake, monitoring of the contractions, checking for signs of infection.

The problem came with the fact that with a leaking amniotic sac, Christine had a ninety per cent chance of going into unstoppable labour over the next forty-eight hours. They didn't have high-level neonatal care facilities here. If the baby was born here, he or she wouldn't survive.

Steve wasn't at all surprised that Sister Shearer had already arranged for a SouthCare helicopter to make a night flight from Canberra to pick up the patient and transport her to Black Mountain Hospital. There the baby would have a fighting chance, at twenty-nine weeks, of surviving a premature birth with no long-term problems. Since the flight was short, Mrs Smith was unlikely to deliver during the journey.

On paper, Steve's job was to keep the patient stable until the SouthCare team arrived, then assist with the transfer. In reality, it was much more about reassurance, listening and answering questions.

'What happens if I get an infection? What are my chances of going to my due date?'

'Can I come with her in the helicopter? If this settles, will she be allowed home? I'm not sure if I can take the time off work...'

Steve fielded all this as best he could. They seemed like a nice family—young and steady, the parents trying to conceal their anxiety from their little boy, whom they'd had to waken from sleep at their motel, and who now looked frazzled and disorientated.

'Mummy,' he was saying persistently. 'Mummy...'

It turned into open crying, and Christine asked, 'Could he come up here on the bed, or something? Neil, should you just take him back to the motel straight away? It's insane for you to wait till I go, and then drive up to Canberra tonight.'

They talked about it, then Christine's face crumpled as another contraction came. 'They're only light,' she said. Saying it so it would come true, Steve understood. 'Seems like they might stop.'

Steve heard Neil mutter through pale, dry lips, 'This isn't fun. I hate this!'

But then the air began to shudder with the sound of the helicopter approaching outside, and everything got hectic. Liam had fallen asleep on his father's shoulder. Christine was coming out with all sorts of distracted last-minute instructions to her husband about her little son's care. His breakfast. His tantrums. Travis the toy tractor.

Steve watched the helicopter take off and was about to leave the hospital himself when he noticed a familiar car pulling up in one of the parking spaces to the side of the emergency entrance. His brother Matt's car.

His heart lurched, but Matt had seen him and was rolling his eyes when he got out of the car.

'Don't panic. It's OK,' he said. 'Annabelle has got a peanut up her nose. Put it there herself, of course, and didn't tell us because she was scared we'd be cross. We only found out about it when she woke up and was crying in bed because it hurt.'

He bundled his three-and-a-half-year-old daughter out of her booster seat and carried her into the A and E department. Wearing a pink dressing-gown on top of flannel pyjamas, she was looking big-eyed and ready to cry.

'Hey, didn't I tell you we might see Uncle Steve here?' Matt told his daughter in a bright tone. 'He's going to get that peanut out, and if you're a big brave girl about it, I bet he'll have a...'

'Jelly bean and a sticker,' Steve supplied.

'Hear that, Annabelle? A jelly bean and a sticker for you.' In an aside to Steve, he added, 'Fun, this is!'

'Do you get much of this sort of fun in the parenthood game?' Steve asked casually, although he knew what the answer would be.

'It's a laugh a minute,' Matt drawled, then took a second look at Steve's face. 'You're not thinking of—?'

'I'm working a few things out,' Steve cut in hastily. His scalp was tight and he was now even more desperate to get away. To get to Candace. To explode at her about rights and decisions and the future. Hell, she'd be asleep by now, probably, but he was too impatient and angry to wait. Too desperately in love with her as well. 'Let's look at that peanut, Annabelle,' he said, his voice a gritty rasp, overlaid with effortful good cheer.

Annabelle was a very big, brave girl, mainly because the peanut wasn't lodged all that far up her nose. Matt or Helen could have got it out themselves, only she'd kicked and screamed when they'd tried, and they'd become concerned about accidentally shoving it further in.

Uncle Steve in his doctor clothes was apparently intimidating enough to induce co-operation. Or perhaps it was the prospect of the sticker and the jelly bean. Matt and Annabelle were ready to leave again in a few minutes, as soon as they'd made a trip to the bathroom.

'What I said before about fun...' Matt said urgently outside the bathroom door, when he saw that Steve was about to head off.

'I know,' he reassured his elder brother. 'Don't worry. You haven't put me off. I know it can't always be fun.'

Over the past few weeks, without him being fully aware of how his attitude was changing, the job description had come to make sense.

'When you're with the right person, you can take whatever comes,' Matt said. 'Helen and I have found that out this year, if we didn't know it before. Don't let Candace get away just because there are a few hurdles, mate. You can get over those.'

He pressed a fist against Steve's upper arm.

'I know,' Steve repeated. 'I know, OK? Let me get on with it, Matt.'

'Now?'

'Now!' he confirmed grimly. 'Should have been weeks ago.'

Although she had craved solitude when she left Steve's, her own house seemed too empty when Candace closed the front door behind her. Elaine's bag no longer hung over the back of a chair. Maddy's magazines had been piled away, and her litter of hair accessories was gone from the bathroom.

Candace wandered through the living room and down to the bedrooms. Maddy and Elaine hadn't vanished without trace, she was reminded when she breasted their doorway. Their twin beds were covered with the many fruits of their shopping expeditions.

There were at least twenty items which Elaine had casually asked Candace to 'mail back for us'. Elaine had gone so far as to acquire boxes, bubble wrap and packing tape, but she hadn't actually done any of the packing.

Candace picked up a heavy kitchen cutting board made of Australian hardwoods, measured out a section of bubble wrap and parcelled up the smooth rectangle of wood. It fitted very neatly into the bottom of one of the boxes, but maybe an extra layer of bubble wrap wouldn't go amiss...

Before she knew it, she was fully engrossed in the job, and decided that she may as well keep going until she'd finished. It wasn't as if she was going to get to sleep yet, and she could think just as well while her hands were busy. Better, maybe. For good measure, she put on some soft music and made coffee as well.

Thinking. Decisions.

Have the baby here, or go back to Boston? Taking Steve out of the picture, only one thing made sense. To go home. The idea beckoned, yet at the same time seemed to suggest bitter failure.

I won't decide yet. I'll leave it a little longer.

No, that was weak. She couldn't afford, emotionally, to keep herself on hold for Steve any longer. If he cared the way she did, surely he'd have said something by now? Her thoughts circled back to the beginning, dwelt on Maddy and Mom, Todd and Brittany and their baby, returned once more to Steve.

It was after midnight when she heard footsteps pounding up her stairs. It frightened her until she recognised their familiar rhythm. Going to the door with some tape and a half-wrapped souvenir mug still in her hands, she knew it would be Steve. Didn't know whether to be angry or grateful.

He was turning up at this time of night? Hadn't she told him she needed to be alone? Hadn't her spirit cried out for him to give her some help? The two sets of feelings warred inside her like hostile siblings.

She opened the door and he strode straight inside, pivoted on one foot and began forcefully, 'I've been thinking about it, Candace, and you have no right—!' Then he stopped abruptly and his face went white. 'You're packing.'

'Y-yes, for my—'

But he didn't give her a chance to finish. Didn't notice, or maybe didn't care, how he'd unnerved her.

'No!' The word grated between his clenched teeth.

He grabbed tape, mug and bubble wrap from her hands and flung them onto the couch. He looked magnificent, hardened by anger, arrogantly certain of himself. Wounded, though, as well. He was like a jungle cat, both enraged and endowed with exaggerated strength because of his pain.

'Don't!' he said. 'You have no right— You can't just leave without some input from me. You can't leave at all.'

His grip closed around both her upper arms, and this close she was frightened at how white he looked. His eyes were like blue flame, blinding her into incoherence.

'Steve, I'm—'

'You can't leave,' he repeated for the third time.

'I'm not,' she gasped at last. 'I'm just packing this up for Mom and Maddy. The things they bought. They couldn't fit them in their suitcases, and I'm going to mail them instead.'

'Uh…!' The breath went out of him as if he'd been struck with a blow. 'That's…a help, I guess,' he said. He was still gripping her arms. 'But, no,' he went on, 'it doesn't change anything. My God, Candace, we're so far overdue for a talk it's not funny! You have no right to make any of your decisions alone!' His voice softened suddenly. 'But, of course, it's at least half my fault that you don't know that.'

His arms slid around her and she was astonished to find them trembling. So was his jaw. Trembling with tension, his whole body.

'I love you,' he said. 'God, why haven't I said it before?'

His kiss was passionate, imperious, sure of its response.

'I love you, too,' she answered, tears burning in her eyes. 'I've loved you for—I don't know when it started. Is it enough? I've been wondering if it's enough.'

'Hell, yes! *Enough?* It's the *only* thing, Candace. Maybe I didn't know it until tonight, but I know it now, and a moment ago when I thought you were packing to leave without even a word of advance warning… Loving each other is the *only* thing. We have to say it to each other—'

'We just did.'

'We have to say it every time we're together, and then we have to talk about the future, knowing that what we decide has to be based on that. The fact that we love each other. Candace, I love you, and I want to be with you, whatever it takes.'

His arms and his lips softened, as his voice had softened, and when he kissed her this time it was sweet and slow and cajoling.

'So do I,' she said, with her cheek pillowed against his chest.

'Whatever it takes?'

'I want to be with you. I want to make a family for this little boy.'

'Here? Do you want it to be here? That's one of the things that seemed like a mountain between us.'

'Anywhere.'

'Anywhere. That's almost as big as "forever"—do you realise that?' he said.

'Are you asking me about forever?' She lifted her head, cupped his face in the palms of her hands and looked deeply into it.

'I don't think I'm asking. I'm telling you,' he said, meeting her gaze steadily. 'Or I'm offering it. Forever. If you want it, Candace. I want to marry you and promise you that it's forever. As for where, it can be wherever you want. Wherever we decide. Only let's decide it together. Let's not second-guess what we think the other person needs.'

'Can it be here?'

'What about Maddy?'

'I've been thinking about that tonight. Really thinking about it, instead of running away from it because it's too confusing and scary. Maddy...' she took a deep breath '...will find it easier this way. To live with Mom, who's so good with her. That's kind of hard for me, because she's growing up and I haven't accepted it yet.'

'Mothers don't, do they?' He smiled.

She nodded. 'It's the same as it was when I first came out here. It was harder for me to leave Maddy and accept that she'd be all right than it was for her to wave goodbye to me. She's going to be sixteen soon. She'll live with Mom for a couple of years and they'll have fewer fights than Maddy and I would have, even without this baby on the scene. Mom will talk to her about the baby, and about you and me, and she'll listen and take it to heart in a way she never would if I said it. She'll make more visits over here, and we'll visit there. We'll talk on the phone and run up huge bills, and stay closer that way, I think, than if she had to live with us.'

'Yeah?'

'Two lovers, their baby and a teen? Doesn't work! That's really why she's been miserable with Todd and Brittany.' For the first time, she spoke those two names together without pain. 'It's not because she was missing me. It's not even because Todd and Brittany are particularly horrible.' Again, she could say it and it didn't hurt.

But he told her seriously, 'Candee, I'm sure they're very, very horrible.'

She laughed. 'Thanks! But when she's older and settled somewhere, could we move close by so that she can get to be friends with her second little brother?'

'I like the idea of that,' he said. 'Living there, when it seems right. I like the idea of not making it an either-or thing. We can do both. There'll be sacrifices. But when I think about what I feel, I can believe they'll be worth it, and they'll balance out.'

'The Pacific seemed so huge to me today when I watched their plane taking off,' Candace said. 'But, yes, when there's solid ground beneath my feet, the solid ground of loving you, and knowing that you feel the same, the distance doesn't seem so important.'

'Nothing else is important, everything else finds its right place, when we're so certain of this,' he whispered, and found her mouth.

EPILOGUE

THIS isn't fun, Steve thought to himself. This most definitely and absolutely isn't fun.

Candace squeezed his hand again. Lacerated it, if he was truthful. Her face was red and straining and sheened with sweat. Her blue hospital gown was limp, and she was very, very tired. Sixteen hours of labour, a quarter past four in the morning, and it wasn't over yet. He hated her pain, and his powerlessness. Hated it. Oh, truly, there were moments in this adventure called love that were definitely not fun!

But at least Candace's pain had been replaced to an extent by hard work over the past half-hour. The baby's head was crowning strongly, and no longer slipping back up into the birth canal between contractions. It wouldn't be long now.

'You're doing so great, Mom!' Maddy said with a sob in her voice. She squeezed Candace's shoulder from her position on the other side of the bed. 'I'm so proud of you.'

But Candace was too involved in her work to respond to her daughter with more than a big-eyed, love-filled, exhausted look, as another contraction came.

She and Steve had both been thrilled and relieved when Maddy had announced over the phone, several months ago, that she wanted to be present for both the wedding and the birth, if possible.

'I've talked about it a lot with Grammy, and I want to apologise for being a spoiled brat, before, when I was with you.'

'Oh, sweetheart...'

It had ended up a very lengthy phone call, and both Candace and Steve had been very happy to accommodate

183

what Maddy wanted. The logistics of distance dictated that both events would have to take place during the same trip, over Maddy's Christmas and New Year break from school.

This had given all of them some anxious moments on 23 December when an hour of false labour made it seem as if the baby might arrive before their scheduled Christmas Eve wedding.

'Really, baby!' Elaine had admonished Candace's round, hard belly. 'It would be a lot more convenient if you would wait. Your big sister might want to see you born—personally, I'll be waiting somewhere civilised, not in the delivery suite—but I'm here to see your parents married first!'

And the labour had subsided, the simple wedding had taken place, outdoors, at seven o'clock in the evening at a local park—Candace had looked huge and fabulous in a simply cut cream linen maternity dress—and now the baby was coming, right on his due date of 7 January. As promised, Elaine was waiting for the news at home in Candace's and Steve's spare room, while Maddy was here, tired but very involved.

'Pant through the break, Candace,' coached the midwife urgently. 'His head is almost out. One more push…'

'One more push, Candee,' Steve echoed. 'You can do it.'

She nodded and gripped her angled thighs, and he held her shoulders and prayed.

'He's coming… He's coming…' the midwife said.

Candace gave a huge sound of effort, half groan, half yell. The head was out…it was rotating…the midwife delivered one shoulder…the other slipped out on its own, followed by torso and limbs, all wet and slippery. Born! He was safely born! Steve's eyes stung then filled, and his diaphragm jerked with sobs of relief that he barely noticed. He was grinning so much that it hurt, was in no doubt at all that this was the best moment of his life.

The baby cried at once, lustily, and waved his tiny,

splayed fingers. Pink spread all over his body, and the midwife cradled him in a towel and laid him at once in Candace's arms.

'Oh… Oh…' Candace said. She was crying, too. 'He's so beautiful! He's amazing! So perfect!'

Maddy had dissolved completely. 'I knew it would be special, but I didn't know it would be like this,' she said. 'Oh, Mom…'

They hugged, clumsy in their emotion, and Maddy touched her little brother's head.

'I'm so glad you were here, sweetheart,' Candace whispered to her daughter. Then she turned to Steve, frowning. Strands of hair clung damply to her forehead, making him itch to smooth them back. 'Is your hand OK? I think I was pulling on it a bit…'

'It's fine.' He hid it from sight, didn't want her to see the stiffness in it or the scratches. 'Everything's fine.'

He leaned across, pushed the hair from her brow and kissed her, then watched as she lifted her gown and gave the baby her breast. He felt a fullness inside him, a physical sensation of love and protectiveness, pride and triumph, which was almost a kind of pain.

'You know, I actually think this was all worth it,' Maddy said. She was laughing now, while brushing tears from her young face with the back of her hand. 'All the horribleness. Everything. Never thought I'd be able to say that. But it really was.'

'Is she right, Steve?' Candace whispered, looking at him across the damp black shape of their baby's head, pillowed at her breast.

'Do you even need to ask?' he whispered back.

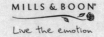

CODE RED

ORDINARY PEOPLE
EXTRAORDINARY CIRCUMSTANCES

Courage Bay...
a community founded on bravery. Meet the town's
heroes – the people of Courage Bay Emergency Services.
Bold enough to risk their lives – and their hearts.

12 high drama romances to collect

Spontaneous Combustion by *Bobby Hutchinson*   4 February 2005

Line of Fire by *Julie Elizabeth Leto*   4 March 2005

Next of Kin by *CJ Carmichael*   1 April 2005

Total Exposure by *Tori Carrington*   6 May 2005

Blown Away by *Muriel Jensen*   3 June 2005

Nightwatch by *Jo Leigh*   1 July 2005

Tremors by *Debra Webb*   5 August 2005

Aftershocks by *Nancy Warren*   2 September 2005

Crossfire by *BJ Daniels*   7 October 2005

Critical Affair by *MJ Rodgers*   4 November 2005

The Trigger by *Jacqueline Diamond*   2 December 2005

Justice for All by *Joanna Wayne*   January 2006

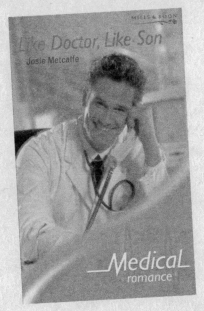

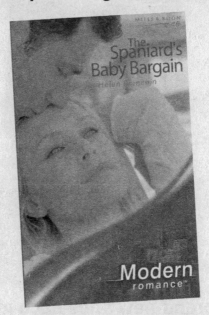

▼ SILHOUETTE®

Passionate, dramatic love stories

Desire 2 in 1

BEAUTY AND THE BABY
Marie Ferrarella

SOCIAL GRACES
Dixie Browning

GEN/18/RTL5 V2

▼ SILHOUETTE®

*Passionate and thrilling
romantic adventures*

Sensation™

NIGHT WATCH

Suzanne Brockmann

GEN/23/RTL5 V2

♦ SILHOUETTE®

Life, love and family.

SPECIAL EDITION™

THE ONE & ONLY

Laurie Paige

⧭ SILHOUETTE®

Super ROMANCE

Right place, wrong time

Judith Arnold

Enjoy the drama, explore the emotions, experience the relationship.